CW00735545

SHADOW

OF THE

NORTHERN ORCHID

Genre: Historical/Adventure/Romance

Cover design created by Cat Petersen

SHADOW

OF THE

NORTHERN ORCHID

Written by Elizabeth Rimmington.

Shadow of the *Northern Orchid*

Published at Ingram Spark
by Elizabeth Rimmington. 2019.
Queensland
Australia

Copyright 2019 © Elizabeth Rimmington
National Library of Australia
State Library of Queensland

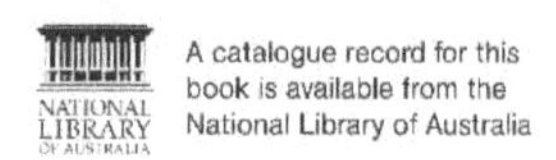

ISBN
978-0-6485257-0-7 (Print)
978-0-6485257-1-4 (Mobi)
978-0-6485257-2-1 (EPUB)

All rights reserved.
Except for purposes of review, no part of "Shadow of the *Northern Orchid*" may be reproduced, stored in a retrieval system or transmitted in any form or by any means, electronic, mechanical, photocopying, recording or otherwise without prior consent of the author. Inquiries concerning publication, translation or recording rights should be directed to Elizabeth Rimmington, e-mail: lizrim007@gmail.com.

Disclaimer
This novel is entirely a work of fiction. While some of the names, characters and business places mentioned may have existed, their interaction with the story characters is pure fiction. All incidents are either the products of the author's imagination or have been used in a fictitious manner. The opinions expressed or beliefs held are those of the characters and should not be assumed to be the opinions or beliefs of the author.

APPRECIATION

To Caroline and Margaret who sprinkled the gloss.

To Tricia who sailed the *Northern Orchid* through the stormy seas of formatting.

To Anne who assisted with the research material.

To Tom who shared his passion for steam engines.

To Jan, who gave me the courage to begin this journey.

To Avril who led me through the maze of publishing.

To the fellowship and support of good friends within the local writing groups.

To the staff at the Gympie Library for their support.

PROLOGUE

THE *NORTHERN ORCHID* 1860

PROLOGUE

Captain William Sloan opened his mouth to shout the order but the bosun's roar, rising above the din of the wailing winds and pelting rain of the storm, pre-empted his call. Miniature waterfalls ran off the dark curly hair and muscled body of Jimmy Dougall, the bosun-cum-carpenter, as he clung to the ship's boat-davit.

"Mast monkey, get yourself up that mizzen mast. Secure that sail boyo, before it tears itself to shreds."

In the wheel-house, the captain and the ship's mate, stood with their feet braced as they fought to control the helm when it threatened to break their arms with each twist of the three-masted barque. Bolts of lightning illuminated the night. Sheets of rain obscured the movements of the young lad now scaling the mizzen mast swinging in wide irregular arcs with the tossing of the ship. The mainsail yard-arm appeared to almost skim the crest of the angry waves seething on either side of the ship. Mountainous seas overwhelmed the scuppers and flowed across the upper decks already awash with the waters from the vengeful skies.

A shiver ran through the captain's body; more in empathy with the boy struggling to tame the recalcitrant sail outside than from feeling any cold himself. It was relatively warm in the wheel-house. The youngster scampered over the spars and sails wearing only tattered shirt and trousers as protection from the icy winds and the rain. His hair may be thinning and grey but the captain remembered his days of dancing the yard-arms and working the sails with painful hands stiff with cold.

The two men strained at the tiller. Captain Sloan grunted.

"How long can she take such punishment?"

Ewan MacGregor, the ship's mate of the *Northern Orchid,* nodded.

"It's a spiteful sea and sky we'll be having this night."

At that moment, a grinding shriek, emanating from the bowels of the ship, assaulted their ears. An ominous shudder ran through the vessel. It was felt above all other of the ship's contortions.

"Mother of God, what on earth is that?" the captain spoke quietly.

Mesmerized, he stared through the flashing lights of the sky, as the main topmast began to twist. The tortuous crack, as the scotch pine finally split asunder, echoed off the wall of sea and sky around them. Ropes strained against the weight as the mast, with deadly spikes of tortured timbers at its broken shaft, began to fall.

From out of nowhere, a weight struck Captain Sloan hurling him through the wheel-house door and onto the catwalk outside. A groan burst from his throat as a streak of pain tore across the side of his face. He clamped his hand over the injury. Unnoticed, blood poured down his chin to drip on to the deck below. When the bow of the ship nose-dived into another trough in the waves, he stumbled. His free arm reached blindly for the rail. An avalanche of saltwater mixed with the rain blinded him for a moment. He shook his head to clear his vision and to help him understand what had happened.

MacGregor lay groaning near his feet. His hair, usually the flame colour of a fire torch, was now a different red. Fresh blood ran from a large wound across the mate's forehead. The stoved-in wheel-house held the shattered lower end of the main topmast. The bloodied upper body of Jimmy Dougall was visible. The lower half was hidden from sight.

Captain Sloan looked down on the deck to see, reflected within the glare from another lightning bolt, the whites of several pairs of eyes staring up at the wheel-house. He glanced up to the mizzen mast where the mast monkey clung like a limpet to the yard-arm. Streaks of lightning lit up the fractured main topmast. The rigging still attached, lay partly across the stays of the mizzen mast threatening to unseat the lot. Screeches of timber on timber filled the air as the huge mast began to slide across the deck threatening to destroy all within its path.

“Axemen! Axemen!” Sloan searched below for the towering frame of a man he had noticed with the group only a moment before. “Evans, cut the rigging from this mast before it drags us all down to Davey Jones locker.” He bellowed the order automatically while still trying to comprehend what had happened. It appeared Jimmy Dougall had shoved the ship’s mate and himself out of danger; losing his own life in the process. “And keep those men on the pumps,” he yelled.

William Sloan struggled over to the body of his bosun. He whispered. “Jimmy Dougall, that was a brave thing you’ve done here today.” He touched the broken remains of his friend and sailing companion of many years. “I’ll not be forgetting this in a hurry.”

ONE

THE DOUGALL FAMILY

BRISBANE 1866

SARAH

Thud, thud, thud; the repetitive banging of the narrow wooden bed on the thin walls threatened to bring the house down. Slowly the grimace of pain on Sarah's pale face eased but the curled lips of disgust remained.

"Is this how Ma felt; her first time?" Sarah asked herself silently. She opened her eyes.

The dust motes still hung in the sunbeam where it squeezed past the piece of hessian tacked across the window. Unpainted walls that did not make it all the way to the unlined roof still closed in around her. How can everything appear so normal when her whole world had so rudely changed? She took some reassurance from the familiar scratching on the outside wall of the small house which told of the gentle sea breeze ruffling the fig tree branches. From where she lay on the bed the clean briny smell of salt was now suffocated by the smell of cheap hair oil, sweat and unwashed skin. Warm drops of perspiration fell from the large grunting male above her landing like snake strikes on Sarah's face. The grimace returned.

"I hope he doesn't disturb Ma?" Sarah's thoughts drifted to her mother who lay semiconscious on the bed next door. Lucy's last coherent words from yesterday echoed in her daughter's ears.

"It is up to you to pay the rent and feed your brothers and sister now, Sarah. Just remember to be polite to Mister Dingle and make sure you get your coin before he enters the room."

She sighed. Was this ever going to stop? Of its own volition, her mind sought an escape from the reality of the moment. Her head turned in resignation to gaze at last year's faded calendar with its picture of Queen Victoria hanging on a nail in the wall. The "1865" was almost undecipherable due to the muddy footprint of a mongrel dog that had contested her ownership of this masterpiece lying in a gutter of Brisbane. Everyday Sarah's stubby finger traced the letters and numbers while she repeated them out loud. The infrequent free time she had was spent struggling to ensure she did not forget the little education received; when their father was alive. Tears of anguish and revulsion trickled unheeded down her cheeks. After the initial discomfort, Sarah now experienced only a dull pain in her lower abdomen and the bounce of the man pushing her onto the hard wood of the bed under the thin horse-hair mattress. This unpleasantness fell far short of the excruciating pain in her heart.

"Oh Da', why'd you have to go and get yourself killed?" A soft groan broke out from between her tight lips. Shame clenched her gut.

The sound of two dogs scrapping in the nearby street floated through the window. The bouncing continued. Her eyes pressed shut. The pain increased along with the tempo of the drumbeat on the wall behind her. Sarah gritted her teeth. Her mother's voice again filled her head.

"Just close your eyes dear and think how best to spend the coin. Remember, it will not last forever."

Retreating further from the present, Sarah focused on the clang of the cans in the milk depot next door. Harnessed horses stamped their feet on the cobbles impatient to begin their deliveries of these empties to the outlying farms.

"Hell; is it that time already? Daisy will be wondering where I am," Sarah thought.

Blue eyes peeped out between her almost closed eyelids. Several long strands of well-oiled mousey hair had become dislodged from their position of sentinel over the large bald patch of the man's scalp. They whipped her nose. Sarah's wicked sense of humour threatened to overwhelm her. She wanted to giggle. Her thoughts rambled on unrestrained.

"I can remember Grannie Dougall always saying that we should look on the bright side of things. I bet this is not what she had in mind."

Memories from happier days came to Sarah of a parsimonious grey-haired lady who was never short of advice to all and sundry, for all occasions; maybe not this one. The overwhelming sudden urge to burst into sobs took Sarah by surprise. She was not sure why. Maybe for the dreams, she had entertained many years ago of handsome princes, large castles and happiness. She bit her lips until she tasted blood.

"That's life, girl; just be getting on with it."

Her mother's voice once again took centre stage in Sarah's thoughts. At sixteen and the eldest, it was now her duty to care for her siblings. Josh, fourteen years of age and Gus, twelve months younger, brought in a few shillings working at Mister Campbell's blacksmith forge; when there was work available. They, being boys, were able to continue their lessons courtesy of the generosity of their father's friend, Captain Sloan. Then there was Daisy; poor eleven-year-old Daisy. Despite being easily distracted, she was an enthusiastic helper in the kitchen; but did require considerable supervision. Daisy lived in a world of her own understanding.

"Oh Daisy, what's to become of you?" Sarah thought.

She froze. The pace of the man had changed.

"Oh no, is Mister Dingle having a fit or something?" Sarah asked herself as the man's flabby body flapped along at incredible speed. Slapping noises sounded as bare skin met bare skin, all awash with sweat. Saliva dribbled from the man's mouth. Sarah had once seen an old lady in Brisbane's street fall to the ground shaking like this. Something horrible it was. By the time the policeman arrived the body lay pale and still.

"No point yer gawkers 'anging about. The old 'ag's carked it. Be off and mind yer own business," was the policeman's instruction to the gathering crowd as he waved them on their way.

Her left arm stretched out removing the florin from the old butter box by her bed. Sarah clasped it tightly in her work-hardened fist as Mister Dingle removed himself from her body and began to rapidly adjust his trousers.

"Same time Thursday, Miss," was Mister Dingle's parting remark as he made haste out the back door.

Sarah ran out to the kitchen. Clunk; the coin landed in the tin on the ledge above the fireplace. A bucket holding a few inches of water stood nearby. She scrubbed her body and her hands until the skin glowed red. There was little left of their home-made soap supply by the time she had finished.

"I guess rendering the fat for soap will need to be done before I get to sleep this night," she mumbled as she moulded the soap remains into a ball. The smell of lye filled her nostrils.

She sat by her mother's pale form, stroking the dank hair.

"Oh Ma, how did you carry on doing that for us these six years past? If only Da' was still here."

The feverish body gave no evidence of response. Rapid shallow breathing barely moved the bony tuberculosis-riddled chest cavity. Maybe the gurgling in Lucy's throat sounded a little moister and louder than it had earlier.

"I'd best go look for our Daisy. I told her to stay with the ducks by the river until the boys or I collect her."

Lucy's dark-rimmed hollowed eyes remained shut; her grey face unmoving.

Elizabeth Rimmington

Lucy's dark-rimmed hollowed eyes remained shut; her grey face unmoving.

DAISY

The ducks were happily pecking through the grasses at the waters' edge in the shade of the paperbark trees. Voices floated across the water from where a group of natives was hunting through the shallows around the mangroves. A piercing yell sounded when one of the hunters waved his spear, showing off to his friends the large fish caught in its prongs. The late sun had turned the waters into flowing liquid gold. Further up the river, several fishermen in small row- boats were beginning to pack their lines and return to the shore. There was no sign of her sister.

"Oh bother, where has that girl wandered off to now?"

Sarah walked further downstream. The sound of banging and hammering along with the jingle of horses' harness came from where workmen were building a new wharf.

"Daisy! Daisy!" Sarah called apprehensively. "That girl's been told a hundred times not to go near the wharves," she mumbled. It was the soft sound of crying that led her to the giant camphor laurel tree.

"What's the matter, Daisy? What's happened?"

She came upon her sister cowered within the protection of the twisted tree trunk. Daisy's dark plaits were falling to pieces. Mud covered her clothes and limbs. Channels of tears ran down the dirty cheeks of her face with its shattered expression. Her right sleeve was torn and the hem of her dress hung tattered beyond repair. Wild blue eyes peered through unfettered hair tresses. Gulping sobs exploded through the open cavity of her mouth.

"Have you fallen out of the tree?"

The sobbing grunts increased. Daisy shook her head from side to side. Her little hands clamped tightly to Sarah's arms. Sarah enclosed her in a hug.

"Daisy, Daisy pet, what's the matter?"

"The man," Daisy stuttered, "He hurt me."

Sarah's flesh crawled as she asked, "What man, Daisy? Who hurt you?"

"The green-grocer man, Mister Bland; he hurt me."

"I'll kill him, I swear," Sarah thought.

"He said to shut up." The words exploded between Daisy's sobs.

"Shush child, now tell me, how did he hurt you?"

Not hearing her sister, Daisy continued with her word explosions. "He said that now our Ma's dying. We'll all be on the game."

Sarah stroked the hair away from the child's wet uncomprehending eyes.

"He put his thing in me and it hurt."

Not really knowing what else to do, Sarah held Daisy tightly.

"What does he mean; on the game? I don't like his game."

Struggling to contain her anger, Sarah replied. "Dirty, perverted blabber-mouth; he doesn't know what he's talking about."

"He said, Ma's dying. Is our Ma really dying?"

Holding Daisy's shoulders firmly, Sarah guided her sister back to their slab hut herding the ducks along ahead of them.

"He is a very bad man, dear. Make sure you keep well away from him in the future. Now, I'll fill a tub for you to clean up in before the boys get home."

JOSH and GUS

"Come on young Gus, put yer back into it," the blacksmith growled. A shower of sweat ran from his blackened face splattering his leather apron and hairy arms. "I could barely fry an egg on this forge, let alone soften steel. I could fart better than yer have those bellows working. And Josh will yer be putting another shovel of coal into it sometime today?"

"Yes, Mister Campbell," the boys said in unison.

Young muscles rippled along his short arms as Gus pumped the bellows furiously. His piercing blue eyes glowed in the fires of the forge. Taller than his younger brother, but no less solid, Josh bent his back to the shovel lifting coal from the large heap in the corner of the blacksmith's workshop and tossing it into the stirring flames. Both the boys' faces, with the hint of early teenage fluff on their chins, were almost as red as the forge itself. Very little breeze made the shortcut through the open awnings on all four sides of the timber slab hut. Shade from the gum trees outside did little to reduce the blistering heat inside the smithy.

Clang, clang, rest. Clang, clang, rest. Clang, clang, clang, rest. The music of the blacksmith's heavy hammer moulded the red-hot metal amidst the accompaniment of original and imaginative curses. Slowly the shape of a horse-shoe evolved. Scars left by previous burns shone white on the back of brown fire-hardened hands. Using his large tongs, the florid Mister Campbell dropped the shaped shoe into the drum of water. Steam rose to hang like a cloud under the bark roof of the smithy. With ease, the big man hung the tongs and hammer on one of the wooden pegs sticking out of the central post.

"I'm going out for a bit to have another look at the hooves on that Clydesdale in the yard. I'm not totally happy with the shape of this shoe." The blacksmith glanced towards the drum where the wispy steam was disappearing. "Don't you lads be nodding off on me now."

"No, Mister Campbell," was the joint reply. No sooner had Mister Campbell's back disappeared than the boys began talking in undertones.

"Josh, you heard what Sarah said happened to our Daisy at the river yesterday. Aren't we going to do something? Can't we report Mister Bland to the coppers, at least?"

"That'll do not an ounce of good. What notice will they take of the likes of us?" Josh shovelled another load of coal into the furnace. "Don't worry; he's not going to get away scot-free, Gus."

"You won't kill him though, will ya? We don't want to see you swing for the likes of him."

"I'd sure like to, but no, I won't be killing him. Sarah'd kill me if I did," Josh laughed. "I was thinking …"

Mister Campbell marched back into the smithy, automatically bending his head at the lintel.

"I pay you to be keeping this forge going; not thinking, boyos."

"Yes, Mister Campbell."

"Go on be off with you and mind you're here at sparrow fart in the morning."

"Yes, Mister Campbell."

Walking home past Mister Campbell's paddock dam was too much temptation for the boys. Not bothering to remove their coal-dust covered shirts and knee-length multi-patched trousers they gingerly made their way through the muddy shallows and into the deeper cool water where their feet just touched the bottom. Laughing loudly, they splashed and ducked each other for some time before resting back to float. They lay on the water staring up at the cloudless sky with its sun approaching the western horizon.

"Josh, is Ma really dying," Gus asked tentatively.

"The doctor reckons she'll not last more than a day or two." Silence hung over the boys. The minutes ticked by. Hidden tears mixed with the mud-stained water.

"What'll happen to us, then?"

"Sarah and us two'll have to keep bringing in the pennies to feed us all and look after Daisy, I guess," was Josh's considered opinion.

"We could run away to sea. Da' loved the sea. The coastal-tramp he worked on still pulls in to Brisbane regularly. I bet Captain Sloan'll take us on the *Northern Orchid*. He and Da' were good friends and the Captain still pays for our lessons."

Gus duck-dived under the water three times before he resumed floating on his back. He spat water from his mouth as he spoke again to his brother.

"You seem to be enjoying the lessons more now that we have Captain Harris teaching us."

Josh floated quietly for some moments before speaking again. "Yeah, I reckon; we're learning important things now. Stuff about the sea and sailing instead of alphabets and tables. I think Captain Harris needs the money too. It can't have been easy for him; invalided out of his job as harbourmaster."

Gus squirted fountains of water into the air for a while before returning to his original subject. "I'm sure Captain Sloan'll give us a chance if we go see him."

"You're serious about this, aren't ya, mate?" Josh grinned.

"I just wish Da' was still alive. Ma wouldn't be dying and Sarah wouldn't have to whore herself too and we'd all be happy again, like before," Gus swallowed a sob and a mouth full of the dam water. He began to cough and splutter.

"You're right there, Gus."

"What about when he took us fishing in the river."

Josh laughed. "Remember the time he caught that monster shark? When Da' gave it to Billie Toe-bite, camped upstream, the blacks had it in the fire so fast the thing was still wriggling,"

"No other dad could make shanghaies like our Da' either. I wish he were still with us," Gus's eyes glowed.

Josh shook himself. "Gus lad, remember what Ma always says when we start wishing for what we can't hope to have. 'If wishes were horses, beggars would ride, my boys'."

"Yeah, yeah, I know," Gus admitted with some reluctance.

Josh continued, "Besides, we can't leave Sarah to look after Daisy all on her own, you know."

Gus frowned. "No, I guess not; but one day I'm going to sea." He pondered on that thought for some moments before asking, "Did you hear Daisy crying all last night?"

"Yeah, that's what got me thinking. It's not right the mongrel Bland gets away without some pay-back. That pervert's got to suffer for what he did." Josh wiped the water from his eyes. "You know how the bastard keeps his three goats in the yard near his shop at night?"

"If Ma hears you swearing like that, she'll wash yer mouth out with soap. Yeah, I know his goats," the younger brother answered slowly. Alerted to the change in Josh's tone, Gus spun himself upright in the water.

"Well, perhaps one night they might just happen to make their way through the gate into the gardens where he grows his vegetables; by accident of course."

Gus became excited at the thought. "Great; I bet those poor goats'd like a feed in the middle of the night. He probably half starves them. Maybe we could let them into his shop too?"

"Nah, he probably keeps that locked. Remember to keep stum now. Not a word to anyone, including our Sarah."

"Friday nights he's always down at the pub till all hours. Blind as a bandicoot he gets, according to Mister Campbell who reckons he stumbles home like a rock-hoppin', dog-barkin' navigator."

Josh grinned. "Gee I haven't heard that expression since Da' died. He was always saying that."

GOODBYE LUCY

Sarah's greeting as they entered the darkening hut sobered their excitement.

"Where've you boys been? I've been out of my mind with worry. You should have been home an age ago." Sarah paced back and forth across the narrow kitchen. Hands raked at her dark hair.

"The Doctor's just been. Our Ma's passed on and Daisy is still curled up in the corner not saying a word. She's been like that since yesterday's attack."

Both boys stood as if paralysed, trying to absorb the expected but still traumatic news.

"What do we do now?" Josh whispered.

Sarah could not answer. She walked over to her brothers and held them both tightly around the shoulders. Sobs filled the small room.

"It's not fair; why our Ma?" Gus asked no-one in particular. "Do you think God killed her because she whored herself?"

"If that were true, He's not much of a God." Josh angrily wiped his face with the back of his hand. "Wasn't her fault she had a family to feed."

Sarah pushed her brothers away roughly. "Ma wasn't a whore. Mister Dingle, our landlord, provided for us and mother comforted him when he needed it. She wasn't a whore. She done what had to be done to look after us."

It was sometime before Sarah re-claimed control over her voice.

"Josh, I want you to run down to Miss Millie's. She'll be at The Rest as usual. She was here visiting Ma this morning. Miss Millie asked that we let her know when Ma goes."

"That's not surprising. Ma an' her were good friends." Josh took the lantern and headed back out the door.

Sarah held Gus's hands. "Gus, I want you to go to Daisy. See if you can get her to talk to you. She might listen to you. I can't get a thing out of her. She hasn't moved or eaten since the business with Bland. I'm not sure if she even realizes Ma's gone."

Sarah wandered around the room with its dirt packed floor, touching things but not really seeing them. She ran her hands along the central wooden table. Crumbs were flicked off the forms on either side. A sigh filled the small room. All this furniture was made by her father many years before. Using a folded dishcloth, she moved the bubbling kettle resting at the fireplace with its wood-box on the floor. Only an hour before, the bucket of water had been filled from the hand-pump out in the street. She leant against the side wall near the bench with one of its legs propped up on a rock. Her mother's rose-patterned wash-basin sat on its well-scrubbed surface. Against the back wall stood the bunk beds built for the boys. Unpainted slab timber walls provided a dismal backdrop. The silence of the dead and a family in shock was heavy.

The clop of the horse's hooves and the jingle of a harness announced the arrival of Millie from "Millie's Mariners' Rest: Hotel and Lodgings" situated on the rise above the wharf. Jewel-adorned arms held exploding skirts and petticoats close, avoiding the frame of the narrow doorway as she bustled into the gloomy room to hug her best friend's daughter. A small black hat sat upon her piled-up henna-enhanced hair. Her painted face had been toned down with a layer of powder; crows-feet thereupon filled to overflowing.

"Sarah luv, I'm sorry about your Ma. Now I'll be making some tea for us all and I've brought a wee dram to build up our spirits at this sad time."

Sarah screwed up her face as the brew smacked her tastebuds. She gasped.

"Drink up now pet, all of it. It will do you the world of good." Millie took a long sip from her own mug.

Josh barged through the door. "I've put the hobbles on Prince, Miss Millie and settled him near the fig tree. He sure loves those figs."

"Thanks, lad, now come and drink your tea. Sarah and I will go prepare your mother's body for burial."

Water splashed into the wash basin. Turning to Sarah she instructed the girl to bring as many clean rags as possible.

Barely able to control her tears, Sarah spoke. "Miss Millie, they are putting Ma in a pauper's grave and still they're going to make us pay through the nose for their scabby pine box. We do not have that sort of money. What should I do? Do you think they'll put us all in the poor house?"

"Now, don't you be worrying about things like that. I have it all in hand. Your Ma will get a decent burial tomorrow afternoon. The priest owes me a favour or two and I owe your mother a favour or three."

As the newly-awakened young woman and the experienced hotelier performed the last preparation on a mother and a special friend, Sarah told of Daisy's attack the day before.

"Holy Mother, there's some bastards about," Millie fumed. "I'm sure we'll think of something that might improve his manners."

Millie spent some time arranging her friend's hands across the silent heart.

"Did your mother ever tell you how we met?"

Sarah wiped her eyes. "No, she did not."

"It was just after my husband died. He was a good man; nearly three times my age, mind you. But he looked after me good. That's how I got the business. He bequeathed it to me; he had no family. Your mother found me sitting on the river bank, sobbing my heart out. I felt I could not carry on. She came and sat down beside me and comforted me. No other towns-woman ever offered any help. They did not want to be seen consorting with a fallen woman. Lucy called in at the hotel every day for weeks until I began to gather my wits together. Six years ago, when your father was killed, I tried to do the same for her. We ended up firm friends. I will never forget her."

The sun was high next day as the grey draught-horse, Samson, pulling the dray with Miss Millie's handyman, Ned Turner, guiding the reins, entered the Dougall's yard. Sitting in the back, beside the modest casket, were three men looking decidedly uncomfortable. Rough-skinned fingers tugged at the white collars already producing reddened skin, unfamiliar with starch. Jacko Benson, the bouncer at The Rest and two of the regular drinkers jumped out. The smell of lye soap and hair grease preceded them inside the dwelling. Ned tailed them in.

Josh whispered to his younger brother as Sarah directed the men into the room where the body of their mother lay.

"Miss Millie must have given them quite an earful to have them spruce up like this."

Pulling up in a flurry of dust beside the dray came the chestnut gelding, Prince. Millie dressed in sober black was in firm control of her buggy with its polished leather and bronze fittings. She arrived at the door just as the men and their burden were on the way out. Under her supervision, the pine box was settled gently onto the back of the dray.

Only the rattle of the wheels on the stony road, the creaking of leather and jingling of bridles provided the lament for Lucy as her body was taken to its final resting place. Millie's four assistants walked respectfully beside the horse and dray, albeit with the occasional groan at the discomfort of ill-fitting dress and shoes that pinched. Millie and the two girls followed closely in the buggy. Prince worried the bit. He preferred more lively trips than this slow march. The two brothers walked on either side of the animal's head.

Holding the little black bible in front of him like a shield, the preacher, with his red bulbous nose and black cassock, provided a short prayer before the casket was lowered into the earth. Everybody jumped when a penetrating scream filled the air. Daisy threw herself onto the casket as it began to disappear. The unsuspecting rope-holders almost lost control. The casket rocked precariously for some moments as Sarah and Josh dislodged their terrified sister from the top of their mother's coffin.

"Hush, hush, Daisy, oh my darling, my darling sister." Sarah held her tight.

Even the tough Jacko Benson wiped at his tears.

The instant the buggy pulled up at the hut, Daisy flew into her room. Once more her dark plaits were burrowed beneath the narrow pillow. The others, including the helpful men from The Rest, joined together in the kitchen to drink from the large bottle of whisky provided by Miss Millie.

"To our Lucy, may she rest in peace at last," Miss Millie said softly.

JOSH and GUS

"It was good of Miss Millie to do all that for Ma's funeral the other day, wasn't it, Josh?" Gus swung at a cloud of mosquitos feeding off his exposed flesh.

"I told you the mozzies'd be bad tonight. Why didn't you listen to me and rub the kero on your skin?"

"It burns," was the younger brother's response.

"Since when have you been such a sissy? Struth, you keep slapping the damned insects like that you'll wake the whole town up."

"Did you bring that scrap of meat for the dog, Josh?"

"Yes, of course, I did. As soon as the cloud goes over the moon, we'll follow these bushes down the fence line to the vege-garden gate. Don't make a noise and keep low."

"Do you think it was us set that damned dog barking his fool head off earlier?" Gus whispered.

After that fright, the boys had stayed longer than planned in the gully across the road hidden by the grasses and shrubs. They waited for the dog to settle back to sleep.

All was quiet when they crawled across the dusty track. They paused in the thick bush only ten yards from their target. Further progress was halted at the sound of a low deep growl of a large dog close by. The boys froze. Josh struggled to remove the piece of meat, which he had flogged out of the butchers' scrap bin earlier in the day, from the pocket of his pants. Meat, with the paper wrapping still attached, flew in the direction of the slobbering jaws. The slab of meat swung from those jaws as the hungry mutt disappeared in the direction of the house.

"Quick, let's get this done before the dog wants more or that mongrel Bland returns," came Josh's hoarse instruction.

The gate squeaked at their touch. Gus nearly ran in fright. Josh's steady hand held his brother.

"This is for Daisy, remember."

Painstakingly they edged the gate ajar as far as it would go. The goats that were munching nearby looked on inquisitively.

"Won't take them long to check this out," Gus grinned. His teeth shone in the moonlight when the clouds drifted on across the night sky.

Like two wraiths the boys returned to the bushy cover from where they could once again reconnoitre the situation before making the road crossing.

"Struth, here he comes," Josh whispered. "He must have left the pub earlier than usual. Don't move. He won't see us here."

A clamped off high pitched yell sounded. The lads peered around the branches. Between the shadows, cast by the moonlight through the trees, they could see what appeared to be Mister Bland in the arms of a very tall and very solid man. It did look a bit like Jacko Benson from "Millie's Mariner's Rest: Hotel and Lodgings."

"Hell, is he going to kill him, Josh?" Gus's voice shook.

"I'd doubt it, but we never tell a soul if he does; agreed?" The boys spat on their palms and shook hands on the promise.

"What on earth's he doing now?" Josh asked quietly.

Even though the moon was greater than half full, it was difficult to see exactly what was happening only a couple of chain down the road.

"He seems to be taking Bland's trousers off. I think he's using them to tie the rat to the gum tree."

"You're right. Couldn't happen to a better man; pervert." Josh laughed softly. "Come on, we'd better make ourselves scarce. I think they're both otherwise occupied and won't notice us slipping by."

Running down the lane towards their hut, the boys slapped each other's back and laughed quietly. This was the first time they had laughed since their mother's funeral less than a week before. It felt good.

"Won't Bland be happy when he's released by whoever happens along the road in the morning and then finds the goats have invaded his garden," Gus whispered loudly. This set them off into a burst of giggles again.

"I do hope it's the widow-lady Horton. She lives just down that road. Won't she give him a tongue lashing; being out in public and undressed," Josh bent over, struggling to control the sound of his amusement. "Now remember, not a word to anyone; not even our Sarah," Josh instructed.

"One day we should tell Daisy; when she's feeling better and wants to talk to us," Gus suggested.

"Maybe," Josh compromised. They both sobered up at the thought of their once happy sister fading away to a shadow.

DAISY

Curled up in the corner of her small bed, holding the horse-hair-filled pillow tightly over her eyes, Daisy flowed with the butter churn that was her head, turning end over end, round and around; end over end, around and around. Mister Bland's broad hands with their soil-filled fingernails spun the wheel. Despite her clenched eyelids, his long-nosed narrow face, with its pointed ears and wide mouth full of teeth, filled her vision. The echoes of his evil laugh reverberated in her ears. *Spawn of a whore should be drowned at birth. You'll all be on the game now; on the game now; on the game now*. A pitiable moan escaped Daisy's throat. The butter churn spun faster.

Sitting on the up-turned box at the bedside, Sarah's earlier enticements of fresh bread and dripping remained untouched. Daisy had not heard the boys leaving for their day's work at the smithy. She had been totally oblivious of Mister Dingle exerting himself in the next room. The clunk of the coin in the tin above the fireplace went unnoticed. Daisy did not reply to her sister, later in the day, when Sarah said goodbye before leaving for her job cleaning Mister Dingle's house in the next road.

A memory of the kinder voice of Mister Barton, the dairyman, rattled in her head. *Not too fast and not too slow, young Daisy or yer'll spoil the butter.* Mister Barton did not call her the spawn of a whore. Is that what he thought, though?

Spawn of a whore should be drowned at birth. Harlot of a harlot, what do you expect? Dirty trollops the lot of you. Mister

Bland's face returned complete with horns protruding from his forehead. *Should be drowned at birth, drowned at birth; trollops the lot of you.* Daisy reached over the edge of the bed and dry retched. Not having eaten for several days only a small spray of clear watery fluid hit the floor. *Dirty, dirty trollops the lot of you, should be drowned at birth,* bounced off the bony walls of her skull.

Like milk in a churn gradually solidifies so too did Daisy's thoughts.

"Drowned at birth," Daisy whispered, "Drowned at birth."

She rose. The hut was silent. Like a sleepwalker, she pulled aside the hessian across the doorway and slowly made her way to the backdoor. With a creak it opened to her feeble push. *Spawn of a harlot, whore of a whore,* was the beat to which she shuffled her bare-feet. Mud squelched between her toes as she crossed the puddle left from last night's rain. *Drowned at birth, whore of a whore, drowned at birth.*

The Queensland summer sun sizzled her bare head. *Burn in hell, burn in hell*, added itself to the mantra. Daisy did not hear or acknowledge the voice of old Tom Barton at the Milk Depot when he called.

"Good to see yer up and about, Miss Daisy."

Neither her step nor her vacant gaze faltered. The incantation accompanied her past the Milk Depot and onto the track down which she had led the ducks to feed every day.

A black snake slithered across the path and into the long grass in front of her. In Daisy's eyes, the reptile raised its long body on the top of which were six heads calling, *S-s-s-spawn, s-s-s-spawn, s-s-s-spawn of whores-s-s-s. S-s-s-smother and s-s-s-sink.*

As she passed under the gum trees, the crows called from the branches above, *Whore, whore, whore*.

Kookaburras in the silver ash trees laughed, *Spawn of a harlot, har.. har.. harlot.*

The hot tongue of the sun blistered on. *Burn in hell, burn in hell.*

As Daisy approached the river, the light breeze rustled the foliage of the paperbark trees. *Should be drowned at birth, drowned at birth.* She did not feel the cool water as it covered her ankles. She did not feel the wavelets lapping her thighs.

The melting sun maintained the beat. *Burn in hell, burn in hell.*

A flock of galahs screeched overhead. *Harlots, harlots, should be drowned, drowned, drowned.*

As the water lifted her plaits and rippled under her nostrils the river current whisked the unresisting young girl off her feet dragging her under the surface. Daisy did not hear the fisherman call from further along the riverbank.

Daisy only heard her mother's voice. *Daisy, Daisy, Oh, how I love you, my little Daisy.* She did not feel the touch of the large fish tentatively sucking at her face. She only felt her mother's soft caress on her forehead.

Daisy opened her mouth. "I love you too, Ma. Don't ever leave me again." The waters rushed into her lungs and Daisy sunk further into the swirling undertow.

Gus stirred the dying embers in the fireplace. Josh moved the kettle of water onto the heat.

"I think we should talk to Captain Sloan when the *Northern Orchid* is back in the harbour." Gus once again broached the subject of going to sea.

"We could go talk to him but that still leaves the problem of who'll look after Sarah and Daisy."

"Between us, we could earn enough at sea to pay for their keep. Sarah won't need to look after Mister Dingle then."

"Speaking of Daisy, is she talking to anyone yet? It's as quiet as the grave in here." Josh spoke quietly. "Go have a look, will you, Gus?"

"Sarah should be home shortly," Gus said as he walked over to the hessian curtain separating the smaller bedroom which held the two cots. He peered in. "That's odd; Daisy isn't here." Gus then moved to the doorway leading into the larger bedroom. Sarah had been taking Daisy to sleep there at nights with her since their mother had died. "She ain't here, either. That is odd. Daisy hasn't moved for weeks and now she's gone. Sarah would never take her to Mister Dingle's house."

"Not a chance. Maybe Daisy's feeling better and taken the ducks to the river."

"No, the ducks were in the pen when we got home. I saw them," replied the younger of the two boys.

At that point, the backdoor squeaked. Sarah entered with her head bowed.

"Where's Daisy?" Josh asked.

Sarah picked up the water bucket from near the stove and passed it to Gus.

"Will you refill this at the pump for me, Gus? I'll be getting our tea." She turned her head to Josh. "What do you mean, 'where's Daisy'? Isn't she here? Of course, she's here. She hasn't moved for weeks."

"No, Sis, she's not here," Josh replied with a frown upon his face.

"Oh God, what now; she's got to be here somewhere." Sarah ran to check the small bedroom. "I don't believe it. Where on earth could she be?"

"Daisy's not outside in the yard or in the fig tree either," Gus added when he returned with the full water bucket.

Three pairs of matching blue eyes looked blankly at each other.

"Where on earth would she have gone?" Sarah asked. "We've still an hour of daylight left if we're lucky. We'd better go find her."

"Look," Gus pointed at the fresh footprint near the puddle at the gate. "That has to be Daisy's little foot mark."

With heads bowed, the three siblings examined the ground leading out from their yard onto the lane. A voice from the Milk Depot called. "You kids lookin' fer somethin'?"

"Good evening, Tom," answered Josh. "We're looking for our Daisy. We're not sure where she's gone."

"She passed here an hour or so back. Seemed to be in a daze; never spoke a word she didn'. Headin' towards the river, I'd be thinkin'."

The searchers ran on fast. They pulled up short at the sight of several policemen, all standing peering out into the water. Neddy Bell was there with his know-it-all sneer. He walked over to the new arrivals.

"Some kid just walked into the river this arvo. Just walked in; never stopped; drowned. A fisherman over there seen it happen; couldn't believe 'is eyes. The coppers're trying to find the body."

Josh, Gus and Sarah stood aghast. Their minds not believing what seemed apparent.

"It can't be Daisy," whispered Sarah.

"Where's the fisherman?" Josh asked Neddy Bell.

The unkempt youth pointed a finger in the direction of a tall bloke standing alone further up the river bank. When the three approached the fisherman, they found him shaking his head back and forth.

"She didn't even stop. She didn't look sideways; just kept going. I've never seen anything like it in me life." Bare knobbly toes scratched in the dirt.

Josh spoke quietly to the man. "'Scuse me, sir, did you say it was a little girl drowned?"

"Just walked straight in. 'Bout ten or eleven she was, with black plaits. I called and called but she just kept on going right in. I couldn't do a thing. She was too far away. I can't swim, ya see." A protruding Adam's apple jumped in his throat as he struggled to find a little spit in his mouth to swallow.

Loud sobs escaped Sarah's hand-held mouth. The three clasped tightly to each other. Tears fell freely down Gus's face. Josh tried to keep up a brave front but huge gasps burst forth intermittently.

"We'll have to go talk to the coppers," Josh reminded them after some time.

"This is not happening; tell me it's a nightmare and I'll wake up shortly." Sarah tried to control her sobbing.

Later at the hut, when the policeman had left and Millie sat at the table with them, the reality of it all began to sink in.

"Oh, Miss Millie, I feel so guilty. I went off and left her alone." Deep choking sobs took Sarah's breath away. "I would never have left her alone if I thought she was going to kill herself."

Millie held Sarah close patting her shoulder. "Sarah, it's not your fault. Daisy hasn't been herself lately, you know that."

"She wouldn't talk to us. We didn't know," the shattered voice of Gus tried to explain.

With his arm resting on the ledge, Josh stood staring into the fireplace unable to speak; unable to understand.

"Maybe we should have told her of our revenge on that mongrel Bland. Maybe she would've felt a little better?" Gus questioned their decisions.

Millie's head lifted and watched the two boys closely. "What revenge would that be, Gus?" Guilty glances passed between the brothers.

"Josh and I let the goats into his vegetable garden the Friday night after we buried Ma. I guess it wasn't much but we had to do something to pay him back for what he did to our Daisy." Josh spoke quietly.

"Aaah!" Millie almost smiled. "That would be the night before Mister Bland was found tied to the tree outside his house with his own trousers shoved down his throat. Not a stitch covering his prized possessions. The widow-lady Horton found him early Saturday morning. She stirred up a right hornet's nest. Mister Bland was on the next ship to Sydney."

This stirred Sarah. "I hope you boys weren't responsible for that, were you? Mind you, it couldn't happen to a more deserving bit of slime though; I have to admit."

"If you can believe what the preachers tell us, maybe Daisy is with our Lucy now and maybe they both know that revenge has been meted out," Millie smiled. She did not reveal that it was at her instigation and by the hand of her faithful Jacko Benson that the deserving revenge had been implemented.

"Oh, Daisy; we haven't even got a body to bury. Maybe she hasn't drowned. Maybe she's been left high and dry on a sandbank. She could walk in that door at any moment." Sarah clung to hopeless threads as the sobs wracked her body once again.

SARAH

The tabletop moved in waves of ants as they scavenged from the unwashed breakfast dishes framing Sarah's head and arms spreadeagled amongst the debris. The glare of the mid-morning sun shining through the gap in the wall near the stove eventually stirred her. Was it that long since the boys had taken their cribs and left for their lessons with Captain Harris? For some time, she fiddled with the ant lines sending the black bodies, struggling with their loads, off on different tracks. With a drum roll, her hands slapped at the table scattering dead little bodies in all directions. She jumped up.

"What would Ma say if she could see me now?" Sarah bustled over to the fireplace and stirred the dying coals before pouring hot water into the basin. She added cool water from the bucket on the floor. Plates rattled as she began scrubbing them before turning her attention to the tabletop.

The knock on the door sounded just as she was in the bedroom cleaning herself up. She froze. Dark blue orbs rolled in the whites of her eyes. Was that Mister Dingle? He should not be here today. Her hands clamped her mouth shut. She wanted to scream. Breathing was almost impossible. She could not handle him just now. She doubted if she would ever be able to handle his needs again; but what could she do if they were to survive? Tears rolled down her cheeks at the sound of Miss Millie's voice.

"Sarah, Sarah, are you there, dear?"

Sarah could not believe that she hadn't heard the horse and trap pull up; particularly with Miss Millie's style of driving. Her arrivals were always accompanied by a cloud of dust, the horse snorting, hooves stomping and the traces rattling and creaking.

She opened the door and fell into Millie's arms.

"Oh, I'm so glad it's you, Miss Millie. I thought Mister Dingle was calling."

"Hush, child; come inside and I'll make us a good cuppa."

Sarah fussed around putting out two cups; the one without the chip for Miss Millie. Next came the search for their one and only saucer. She poured the boiling water over the leaves in the cream china teapot with its lavender flowered pattern. This had been a wedding present to her mother from their father.

Millie sat in deep thought while watching the younger woman preparing the tea. She made patterns with a few spilt drops on the wooden table top.

"So, Sarah, Mister Dingle is expecting you to take up where your mother left off, is he?" she asked.

"I have no choice, Miss Millie. We owe him the rent and he gives me extra for food. I am to clean his house once a week and provide him comfort twice a week. As Ma said, he needs someone to provide this service since his wife died."

"Hmmm." Millie began to sip at her cup.

"Miss Millie, how do the girls at your place do that all the time?"

"Aah, my child; there are as many reasons as there are ladies of the night. Some hate it. They have had no choice in their lives. They usually keep a gin bottle as their closest companion. Some actually choose that way of life. Others grow fond of the quick cash they can make."

They listened in companionable silence to the rattle of the wagons next door returning with the morning milk from the local farms.

Millie chewed at her bottom lip while she pondered how best to say what she wanted to say. She knew that she had to be tactful. Young Sarah was just as proud as her mother had been. She would not take charity if she thought that was being offered.

"Sarah, I was hoping you might see your way clear to help me out. As you know, I am not getting any younger and I need to train someone up to run The Rest for me in my old age."

"Oh, Miss Millie, you'll never grow old. You could live to be one hundred but you'd still be young," Sarah smiled.

"I don't know about that, dear, but I do know I have slowed down a lot in recent times." Millie took a long sip of the tea. "Anyway, I need someone I can trust. I was hoping you might consider coming to work full-time at The Rest."

Millie saw the look of horror flash across Sarah's face. "Oh no, I don't mean that side of the business, dear. No, I want you to learn everything about running the hotel. You've already helped me out occasionally relieving staff when required. I need you to continue filling in where necessary and when you feel confident you can help me in the bar and the office. Your mother always said you were better than the boys at reading and writing."

"But Miss Millie, I have only just turned sixteen. Surely that is too young to take on such responsibility?"

"Let me be the judge of that. I think you have proven that you can accept responsibility. Did you know, I was not much older than you are now when my dear husband brought me to The Mariner's Rest to help him? He had to teach me to read and write too."

"Will I earn enough to pay the rent here?"

"I was hoping you might come and live at the hotel."

"But what about Josh and Gus. Where would they live?"

"You know the small hut at the back of The Rest? That is where my husband and I first lived. After his death, I moved into a suite of rooms inside the hotel. The hut is used more as a junk room than anything else lately. I hoped we might clean it out for you and the boys to live in. I'd be really grateful if you'd consider this. The boys could give it a coat of paint. It has timber floors too, you know."

"But if we left this hut, Daisy might come back here looking for us? Her body has not been found yet. She might not be dead at all."

Millie reached over and took Sarah's cold hands in her own. The stones in her rings glittered in the strip of sunlight across the table.

"Sarah dear, you heard what the policeman and the witness said. Poor little Daisy had no chance. She walked right into the river without looking back. The sweet little thing was not in her right mind at the time; we know that. With all she had been through at her age, is it any wonder?"

Millie took another long swallow of her tea. Sarah stirred her cup first one way and then the other.

Millie offered another incentive. "Meals will be thrown in too; for the three of you. The boys can give old Ned Turner a hand in the stables and garden; if they have time. Billie Toe-bite comes sometimes but he is often away on walkabout."

"I thought men were crying out for work these days. There's a lot of unrest in the streets."

"You're right, but many of them are not too fussed on work. As a woman trying to run my own business, I need people about me that I know I can rely on."

Sarah grabbed the rag she had used earlier to dry the dishes and began to mop the tears flooding from her eyes.

"And what about Mister Dingle; what will I do about him?"

"Don't you give him another thought; I will sort him out for you. Now, what do you say? Can you come and help me out?"

"Miss Millie, it sounds wonderful but I had best talk it over with the boys first. They will be home from their class soon. They have to go to Mister Campbell's to work in the smithy this afternoon. Can I come down to The Rest later and tell you my answer then?"

The powder-filled crow's-feet on Millie's face deepened. "That is very good of you, Sarah. I will really appreciate the help."

Sarah breathed in the evening sea breezes. Laughing out loud she spread her arms and swung around. The Brisbane River in front of her was a forest of ships' masts. The late afternoon sun striped the walls of The Rest in gold as it shone through the trees. Branches soughed in wind. The industry noises from the wharves, the foundry and sawmill across the water faded as the day receded.

Her nose twitched when the wind drifted a little north bringing the odour of the tannery. With a shake of her head, she returned her thoughts to the here and now. The dreadful year of 1866 must be put behind them. A new year filled with new hopes had arrived. Holding her stirring stomach tight, excitement and nervousness fought for supremacy. Tomorrow would be her first day of regular work.

Earlier today, Miss Millie had walked her through the two-story building describing what would be expected of her. The Rest consisted of a large central block from which two wings extended from opposing sides. The central section held the foyer, the public bar and the kitchen on the ground floor. Above this was the private lounge, for the more privileged guests and a linen store area at the back. The A-wing, overlooking the river, provided private accommodation of seven rooms on the top floor and four rooms on the bottom floor. The remainder of the bottom floor held the private dining room, private drinking lounge and the foyer lounge. The B-wing, which looked out over bushland held the public dining room as well as six cheaper-class guest-rooms on the bottom floor. On the top floor of this wing, Miss Millie's apartment separated the private guest lounge from her more questionable income stream. Six rooms were occupied by the better class ladies-of-the-night. Access to this area was via an outside staircase discreetly concealed by a dense green vine reaching as high as the roof and producing never-ending gold blossoms. A small staircase behind Millie's apartment led down to the kitchen where these ladies and the hotel staff ate their meals.

The wash-house, the male & female outhouses, the hut where Sarah and her siblings now lived and the stables, where Ned camped in the tack room, were the other buildings on the block of land. Sarah had been thrilled to discover the fenced poultry run at the back of the stables where chooks, ducks and geese scratched amongst the kitchen scraps.

Over the past two days of hard work, Sarah and the boys cleaned up Miss Millie's hut. They brought their little bit of furniture here on Miss Millie's wagon. Jacko Benson had let Gus drive Samson, the grey horse, there and back. Her brother had not stopped talking about it.

Sarah's day-dreaming was rudely interrupted.

"Come on, Sis." Josh caught her arm as he raced out of the hut. The boy's shiny face glowed beneath combed damp hair. "That bathtub is great. A person could spend all day lying in that."

"Here I was thinking boys hated water. Don't imagine for one minute that's what you're going to do; spend all day in a bathtub."

"Come on you two slow coaches, let's go get a feed." A wide grin split Gus's face from ear to ear.

"Yes, come on." Josh agreed. "We don't want to be late. I'd hate to get on the wrong side of Mrs. Hamilton. She's a great cook but her face could turn the milk sour."

Sarah tried not to laugh out loud. "Hush now, the both of you. Whatever you do, remember all the manners that Ma taught us."

JOSH and GUS

"There she is," yelled Gus enthusiastically to his brother.

He pointed to the triple-masted ship tied up at the next wharf. Wind blowing off the sea cooled the perspiration on their bodies. Impatient horses stomped their feet while others waited submissively with their wagons in the process of being loading. A recently acquired steam-driven crane, the first on this wharf, belched smoke into the salty breezes while growling ferociously at its task. Seamen and stevedores yelled orders, insults and ribald jokes across the gap between the wharf and ship-decks. Seagulls squawked and fluttered above.

"There she is," he called again. "The *Northern Orchid*. That's Da's old berth."

Josh stood, unmoving for some time, absorbing the noise and movement about him. Scenes of his mother and siblings waving goodbye to their Da' as the *Northern Orchid* left the wharf on another exciting journey, flooded his memory. He recalled their Ma bringing them to greet the ship's returns; not that last fatal trip. Word had reached them the day before the *Northern Orchid* was due to dock. The harbourmaster delivered the news, having heard from the crew of the *Eagle* which arrived two days earlier. For many months after his father's death, Josh had returned alone to watch the ships coming and going; waiting in vain for his father. He shook himself from his musings.

“Well, come on then Gus, let’s see if Captain Sloan is aboard.”

They wound their way around the traffic and workers, being careful not to trip on the rough-hewed timber planks of the wharf or the bollards with large lines wrapped around them to secure their floating charges. A nervous glance passed between the brothers as they stood at the bottom of the *Northern Orchid’s* gangplank. They stared at the ship with its furled sails. Orders rolled from the mouth of a huge man with his dirty blond hair tied in a queue. Sweat-streaked men loading the aft hold, jumped to his command. Another man, whose hair was as red as Mister Campbell’s forge, sat on an upturned barrel in the shade of the mast. The pen in his hand dived into a bottle of ink beside him before scratching entries across the page of a large book. The boys paused in unison. If they wanted to change their minds, this was the time to do so. The moment passed when a loud voice called from the deck.

“Well me hearties, plannin’ on runnin’ away to sea then, are yer? Don’t be shy. Come along up.”

Warily the boys eyed the stranger in his patched canvas trousers and bright red shirt as he spliced the ropes stretched out on the deck. Unruly hair that was unlikely to have ever seen a comb was restrained by a dirty brown bandana.

“We wanted to see Captain Sloan, please, Sir,” Josh asked.

“Oh, you’d be knowing the Captain then, would yer lads? I’m not sure if he’s up for visitors this morning; busy man is our Captain.”

Josh was not sure whether the seaman was teasing him or not.

“Can you tell us when we might see the Captain, then?” he asked.

A voice roared down from the wheel-house above.

"What do those sprats want around here, Sykes?" A grey-haired man with his once-white shirt billowing in the breeze stood with his hands resting on the rail.

"They want an appointment with our Captain Sloan, Sir," the man named Sykes responded.

"Do they now? Well don't muck about, send them up."

At first, when Josh and Gus entered the wheel-house, they did not see the man who had demanded their presence. A deep voice coming from behind the massive wooden wheel made them jump.

"What did you want to see me for?" Before either boy could catch their breath, the man went on. "Here, hold this chock will you, lad or I'll never get this new spoke back in this wheel."

Without thinking, Josh did as he was told. Without needing to be asked, Gus bent down and handed the man the mallet with which to pound the timber into place. A fit of coughing took Gus as he tried to cover his swallowed gasp. He had caught his first sight of the thick white scar laying like a bleached rope down the suntanned face from the corner of the man's left eye, down the front of his left ear, and into the leathery neck.

Windows allowed observation from three sides of the wheel-house. Below the windows, towards the ship's bow, a chart cupboard ran the width of the room. Doorways on both the port and starboard sides led out onto a narrow walkway surrounding the wheel-house. A tall cupboard filled the starboard corner towards the ship's stern.

"Handy pair aren't you; twins? Done a bit of carpentry have you?"

Josh held firmly to the chock as shown. "I'm Josh and this here's my brother, Gus. Our Da' was the carpenter on this very ship. Jimmy Dougall was his name."

Peering around the helm, Captain William Sloan looked long and hard at the boys.

"Aah, I thought there was something familiar about you lads. You've grown a bit. Four or five years now, isn't it?" The Captain went back to his work. He gently tapped the wheel-spoke into its final resting place.

"Five, going on six years, Sir," Josh spoke.

"Sad day when we lost Jimmy. He saved my life, you know. How's your mother keeping then?"

Gus concentrated on tapping the mallet as indicated leaving Josh to answer.

"We buried our Ma a couple of weeks back."

"I'm sorry to hear that. She was one proud woman." He paused deep in thought. "Do I take it that you want to follow in your father's footsteps?"

"Yes, Sir," Josh replied. "Gus and I want to get a berth on the *Northern Orchid.* We are good workers. We've been helping Mister Campbell at the smithy most days.'

Gus joined in. "We can read and write too, you know and now we're learning from Captain Harris all the things we need to know at sea. Ma told us that it's you who's been paying for our lessons since Da' died. We'd like to thank you for that, sir."

"Hmm. I have been after a young lad to give the bosun a hand maintaining the sails and rigging. Do either of you know the nautical knots?"

Gus spoke up, "Yes, Sir, our Da' taught us all the seaman's knots before we could walk, just about."

"We understand semaphore signals too," Josh butted in.

"Ha, that'd be Jimmy; always said his boys were going to be seamen."

Rubbing his chin thoughtfully, Captain Sloan spoke slowly. "I don't know if I really need two of you though; that's the rub."

"I'll work for just my tucker and a corner to sleep, Sir," said Gus before his brother could say a word.

"Hmm. Don't suppose you know anything about these new steam engines at all?"

The boys' faces dropped. The sparkle left their eyes. They had only ever seen a steam engine from a distance; the one on the wharf and the other on the river tugboat. Mister Pettigrew had a steam-powered sawmill but they had never been allowed in there.

"No Sir, but I'd like to learn. I learn real fast, Sir. I'm good at 'rithmatic." The usually reticent Gus continued with his spiel.

"Hmm. Well, you might get your chance. Once we get loaded here, the *Northern Orchid* will be setting sail for Sydney. We leave on Friday morning's tide. While there, she is going into dry dock to have a steam engine with a screw propeller fitted."

"Well, Sir, I'm your man." Gus poked out his chest and stretched his body as high as he could, without standing on tiptoes.

The Captain put down his tools and rested his back against the map cupboard. Taking a rag out of his top pocket he rubbed the sweat from his face hiding his grin at the boy's enthusiasm.

"Doesn't he sound like his father?" Captain Sloan mused.

"Let me think on this for a time. Do you know 'Millie's Mariner's Rest', up the hill?"

"Yes, Sir. Miss Millie is, was, a friend of our Ma."

"Yes, I remember that now. Meet me at The Rest tonight at eight o'clock. I'll have an answer for you then."

"We'll be there, Sir. Do you need any more help with this, before we go?" Josh offered.

"No boys, I've got it from here." The Captain turned to read a large log-book lying open on the top of the cupboard.

With eyes shining, the boys made a slippery exit down the gangway to the deck. As they approached the gang-plank they noticed the seaman called Sykes had been joined by a brown-skinned muscled man with a four-cornered-knotted cloth on top of what appeared to be a bald head. This fellow gathered the heavy rolled-ropes from the deck and tossed them over his shoulders like they were nothing more than pieces of string.

"Now there goes a nice pair of bum-boys, Bony," Sykes spoke in an undertone but the words did not escape the sharp hearing of the young lads.

"We'll need to keep an eye out for them two, I reckon," Josh warned his brother.

TWO

MILLIE'S MARINER'S REST HOTEL

BRISBANE 1867

MILLIE

Dancing shadows cast by the flickering candlelight lessened the impact of Captain William Sloan's facial scar. The wooden chair creaked as he turned sideways and stretched his legs. He glanced fondly at his companion.

"Do you remember Jimmy Dougall, Millie?" Sloan asked.

Millie handed her long-time customer and good friend a glass of whisky on a silver platter. She paused for some moments. Her eyes saddened.

"Jimmy? Yes, very much so. He was my best friend's husband, but you know that. Lucy died recently. It was all so tragic at the time. Lucy died and a short time later her youngest daughter drowned; seems like it was suicide. Why do you ask?"

"I had the boys, Josh and Gus, out on the *Northern Orchid* today, wanting a berth. I told them to meet me here at eight o'clock tonight, for an answer. I hoped to talk to you first. I thought you might know them."

"They are fine boys and hard workers. The family did not have it easy when Jimmy died."

"I am sorry to hear that. As you know, I tried to offer his wife financial support but she refused to accept what she thought of as charity. She did accept the tuition for the boys. Mrs. Glendenning always sent favourable reports and now Captain Harris seems to think they will make worthwhile seamen."

Millie's soft white hand, with its jewelled fingers sparkling in the lamp-light, covered the salt and sun-hardened wrist of her guest.

"You will have to go a long way to get a better pair of lads. That family could well do with a change in fortune. I have the eldest girl taking over the housekeeping duties here this week."

"Oh, what happened to Mrs. Chapman? She was always such a dragon lady. You never needed a guard dog with her around."

"That may have been but she knew how to keep her lip buttoned and the place was always clean. Her husband died of typhoid recently. She's going to family in Sydney; on the *Northern Orchid* I believe; this Friday." Millie rose and picked up the Captain's glass. "Another, dear?"

William Sloan nodded.

"Now, it is nearly eight. I'd best nip downstairs and bring the boys up here for you. Have you decided what you will do with them?"

"What else can I do? I will take them under my wing. It's the least I owe Jimmy Dougall. They are better off here in Brisbane, learning all they can from Daffy Harris for the moment, though. There is little they can learn on the *Northern Orchid* while she's in dry dock in Sydney; except how to get into trouble, maybe. I do have a little scheme up my sleeve for them. I hope they won't be too disappointed. Where are they living, anyway?"

"They and their sister Sarah are staying in the hut at the back of the hotel."

"What, in the old love shack?" Captain Sloan roared with laughter.

"That's enough out of you, Billy Sloan." Millie tried hard to look serious. "The boys give old Ned a hand in the garden and the stables. It works out very well."

The bar downstairs had closed and the quiet of the night settled around them. Millie sat contentedly in her private boudoir at her large mirror. William Sloan repeatedly drew the brush through her long hair marvelling at its softness and gleam.

"Ah, Millie, this hair is more beautiful than a sea chest full of gems."

"And you, Captain Sloan, are always ready with my sea chest of gems," she said dropping her hazel eyes.

"Hah woman, always the flatterer? Come to bed now; my gems need polishing I think."

Millie rose from her padded chair and turned to hold her lover. She kissed his forehead, his eyes, his lips, his scar.

"Mmm, Will, it's always a pleasure to welcome you back." The bed creaked as they slid over the satin sheets.

JOSH and GUS

The soft light of the candle cast a pale glow through the window of the hut. Josh, Gus and Sarah, with their heads close together, talked of the day's events.

"So, what is Captain Sloan saying exactly? He's going to take you on the crew of the *Northern Orchid*, isn't he?" A furrow deepened between Sarah's eyebrows.

"Yes, but the ship is going into dry dock in Sydney. There is nothing for us to do there. The *Orchid* won't be back for at least six months." Josh began the explanation.

"He has organized for us to continue our lessons with Captain Harris. He has also spoken to the captain on the steam tug and the engineer in charge of the steam engine on the crane." Gus broke in.

Josh took back his tale. "They are going to employ us as coal shovelers for a couple of days a week. We are to learn all we can about, what Captain Sloan calls, 'these new fandangle machines'."

Gus patted Sarah's hand. "And, Captain Harris is going to teach us all about the different types of ships and all about how to sail them."

Sarah laughed and turned as Josh spoke.

"He'll show us how to use the sextant too."

Sarah held up her teacup in salute.

"Here's to 1867 then, boys. It's made a good start."

The gas light near the harbourmaster's office illuminated the shadowy figures of workers beginning to stir along the wharves. Sunrise was barely a thought in the sky when Gus clambered aboard *The Lion.* Thick mist blanketed the river. Steam drifted up from the pannikin held in the captain's hand.

"Good morning, Captain." A grin filled Gus's face.

"Yeah; the engine's waiting," came a husky reply, followed by a deep rattling cough. A dollop of phlegm glistened in the glow of the hurricane lamp before landing with a plop in the river. "As soon as you've a head of steam I want to know. We need to be at the north passage at full tide. *The Miracle* needs all the water we can give her unless you want to see her on the sand. With a bit of luck, we may be finished with her in time to pick up *The White Southerner.* I'd like to see the look on the faces of those other scavengers if I can snap her up from beneath their noses."

With a thump, Gus jumped down behind the bulkhead that offered protection to three sides of the engine and boiler area. His grin widened even more as he caught the captain's words. It was a well-known fact on the wharf that Captain Tobias Johns would sell his own grandmother to beat his rivals to a tow job. Woe betides any other tugboat trying to sneak in under his guard. Some even said he'd been known to ram his floating competition.

Coal rattled in the bin as Gus shovelled with relish. While the pressure in the boiler built up, he checked and greased every moving part on the Grasshopper Steam Engine that powered the river tug. Steam-engine oil was fed in where necessary. As he lay on his back inspecting the attachment of the connecting rod to the lever, the sound of the engineer stumbling down the three steps from the deck caused him to lift his head. Pain shot through his skull when his forehead connected with the rod, making an audible sound.

"Damn." Rubbing at his forehead, Gus groaned as he watched the old man's shaky legs carry him over to the narrow bunk against the bulkhead on the starboard side of the engine. The engineer landed with a crash on its boards. After patting the pockets of his large coat to ensure his liquid lunch was on hand, the man threw his head back and began to snore. One of the deckhands bent down to speak to Gus through the doorway.

"Delivered with our compliments. We found him on his hands and knees at the gates. Don't know that you'll get a lot of help from him today."

Gus raised his finger in acknowledgment. These past four months he had been doing this work. He was unperturbed at the thought of being in charge of the engine; in fact, he preferred to be left alone with his precious machine. When the boiler pressure was ready, he cranked up the engine before signalling to the captain above. Another workday on the river was to begin. The paddle wheels churned the river to frothing white water.

As Gus leant out past the bulkhead, he watched the process of securing the ship's hawsers to the bollards on the tugboat. *The Miracle* towered above *The Lion*. He savoured the smell of the salt, the burning coal and the engine oils. The steam engine ticked away quietly as it exerted just enough power to keep the tugboat in position. From the ship's deck above, he heard the bosun direct his crew to discharge the smaller hauling lines. On the tugboat, Captain Johns swore fluently in three languages at his deckhands who were, according to him, not using enough effort in dragging the lines over to the tug. Once the cables were secured, Gus jumped back inside to add more coal to the boilers. Now his little engine would show them all how it's done.

Gus's teeth gleamed white in the black soot covering his face. He felt good after a successful day. *The Miracle* had been delivered out to sea and they had towed *The White Southerner* back through the passage with plenty of water under her. Gus laughed out loud when he recalled Captain John's sparkling eyes and his teeth chomping the cigar as they passed the opposition tugboats. *The Lion* had been just off Lytton at the entrance to the Brisbane River and heading in to harbour with *The White Southerner* in tow. Gus released the grubby scarf from around his neck and rubbed the blackened sweat from his face. He watched the water and pressure gauges on the boiler. His eyes then turned to the engine. The whoosh-whoosh accompanied by the hushed clickity clackity ticking of the piston pumping was like the sound of angels singing; to Gus's ears. The engineer had surfaced twice during the day to teeter around the engine, take several deep swallows from his bottle before landing back on the bunk where his snoring competed with the tug's motor.

The sun was low in the sky when they approached their anchorage. He felt the shudder as the Captain nudged the tugboat in beside their jetty which was no more than a huge tree lying on its side. In turn, Gus nudged the engineer. Without a word of thanks, the sour man with his red face and bulbous nose proceeded to make his way onto the deck. Gus hardly noticed as he closed the dampers to reduce the air flow and settle the fires. He took a final look to ensure the engine and boiler were left as they should be.

As Gus's feet hit the firm ground, the Captain of the tugboat called him back.

"Working down there with the engine, on your own, has not gone unnoticed, lad. You're doing a good job."

With a light heart and his belly rumbling Gus stepped out for home. Dusk approached fast. Soon the night watchman would fire the gas lights. Gus scanned the area, in the hope that his brother Josh may be late finishing his job on the steam crane. There was no sign of him.

Unseen, behind a mountain of crates, Head-breaker Anderson and his six cronies watched as Gus Dougall jogged through the gates.

"That's the younger'un. 'E'll make a good punchin' bag. 'Im and 'is brother think they can just walk onto the wharf and take our jobs. 'Bout time we taught 'em a lesson." Head-breaker stirred his fellow hooligans on. "Let's go get 'im."

The seven men were just about ready to bounce Gus when the second brother stepped out from behind a tree.

"G'day mate, how'd your day go?" Out of the corner of his eye, Josh caught the movement of the fast-approaching danger. "Look out; here's trouble."

Josh ran the last few yards and stood back to back with his brother. Gus twisted about to see the attackers surround them, like blowflies targeting a boiling cabbage.

"Remember what Da' always said, 'Chin down and guard up'."

There was no chance to say anything more. A fist like a rock slammed into Gus's head. He felt his body shudder. The world spun for a second. Instinctively he ducked as another jab shot over his head. After that, it was hit what he could when he could. Some connections were solid. He desperately wanted to rub at the pain in his hands but there was no time for such luxuries. It felt like every bone there was broken. The sound of flesh on flesh came from behind him. He hoped Josh was making out okay.

"Hoy!" A shout went unheard amongst the brawlers.

After riding across the river on the ferry nearby, six deckhands approached.

"Ain't that Head-breaker Anderson?" The blond giant asked his mates.

"Yeah, heroes as usual. Looks like seven on two, to me." The wiry bloke with the long black hair answered.

One of the aggressors lay face down in front of Josh. He struggled to raise his body but each time his arms would not hold him and he collapsed into a heap again. Another one of the gang had stepped back, away from Gus. Strident breaths whistled through his bloody mouth as he bent over gasping for air. Gus stepped forward, grabbed the man's shoulders and brought his knee up hard. The squeal was like that of a stuck pig. The fellow fell to the ground moaning. He curled up in the foetal position, hands cradling the soft bits between his legs.

"That's Jimmy Dougall's two lads; they stay at The Rest. Looks like they're chips off the old block, I reckon. They're not doing too bad a job." The grey-haired fellow in the middle of the group from the ferry piped up.

"Well, come on then. A friend of Millie's a friend of ours." The blond giant spoke again.

With a shout, they joined the melee. The giant copped a thump right between the eyes as he barged in. He stood upright and shook his head. The blue eyes swung left and right for a moment. The man's mouth opened wide and burst out with a roar that a prize bull would have been proud of. His thick long arms reached out and snatched up the first fellow he managed to take a hold of; which happened to be Head-breaker Anderson himself. The giant lifted the lout high over his head; well above those around him.

A voice from within the group yelled. "Lookout fellas, Snow's gonna throw the Caber."

Following that introduction, Snow leant back balancing his feet before tossing his burden as if it was little more than a feather pillow. A blood-curdling scream blanketed them all as the body passed over the group before landing, with a crash, against the wall of the maintenance shed. A slab of timber broke away from the wall and dropped with a thud on Anderson's head. He lay quiet.

The fight went out of the trouble makers. They slinked away nursing their wounds and dragging Anderson with them. Gus was still swinging. He nearly slugged one of their rescuers.

"Jeez, hang on there, bruiser. I'm not the enemy. How's the damage report?" Snow laughed.

"Thanks for coming by, Mister." Using the tails of his shirt, Josh wiped at a fast-swelling eye into which blood dribbled from a cut above the right eyebrow.

Gus stood with his shoulders slouched. His thumb and forefinger prodded at his bent nose with great care. Blood dripped onto his feet. He sucked at his split bottom lip.

"That's not gonna do much for your beauty. That nose could be broken or maybe just bent. I could have a go at straightening it for yer; if yer want." The wiry man suggested.

"She'll be okay, thanks. Come on Josh, let's get home. Sarah'll be wondering where we are," Gus mumbled.

"We'll walk along with you. I wouldn't put it past Anderson to jump you between here and The Rest if he thought you were alone," the black-haired man said. "Come on fellas; if we get a move on, we may get a drink before Miss Millie closes the pub."

Snow and his mates were all for shouting their new friends a pint but Jacko, who was behind the bar this evening, had other ideas.

"Miss Millie'd tear strips off me if I served under-aged drinkers." He pointed a finger at Gus and Josh. "Besides, your sister'll give you a few more bruises if she catches you in here having an ale."

"Jacko, do you want me to let Miss Sarah know her brothers are home battered and bruised? She's still up with Miss Millie." Ned spoke up from where he sat in the corner nursing a drink.

"Yeah, mate." Jacko then turned to Snow and his group. "So, I take it you helped the boys out of a tight spot."

"Ooh, I don't know about that; they were doing all right on their own. Head-breaker Anderson and his cronies jumped them near the river. We just evened up the odds a little."

"Thanks, fellas; 'ave a drink on the house and then I must close. It's nearly time."

SARAH

"Ooh, Sis what is that stuff? It feels like acid." Josh complained as his sister put a friar's balsam poultice on the cut over his right eye. Ned stood at the door watching. He offered advice to Sarah while she administered treatment.

"Boys are such babies. Now keep still. If this stuff runs into your eyes, you'll really have something to worry about." She began to rinse Josh's bunged up eye with salty water.

"What are you doing now? Is that a shovel you're using to open my eyelids?"

"Bah, I bet if it was Mavis Navin from the butcher shop fixing your wounds, you'd be the big brave hero. You'd never let her see you whimpering like a scaredy-cat."

Josh blushed a bright pink. Sarah grinned as she wiped the eye dry with a clean cloth before painting the grazes on his knuckles with iodine solution.

"Now, Gus, let me have a look at you."

Gus hesitated in approaching his sister's tender mercies.

"Don't muck about. It's getting late and I have to take eggnog up to Miss Millie shortly. She's been feeling poorly today."

Rubbing his hands, Gus came and sat on the chair in front of Sarah.

"Miss Sarah, you need to feel the bones in the lad's hands. Wiggle the fingers to make sure nothing is broken inside," Ned advised. "Humans ain't a lot different to animals, yer know."

Sarah picked up Gus's hands and ran her fingers lightly over the long bones; one hand at a time. She bent each finger in turn; in and out. "Is that right, Ned?"

"Yes, Miss. It don't look like you've broken anything there, Gus, but those hands will be black and blue tomorrow."

"How on earth did the pair of you get into a fight?" Sarah did not give the boys a chance to answer. "It's those louts that have been stirring up trouble since the food riots in September, I'll bet. Half of them aren't interested in working anyway."

Gus rolled his eyes at Ned as he listened to his sister getting on her high horse. His grin quickly turned to a grimace when she painted his knuckles with iodine.

"We didn't start it." Gus piped up.

Josh brought a pannikin of tea to the table and began to sip.

"We didn't start the fight, Sis. It was like Da' always said, 'Don't go looking for a fight but if one comes lookin' for you, don't be a coward'."

When Sarah applied a little of the poultice mixture to the split on his bottom lip, Gus jumped up off the stool with a howl of pain.

Sarah sighed. "Okay, okay, I've done now. There's some left-over stew on the stove. You'll have to look after yourselves. Mrs. Hamilton has been unwell today, too. She won't be in tomorrow. I'll have to be up before the crack of dawn to prepare the breakfasts. Now, I'm going back over to the pub to settle Miss Millie for the night, then I'm going to be looking for my bed."

Sarah stood by the window in Miss Millie's room gazing out across the river. A few lanterns glowed through the house windows on the town-side. Hurricane lamps swung in the hands of some pedestrians out braving the chilly evening. Lamps also hung from the carriages as they moved about the town. Lamps on the vessels in the river swayed with the movement of the waters, their reflections dancing across the surface. The rustling of the leaves in the trees drifted up through the open window. A dog barked nearer the riverbank. The smell of wood-smoke hung in the air.

She turned to move back into the room. Heavy dark blue curtains divided Millie's room into three sections. The front area was accessed from the private lounge next door. It was furnished with two comfortable armchairs and a small table. Millie now sat in one of these chairs sipping slowly at the drink Sarah had delivered. A large four-poster bed covered with a bright scarlet bedspread took centre place in the middle section. Drapes had not been pulled completely across the bathtub and commode in the rear section. A narrow doorway opened out onto the back steps.

"Thanks for this, dear. It's a long time since someone has waited on me."

"Miss Millie, it's my pleasure to look after you. Me and the boys really appreciate what you've done for us, you know."

"I know, lass. Will you be alright with just you and Meg in the kitchen on your own, tomorrow? We have that group arriving from London around lunchtime. A Doctor Goldfinch and his manservant." Millie wiped her finger around the inside of her eggnog glass before putting it into her mouth and sucking off the dregs. "Who on earth has a manservant these days?" Her hands trembled as she placed the glass on the small table. "His sister, Mrs. Baldwin, with her companion and a maid will be accompanying the doctor, Sarah. I've booked them into the top floor rooms. I'm not sure where they'll want their hired staff to be accommodated. You'll have to sort that out when they get here. There's still plenty of rooms downstairs."

"Now, don't you worry about a thing, Miss Millie. The boys have their lessons with Captain Harris in the morning. They'll help with the kitchen duties in the afternoon." Sarah began to turn down the bedclothes. She swung back with a rush. "Oh, Miss Millie, should I be doing anything with the ladies next door?" She nodded her head in the direction of the rooms beyond the apartment's wall.

Millie smiled. "No thanks, Sarah. The girls can look after themselves. I'm very selective with whom I chose to have there. The girls are usually pretty honest with my percentage. They come to me recommended by my friend in Sydney." Millie stood up with a grin on her face. She crooked her little finger at the younger woman. "Come here, Sarah. I'll show you how I keep track on what is happening; if I am a bit suspicious."

She led the way to the wall where a large painting of a forest hung. Millie swung the frame to the side. A small piece of raised timber stuck out of a knot in the wall plank. She twisted the knob back and forth and it popped out leaving a small hole.

"Look through there."

Curiosity moved Sarah forward. She held her eye to the hole in the wall. A clear vision of the lantern-lit hallway between the rooms in which the working girls lived and carried on their trade opened up to her. She was able to see all the way down to the sitting room and entrance door at the other end.

Millie stood at her shoulder. "I'm able to see visitors entering and for how long they stay. It's not too hard to work out what the girl should be earning and what my percentage should be at the end of the week."

With a laugh, Sarah replaced the wooden plug. "You're no one's fool, are you, Miss Millie?"

"They'd have to get up early in the morning to put one over on me." She laughed also which set off a fit of coughing.

Sarah helped her over to the bed. "Let's be having you up into bed, I think."

After leaving Millie, Sarah exited down the back steps and collected the large brass key hanging from the nail in the post beside the pantry. The bolts rattled in the doors of the kitchen and central area as she checked each one. She then slipped out through the back door locking it securely with the large brass key. A horse snorted in the stables and stamped its hooves. Either Prince, Emperor or the draught-horse, Samson seemed a little restless tonight. No lamp- light shone from Ned's room at the back of the stables. A tired smile lightened her face when she noticed that the boys had left the lantern alight for her return. As she tucked the key into her pocket, her hand touched a large envelope that had arrived earlier for Miss Millie.

"Oh bother." She paused and turned. "No, it can wait until morning. Miss Millie should be asleep by now. I won't disturb her. Time enough for business in the morrow."

Sarah yawned and rubbed her arms as she made her way across the back yard. Winter was not far away. She felt as if her head had barely hit the pillow when it was time to get up. The sound of several roosters crowing in the area heralded the promise of dawn. The ammonia-like odour of the horses in the stables drifted through the open doorway. Ned was up and about. She patted the pockets of her jumper to ensure that Miss Millie's envelope was still there. A mopoke called from the tree near the stables as she scraped the brass key across the lock, struggling to see the keyhole in the dark. Disturbed by her approach, an animal shot off over the box of wood chips and into the garden of geraniums. Sarah preferred to think of it as a cat or a possum. The thought of a rat that big sent shivers down her spine. With her hands full of wood chips from the box near the door, she entered the kitchen. Her sigh filled the room as she rubbed her cold fingers together over the warmth still present in the woodstove. The handful of woodchips soon burst into dancing flames. Larger pieces of wood were then added. With two hands, she lifted the kettle onto the heat. It took but a minute to fill a small pan with oatmeal and water and place it on the stove. She planned to eat with Josh and Gus before they set off to their mystery meeting with Captain Harris at 6 am. A larger pot of oatmeal stood ready to cook, for the later breakfasts.

As Sarah prepared and kneaded the dough for the bread-making she read the list of current guests.

In the room A-9, Mister Boris, the Prussian, with the unpronounceable last name, had not changed his breakfast order during his four-year stay. Mrs. Keppel on the top floor room A-7 had never changed her breakfast menu in six years. The B-wing, bottom floor, currently housed three male guests; all drummers.

Sarah gave her dough one last thump and a roll before placing it in the large china bowl. She covered it with a clean cloth. Steam rose from the bubbling kettle. With a last stir, the small pot of oats was removed and served into three bowls just as Gus entered through the back door followed by Josh swinging the milk can.

"Mister Barton just delivered the milk. He sends his regards, too." The large lidded can landed with a dull thud on the table.

As Sarah spooned the oats into her mouth, she resumed checking the guest list.

Five working girls were in residence. They usually wandered down late in the mornings with blotchy face paint and bleary eyes. Each one ate the basic breakfast with tea to which some of them added generous dollops of liquid from small bottles secreted within the folds of their wraps.

Jacko and Ned always had oatmeal and eggs with charred bread and copious amounts of white tea with sugar. Sarah stirred her large pot of oatmeal. The pantry door opened with a squeal as she poked her head in to check her supplies for the dinner today and tea tonight. It would be after ten this morning before the Londoners were collected from their ship anchored off Lytton and delivered on *The Platypus,* to The Gardens. They then must make their way through customs. Sarah did not expect them here, at the hotel, before 1 pm. No doubt they'd arrive famished. Ned was to take Samson and the dray to collect their luggage. Jacko had Miss Millie's instruction to use the carriage with both Prince and Emperor. He was to ensure the group encountered no difficulties with the formalities.

Wooden chairs dragged on the floor as the boys finished eating. They dropped their dishes in the sink.

"Don't go running off. Miss Millie wants you to take this bag of biscuits over to Captain Harris." Sarah took up a large brown packet from the end of the table and passed it to Josh.

"Bye, Sis," they called as they made a quick exit into the brightening morning.

"Bye, Gus. Bye Josh. And don't go eating those biscuits on the way. And don't forget you have to help me in the kitchen this afternoon." Sarah called to their backs.

Footsteps from upstairs signalled that Miss Millie was awake. Sarah busied herself preparing a tray. Cockroaches scattered as she dug into the box under the sink. Yesterday, she had hidden an orange given to her by Billie Toe-bite. She knew not to ask where he may have gotten it from. With the help of a sharp knife, she lifted the skin in one long narrow strand. A bloom from the garden was set on top of the letter that had been burning a hole in her pocket all morning. Sarah was half-way up the stairs when Mrs. Hamilton's daughter entered the kitchen shutting the door with a bang. The young girl's face looked as sour as a jug of one-week-old milk. Meg was not an early riser.

"Hush, Meg." Sarah admonished. "The guests are still sleeping and will not thank you to go around slamming the doors."

“Sorry, Miss.” The lips remained pouted.

“You can stir those oats and begin setting out the trays.”

JOSH AND GUS

"I hope you boys know how to row a boat." Captain Harris greeted them at his back door looking every bit the retired sea captain. He wore a white shirt and a pair of trousers with a navy jacket all neatly pressed by his housekeeper. Frayed edges trimmed his British navy cap. Scrubbed white canvas shoes covered his feet. Aging brown eyes lit up at the sight of the packet of biscuits.

"That Miss Millie is a gem." He stashed the bag in the kitchen cupboard. "Come on then, don't dawdle." He pointed to a large box on the end of the kitchen table. "Bring that along, will you? Be very careful with it. It is worth more than your life probably. Oh, and bring that waterbag at the door too. It may be winter but rowing is still thirsty work."

The two walking sticks clicked and clacked along the path as he made surprising speed towards the river. His feet stumbled when he turned his head around to speak again.

"So, can you boys row a boat?"

Josh supported the man's arm for a moment before answering.

"Yes, Captain Harris. Our Da' often took us out fishing in his friend's boat. It has been a long while though."

"Well, you'll have a few blisters to add to your bruises by the time you finish rowing today, I'm thinking."

Josh and Gus rolled their eyes behind Captain Harris' back.

"You boys will have plenty of time to explain the bruises while you are pulling on those oars. On the way, you can stop and take sightings with the sextant. We'll see just how accurate you can be."

The boys' eyes glistened with anticipation. Figuring their own position with a real sextant and not just in theory sounded a great lark. The smell of sea-salt was strong on the early morning breeze. Water lapped the side of a wooden dingy tied up to a ti-tree. Three inches of dirty water and leaves lay in the bottom of the fourteen-foot-long boat. An old frayed rope, with what looked like a cut off piece of railway track attached, represented the anchor. A re-fashioned kerosene tin provided a bailing can. Two oars with their rusty rowlocks attached, looking like they might have been rescued from the town dump, lay in the bottom of the boat.

"This is it." Captain Harris told the boys. "The man, who owns it, calls it *Perfection*. He must have been looking into the bottom of an empty rum bottle when he named it, I think."

With the captain's precious box resting on a seat, Josh and Gus untied the boat from the tree and pushed it further out into the shallow water. Gus began to bale while Josh helped Captain Harris into the small vessel. He settled on the seat at the stern with the box in his lap. The Captain dipped his good hand into the water on the starboard side of the boat. He then licked his fingers.

"Aaah; salt water." He sighed.

Josh and Gus reached for an oar each as they sat on the middle seat.

Captain Harris laughed until tears poured down his face, while the novice rowers tested their skills.

"I do hope I remember how to swim," he chuckled. "I think I may be doing so before the day is out. On the other hand, we may never leave this spot."

Gus and Josh flushed red. The little boat went around and around in circles before threatening to settle on the shoreline. The oars clattered in the rowlocks. Josh and Gus argued over who should be rowing this way or that way.

"If you boys stop arguing for five minutes, you may need to figure out how to avoid running into the *Kate*. She is rather bigger than us. The Queensland Government will not take kindly if you bump into their pride and joy while she's anchored in the Brisbane River."

The row-boat rocked rather wildly as the incoming tide pushed it closer and closer to the port side of the large boat. Just as it seemed a crash was inevitable, Gus reached out and pushed hard against the hull. His hands walked their dinghy along the length of the *Kate* that seemed to look down upon them with a baleful glare. When the tide spat them around the bow of the *Kate,* they all bent their heads as the dinghy slipped under the anchor chain and bounced along up the river.

To add insult to injury, several native children who had been checking fish traps at the river's edge saw the antics of the amateur rowers in the dinghy. Fingers pointed in the rowboat's direction while squeals of laughter echoed across the waters.

The next obstacles were the timber pylons of the Victoria Bridge. The captain grinned as he commented again.

"Don't bump that bridge whatever you do. It's so eaten away with the cobra worm you could bring the whole thing down upon our heads. And look out for John Williams' ferry heading this way. You should have plenty of time to evade it. There is a good reason why the folks call it *The Time Killer*."

Eventually, common sense took over and Josh and Gus began to synchronize. At long last, the dinghy headed off upstream, with the tide, as intended. The Victoria Barracks had only just disappeared out of sight when Captain Harris called the first halt.

"Ship oars, lads." They sat drifting for a few moments watching fish jumping in the shadows of the mangroves that were growing near the banks.

The captain then slid the lid of the box open. As if a precious jewel was inside or maybe a deadly snake, he carefully pulled aside the oilcloth and withdrew the sextant.

"My father gave this sextant to me when I first became a midshipman. I have never broken any part of it in all that time; including the mirrors. I do hope we are not going to break anything today." He took a white handkerchief from his top pocket and reverently wiped the already shiny instrument.

Josh and Gus looked at each other nervously. Would they be the cause of damage to Captain Harris's prize possession?

"Right, you have already learnt all the theory about the sextant; why you use it and when you use it and how you use it. Now you **will** use it." He held the brass instrument out to Josh. "I have the timepiece and the logarithmic table book here in the box when you are ready."

Josh's eyes widened. The blue eyes stared in awe at the triangular instrument in the captain's right hand. The captain's left hand, which had lost the art of finer touch since his stroke, rested on top of the open box.

"Take it lad; it won't bite."

Josh held his breath and he willed his hands not to shake as he lifted the instrument across to his own lap. So far so good. He did not drop it into the bottom of the dinghy and he did not drop it over the side into the fast-flowing water. He began to relax. He looked at his brother for support. Gus winked. Captain Harris took a small pad and a pencil from the top pocket of his jacket.

"Now Josh, I want you to take it up to the bow and work from there. Gus you can work both oars to keep the boat as steady as you can."

Horror filled the boys' faces at the thought that one way or another they might be responsible for damaging the sextant. The boat rocked as Josh, with gritted teeth, moved carefully up to sit on the nose of the dinghy. He kept his hand holding the instrument well within the confines of the little vessel.

"Anyone might think you are delivering a baby there, boyo. How long are you going to take to tell me where we are?"

Josh took a deep breath and began to do what he had studied so hard in theory.

As he gentled the oars against the tide pressures, Gus turned his head to watch his brother. His stomach churned. He wished Captain Harris had not mentioned his attachment to the sextant. It only made them both nervous and surely one or the other would manage to sink the blasted thing. He began to wish that at that moment, he was aboard *The Lion,* breaking his back, stuffing coal into its boiler.

As Josh called his findings, Captain Harris wrote carefully in his notebook. When Josh had completed his readings, it was Gus's turn. Again, the dinghy rocked as they changed positions. Josh's fingers were white around the frame of the sextant as he handed it over to his brother. Gus's fingers fumbled as he took the instrument. Josh threw out his hand saving it before it fell into the water that was now filling the bottom of the boat. Both their faces were white. Gus swallowed his fright.

"Gentle Gus, you have the grip of a beggar on a lamb chop there. Don't hold it so tight. You might crumble it." The Captain smiled; a tight smile. "Come on, Josh, can you bale and keep us steady at the same time?"

Gus felt as though the captain's eyes were boring into him like the cobra worms penetrating the timbers of the Victoria Bridge. He heard his father's voice in his head. *You can do anything you want if you want it enough.* His hands stopped shaking. He took a deep breath and proceeded to take his readings and call the results out to the captain.

Three more times on their journey upstream this process was repeated. Each time the boys' confidence lifted a little more. At the top of the tide, the captain called a halt.

"The tide is about to turn, boys. I think we can row for home. How are the blisters on your hands?"

Both Josh and Gus looked down at the back of their hands resting on the oars. The bruises from last night's fracas were turning a dark purple. Four palms were then turned upwards. There were no blisters. Instead, hard calluses built up from shovelling coal; first at the smithy and more recently for the steam engines, covered their palms.

Captain Harris shared the water bag with the boys. After the boat had been baled again, they set the rowlocks grinding in a regular rhythm. The boat headed downstream. Josh and Gus assisted Captain Harris back to his house before setting off, at a run, for The Rest. The gunshot from the old windmill signalling 1 pm, added wings to their feet.

THE IMPOSTER

Mrs. Lawson, one of the two cleaners, arrived just as Sarah removed the first batch of bread loaves from the oven. Peggy Lawson, as usual, wore a dull grey cloth to secure her grey hair. The dark green dress was covered with a grey pinafore. Sarah tried not to stare at the black eye which was quite visible under the coating of face powder. This was the third time within the past few weeks. A wave of burning anger stirred deep inside her belly. How could a man do this to his wife?

When the other cleaner, Mrs. Randal, entered the kitchen she was not so reticent.

"Peggy, I don't know why you let that so-and-so do that to you. Can't you keep him away from the grog?"

The pair were as opposite in character as they were in dress sense. Lizzie Randal wore the brightest of clothing combinations available. Today a scarlet cloth bound her wild brown curls and an orange pinafore covered a sea-blue dress. Both women were good workers whom Miss Millie valued.

"Lizzie, if only I could. He is a good man really. He is just weak for the grog."

"Just a big bully, if you ask me," Lizzie mumbled as she took up the cup to drain the dregs.

Meg was in the process of delivering the breakfasts. Door handles rattled and windows scraped as Sarah began opening all avenues to vent the rising heat in the kitchen. Everyone's gaze turned to the apartment above as a wail split the air. Sarah took off up the backstairs to Millie's room. She found Millie bent over the back of her chair coughing vigorously. Eyes bulged in her red face. A strident intake of air followed each coughing fit. The teapot lay overturned on the breakfast tray. Everything was saturated in the brown liquid. Miss Millie waved some papers wildly above her head with one hand. It was nearly impossible for Sarah to understand the words that she was trying to say.

"Who in the hell is this person? I've never heard of him. What does this all mean?" Her face began to turn blue. Sarah was at a loss. It eventually came to her that the papers Miss Millie verbally berated were from the letter that arrived yesterday. She wished she had burnt the darn thing. Then a calmness settled upon her young shoulders. Jumping forward she took the pages out of Millie's hand. After pulling the chair well away from the table, she sat her friend down.

"Forget the letter for the moment, Miss Millie. Take slow deep breaths. I'm going to run down and bring up a drink of warm honey and brandy for you." Sarah's feet hardly touched the stairs as she ran back to the kitchen.

When Sarah returned, Millie's coughing attack had settled somewhat. Sarah's anxiety lessened when Miss Millie began to sip at the drink offered. While Miss Millie's breathing returned to normal, Sarah began to sort out the mess of the breakfast tray. She rescued the papers from the floor where they had fallen.

"Do you want to talk about whatever has upset you, Miss Millie?"

"That letter you sent up this morning, where did it come from?"

Sarah had to think for a minute.

"Spud Murphy gave it to me; after closing time it was; last night. Someone had just left it on the bar-top." She paused as she remembered the worried look on the Irishman's face. Spud had only been working full-time at The Rest since Christmas. He did not want to get into trouble. "Spud assumed the letter carrier had delivered the envelope earlier without telling him about it. He found it when he was cleaning up."

"The letter is supposed to have come from my dear husband's brother, Edward Carson. My husband did not have a brother called Edward or any other name. He only ever had two sisters who both died with the smallpox when they were only youngsters. That's what he always told me, anyway." Millie shook the recovered pages again. "This letter goes on to claim that, as the writer is the nearest male relative to my dear Christopher, he will be taking over control of his brother's assets. He will arrive at the hotel sometime today."

"Today, but Miss Millie, can he just do this?"

"According to this fellow's letter he wants to have the best hotel room put aside for him. We'll see about that." Millie's lips tightened. Tram tracks appeared across her forehead. Her hazel eyes spat fire. "He'll be in for a shock if he thinks he can put one over on me. I've met some dubious characters in my life and each one has taught me a thing or two. My husband consulted three solicitors when he prepared his will. He was determined to ensure that the arrangements he put in place to protect me were all above board." She sipped on the honey and brandy drink. "Sarah, I want you to send Ned to ask Mister Rankine to call; this morning if possible."

Sarah was pleased to see Miss Millie calmly take up the pen and begin to write.

"Can I bring you up another breakfast tray?" she asked.

"No dear, I have enough food for thought here." Millie grimaced.

Sarah felt as if she had been running all morning. She glanced at the clock above the kitchen sink. It was only 8.30am. That couldn't be right; was it slow? It must be much later than that. She must ask Meg if she wound the clock on Monday morning. The sink was full to overflowing with unwashed dishes. Sarah wondered where Meg was. This should be almost cleaned up by now. She stopped at the sink and drank a large glass of water before poking her head through the door into the A-wing dining room. Mister Boris and Mrs. Keppel had returned to their rooms. Instead, sitting at the table in the corner was a stranger, who was giving young Meg a mouthful of instructions.

"You do not have to talk to Miss Millie first. If I tell you what to do, it will be done immediately. You will learn shortly that I am to be your employer from now on. So, bring me a breakfast tray and while I am eating, you will go prepare the best front room for me."

Sarah's blood boiled. This rat-faced, moustached, pompous, skinny streak must be THE Edward Carson. She bit her lip. How would Miss Millie handle the situation? Sarah had to stop herself from grinning as she remembered Miss Millie's mood earlier. Maybe Miss Millie's tact might be in short supply at the moment. Sarah took a deep breath and stepped forward.

"Good morning, Sir. I am Sarah Dougall, the housekeeper. May I help you?" She nodded a sympathetic dismissal to Meg.

"Yes, you can. I want a breakfast tray immediately and the best room in the house; permanently. I am the new owner of "The Mariner's Rest."

"Yes, Sir, of course. Breakfast will be served; on the house. By the time you have eaten, Miss Millie's solicitor will be here to discuss the situation and the necessary papers with you. I shall just go myself and put on fresh bacon and eggs."

Mister Edward Carson sniffed and offered a tight smile before he sat up higher, adjusting his jacket as he did so. Sarah's hands trembled as she closed the door behind her. In the kitchen, she pulled the curtain around the staff dining corner to prevent Mister Carson from viewing the working girls arriving for their breakfast.

Mister Edward Carson was just finishing his breakfast when Millie received Mister Rankine to her rooms. Twenty minutes later the solicitor entered the dining room just as Edward Carson was berating Sarah for not having his room prepared.

"Mister Edward Carson, I am Arthur Rankine, solicitor for Mrs. Millie Carson." The well-dressed gentleman pulled out a chair and folded his legs under the table. Sarah disappeared into the kitchen. It was only a few minutes when she returned with a tray of freshly steeped tea and clean crockery. Buttered scones sat on a large plate.

"Thanks, Miss Sarah." The solicitor smiled. Mister Edward Carson frowned.

"What on earth does that woman want a solicitor for. I am the brother of her supposed husband, Christopher. That scarlet woman bedevilled him until he lost all reason. I am here to look after his assets, now that he is dead."

Sarah fled the room.

A mottled shade perfused Ed Carson's face as Mister Rankine spoke quietly to him.

"You see Edward, may I call you that, things could become quite confusing if I call you Mister Carson. My firm will need to investigate the authenticity of the birth papers, marriage papers and other family documents that Mister Christopher Carson has always kept at our office. Your own documentation will need to be authenticated also. This, of course, may take at least twelve months."

"That will be no trouble. I'll manage this hotel until that is completed and I then become the owner of the establishment." The rat-face blustered.

"Well no, sir, the status quo cannot change until things become clearer. Miss Millie will continue in her position until then. You see, Mister Christopher Carson went to great lengths to ensure that all incomes from his assets were to be enjoyed by his wife, Millie. We hold these papers at my office also."

Edward Carson jumped up waving his arms in the air.

"That is ridiculous. Whoever heard of a woman running a business of such value? Women, particularly that sort of woman, have not the brains for such an endeavour."

Mister Rankine gave a discreet cough. "Edward, you seem to have forgotten that Miss Millie has done very well in the past ten years, since the demise of her husband, Christopher."

"Well, it should not be allowed. The law says that women should not be in charge of their money. It is for the male member of the family to do with it as he sees fit."

"Actually, that is only if the husband is on the scene. Now, Edward, I must go to my office. I will give you a lift to the town centre where you will be able to seek legal advice from one of several law firms. You will find suitable accommodation while you are there. Of course, while the legal process inches forward, you cannot be residing here on these premises. My horse and sulky are out back."

"Humph." Mister Edward Carson walked into the foyer where his bags were stacked near the brocade sofa. Mister Rankine ran up the foyer stairs to Miss Millie's apartment. Unaided, Edward Carson with his nose in the air, dragged his luggage out to the sulky. From where Sarah was busy putting the roast in the oven, the departing visitor's voice was heard calling loudly.

"I'll be back, just you wait and see. Every one of you lot will get your comeuppance."

Sarah was too busy to take a lot of notice. It was later than planned and she worried that dinner may not be ready on time.

"What's eating that chap?" Spud Murphy asked.

Sarah only rolled her eyes and smiled at the barman as he limped off to the public bar area.

"Leave the door open please, Spud. There is a lovely breeze coming through from the river. This kitchen is a furnace today." She stood enjoying the draft of air and watched as the once-upon-a-time jockey set up his bar. He had a small ladder which he used to access many of the drinks, bringing the bottles down to a more comfortable level within his reach. "Do you need a hand with anything?"

"Thanks, Miss Sarah, but I've got it all under control."

END OF ANOTHER DAY

Jacko sat at the end of the kitchen table with his legs stretched out in front of him. He enjoyed the repetitive scrape, scrape, scrape of the spoon in Sarah's hand as she stirred the hot cocoa. His glance moved to Millie, sitting near him, he smiled. She did look much better tonight; all be it, she was robed in her dressing gown. He reached over and touched the hand of the person who was more mother to him than anyone he could remember.

"It's good to see you about, Miss Millie."

Millie smiled as she touched the back of his rough hands. Millie and Jacko thanked Sarah as she poured her mixture into three cups.

"It takes more than a bit of a sniffle to knock me off my perch, you know." She sipped at her nightcap. "The new guests seem a nice lot. What do you think?"

"Doctor Goldfinch and his group? Yeah, they're all right, I guess. I thought they'd be a bit snobby, you know, with a manservant and all." Jacko sipped his hot drink.

The chair screeched on the floor as Sarah drew it out to sit. "I think they're lovely. They didn't look down their noses at all and Thomas, the manservant, was very helpful." She drank from the cup. "Mrs. Baldwin is beautiful and so brave to travel all this way in her condition."

"What condition's that?" Jacko raised his eyebrows.

Sarah blushed. Millie smiled. "She is with child, Jacko." She sat thoughtful fiddling with the teaspoon. "I wonder where Mr. Baldwin is?"

"Well, it's none of our business. Miss Jane and Eve did seem rather protective of her, now I come to think of it." Jacko nodded.

Millie reached into the tin of biscuits which Sarah had placed in the middle of the table.

"All round it was a successful day. Arthur Rankine has got the measure of our Edward Carson, or whatever his name might really be and our guest list is rather full."

"Remember, Miss Millie, my offer to assist in the solution of that fella's still open."

"No, I don't think so, thank you, Jacko. We'll keep on the side of the law in this matter." She turned her attention to Sarah. "Now, young miss, I do hope that Arthur is not going to spend all his time sitting at this table drinking tea and eating me out of house and home every day? Good looking chappie, is he not?"

Jacko looked up in surprise. Sarah was just a kid.

A flush raced across the girl's face as Sarah stammered. "Oh, Miss Millie. I thought you'd want me to feed him, given that he missed breakfast at his boarding house to answer your call this morning."

Millie laughed. "I was only teasing you, child. But he did ask more questions about you than he did about Edward Carson, I think."

Jacko looked more closely at Sarah. She had blossomed since joining Miss Millie's family here at "The Rest". There were curves that he had not noticed before. When did that happen? How old was the girl now? A frown crossed his brow while he considered. As far as he knew she must be sixteen or seventeen this year; just over half his age.

"Oh, Miss Millie, Mister Rankine is an important man. He's not going to notice a nobody like me. When he's ready to take a wife, he'll want someone important, like himself."

"Hmmm," was all Miss Millie said with a gleam in her eye.

Jacko sighed. Suddenly he felt every one of his thirty years.

THREE

THE *NORTHERN ORCHID*

SYDNEY 1867

CAPTAIN WILLIAM SLOAN

William Sloan lifted his stockinged feet up to rest upon the wrought iron balustrade. He relished the feel of the warm sun on his face. Smoke dribbled from the side of his mouth. He tapped the bowl of his pipe on the edge of the table. There was no one here today to criticize this habit. His other hand rubbed at the scar running from his left eye down his face to disappear under his strong jawline. Only his subconscious observed the ships in the Sydney harbour below. Perhaps he should be feeling guilty, but right at this moment, he savoured the feeling of relief flooding his body.

These past six or seven months had been trying, to say the least. The fitting of a steam engine and screw propeller into his ship had not gone as smoothly as promised. One consolation had been that the examination for woodworm had revealed nothing startling and only minor repairs had been required. Every week there had been reports of delays for one reason or another. At least he had no difficulty in accessing and completing the Extra-Master's Certificate. This had been a recently introduced competency requirement for those in charge of a ship driven by steam engine power. The British Royal Navy might be of the opinion that the colonial examinations were less stringent than their own but as he had no intention of returning to the Royal Navy this did not bother him in the least. Then yesterday, the news that he so desperately awaited, arrived. The *Northern Orchid* would be ready for trial runs in two days' time. He looked forward to being out of this cage of a harbour and to pit his skills against the many and varied challenges of the seas once again.

Since this enforced stay in Sydney, things between himself and his wife had been tetchy. This morning, he had waved farewell to Catherine and their two daughters as they sailed out of the harbour en route to England.

"To give the girls the experience of a season in civilized London," were her words.

Both of them knew full well that she and the girls would never return to Terra Australis. He did not blame her, really. He had no right to blame her, probably. Catherine had married him expecting her Royal Naval captain would go on to master ships in the Sloan family shipping company or at least work within her father's shipping interests. To have him thumb his nose at both and choose to buy a humble trading vessel bumbling its way up and down the coast of eastern Australia was too much. In her world, where appearances meant everything, the shame for Catherine was overwhelming. He sighed. Perhaps if they had produced a son or two, he may have been inclined to endure the restrictions of a traditional career; for their sake.

A small whirlpool of anxiety nipped at his stomach. Her last statement, as he bid her farewell in the ship's cabin, concerned him. Hate spat from her eyes like fiery lava from a volcano.

"Don't think for one minute, William Sloan, that I don't know all about your dalliance with Miss Millie at that questionable hotel in Brisbane. You have spent more time with her, these past years, than with your family in Sydney. Well, she is in for a big surprise; you can rest assured of that. Your floozy will have her work cut out, trying to handle the load of trouble I have sent her way."

Those were the last words spoken between them. What had that witch, Catherine, done? He really needed to see Millie as soon as possible. To wait for the *Northern Orchid* may take weeks. The tiles under his feet felt cool when he began pacing the small landing. Long tanned fingers raked his grey hair. There would be no chance the trials might include an emergency trip to Brisbane. A trek on horseback was hardly worth thinking about. His body was more used to the battering of a rough sea than that of a saddled horse. The new fancy telegraph system provided no privacy.

"Oh, Millie."

He flopped back into his chair and put his head in his hands. The sounds of the wind in the trees, the shouts from the riverbank below and the laughter of children playing in the bushland next door faded. The fragrance of flower blossoms and salt spray from the sea retreated. In the place of these things, he saw his beautiful Millie with her red hair spread out on the silk sheets behind her. He smelt the perfume of her eau-de-cologne drenched body. He saw her hazel eyes change, as they did, with her moods: limpid pools, blazing bushfires, sparkling laughter and glistening with tears of sorrow. All of these things could happen in the time the grains took to drop through the waist of a sandglass.

He straightened up. There was no point worrying about something that might never happen. Catherine was most likely making idle threats. Besides, his Millie had an army of loyal supporters at The Rest. Whatever troubles Catherine may have sent her way, Millie was well protected. Jacko Benson, the young boy Millie and her husband rescued from the streets of Sydney, now a man. He would gladly lay his life down for Millie. Ned, the aging horse-trainer, who was taken out of the gutter and given back his self-respect. He would stand by her to the end. The family of Jimmy Dougall would not hear a word against her. If there were any legal issues, he knew Arthur Rankine would fight tooth and nail for the lady who set him up in business. He walked back to the table and poured another nip of whisky. There was really no need to worry. Millie would be fine, but come hell or high water, he planned to get himself to Brisbane as soon as possible.

A tap sounded on the door. The housekeeper entered the sitting room.

"Will I serve your tea here, Captain or would you prefer to eat in the small dining room downstairs?"

"Downstairs will be fine, thank you."

"Will you be going out later?"

William Sloan stared at the lady for a moment. Was she his jailer? Before she left, Catherine had shut the rest of the house up and dismissed all of the staff except this woman. She usually remained hidden in the bowels of the kitchen somewhere. A loyal servant of Catherine's, no doubt.

"Sorry, Sir, I did not mean to pry. It's just; will I leave a door unlocked for you?"

"Thank you; Mrs. Smith, isn't it? Thank you, no. I have the spare key to the butler-door if I want to go out."

The lantern flickered as Captain Sloan blotted the ink on the completed letter to Millie. Tomorrow, at first light, he planned to row the ship's tender out to the *SS Lord Ashley* to renew his acquaintance with the captain. If he judged correctly, a bottle of the finest whisky available in Sydney would see this letter delivered, by hand, to Millie Carson in Brisbane within the fortnight. He rubbed his eyes. He felt better for having made an effort to inform Millie of Catherine's threat.

Now he must concentrate on getting the *Northern Orchid* seaworthy again. Tomorrow, he planned to talk further with Guthrie Winston, the engineer he'd signed on to run the Maudslay oscillating steam engine on the *Northern Orchid*. Old Guthrie's years working with the steam trains in Britain followed by time served in the engine rooms of the paddle steamer, *Young Australia,* should come in good stead. His slowness of step and thinning hair were the only indications that his years of active work on a ship were limited. Hopefully, the two Dougall boys would have been trained in the mysteries of an engine room before that day came.

William Sloan prepared himself for bed where he lay thinking about the two loves of his life; the *Northern Orchid* and Millie Carson. He admitted to himself that he would be hard pressed to make a decision on which one was to be named the favourite. And what of the *Northern Orchid*'s trials? Would she be as accommodating as she always had been when she felt the alterations in her balance and the surge of her new propeller?

The following Tuesday, in the pale glow of the morning dawn, Captain Sloan, at the helm of his *Northern Orchid*, watched closely as the crew prepared to winch in the anchor chain. A light breeze rippled his partially buttoned white shirt with its sleeves rolled above his elbows. His facial lines of the past months were gone. His lips smiled and crinkles teased the corner of his grey eyes. A well-worn naval cap covered his thinning grey hair. Having spent the past two nights back in the familiarity of his cabin, the weight on his shoulders had disappeared along with the sea mists of the early morning. Guthrie Winston was out of sight in the engine room along with a deckhand employed to keep the coal supply up to the boiler's fire. Cluttering up his wheel-house was the pilot supervising their exit from the harbour, the supervising engineer in charge of the installation of the new engine and the harbourmaster, Mister Turnbull, who had, 'Just come along to give my sea legs a bit of an airing.' The ship's mate, Ewan MacGregor, stood hugging the corner. His face was nearly as red as his hair. A sure sign that he was not too happy with the crush of visitors. A thick lock of that hair covered a fine white scar which had been acquired on the same day as William's own more obvious scar.

Captain Sloan sniffed the air. Wind dragged the smoke spewing from the funnel away from the wheel-house but the distinct smell of burning coal could not be ignored. Was it his imagination or did he really feel the extra weight in the altered balance of the ship's keel? He desperately wanted to call the bosun for sail but this short trip was for the purpose of testing the performance of the new engine. Sails were not allowed. His only purpose here today was to steer the ship. Hopefully tomorrow they would be ready to give the *Northern Orchid* a trial using both the engine and the sails in unison. Unless of course, all the sea gods were with them and it could all be accomplished before the light faded this evening. Today all the commands were to come from the engineers. This did hurt his pride somewhat.

Captain Sloan's eyes scanned the seamen on the foredeck below. When the *Northern Orchid* had gone into dry-dock, the regular crew were disbanded to go on to other jobs. He had been fortunate in reclaiming most of them when the news had gone out of the ship's imminent release. He glanced to his left. Ewan Macgregor, Mac, grinned ruefully. They had sailed together for more years than he could remember. Mac had spent the past seven months working the immigrant ships to and from Europe. Sykes, down below, was lining the new sailors up around the capstan. Was that the same dirty bandana the man had worn since he had first laid eyes on him? Standing near Sykes was his friend, Bony. Neither man appealed to the captain but they had always done a fair day's work. Was Bony's skin darker than when he saw him last? That four-cornered knotted cloth covering his bald head might never have been removed. Neither really did say where they had been for the past months and he had not wanted to press the point too much. He just wanted a crew to sail his ship. He nodded and smiled when he caught the eye of Evans standing below awaiting the order. As always, Noel Evans' muscles challenged the seams on whatever shirt he wore. The man's sandy hair was secured in its usual queue. Jimmy Dougall always said Evans had the makings of a good carpenter. He was right. Evans was now officially his bosun as well as the carpenter. Several other new crew members were tidying up the decks under Evans' orders. No doubt he would get to know them in the days to come. A frown deepened his brow. He leaned forward.

"What do you make of that, Mac?"

Down below the deckhands were laughing and pointing off to starboard. Shouts and whistles floated up to them on the breeze. A Chinese sampan approached the *Northern Orchid*. The front of the small craft was loaded with large baskets of what appeared to be vegetables. Two young Chinese men, dressed in what looked like grey pyjamas, propelled the vessel using a long single pole extending out from the stern. An older Chinese man wearing a pointed straw hat sat almost hidden amongst the baskets. He could be seen talking sharply at the younger men while his slim hand gestured frantically at the ship.

"Stone the crows," Captain Sloan laughed. "Is that Chinaman Ching? I thought he must have died. Last week I had people out looking everywhere for him; all to no avail."

Ewan MacGregor spun around to see what had amused his captain. "Yes, you're right. That is old China. Thank goodness, at least we'll get decent tucker again. I feel better already. I can tell you, the thought of eating too many more meals cooked by Bellyache Basil had me worried."

"Mac, you'd better go down and welcome China aboard? You know, make him feel important. I don't want him getting his nose out of joint when we have him this close to our galley."

By the time Mac had reached the side of the ship, Evans had a line to the sampan and tossed over the Jacob's-ladder. The short old man with the single grey plait swinging over his back issued orders left and right in his broken English. A folded black umbrella emphasized the meaning of all he said. Small ropes were sent down from the deck and tied to the handles of the large woven baskets. These were then hauled up under instruction. China literally danced back and forth in the wildly rocking sampan threatening devil's curses on anyone who caused one leaf of a lettuce or one small tomato to fall overboard.

Peace had only just been restored to the ship when everyone in the wheel-house tensed. The whistle sounded from the speaking tube which had direct access to the engine room. The supervising engineer bowed his head to Sloan before removing the wooden whistle from the end of the tube. He listened to Guthrie Winston, the engineer, down below. The steam pressure was up. Captain Sloan bit his lip to prevent himself from giving the orders. The supervising engineer called for the engine to be started.

"Mister Winston will ensure the correct combination of steam pressure and engine revolutions are applied to ensure efficient thrust." The supervising engineer enlightened anyone who may have been interested.

A collective sigh filled the confined space as the vibration of the steam engine was felt through their feet.

A powerful vibration, Sloan conceded but not all that different to the vibration of a brisk breeze on the full complement of sails or the rhythm of a running sea on the hull.

"Captain, can we have the anchor up now?"

Sloan gave the order. The capstan creaked as the men bent their backs. The pawls used to prevent the recoil fell into place with a clunk. The cable clattered through the hawse-hole. The ship's timbers, too long away from the water, groaned. Sloan smiled and relaxed. These sounds fell like angel dust on his ears.

The supervising engineer then spoke into the speaking tube once more. He ordered the engine slow ahead. The engineer turned to Captain Sloan.

"You and the pilot have the wheel, Sir."

The pilot deferred to the captain.

"You have been in and out of this harbour more times than I, Sir. I will just stand by here." The younger man nodded and took a step back out of the way.

The captain's hands fondled the wooden spokes of the helm. He knew every little bump and scratch in their worn surfaces. He tried to look nonchalant, but his eyes sparkled.

"This is a quicker departure than waiting for the tugboat, I have to admit." He looked wistfully at the masts with their furled sails. He breathed in deeply, sucking up the salt air. "Though, on a day such as this, with a stiff breeze and the sun glinting off a blue sea, I think you would be hard pressed to get more pleasure from anything other than a ship under full canvas."

The pilot smiled but the supervising engineer only pressed his lips together.

"On the other hand, Captain, the advantage of a powered engine is that you do not have the worry of being unable to tack if caught on a lee shore by the north-easterlies in the cooler months."

Did he actually humph after that little speech? Sloan thought it possible.

As the *Northern Orchid* steamed slowly across Line Zulu, the invisible line between Sydney Harbour Heads, the older crew members gave a cheer. It felt like such a long time since they had brought the *Northern Orchid* to Sydney for refitting. Within days they should be heading north again. The south-east swell lifted her bows and the stern followed obediently behind. The breeze whistled through the narrow gaps around the casements of the wheel-house. Sun glinted off the white crests of the waves. William Sloan could not think of a better day. Down below, the engine whooshed-whooshed and clickity-clanked. His fingers twitched restlessly. He so wanted to spread the sails and fly over this sea and not plough through it with all the grace of a Southern Ocean ice floe.

Dusk engulfed the harbour and its environs. The waves of the changing tide lapped against the hull in the calmer waters of their moorage. The *Northern Orchid* tugged impatiently as if resentful at the restraint of her anchor. She had only been released this morning and now here she was confined once more. In the wheel-house, William Sloan poured shots of whisky into four glasses. He had just bid goodnight to a very satisfied supervising engineer, the returning pilot and to Mr. Turnbull as they headed off for shore in the ship's jolly-boat being rowed by two of the new deckhands, Adams and Tanner. As well as the captain, the wheel-house now held Mac, Noel Evans and Guthrie Winston; a very puffed up engineer.

"Well lads, a toast I think." Captain Sloan held up his glass. "To the *Northern Orchid*, her new engine and her graceful wings."

"The *Northern Orchid*." All the men laughed and patted each other on the back.

"You will be pleased with the trials today, Captain." Evans took a deep swallow.

"Yes, I had not dared hope that we might get them all over in one day." William Sloan turned to the first engineer to be employed on the *Northern Orchid*. "What did you think of the engine, Guthrie; will she do?"

"That is one fine engine, Captain, Sir. I think you'll be very satisfied."

Mac ran his fingers through his hair as he spoke. "Captain, how did the ship handle when both the sails and the engine were employed in unison?"

"Och Mac, it was like driving two unbroken young horses in an old dray. No doubt both the *Orchid* and I will come to some compromise." He stood up straight. "Now, while I've got you all here. Do you think we can up-anchor for Brisbane in two days?"

Guthrie rubbed the grey stubble on his chin. "I'll have to chase up the coal carrier and ensure all the water tanks are full. You will notice the increased use of water even though you have got compound expansion steam cylinders. With a bit of luck, it should not be impossible to leave on Friday's tide, Captain."

The captain turned to his ship's mate. "Mac, what do you think?"

"Tomorrow we'll load the steel going to the Brisbane foundry. The harbourmaster has held it for us. There's nearly twenty-five tons in that lot. They also have several hundredweight of crates waiting to go to Pettigrew's sawmill. The harbourmaster also mentioned he has a load to go to the Queensland Government House building site. He thinks he can see that coming our way. If Guthrie here, can make his toy machine take us to where we are to load, then there's no reason why that lot can't be on board by tomorrow night, Sir."

"What do you think Evans, can we do it?"

"If there is no trouble with the stevedores, we'll certainly give it a good shot, Sir."

"You have all forgotten the most important thing," Sloan said with a wide grin. The men looked blankly at each other. "The most important thing; our stomachs. I'll go down and welcome China personally and ask him what he needs. Do you chaps want me to order your meal served in what is left of the chartroom or in your cabins?"

"The chartroom will be fine, Captain, though we will miss the space that Guthrie's engine funnel has commandeered." Mac laughed and slapped the engineer on the back to show no hard feelings.

"What are you going to do with the Captain's Cupboard?" Evans asked curiously. He was referring to a small room adjacent to the captain's cabin. It was barely larger than a cupboard but had always been a part of the *Northern Orchid*. "Gossip has it that previous captains on this ship kept their sweethearts hidden away in there." Evans went on to explain to Guthrie.

The captain laughed. "All I'm admitting to is old charts, log books as well as new canvas for sails, secreted therein."

"Don't think it'll make much of a cabin for you, lad. You'd never fit in it." Guthrie smiled at Evans.

"I have plans for that cupboard, as you call it." Captain Sloan tapped the side of his nose but he did not expand on those plans.

CHINAMAN CHING

William Sloan could hear China berating some unprepared deckhand within the galley before he even climbed down the companion-ladder. The reedy voice with its thick accent penetrated through the bulkhead like a sharp knife through a pig's gut. Following this drifted the wonderful aromas of good food.

"You son of a two-legged camel. You no complain about tucker when I cook. I cook good tucker. Millions hungry Chinee people be happy to eat this rice. The green is vegables. You have lucky country with vegables. Eat up and shut up mouth or you clean the galley out tonight. Salt beef junk all time no good for you."

Captain Sloan took a minute to straighten his face before entering the galley. At first, he was amazed at the changes that China had made is such a short time. Bellyache Basil had only worked here for two days but in that time, he had covered everything in dirt and grease. One could now see the timber grain in all the benches and seats. The stove shone.

He sighed. He was the luckiest ship's captain in the world to have such a cook on board. How many times have others tried to bribe this little cyclone away from the *Northern Orchid;* all to no avail. How this ship entwines us all within her spell?

Chinaman Ching rushed over and grabbed Sloan's calloused hand in his small clasp and began shaking it enthusiastically.

"Mister Cap'n, Mister Cap'n. You are well, yes? What you like to eat?"

William Sloan extricated his hand gently and patted China on the back.

"It is good to see you, friend. How have you been and all the family?"

"Good, good, all good. Now I feed you. You thinner, I give you good food."

"I'll have whatever's cooked; as will the ship's mate and the bosun and our new engineer, Mister Winston. Can you get one of the lads to set it up in the chartroom for us?"

"Will do, I get these useless men working. Mister Cap'n, you go and sit down."

Early the next morning, William Sloan sat in the doorway of the wheel-house reading the latest updated reports on the reefs and other dangers along the coast from Sydney to Brisbane. He'd learnt early in his career that it was always good policy to ensure a bottle of whisky goes to the harbourmaster in whatever port one found oneself.

It took some time but eventually, China's screech penetrated his concentration.

"What on earth is all the fuss?"

He pulled himself to his feet and peered over to where China was hanging over the bulwarks on the starboard side. There was every risk the little man might dive headfirst into the water. Once more he was directing the loading of supplies. William watched the process with a smile. There was little that he would want to refuse this man. He recalled one exception; the time in Melbourne when China was going to kidnap a beautiful Chinese girl. She was actually on board and in the cook's sleeping area, off the kitchen, when William rescued her. China protested loud and long. This was a bride for his son, China had informed him. The whole crew ate poor fare for three days.

Evans was on deck when the sampan approached the *Northern Orchid.* He scratched his head amazed at how the little vessel remained above water. There was no more than a couple of inches' free-board on the overloaded vessel. Piled higher than the Chinese man on the pole were several large wire netting cages. Evans grinned. It appeared that the officers would be having fresh eggs for breakfast each day. He would need to send one of the deckhands down to the aft-hold and retrieve the framework that had been set up the last trip to hold the hen cages. This made for much easier cleaning. Quite a few large lidded woven baskets appeared over the bulwark. No doubt somewhere in all that lot was the ship's cat. China always insisted on a cat to control the mice and other vermin. Evans knew full well about the cat. It had taken a liking to him and insisted on sleeping on his bunk when not on China's sleeping roll. Some weeks after one sojourn in Brisbane, where the cat had disappeared for two whole days the darn thing had whelped on Evans' blanket. China nearly had a stroke when he found out the captain had drowned the kittens. Bets were taken on whether China's fury was due to his love of the cute kittens or to the fact they may have made excellent fresh meat. One thing about China though, he did keep the animals clean. Evans grinned in anticipation of the expressions on the faces of their new crew members when they encountered China.

"Mister Evans, Mister Evans, Sir. Come, you meet my big son. He named Chinaman Ching too. When I too old he come work on the *Northern Orchid.* He good cook, like me and clean. Not like these unwashed offspring of the pigpens. And see; see, we have the hen eggs for your breakfast tomorrow."

Evans knew it was more than his life was worth (well the comfort of his stomach at least) to ignore the invitation. He walked over and waved down to the man. He wondered if Captain Sloan might know of these arrangements that China had for his son but his musings were interrupted by a hail from an approaching row-boat.

CAPTAIN WILLIAM SLOAN

"Ahoy the *Northern Orchid*; permission to come aboard?"

This is becoming as busy as the entrance to a whore's parlour on Saturday night. It's time we set sail north were the thoughts in Evans' head as he answered. "For what purpose?"

"It's the clerk from the harbourmaster's office. I have a message for Captain Sloan."

"Permission granted." Evans sighed. "At this rate, we'll never start loading cargo," The wind dispersed his whisper.

Hearing the loud voices calling across the water, William finished wrapping the report he had been reading in its oilskin satchel and secured the ties. He let his head drop back against the doorframe and listened. By the time the clerk made it to the wheel-house, the captain was on his feet waiting to hear the message.

"Captain Sloan, Mister Turnbull's greetings, Sir. He asks if you would be interested in taking four passengers to Brisbane with you? The agent told him that two are first-class passengers and two for steerage."

"Yes, but they'll need to be on board before dark tomorrow night. We'll be leaving on Friday's early morning tide." Captain Sloan held out the oilskin satchel. "Will you return this to the harbourmaster, with my thanks?"

"Certainly, Captain."

Excitement filled the air along with a distinctive winter chill. Even the scuds of light rain that thrummed across the deck at irregular intervals failed to dampen spirits. The *Northern Orchid* was heading back to Queensland. The sound of Evans' intermittent orders rose above the jocular banter between the crew members. In the wheelhouse, William Sloan's white teeth shone within a grin as wide as his tanned face. Standing by his side, Mac laughed; as much at the captain's joy as at anything else. The pilot standing beside him watched and smiled too. As the ship exited the Sydney Heads, all thoughts turned to the many ships that had come to grief near here.

"Mac, you take the wheel. Perhaps we might dispense with Guthrie's stinking engine and open up a few sails. Let's smell the sweet taste of the sea."

"Right you are, Captain. I'll tell him to keep the pressure up in his boilers, just in case, will I?"

"That's a good idea. Remind him to watch his water and pressure gauges and vent the safety valves if needed."

"That'll get his own boiler steaming; me, giving him orders for his precious engine."

"He'll get over it. Now, I'd best go down and be polite to our passengers. Remind me again, why do we take passengers? Cargo is much less time-consuming and it doesn't usually complain."

"Because they help pay the bills."

"Aah money, money, the root of all evil."

Sloan did not go immediately to the top-deck stern where the first-class passengers had three cabins and one dining-lounge room. Nor did he go to the lower-deck stern where the steerage passengers were accommodated in two dormitories; male on the port side and female on the starboard side of the ship. His casual amble around his ship belied a sharp eye for detail. He was pleased to see that someone had secured canvas protection over the hen cages. By the time he arrived at the first-class passenger's lounge, he was a satisfied man.

His knock was answered by a mature gentleman, short of stature with sharp intelligent eyes. Sitting in the chair by the doorway was the second passenger in this area; the man's wife; according to the manifesto. At first glance, she looked rather a flighty old girl but when observed closely one could not help but notice the alert blue eyes. Mister Arnold Worthington, Judge at Law and Mrs. Marigold Worthington were his guests on the run to Brisbane. William Sloan wondered briefly what a Judge at Law might be doing cruising around on a coastal trader but he was not going to lose any sleep over it.

"May I come in?" the captain asked. At a nod from the Judge, he slipped inside quickly before closing the door against the wind and spits of rain behind him.

"Good morning. I'm Captain William Sloan. Sorry, we couldn't provide better weather for your journey. I do hope it's not too uncomfortable for you?" William felt the judge and his wife look askance at his casual dress. As usual, he wore white corduroy trousers and a white linen shirt. At least all the buttons were done up this time but the sleeves were rolled to above his elbow. He did have clean white canvas shoes on his feet. Their opinion of his dress did not bother him too much.

The Judge collected himself. "Good morning, Captain. This is a very comfortable berth. Much better than we had been led to expect; for a cargo vessel."

"Have you sampled our galley delights, as yet?"

"Oh, yes, Captain." This time it was Mrs. Worthington who spoke. "We have had an admirable breakfast. Please relay our compliments to the chef."

"It will be my pleasure."

"Captain Sloan, do not worry about us on the high seas. I do tend to seasickness but my doctor in London provided me with ginger tonic and luckily, I have been able to refill my supply in Sydney. It is a marvellous remedy for the ailment." Mrs. Worthington folded the paper that she had been reading on her lap.

Captain Sloan nodded. "I believe you have Crewman Adams looking after all your needs. Do not hesitate to notify him of your requirements." William did not add Adams was allocated the task because he was the only hand on board with clean trousers and shirt. He gave himself a mental reminder to address the shortcomings in the hygiene of the crew tomorrow.

The Judge re-joined the conversation. "He is a very personable young man and very attentive; thank you, Captain."

Mrs. Worthington twiddled with a fan that she held in her hands. "The Judge and I are travelling the world while we are still young enough to do so. All our children have grown up and left home, you see."

"My wife is an adventurous young filly, aren't you dear?" Mrs. Worthington's many wrinkles and dimples crinkled as she smiled benignly at the judge patting her hand. "She refuses to travel on the larger passenger ships."

"I may as well have stayed in London. Those large ships are full of the same people we met every day at home, doing the same or similar things that we did there. I wanted something totally different. Smaller ships and cargo vessels offer lots more adventure, I think; don't you Captain?"

William Sloan raised his eyebrows and grinned. "I hope we don't provide too much adventure, Mrs. Worthington."

She tapped the back of his hand with her lace-edged fan. "Will you be joining us here for dinner tonight?" Mrs. Worthington asked.

"That is most unlikely as Mister MacGregor, the ship's mate, will be sleeping at that time in preparation for his nightly watch. I will need to look after the *Northern Orchid.* If I see your lantern-light later as I go off duty, I will drop in to say goodnight." This was the best William was going to offer in the social graces.

From here the captain made his way to the lower deck. His first port of call was the galley where he found China supervising Bellyache Basil in the art of finely chopping carrots. The man's face was as long as a Sunday sermon; Basil's that is. China had a glint of determination in his eye. It appeared that he had no intention of failing in teaching this man how to cook. Several fresh fish were lying on the bench near a large tin tub. Captain Sloan was greeted enthusiastically before he passed on the Worthingtons' message to the chef.

His next port of call was to the male steerage dormitory where he found Bill Gaskin and Toby Knight sitting on their swags sharpening their tools of trade; shovels and axes. According to Ewan MacGregor, these men were gold prospectors who had left the southern fields for what they hoped might be fresh gold country near Maryborough, north of Brisbane. William enjoyed talking to them and spent more than half an hour listening to their stories.

From here he poked his head into the crew quarters where he found the bosun constructing the bulkheads on his new cabin.

"How's it going, Evans?"

The big man paused in his work and answered. "Good, Captain. I'll be getting a swelled head having a cabin of my very own. Thank you again, Sir."

William Sloan grinned. "I think after nine years of loyal service you deserve your own cabin now that you have extra responsibility. That reminds me. How would you like to take a turn on the helm this evening?"

"What, on my own, Captain?" Evans' face was aghast.

"No lad, I'll be with you in the wheel-house. I have no wish to wake up to find my ship halfway to South America or up on the sandy beaches of some never-seen-before rocky outcrop."

"If you think I can do it, I'd like to try, Captain."

"Midnight, we'll take over from Mister MacGregor."

The heat from the boilers greeted the captain as he weaved his way around the bulkheads to the engine area. Guthrie was in the process of spitting on the pencil-tip in his hand before entering data into his hard-covered journal. He looked up as the captain approached.

"Morning, Captain. This little beauty brought us out of The Heads without any problems, did she not?"

"Yes, Guthrie, she did that. It is still very hot in this engine room. Do you think the ventilation shafts, the maintenance crew at Sydney put in, have done any good?"

"Much better, Captain but I did think maybe we could do with another." He pointed to the further corner.

"Talk to Evans and see what he thinks."

"Thanks, I'll do that today."

From here the captain went and stood at the bow of his ship staring into the waters. As one with the ship, his body rose and fell and rocked with the waves. Silver flashes zipped through the water as half a dozen dolphins emerged from under the boat. In formation, they preceded the vessel like marine horses hauling the ship behind them on invisible traces. He barely noticed their antics. It was as if he was unaware of the cold breeze rippling his shirt and the odd shower that dampened his hair. Even the whistling of the winds through the rigging and sails failed to attract his attention. In the blue-green sea, he saw Millie's eyes. The fronds of floating seaweed became the russet red of her hair framing her precious face.

FOUR

MILLIE'S MARINER'S REST HOTEL

BRISBANE 1867

JOSH & GUS

Josh placed the pencil on the table and tucked his fingers under his armpits. He and Gus had been at this since early morning and his fingers were still stiff with cold. Captain Harris had volunteered their labour to the harbourmaster, Mister Burkitt. They were making copies of the latest map-changes to ports, shipping lanes and channels along the Queensland coast. It was time-consuming work. He bent his head back to the task. At the other end of the long table, Gus had not moved. Captain Harris continued reading some of the reports he had found on the unpainted shelves in the chartroom of the harbourmaster's office.

The sound of an explosion emanating from the docks nearby, burst through the window. The three heads snapped up. Chairs scraped on the timber floor. One fell onto its back unnoticed. Both Josh and Gus flew to the window. Captain Harris made a slower approach.

"It's the boiler on the steam crane. I bet Dozy Davis has forgotten to check the pressure gauges; again. He's always forgetting the gauges. He's sure done it this time," Josh yelled as he ran through the next room on his way outside.

Gus followed right on his heels along with Mister Burkitt and the clerk. They slid to a halt at the bottom of the three steps. The drumming hooves of four runaway horses with an attached out-of-control wagon raced towards them. Two large crates that had not been transferred to the ship were hurled off the side of the wagon.

One hit a tree trunk spilling bolts of cloth sending white linen tails waving in all directions. The other landed with a thud that frightened the terrified horses further. The boxes of bolts, nuts and nails sprayed out like oversized pellets from an oversized scattergun. The voice of the driver trailing in the dust behind was heard screaming.

"Whoa, Ned. Whoa, Bess."

The horses thundered on with their necks extended, their blood-stained nostrils flared and the whites flashed as their eyes rolled in their heads. Fear-filled squeals through froth-ringed mouths accompanied by loud rasping snorts flooded the air. Their large hearts pounded in their heaving chests. Sweat glistened over their bodies. At the corner, the wagon rolled dragging the horses down in a conglomeration of squealing panic-stricken animals, flailing hooves, enwrapping traces and thick clouds of dust. The upper shaft of the vehicle snapped with a loud crack. Its splintered ends threatened the wildly threshing legs of the rear horses.

Gus veered off to see what he could do to help the animals. Josh, Mister Burkitt and the clerk ran down to where a large cloud of smoke hung over what remained of the crane. The body of a man was on his hands and knees attempting to rise. Blood could be seen spreading across the back of the tattered remains of his shirt. A puff of dust burst out from under the man as he collapsed with a thud. Josh squatted down and gently turned him over. As the body rolled to the supine position, Josh fell back on his haunches with a gasp. The tart smell of the clerk vomiting behind him hardly registered above the smell of burnt human flesh. Blackened charred flesh dribbling serous ooze was all that could be seen of the front of the man's body. An expulsion of air burst from his gaping mouth, with its lips cooked beyond recognition, before the body lay still. There was no movement of the chest wall at all.

"Strike a light." Josh was grateful for the steadying hand of the harbourmaster on his shoulder.

"He's gone, son. There's nothing that we can do here."

Josh looked up to see the blackened bottom half of the boiler which sat like a macabre flower. Its petals of metal reached out and upwards to the sky. The top half of the boiler had been caught up amongst the twisted pipes as if held by the limbs of a giant black metal octopus. The dislodged boom floating on the water knocked rhythmically against the jetty pylons; a mournful dirge. The jib lay broken on the ground beside the body. The engine lay twisted on its side.

Deckhands threw buckets of river water onto the numerous hot coals smouldering on the wooden fore' deck of the ship that had been in the process of loading. Filaments of smoke rose from several rigging lines tied to the bulwark of the vessel. White water parted around the bow of the approaching water police boat.

"I cannot be sure if it is Dozy Davis, or not," Josh choked out.

Meanwhile, Gus and the driver were doing what they could for the horses.

"Be careful, lad. A belt with one of these hooves will send you to kingdom-come quick smart."

The driver drew a long knife from a sheath within his boot as he spoke. With Gus's help, he began to cut what traces he could. They unwound or unbuckled those that they could not. The protest and panic of the horses were deafening, making it hard to concentrate. Gus heard the whistle of the wind as a shod-hoof of the draught-horse whizzed past his ear.

"Easy Ned, easy," the driver murmured to the black gelding; one of the two leading horses. The horse threw himself upwards when the last restraint was removed. The animal trembled and snorted while the driver patted him down checking for any damage. When he was settled somewhat, the horse was led into the small enclosure near the maintenance shed. Gus was ready to remove the last trace from the other leading horse when the driver returned.

"Easy Bess, my beauty. Easy girl." She also bounced up once she felt the ties removed. The driver again checked his horse for damage, talking softly all the while as the tremors passed.

The two rear horses were almost immobilized within the reins and traces. Blood poured from the one leg of the horse underneath. The pale face of the driver looked up at Gus.

"Lad, run down to the ship at the jetty. Ask the captain if he has a gun. This horse needs to be put out of its misery." His hands remained busy striving to release the grey horse. The mare was slow to rise and stood head hanging for some time before she followed the man to where the other horses stood stamping their feet.

After passing the gun over to the driver, Gus looked away. He flinched as the shot rang out. After a big swallow and a deep breath, he turned to once again help the driver. This time the task was to release the wagon from the horse's body.

THE DOUGALLS

Sarah helped Blossom finish up the day's work in the wash-house. Blossom bucketed out the hot water from the copper boiler in which the white cottons and work clothes were boiled each day. Her small black frame threatened to snap in two as she carried her load to the dunny house. Her wild black curls bounced with each torturous step. The soapy contents of the buckets were poured over the wooden seats. She then took, from the nail on the outside wall, a large wooden-handled brush which she employed scrubbing the timber of each seat to within an inch of its life.

On the long table in the centre of the wash-house, Sarah folded towels while Blossom's daughter rolled up the face washers. The six-year-old carefully placed all the ones of similar colour together in their separate heaps. Her work was interrupted regularly to jump down from the stool and admonish her younger brother who entertained himself with a small pile of coloured rocks. He sorted and re-sorted the rocks into different arrangements, yabbering away to himself as he did so. When Blossom returned, the two women began folding the clean sheets draped over two long railings against the back wall of the room. These were placed in the large wash baskets for delivery to the linen storeroom inside the hotel.

Sarah removed the irons from the hot surface of the small stove and damped down the fire for the night. Just at that moment her brothers, Josh and Gus, burst in. Both their faces were sombre. Their expressions were grim. Sarah turned to Blossom.

"Blossom, you may go now. Josh and Gus will help carry the wash baskets."

"Ta, Miss Sarah." Blossom wasted no time gathering her offspring and scooting out through the side doorway.

It was Josh who began. "Sarah, you would never guess what happened today."

"In that case, there is no point in my trying to guess. So, what have you been doing today?" With a smile and a nod of her head, Sarah directed her brothers to the wash baskets. The both lifted together.

"And be careful you don't touch anything with your dirty clothes and hands." With that warning echoing in their ears, the boys headed over to the back door of the hotel.

Josh twisted his head back to talk to Sarah as she followed them. "I'll be working at Birley's Sawmill, at Kangaroo Point, tomorrow."

"What's wrong with the steam crane at the jetty?"

Gus butted in. "Haven't you heard, Sis? The boiler blew up this morning. Dozy Davis was killed. I thought the whole town would know by now."

"Heaven forbid; no one told me your work was going to be this dangerous."

Josh was quick to defend their jobs. "It's not dangerous if you keep your wits about you. The engineer was always going crook at Dozy for not watching the pressure gauges. The thing just blew up and took him with it."

"What will happen to your work now, Josh?"

"Mister Burkitt, the harbourmaster, pulled a few strings. He's secured me a few days a week at Birley's sawmill. They've a couple of steam engines there. I can go back to the crane on the jetty when it's repaired but that may take some time; waiting for a new boiler and parts."

They sidled through the back door and headed upstairs to the linen storeroom. Josh looked down at himself.

"I guess there's no point our offering to help with putting this lot away then, Sis."

"Be off with the pair of you. Go and have a good soak in the tub." Sarah began to empty the basket adding to the tidy heaps of linen on the shelves.

As the boys exited the rear of the building, they waved to one of the guests, Doctor Goldfinch, who was in the process of having his hair cut. Josh stopped suddenly and swung around.

"Doctor Goldfinch, I just remembered. There is something I wanted to tell you. It's a bit of gossip I heard today."

"Gossip; I am not too good with gossip, young Josh."

"This bit of gossip may be something you'll enjoy hearing. Do you know Southern Cross House just up the end of this road?"

"Doctor George, if you don't want your ears lopped off you really must stop moving your head around like that," Thomas, the manservant, grumbled.

"Sorry, Thomas. Josh, I think I know the one you mean. It's well hidden amongst those large fig trees."

"Yes, Sir, that's the one. The old couple who own the place are going back to England. One of the fellas, who was talking about it today, thought the people were going to sell up but another fella said it was going to be leased for several years."

"That would be wonderful. Thanks, Josh."

An apricot dawn trimmed the few clouds in the sky. A scant cold mist hung over the river. Water lapped the sides of the tugboat where it floated, tied-up at the log-jetty.

"Hey, Josh! You doing anything today?" Captain Johns threw the butt of his rolled smoke into the water as he called out.

Josh, having just said goodbye to his brother Gus, swung about.

"Not really, Captain Johns. I was heading over to see if Captain Harris wanted a hand with anything."

"Good, I need a deckhand. It seems I'll be one short today. Can you take his place?"

Josh needed no second bidding. Even a job on a simple tugboat beat weeding a garden.

He ran back to the jetty and jumped on board.

"What can I do?"

"As soon as young Gus is happy with his engine down there, we're heading down to Petrie Bight. A ferry-boat slipped its mooring last night. It's caught up on the riverbank. We're going to winkle it out and secure it before the high tide takes it off into the channel. It's sure to collide with another vessel out there. Oh, I forgot to ask. Can you swim?"

"Like a fish. I'll go down and shovel some coal, then."

Gus, who was in the process of opening the damper on the boiler and stirring the coals to a flame, looked up when Josh landed, with a thump, beside the engine. The brothers grinned at each other.

"Like a fish?" Gus asked quietly. "You can barely keep your head above water."

"Rubbish; anyway, I gotta learn some time."

Josh took up the shovel and dug deep into the coal sack. Gus tapped the glass front of the pressure and temperature gauges on the boiler.

After half an hour, Gus nodded his head and set the engine ticking away in neutral. Josh jumped up to the deck where he let the captain know the pressure was up and the engine was ready.

"About time too. Let's get a move on, then. Cast off, will you?" Captain Johns was not a patient man.

The bowline landed on the deck with a thump. Josh landed in a heap right beside it when the tugboat propelled forward towards the middle of the river. The morning sun glistened on the waters running from the blades of the paddlewheels as they turned. *The Lion* began the short journey towards Petrie Bight.

"Hold 'er there, Gus." The captain's voice roared above the engine. Gus stood with his head peering around the engine bulkhead. "Can you hold 'er there?"

"Aye, Captain."

Captain Johns and Josh contemplated the problem that they had ahead of them. Gus waited for the next instruction. The night tide had left the thirty-foot ferry well up the bank. Its bow appeared to be caught between two tree trunks. The rudder had smashed against some large rocks within the bank. The morning tide lapped the keel under the aft of the vessel. A middle-aged man with brown curly hair sticking out from under the edges of a marine cap scrambled down the bank near the boat. His cut-off trousers and dark shirt with its sleeves rolled up were coated in mud.

"Ahoy there, Captain. Thanks for coming. Bill Greenway, this is my boat, the *Marcia*." The voice drifted over the water to where Captain Johns stood at the helm of the *Lion*.

"How's the keel? Will she float?" *The Lion's* captain yelled back.

"Good as gold. Only the rudder's damaged. She'll float good."

"I'll come in close then and throw a couple of lines." Captain Johns turned his head to call down to Gus. "Dead slow, boy; keep it slow."

Josh stood with two stout lines ready as the boat made sternway into position. He looked at the cold water washing around the tug. A dunking was not what he wanted right now. His throwing arm had better do him proud or he was going home wet and cold.

Once more the captain called a halt to Gus. He nodded to Josh who began swinging the heavy end of the rope back and forth. He bent backwards then snapped forwards sending the first rope hurling towards the bank. It fell short by a few feet.

"You're going to have to put a bit of oomph into it, boyo." Came the non-sympathetic voice of the captain behind him.

Hand over hand, Josh pulled the line back on board. He shivered as the cold water dripped from the rope and onto his body. Again, he sent it hurtling off to the riverbank. It landed right in the middle of several small mangrove bushes. The man on the bank slipped and slid down to retrieve the end while Josh fed the line out to him. Josh turned back to the captain.

"Will I send out the second line, Captain?"

Johns thought for a moment as he manoeuvred the tug back into position against the run of the tide.

"Nah, I think we'll give it a go with just the one for now."

It took some time for the man on the bank to secure the line. The tide had now risen considerably and the aft half of the boat rocked in the water. He gave the signal to the tug.

With extra power ordered from the engine room, Captain Johns began to slowly nudge his vessel out into the river. White water frothed vigorously around the paddlewheels. Tension built up within the thick rope. The tug growled. The paddlewheels creaked and groaned. The *Marcia* did not budge. Captain Johns watched the rope vibrating with the pull.

A voice came across the water. "She's caught up on the trees. I'll have to get an axe and chop one out."

The tug was brought to rest. Josh hauled on the rope, rolling it on the deck as they neared the shore. Bill Greenway had boarded his wounded vessel and was now waving a large axe in the air. Josh cringed at the next instruction from Captain Johns.

"It's your lucky day, Josh. You get to have a swim. While you're out there, you can give the old fellow a hand to chop that tree down. And seeing as you're going that way, you may as well take that second line with you." The captain's chest rattled as he began coughing repeatedly. He leant over the starboard side and sent a dollop of phlegm into the river.

A sombre, "Aye, aye, Captain," was all Josh could manage.

He took hold of the second line and stood staring at the water. A cool breeze was now coming in from the south-west. It fluffed up his shirt. Were there icicles on the water? No, but he thought it a possibility.

"Garn, in you go. The longer you think about it, the colder it'll get." Came the voice of encouragement followed by more productive coughing.

With one big breath, Josh jumped. Gus swung his attention from the boiler gauges to his brother's progress and back to the boiler again. Josh went deep. The cold crushed him until he thought he would never breathe again. He struggled to contain his panic. Frantically his left arm searched the waters for the first rope as he kicked his way to the surface. His right hand gripped the second line. He drew a loud rasping breath as his head broke water. The weight of the second line threatened to take him back down into the depths. His heart felt ready to burst when his fingertips touched the first line. He grabbed tightly and hung on. Slowly he followed it hand over hand to assist his journey to the river bank.

Bill Greenway was grateful for the help with the tree. He tied the second line while Josh hacked at the timber. The axe work soon warmed Josh up but he knew he had to return to the tug and the only way was via the water.

The incoming tide had delivered the water under the complete keel of the *Marcia* by the time Josh was safely back on the *Lion*. The captain once more set the tug to work. Slowly at first, the ferry began to edge out after the tug. Bill Greenway jumped up into his boat as she slipped from the muddy grip of the river bank.

During the journey back to the Town Reach of the river and the private wharf there, Josh kept an eye on the ferry following behind. With its rudder unsecured, it tended to pull first one way then the other. Bill Greenway stood against the cabin structure at the bow of his vessel. It was Captain Johns who first drew Josh's attention to the three-masted four-hundred-ton barque with a shiny new funnel that was weighing anchor in the Shafston Reach of the river.

He pointed as he asked. "Any idea what ship that is?"

Josh glanced over then returned his gaze back to the ferry coming behind. It took a second or two before he realized what he had seen. His head snapped about again. He punched his fist into the air and cooeed.

Gus poked his head out, wanting to know what had happened.

"It's the *Northern Orchid*; she's home. Look, over there." Josh pointed.

"Wow, Captain Sloan is back."

MILLIE

After tea, Millie lit the lantern in her office. She sat at her desk and let her mind drift through the day just past. It had been an eventful afternoon. Her conversation with Thomas, while they awaited Abigail Baldwin's delivery, had revealed a man of great artistic talent and a member of Egyptian royalty. Not criteria required in the normal manservant she would have thought. A warm sensation still bubbled inside her following the childbirth and having the infant named in honour of her. She looked up when a tap sounded at the door. The Dougall boys stood on the doormat looking very pleased with themselves.

"Hello Josh, hello Gus. What have you pair been up to today?"

The boys shuffled into the room. Their eyes glistened. White teeth shone in the light.

"Miss Millie, can you guess what we saw today?"

"I could say the same to you, boys. Can you guess what I saw today? Miss Abigail had her new baby, a boy, born this afternoon."

"Wow, was that here at the hotel?"

"It was upstairs in her room. Her brother, Doctor George Goldfinch, Eve and I helped. Now can your news trump that?" Millie was just in the process of retreating into her tender memories of helping Abigail get through a difficult birth when her head snapped up at Josh's next words.

"How about a sighting of the *Northern Orchid* anchoring in the Shafston Reach?"

Millie jumped up out of her chair.

"When was this?" She strived to look calm but inside she felt her heart pound and her mouth just wanted to grin until her face split.

Josh looked at his brother for confirmation. "About midday, maybe a bit later."

Millie held her chest while her mind swirled. What to do first? Definitely a tub bath then a full makeup. A trembling hand reached up to touch her hair. Should she wash her hair now? It was a bit late. He might be here at any moment; if not this evening, then tomorrow sometime. She did not hear the boys say goodnight before leaving to find their sister, Sarah. When her racing feet reached the top of the stairs, she did what she never allowed anyone to do. She yelled inside the hotel.

"Jacko! Jacko! Where are you?"

A door slammed down below and heavy feet pounded up the stairs.

"Miss Millie, what's wrong? Are you all right?"

"Yes, yes, Jacko, I'm fine. Can you ask Ned to bring up a kettle of hot water for a wash?"

"No trouble at all, but at this time of night?" Jacko was at a loss. This was most unusual. His frown disappeared. He remembered Josh telling Spud Murphy, in the bar, that the *Northern Orchid* was on the Brisbane River. All was clear. "Yes, Miss Millie. Between us both we will fill your tub with warm water."

"Thanks, dear." She took up the lantern and made her way to her apartment to look through her clothes.

The hotel was quiet. Only the noises of the night drifted in on the gentle breeze. Pale beams sprayed across the landscape as the moon rose above the tree-line. At the table in her rooms, Millie used the file that she had been reading to brush away some of the numerous insects battering against the glass of the lamp. Common sense told her that it was too late for the captain to be calling but her wishful heart slowed her hand as she reached out to kill the flame. Darkness was thick about her for a moment as her eyes adjusted. The moonbeams crept through the window revealing her room once more. She closed her eyes and sat alone with her despondency.

The rattle of small stones bouncing off her window lifted her from the seat. She threw the casement open. There in the carriageway, he stood; draped in the moonlight.

"Oooh."

Millie's feet flew through the open door, into the private lounge and down the staircase that led into the main foyer. Her fingers fumbled with the bolts on the entrance door. Impatiently she threw the heavy doors open. The three front steps drummed a quick tattoo as she raced out with her arms wide. Over six months of separation melted away as they clung to each other. Eventually, William Sloan lifted his head from its nest in her thick curls.

"Am I going to ravage you right here in the front of the hotel or will we go upstairs where we will not draw an audience?"

Millie giggled. "Billy Sloan, you behave yourself in the front garden of my hotel." She stepped back and took a grip on his arm. He stumbled as she pulled him forward, with surprising force, towards the entrance. The door bolts, when thrown home, sounded like a short volley of muted gunshots. Struggling to control her excitement, she led him up the stairs and into her room. William's boot kicked the door shut. He drew her back into his arms and their kiss was long and sweet.

Slow at first, their passion soon became a fiery thing. His fingers pulled pins from the roll of hair at the back of her head. They flew like missiles in all directions. Millie felt his warmth on her lips like hot chilli peppers. The heat drifted down through her chest. It stirred the sensuous wings fluttering within her stomach. Her mouth opened to receive his inquisitive tongue. The hot lava flowed from her belly, lower and lower until her secret lips throbbed with the yearning. Her fingers now fumbled with his buttons. Somewhere inside her head, she complemented her choice of clothing as his sun-browned hands eased the silk over her shoulders. She almost tore the remainder of his clothes from his body. A soft moan escaped her throat as his lips caressed her nipples. Work-hardened hands gently lifted her heavy breasts and he buried his face. The pair shuffled towards the bed. As if she was but a doll, he lifted her up and lay her gently upon the eiderdown. Her body and soul reached out for him. He groaned as he joined her in mutual desire. The world around them receded as they gave to each other completely.

With their sexual appetites of the evening sated, their lovemaking progressed into the languid sensuous pleasures of the early morning. It was the rattle of the fire grate in the stove below that disturbed them. William parted the curtain of hair from Millie's face. He noted that her hazel eyes were more green than they were brown this morning. He kissed them both.

"Is that Mrs. Hamilton in the kitchen?"

Millie moistened her mouth and lips with her tongue.

"No, it'll be Sarah today. She'll be getting breakfast for her and the boys. They have class this morning with Captain Harris. I'll throw on my gown and ask her to prepare a tray for us."

Millie looked about her at the wreckage of the room. As she moved around, she lifted items from the floor and tossed them over the bedposts. Any article of her own clothing, when discovered, was dragged on her body. With her dressing gown in place, she tip-toed down the back stairs to the kitchen. Sarah was just in the process of preparing the small saucepan of rolled oats for herself and her brothers.

"Sarah, be a dear and put enough porridge on for another two people? How's the kettle going? I'm desperate for a cup of tea."

Other than the sparkle in her eyes, Sarah's face remained deadpan. She gave the pot a shuffle around on the stove.

"It'll be a few minutes yet, Miss Millie. Would you like me to bring the tray up when it's ready?"

"Yes please, dear; if you don't mind."

When Millie slipped silently into her room, it was to find the bed made and things tidy.

"If you want to give up the sea at any time, you can have a job here making beds, Captain Sloan," Millie said with a laugh. "I'm sure the pay will please."

He kissed her soundly. "Wicked wench you may be, but the sea is always my other mistress."

Millie sighed as she turned back to the door ready to take the tray from Sarah who was heard climbing the stairs. After they were settled at the table, Millie poured two steaming cups. She drank thirstily. William took her hand and sat her on his knee.

"Millie, we have to talk about that letter I wrote. You did get it, didn't you?"

Millie kissed his forehead. She told him of the visit from the man, Edward Carson, who claimed to be her husband's brother. She explained that Christopher Carson never had any siblings. He laughed out loud when she told how Jacko was all for taking the imposter out in a row-boat and feeding him to the sharks in the middle of the Brisbane River.

"Arthur advised strongly against such action. You remember Arthur Rankine, my solicitor, don't you, William?"

"Yes, my dear, a good man." William sat thoughtfully for a moment then spoke again. "Millie, I'm sorry that all this has come upon you at the behest of my wife. Catherine found out about us recently and wanted to strike out, I guess. I should have told her long ago. I blame myself for everything. As I said in the letter, she has gone and taken the girls with her back to England."

"I'm sorry that the girls have left too, William. As for Edward Carson, Arthur says there is no way he has any claim here. No doubt it will all blow over."

"Jacko and I could go and lean on the man somewhat if you wanted. Not feed him to the sharks, mind you, but show him the error of his ways. Impress upon him how he would enjoy another clime much better than here."

Millie grinned.

"You really are as bad as Jacko. No, we'll leave it to Arthur and the law." She snuggled in close to his chest resting her head in the crook of his neck. They held each other close. When she stood to tidy the tray, Millie asked quietly.

"Will you be seeing Josh and Gus Dougall today, William? They are like a pair of cats on hot bricks since they saw the *Northern Orchid* anchoring yesterday."

Captain Sloan held her hand. "You have really taken those kids to heart, haven't you, Millie?"

"It's not just that. I owe it to their mother to look out for them. They have been very good to me; the three of them. I will miss the two boys when they go to sea but that's what they want. I'll not stand in their way."

"We'll see how they go. They might be most unsuitable, you know. How will you feel about me, then?"

"Billy Sloan, one is not dependant on the other. You and I are a pair; aren't we?"

"Yes, my wicked wench, we are." He wrapped his arms more tightly around her comfortable frame. "The reports on the boys' progress from Captain Harris have always been favourable. He is not one to give praise lightly. If the boys are anything like their father they'll do very well."

Millie ran her fingers down the scar at the side of William's face.

"We both owe that man so much. Without him, you would not have your life and without you, I would not have a life."

He caught her hand and brought the fingers to his lips. His kisses were soft as a butterfly's touch.

"What will the boys be doing today?"

"Well, they have the class with Captain Harris this morning. It's usually about one o'clock when they get back here to the hotel."

"Tell them to come to the ship and to bring their gear. If we're not at Queen's Wharf loading, they can give the ship an ahoy from the bank. I'll send the tender to collect them. By the way, an extra set of clean clothes would be a boon. Looking for a crew-member who owns a decent pair of trousers and shirt is almost impossible. On those occasions when we have first-class passengers, it is not a good look to have the crew dressed in muddy, greasy or torn and tattered clothes, even if we are only a cargo vessel."

"They have presentable clothes." Millie's smile was brief. Her face fell as realization struck. "Oh, so soon. Will you be sailing so soon?"

"Not immediately. This will give the boys a chance to get used to the ship and learn what will be expected of them, Millie my darling."

"Of course. We will miss them; and you. Sarah will be really lost without her brothers. She still feels the absence of poor little Daisy." A gentle hand reached over and wiped some porridge from his bottom lip. A soft kiss fell upon his smile. "So, when will you be sailing?"

"Not too sure yet. We have cargo to unload and I'll have to talk to the agents sometime today about what cargo they have going north. A few days maybe. Now, I'd best get a move on. Mac will be wanting some time on shore today and tonight. I'll see you tomorrow, my love."

Millie stood at the window watching the captain stride off towards the river. She hugged herself and smiled. Once he had passed out of her sight, she began digging around the bottom of her wardrobe.

"Aah, here you are." She drew out two identical canvas sea-bags with drawstring necks and a name painted on each one. 'Josh Dougall' and 'Gus Dougall' stood out starkly on the pale new canvas. Millie felt sure the boys would be pleased with these. The sailmaker had done a commendable job.

FIVE

THE *NORTHERN ORCHID*

Josh and Gus gingerly made their way across the remnants of the worm-eaten Victoria Bridge on their way to the town side of the river. They strove to appear relaxed; like they were old hands from one of the boats. Their unblemished sea-bags screamed, novice. Together they caught sight of the *Northern Orchid* moored at the wharf, with her recently painted hull a deep blue. The white upper trim matched the bold name scripted across both port and starboard bow. Like a spider web the forestays, backstays and shrouds spread from the three masts to their anchor points on the ship. Braced at an angle against each mast were solid yards. At the upper ends, pulleys with dangling ropes swayed in the wind. Hatch covers were off both fore and aft holds looking like open mouths hungry for cargo to fill their bellies or waiting for their belly contents to be disgorged.

Men climbed all over her like ants disturbed from their nest. Cranes were in use over the fore and aft holds of the ship. Raised voices filled the air as orders were flung about. A thin stream of smoke dribbled from the funnel before being carried away on the gentle breeze. On the hewn-log structure of the wharf, two separate horse teams stood harnessed to large wooden drays. The animals' tails whipped over their backs. The horses' heads swung up and down in an attempt to clear the flies from their eyes. In response to a biting horse-fly, a shod hoof stamped irritably. Occasionally, the drivers repositioned their charges to suit the loads they were receiving or delivering.

The boys watched enthralled. They were here, on the wharf, watching a ship, they were to sail on, being loaded. Many times, in the past months it had seemed like this day was never going to arrive. Now they were here. Their daydreams were interrupted by a call from above.

"Ahoy, my innocent hearties. About time. Stow those kits and give a hand here."

They looked up to see the mountain of a man who had been on the ship when they first approached Captain Sloan last year. It did not take a second telling before Josh and Gus raced up the gangplank onto the ship. They looked about at a loss to know where exactly they were to stow their sea-bags. A man, with thinning grey hair, spoke up from the door of the wheel-house.

"Here lads, toss them up here. They'll be safe with me. I'm the corduroy mechanic, your engineer, Mister Winston. Now, you'd best dash over to the bosun, Mister Evans, and see what you can do to help."

Mister Evans pointed to numerous water barrels scattered along the edge of the upper deck.

"Lash those barrels against the bulwark and mind you do a good job. We don't want to go thirsty because we lost our extra water supply overboard."

"Yes, Sir." They replied in unison.

Josh and Gus found numerous hemp lines hanging in bundles along the inside wall of the ship's upper deck. Each barrel was manhandled into position and tied securely using the knots they had been taught by their father many years before. Hardly had they completed this task when Mister Evans issued a further instruction. He threw a line to them.

"Here, grab this; the pair of you, together. I want you to ease this lot a little to the stern." The line was attached to the load dangling over the open hold from the crane above. “Not too much; just ease it to the side a foot or so.”

With the grind of metal joints, the rattle of its pulleys and the creak of taut ropes the crane lowered the load through the entrance of the hold. A voice drifted up from inside the storage area.

“That’s it, Mister Evans; sits just neat in that space. Can yer send someone down to tidy up the starboard corner? Those smaller crates’ll fit in there with some dunnage around ‘em.”

Mister Evans turned to his two new-comers.

“Get down into the hold and give Sykes and Bony a hand there.”

They discovered, at the open hatch of the hold, a length of rope hanging down into the storage area below. It had been knotted at intervals of about two feet. Neither Gus nor Josh hesitated. They flew down it without a pause. As part of their lessons, Captain Harris had set up similar ropes and netting ladders from the two large gum trees in his back yard. The boys had spent hours racing up and down them.

Their bare feet whispered as they landed on the timber deck at the bottom of the hold. Both boys came to an abrupt halt when they turned to see what awaited them. Standing side by side with hands on their hips were two men. Josh and Gus looked at each other. A flash of acknowledgement passed between the brothers. They recognized the two men as those who had made the veiled threat when Josh and Gus first boarded the *Northern Orchid* the previous year.

“Aah, the cap’n’s bastards; a right pair o’ monkeys we ’av ’ere, Bony.” The skinny man wearing a bandana spat on the floor between Josh’s feet.

A four-cornered knotted cloth covered the head of the large brown man who landed a dollop of phlegm at Gus’s feet. The two older men appeared disappointed when neither lad rose to the bait.

Sykes glanced up through the open hatch to see Captain Sloan standing beside Mister Evans, watching. Sykes turned and pointed the boys to a corner where firewood timber for the galley stove lay around higgledy-piggledy.

"Tidy up that lot into the smallest space you can, monkeys. Come on Bony," he said to the brown-skinned man. "We'll get those smaller crates into place."

As they stacked the timber, Josh and Gus watched what was happening around them. Sykes and Bony, with two other men, were using pulleys and cables attached to the large crossbeams above to lift and shift some of the cartons and crates that filled the hold. They heard the skinny man with the bent legs, called Bandy. The other one, built like a water barrel, Sykes addressed as Rollins.

No sooner was the timber stashed than Mister Evan's hail came from above.

"There's work up here for you fellas now." As Josh and Gus poked their heads through the hatch, Evans asked. "Which one of youse is called Gus?"

"I'm Gus." The shorter brother pointed to his sibling. "That's Josh."

"Right, Gus. You're to go to the engine room and look after the boiler for Mister Winston." Evans turned his attention to Josh. "You're to go into the galley and give old China a hand." The bosun turned to hail a young man slithering down a line from the foremast. The man's long sandy-coloured hair lifted into the air before collapsing about his pale face as he jumped the last six feet to the deck. "Here, Andrews, show these lads around, will you? The big one's to help China and the other's to help Mister Winston."

Andrews only came to Josh's shoulder. He looked up at both boys as he instructed them.

"Follow me. Where ya from?"

"Brisbane." Josh tried not to stare at the skinny Andrews with his monstrous nose surrounded by a forest of pimples. He looked like he might be only a year or two older than himself.

"Oh, I'm from Sydney. I've just joined the *Northern Orchid* too." He continued with his life history as he led the boys towards the companion-way. Dirt stained hands with broken fingernails pointed out the nest of cabins huddled near the funnel. They learnt that the captain's and the mate's cabins were on either side of the wheel-house that rose above them. The engineer's cabin was behind the mate's cabin and the chartroom was situated behind the captain's cabin.

As the three rounded these cabins, on the starboard side, they nearly fell over a small man hidden under a large cone-shaped hat. He was fussing around several cages lined up in a frame outside the chartroom wall. The three young men jumped back. Andrews held his arm over his face.

"Be careful, the old devil'll put a Chinese curse on ya." He warned Josh and Gus who both stood there speechless as the little man jumped up at them.

"Why you not looking where you going for? Give no warning. You want kill me. You'll get a bad Chinee curse one day Andrews, I swear. Who's these new men? More for an old man to cook for. What, you think I got nothing better to do all day but cook for useless men don't know good food?" The little man with the narrow eyes had barely taken a breath through this whole outpouring.

"China, this's Josh and Gus. Josh's come to help ya in the galley this evening."

"What you know about cooking? I hope you wash dishes clean. Andrews can't wash a dish to save his life. Come, first, you must learn to feed and clean the chickens."

Josh stared harder at the cages where he noticed each of the four latticed containers held four hens. All sixteen of the feathered animals stood with heads cocked watching the interaction of the humans. Looking down upon the Chinese man, Josh spoke before even thinking.

"Chooks! On board ship!"

"So, you want Chinee curse too? You show honour to chickens. They lay good eggs for Cap'n Sloan and Mister MacGregor."

"Sorry, Mister China. I've never heard of pet chooks on a ship before." Josh tried to back pedal.

"They're not pets. They're here to work, the same you; and not give cheek. If they don't work …" China drew a long-nailed finger across his throat. "Sheesh; chicken soup. Watch you don't end up in soup, Mister Josh."

Andrews tapped Gus on the shoulder and whispered.

"Come, I'll take ya to the lower deck, to the engine room and Mister Winston."

With a rueful grin at his brother, Gus escaped while Josh tried his best to placate China. He watched attentively as the little man fed and watered the poultry. Four eggs were removed from each pen and placed into a cane-woven basket. A gentle hand caressed and smoothed each feathered neck. After passing the egg-basket and a baleful look to Josh, the man called China, reached up to the strip of worn sailcloth spread across the top of the cages. He tied the corners into cleats within the timber deck. The man rose to his feet with his hand pressed to his lower back. An involuntary hiss escaped through his pursed lips.

"We go to the galley now. You can cut up the vegables for tea. I think we have rice tonight. And don't lose eggs."

A bemused Josh followed obediently carrying the egg-basket.

On the lower deck, Josh breathed deeply at the galley doorway. Whatever was on the stove, smelt as good as or even better than Sarah or even Mrs. Hamilton cooked. Two long tables with wooden forms attached stood on one side of the long narrow room. In the corner near the door on the opposite side of the room was a round table with four moveable chairs tucked neatly underneath. China flung out a hand in that direction.

"The officers' table. Sometimes they eat in the chartroom on top deck; sometime eat here."

As they moved to the back of the room near the two portholes, Josh looked for a suitable place to leave the egg-basket. One bench against the wall held two large tubs with many dents in their sides. Between that and a second bench holding a large chopping board and three long sharp knives, stood two water barrels. In one corner, surrounded by a wall of tin sheeting, a blackened wood stove held a large cooking pot and a kettle. Steam poured from under the loose-fitting lids of both.

"You wait." These were the instructions from China as he took the basket of eggs and disappeared into one of two small rooms leading off the other side of the galley. It was plain, one of these rooms was China's sleeping cabin. A sleeping mat could be seen rolled up in the corner. A hook in the wall above held some clothing and now the cone hat. A tall pile of woven baskets stood in the other corner. The second door was shut. China did not leave it open any longer than was necessary as he slipped through into the room beyond.

Josh began to rummage around the shelves under the benches. As he stood to poke his head out of the open porthole, he froze. The touch on his leg was as soft as a feather but warm. It slithered up his leg. He did not know if he should jump away or stay still. He lowered his eyes and burst out laughing; a cat. Chooks and a cat, whatever would he run into next?

"That is Confucius. He bring good luck and no big mice on *Northern Orchid*."

"As you said before, Mister China, 'No pets.' Everyone and everything must work on the ship." Josh laughed again. China grinned. His eyes scrunched up until they were all but closed.

"Come, you funny man. We chop vegables and boil water for the rice."

The egg-basket now held green beans, carrots and onions as well as several items Josh could not identify. The little man dug deep within the basket bringing out a brown paper packet. China held it open near Josh's nose. He sniffed. The smell was strong but not unpleasant. Inside the packet he could see what appeared, to his untrained eye, to be dead leaves.

"Herbs, dried herbs. Not as good as fresh herbs but they not too bad."

"I suppose one day we can expect to see a garden growing on the upper deck?" Josh grinned at the cook.

"Nah, Cap'n say no. I ask. Is alright. I have many cousins live at every port. They all grow the vegables and the herbs."

Steam gushed from the pot when Josh lifted the lid to give the soup a stir. He watched fascinated as, next to him, China blended vegetables and rice around in a big oval pot he called a wok. The little man's nimble fingers danced the wok around and around over the hot flame using one hand. The other hand stirred the contents strenuously with a wooden spoon. A voice from the door drew both their attention.

"The Captain wants tea for him and Mister Winston in the chartroom, China."

A deckhand disappeared before China could take any grievance out on the messenger.

On their way to the engine room, Gus sniffed the aromas of cooking food as they passed the galley on the lower deck. This was in the midsection of the ship, on the port side. From there Andrews showed Gus to the crew's quarters. This was on the opposite side of the ship. Between the two, heat radiated through the bulkhead of the engine room. The man who had greeted Josh and Gus earlier stood at the open doorway.

"Aah, there you are. Gus, I believe."

Gus turned to thank Andrews for his help but the fellow had disappeared back around the corner. He faced the engineer.

"Er yes, Sir."

"Well, don't just stand there, boy. I hear you are mad keen on engines. I'll see if I can break you of that fantasy."

Mister Winston pointed to where many blackened bags of coal were stowed against the wall of the ship near the bosun's cabin; adjacent to the crew's quarters. The engineer then moved inside the engine room and pointed to a tall metal tank.

"It seems we're stuck here at the wharf for the night. I've already damped down the engine. You can up-end some of those bags into this coal drum. You'll find it takes about four bags to fill it."

"Yes, Sir."

Guthrie Winston and Gus Dougal were lying down under the engine as Gus investigated every moving part. He was never short of a question to ask. Only their feet were to be seen when Captain Sloan banged on the side of the coal bin.

"Time to call it a day, I should think. Mister Winston can I see you in the wheel-house when this young fellow gives you a break?"

The activity of the ship's loading had ceased. The sun was low against the skyline. Captain Sloan and Mister Winston stood in the wheel-house with a glass of rum each.

"You sure you don't mind doing the first watch, Guthrie? I've given you Sykes and Bony. They've been with the *Northern Orchid* for a couple of years now. They know the routine of the ship. Never hurts to keep an eye on them both, though. There's usually nothing too much happening while we're in port but I still like to keep a watch out. Mostly it's our own crew that needs herding when coming back with a skinful. I'll take over at midnight to morning. Maybe I'll drag those two new lads out of their slumbers to stand watch with me."

"I'm sure I can manage. I've got nothing else to do. A bit like playing nursemaid, really."

"Mac will be back tomorrow and I've given Evans tonight off. We'll move back out and anchor in the river tomorrow after we've finished loading the cargo here. The lighterman's skiff with our coal will find us there. All going well, we should get away on the tide, the day after. I'll sort the pilot out in the morning."

The hurricane lantern hanging from the mast sent shadows dancing across the deck where the crew, that cuddled around the capstan, leant into the bars. Feet slipped on the timber deck as they strained to gain leverage. The anchor was stuck in the river mud and reluctant to re-join the ship. They were all pleased to feel the vibrations rippling through their feet and the whoomp, whoomp, whoomp of the engine down below. Inch by inch the ship edged forward in an attempt to overrun the anchor and break the suction holding it. The sudden release of pressure sent them hurtling forward onto the horizontal bars in the capstan's circle. They struggled to maintain their balance. Gus and Josh were not too happy to find they had Sykes and Bony as close company. Sykes pushed in hard against Josh forcing his ribs to massage the capstan's core. Josh felt the bruises developing deep in his skin tissue. He gritted his teeth and pushed back with all of his weight. Gus was also involved in a push-shove competition with the monster, Bony; and coming off second best.

The anchor cable clattered up through the hawse-hole dribbling salt water over the deck before being stored. Clouds that had delivered an early rain shower were clearing from the sky. Stars were seen briefly as they began to retire. The ship continued its slow progress as it approached the sharp bend in the river at Petrie Bight. Standard whistle signals split the air announcing their presence to any vessel making its way upstream. There was no room for two large vessels to pass at the Bight. Having negotiated that tight river bend and the mud bank mid-stream in the Shafston Reach, they poured more coal on the fire. Smoke billowed from the funnel of the *Northern Orchid* as she made her way the twenty miles downstream to the river-mouth. The partially developed banks of the Town Reach and Shafston Reach gave way to flourishing mangroves that protected multitudes of prawns and crabs. Mud banks reached out into the river; a hidden trap for unwary helmsmen.

Josh and Gus saw little of Brisbane as they, along with two other deckhands, Tanner and Andrews, were put to scrubbing the top deck. Andrew's nose had not got any smaller and Tanner, whom they had not met before, was a squat man who said little but worked hard. Bandy the fellow that they had seen yesterday, working in the hold was now assisting Mister Winston in the engine room. Bellyache Basil did his best to evade the mouth and serving spoon under China's rule in the kitchen. Sykes, Bony and the other deckhands Adams and Rollins danced attendance on Mister Evans who relayed all instructions thrown down from Captain Sloan and Mister MacGregor in the wheel-house.

The rising sun sparkled in the last raindrops dripping from the rigging as the boys secured their cleaning equipment. Mister Evans called Gus and Josh to help with the Jacob's-ladder. Josh was just about to toss the roll of rope ladder, with its wooden rungs, over the side of the ship when his hand was halted by the sharp hail from the bosun.

"Hoy, make sure that's secured this end or you'll be diving over to collect it, boyo."

The second warning from Mister Evans was a little late.

"And don't clobber the coxswain of the pilot's boat or you won't be too popular either."

Josh and Gus looked at each other aghast; neither really wanting to look over the side of the ship. When there were no angry protests from below, they chanced a glance. The pilot's boat was keeping abreast about twenty yards from their beam waiting to collect the pilot and deliver him back to Moreton Island. They breathed joint sighs of relief.

"Keep a tight hold this end now, boys." The small man with the permanent frown instructed as he swung himself up onto the bulwark and over the side. He slipped his arms around the ropes and his feet curled onto the rungs. "At least it's good weather today. I won't have me brains smashed out against the hull of a crazy bucking ship."

Up in the wheel-house, the captain, with a sigh of relief and a grin, called for the sails to be unfurled. All the crew topside worked on the rigging to release the main sails, the topsails and the gallant sails on the mainmast and foremast. The mizzenmast carried fore and aft sails. Remnants of the rainwater sprayed over them, cooling their bodies.

As the wind caught the unfurled sails, the sky filled with a volley of cracks like a teamster's whips. Captain Sloan took up the speaking tube and whistled for attention from the engine room.

"You can dampen the boiler, Guthrie. I'm going to bend the sails for a bit."

His hand rested lightly on the helm. The wind blew from the south-east taking them along at a goodly clip. Like a fresh stallion released, the *Northern Orchid* bolted across the waves. The captain's wide grin matched that of the mate who had only just joined him in the wheel-house.

"I've inspected the holds and cargo. Everything's shipshape. I had Evan's add extra dunnage around those crates of medical supplies. What was the weather report from the pilot before he left us?"

"He reckoned we can bank on clear skies with ten to fifteen-knot winds."

"At this rate, and considering there'll be little to no moon, we should be close to Double Island Point when we're ready to anchor up tonight. It will be a short run to Inskip Point first thing in the morning. With any luck, a pilot's boat might be working at the Wide Bay Bar. We may even get to Maryborough harbour before tomorrow night."

"There's a few mights and maybes there, Mac. Pigs may fly too so don't go looking up."

Mac gave a rueful grin and shrugged as he pointed through the window to where the latest recruits were tottering across the yardarms of the foretopsail.

"Your friend, Daffy Harris has certainly taught the lads to flutter around the sails and rigging like a pair of seagulls."

The captain laughed. "Daffy was one of the best. On more than one occasion, when we were midshipmen together, I swore he'd end up in the water. He'd literally fly from one sail to the next. We all did crazy things but he was crazier than all of us put together."

The voice of the bosun drifted up to the wheel-house.

"I'm sure there's work down here for you two smart alecks."

Mac and William Sloan burst out laughing.

The captain asked, "Can we assume Evans is talking to the two seagulls on the topsail and not to us, do you think?"

With rumbling bellies, the first shift welcomed Mister Evan's instructions to go to the galley for their breakfast. China was hidden in the steam rising from the pot of burgoo set to keep warm on the edge of the stove. Four eggs and bacon rashers spat at him from the frying pan. Bellyache Basil cut slices of freshly baked bread at the bench. China smiled at Josh when he arrived.

"You take tray to the Cap'n and Mister Winston, Mister Josh. The breakfasts'll be colder than a whore's smile if I wait any longer. This Bellyache man slower than a turtle today."

Josh was not too sure what to do. He hoped Bellyache Basil did not mind. The man certainly was not rushing to intercept. Josh stood with his hands on the handles while China loaded the large wooden tray. As he lifted it from the bench, he looked up to see a glaring Sykes approaching him.

"So, it's the Cap'n's bastard being a good little boy again, is it?" The man sneered. "Whatcha gonna do if I tip the tray all over the floor?" He feinted to the left, then to the right. His hands threatened to upset the breakfast tray.

With a speed that defied the eye, China slipped in front of Josh and took Sykes by the elbow. If it wasn't for the look of pain contorting the man's face, one might assume a friend was offering guidance. Josh only caught a few of the words China whispered into the ear under the bandana. Threats of curses and not seeing good food wasted and overworked cook drifted through the rattle and chatter and heat in the galley. Josh did not stop to ask questions. As he slipped out through the doorway, China's high piping voice caught his ear.

"Don't forget high coaming at top of companion-way."

When he reached the top deck, Josh lifted his feet carefully over the coaming mentioned before making his way to the chartroom. The captain and Mister Winston were scrutinizing several reports scattered across the table.

"Thanks, lad; put it down there." Captain Sloan made space available for the tray. "You managing your first day on the high seas?"

"Yes, thanks, Captain." Josh was glad to lay the tray on the table with everything still in place. The smell of the cooked eggs and bacon sorely teased his nose and made his mouth water.

The captain and Mister Winston pulled in their seats and began to sort the meals. As Josh made to go out through the doorway, Captain Sloan called him back.

"I want you and Gus in the wheel-house at six bells of the forenoon watch. Let's see if you remember everything Captain Harris taught you. We'll see how you go using the sextant and the chronometer."

"Yes, Captain, Sir." His hunger was almost forgotten and his feet barely touched timber as he returned to the galley.

They came to a skidding halt at the wheel-house door just as the sixth bell sounded. Gus's victorious smile disappeared as they looked in to see Captain Sloan engrossed in a map spread out on the cupboard under the front windows. Mister MacGregor, at the helm, had his attention on the sails and the two deckhands making adjustments under Mister Evans' eagle eye.

"Looking at this map, the markers in the Great Sandy Island region have not changed since we last made this trip, Mac."

"Aye, aye, Captain."

The captain turned towards the boys standing wide-eyed at his wheel-house door.

"Right; come on in and I'll show you our chronometer and the sextant. I know Captain Harris has drummed it into you how these two instruments are a sailor's closest friends and must be cared for as such."

"Yes, Captain." In unison.

Taking a key from his pocket, the captain unlocked the cupboard in the starboard corner of the room. One at a time he took out two small wooden boxes and placed them on the front bench. The sextant did not shine like Captain Harris's had but the boys could see that it had been well cared for. The chronometer floated in its frame designed to absorb the ship's movement and thereby prevent damage to the delicate mechanisms within.

The next hour passed swiftly for Josh and Gus as the captain went through the features of these two instruments. He then led them out to the narrow walkway on the starboard side of the wheel-house. Here the boys put into practice what they knew of taking sightings and figuring the ship's position. Captain Sloan used a blunt pencil to write their deductions in a small notebook. When he was satisfied, he watched as the boys replaced the instruments into their protective containers.

"Follow me," he threw back at them as he nimbly descended the half dozen steps from the wheel-house to the corridor between the cabins. But the captain did not stop at his own cabin. He led Josh and Gus to the door next to his own. When he turned the catch, the door groaned and scraped as he pushed it open. This narrow room was commonly referred to by the crew as 'The Captain's Cupboard'.

Inside an untidy heap of new canvas filled one corner near the only porthole. Behind the door was a bookcase with several large tomes on nautical topics. Some, the boys recognized having seen the same in Captain Harris's cottage. A long slab of timber had been hinged to one wall. When Josh swung it down, it produced a writing bench.

"You'll find pencils, pens, ink and blotter in the bookshelf. There is also a journal book for each of you. Every day I want you to write down everything you do and everything you learn in the day. When you have any free time, I expect you to be in here learning everything these books can teach you. If you have any questions, you are to ask Mister MacGregor or me for the answers. Is that clear?"

The boys looked at each other. They could hardly speak. "Yes, Captain." They whispered.

Captain Sloan swung about and made his way to the door. "Right; now clean this room up before you go to eat."

"Yes, Captain, Sir."

SIX

THE MARINER'S REST

Millie stood, with Sarah at her side, looking out towards the river. The calm waters captured the early morning sunlight. Teardrops of moisture from a predawn rain shower fell from the leaves and golden blossoms of the vine twisting through the verandah rail. Teardrops were not too far from the eyelids of the pair watching. Even though the *Northern Orchid* had not been moored within sight of The Rest, Millie and Sarah each saw, within their mind's eye, the ship weigh anchor and move towards the mouth of the river. Millie blew a kiss to the tall captain with the fearsome scar on his face. Sarah prayed a silent prayer for her two brothers; the last of her family.

"Too many goodbyes, I think. Firstly, the Goldfinch entourage to their own home and now the boys."

"Miss Abigail is such a nice lady, don't you think, Miss Millie?" Sarah did not give Millie time to answer before continuing, "And the Doctor is such a gentleman. Miss Jane, Eve and Thomas are devoted to them, I think. At least their house is not too far away and we will see them and the baby frequently."

They both stood silently for some time pondering on their recently acquired friends.

"This will not get breakfast then, will it?" Millie turned reluctantly and took Sarah's hand. "Come, my dear, we'll do the trays together."

As they came down the stairs, Jacko stepped through the doorway from the bar room. "The ship's sailed without any trouble then, has it? It's sure going to be quiet around here without Josh and Gus."

Sarah's smile was wan. "You having breakfast now, Jacko?" She really did not feel like talking at all.

"Yes, thanks, Sarah. I'll put out the plates."

Jacko was still helping in the kitchen as Sarah loaded the bread into the oven to bake. She did not comment when he took up the towel and began drying the dishes while she washed. If she had not been otherwise distracted, Sarah may have commented on the fact that Jacko did not usually hang around the kitchen to help with the dishes. A clatter of horse's hooves outside sent Jacko peering through the back doorway.

"Who is it?" Sarah asked. Jacko's tightened lips told her it was not one of his favourite people. She shrugged her shoulders. Whoever it was would make themselves known, no doubt. As the crunch of footsteps approached, Jacko answered Sarah's question.

"It's that Arthur Rankine, again. What does he need to see Millie about at this hour? Looking for breakfast, I'll be betting."

"What's the matter with you, Jacko? I thought you liked Mister Rankine. He's been very good to Millie. It's no trouble to give him a decent breakfast when he comes to see her. Millie said he doesn't get fed well at his boarding house."

"So, he should look after Millie; she's done enough for him. Sniffing around you is why he's here, I reckon." Sarah never caught what it was that Jacko mumbled as he stomped back into the bar area.

She shrugged. Men, they were impossible to understand.

The wooden spoon in Sarah's hand scraped around the edges of the bowl as she folded the flour into the mixture of biscuits. She looked up as Millie walked in with Arthur Rankine. The wide smile on Miss Millie's face told her Mister Rankine must have been the messenger of good news.

"Sarah, I'm just going to put together a quick breakfast for Arthur. I won't be in your way, will I?" Millie pointed her guest to a chair.

Sarah edged her seat to the far corner of the table and resumed her mixing.

"Of course not, Miss Millie."

"Good morning, Miss Sarah." Arthur Rankine smiled. The chair dragged on the wooden floor as he pulled it out to sit.

"Good morning, Sir."

"Please call me Arthur, Miss Sarah."

She felt the pink flush creep up her neck and face.

"Oh, Mister Rankine, Sir, that wouldn't be right. I couldn't do that."

The smile on Arthur's thin lips did not reach the depths of his eyes.

"Miss Sarah, here I was hoping we may become good friends."

The spoon in Sarah's hand attacked the biscuit mixture. "Mister Rankine, you are an educated man. What would you want with the likes of me? That would never do."

With raised eyebrows, Millie looked up from where she was placing toast and eggs on a large plate.

"Arthur, you do know that I am as good as Sarah's guardian. You may like to remember that."

"Yes, yes, Miss Millie; of course. I didn't mean any harm. I just thought we could be friends."

"Hmm, as long as you keep things above reproach." Millie knew that Arthur frequented the ladies on the top floor.

Sarah felt the rosy glow of the flush turn to a raging inferno. Her hot scalp set the roots of her hair tingling. A thick dry tongue filled her mouth. She aimed her glare at her fingertips while she struggled for an adequate response. When she did speak, her voice trembled.

"I think Sir, that I should continue addressing you as Mister Rankine." Sarah also knew of Arthur's nocturnal visits to the premises. Her hands shook as she stood up and began to roll pieces of her mixture from the china bowl and lay them rather haphazardly on the greased and floured oven tray sitting on the table.

Mister Rankine nearly choked in his haste to swallow his meal. He stood up and made a feeble excuse as he retreated. A soft cackle drifted into the kitchen from the bar room.

"And that's enough out of you, too, Jacko," Millie retorted.

THE *NORTHERN ORCHID*

A light breeze and a gentle ocean swell nurtured the *Northern Orchid* as she lay quietly at anchor well off the long sandy beach five hours south of the Wide Bay Bar. The night was dark with only the stars offering any glimmer of light. Josh and Gus stood on the deck vying with each other as they identified the star formations. Gus grabbed his brother's arm. He pointed to where spirals of luminescent lights in the water bubbled up in the mini bow waves of a group of dolphins playing around the vessel like guardian shadows of the night. A wide smile split Josh's face. They stood on the starboard side not too far from the wheel-house where Captain Sloan kept a lonely vigil. The fourth man on watch with them was Andrews who was at present finishing the cleaning of the first-class cabins. They were expecting to take on board two guests when they reached the Wide Bay Port.

"Come on, we'd best do another round of the lower decks and then we'll see if Andrews needs a hand." Josh pushed himself upright. "Don't go around that way." He pulled his brother back and dropped his voice. "We'll go this way." He led off down the starboard side of the ship.

"What's wrong with the other way?"

Josh dropped his voice further. "Didn't you see? Sykes and his offsider Bony are sleeping on mats, up in the bow, under the ship's tender-boat."

Gus looked back, but of course, he could not see anything in the shadows. He whispered. "Why do they do that, do you think? Why don't they sleep in the crew's quarters?"

"Don't question it. At least we don't have to worry about sleeping near them."

"They give me the creeps. I feel like I have to sleep with my eyes open, with them two."

Little light flowed in through the open portholes. They had to feel their way around. Gus checked that the dampened down engine boiler fire was contained. Taking the lantern from where it hung on the wall of the crew's quarters, Josh used its glow to make his way down to inspect the level of water in the bilge. Satisfied that all was well, they headed up to the top deck. At the first-class cabins near the base of the mizzen mast, Josh pushed open two of the cabin doors before asking, "Where's Andrews?"

Gus held his finger to his lips and pointed. Andrews was curled up on a couch in the lounge room snoring softly. Josh moved in close and slapped his hands close to the sleeper's ear. It sounded like a gunshot. With limbs flailing, Andrews fell off the couch and onto the floor. He tried to gather up his body and his wits.

"Geez, why'd yer have to do that? Yer frightened the bejabbers out o' me."

Gus laughed fit to burst. "If the captain had caught you, that might have been a real gunshot, Andrews."

Josh began to retreat out of the doorway. "Come on you two, we'd best go make the captain a strong brew. Don't want him dozing off too."

The faintest glow had crept into the sky when Ewan MacGregor announced his arrival at the wheel-house door with a noisy yawn. Steam rose from a pannikin in his hand. His face looked pale in the light of the hurricane lamp hanging from the wall behind the captain.

"So, how's it going, Captain?"

William Sloan rubbed his own tired face. His fingers left his salt-encrusted hair standing at attention on his head.

"An uneventful night. The Dougall boys are stirring the crew out of their slumbers right now. It'll be light enough to weigh anchor very shortly. By mid-morning we should be at Inskip Point as you predicted. I'm off to catch an hour or two's sleep. There is no point waking Mister Winston. Once we get underway, he can organize Bony onto coal shovelling duties. I told Guthrie to have the pressure in the boiler up by the time we reach Wide Bay Bar on the off chance that a pilot might be in the area. It will be a boon if we get an early passage through."

"And if the pilot is nowhere to be seen? Shall I take the jolly-boat up the straits in the hope of finding the pilot vessel or do you plan on taking the *Northern Orchid* through that bar alone? You know, even if we make it through the bar alright, we still have to face those fickle sandbanks up past Great Sandy Island."

The captain stood tapping his fingers against the door frame for some moments while he thought of his choices. "There is always the option of going the extra one hundred and sixty miles up the east coast of Great Sandy Island to the Breaksea Spit and in through the north channel, remember Mac."

Mac laughed. "Since when have you ever done that?"

"The sooner they have the pilot stationed out at Hook or Inskip Points the better. The authorities are always talking about it but nothing gets done. I'll be old and grey before that happens."

Mac raised his eyebrows and glanced at his friend's silver hair. He smiled.

"Enough cheek out of you, you ginger headed fireball." Both men chuckled.

They watched below as Josh and Gus were seen heading off to the crew quarters having been relieved by the morning shift.

"How did the boys go?" Mac asked.

The captain threw his jacket over his shoulders as he prepared to leave.

"Considering neither's voice has broken properly yet, they did alright. Daffy Harris has done a great job with them. They may have a future on the sea; poor sods."

Sykes spun the two Dougall lads, along with the Andrews boy, right out of their hammocks. It was the hard fall on the decking plus the sound of the order for furled sails and the whisper of bare feet above them, that brought them to a conscious state. They scrambled to their feet and raced up to the top deck where they were soon put to work hauling on the halyards while others high above their heads hung over the yardarms dragging up the loose canvas and securing it in place. There was already enough warmth in the sun to heat up the deck timbers burning the soles of their bare feet. After the clatter of the anchor cable and its roar through the hawse-hole, they felt the ship spin about her tether with the wind and the tide before settling into position.

Bloodshot eyes peered between the slits of his eyelids as Captain Sloan leant against the doorway of the wheel-house. The ship's mate sent Bandy up to the crow's nest to see if there was any visible sign of the pilot and his boat. The man had not reached the yardarms of the topsail when he called down.

"Ship approaching the bar from the Straits." He pointed at the Wide Bay Bar. "Pilot's boat following."

Ewan MacGregor smiled at his captain. "You're a lucky blighter, Sloan. Some ships wait here for days before they catch even a glimpse of the pilot."

With a grin, William Sloan touched the wooden door frame.

"The devil looks after his own, Mac. Now we just have to hope that he'll take us back in with him."

THE MARINER'S REST

Millie, wearing her dressing gown and slippers, stopped at the kitchen door. Sarah had not heard her arrival. The young woman stood forlornly stirring the small porridge pot. This was going to be her third breakfast without her brothers beside her. No doubt, there were going to be many more. Millie entered the kitchen and put a hand on the girl's shoulder.

"Care for a bit of company? I could do with a bowl of that porridge."

"That'll be nice, Miss Millie. I'll just put a bit more in the pot. The tea's hot if you'd like a cup?"

"Thanks, dear. You know, they'll be at Maryborough today. I bet the boys are jumping out of their skins with excitement."

Sarah laughed. "You're right, you know. Here I am moping about but they'll have too much else going on to even give me a thought."

Millie sighed. "That's the sea for you, love. It has that effect on strong men." She went to the cupboard and put out two bowls for their oatmeal. "Anyway, we're going to be busy today ourselves. We have three drummers coming in from Sydney and two ladies from Rockhampton. The men will be here for about a week. The ladies plan on being here for ten days, the agent tells me."

SEVEN

THE *NORTHERN ORCHID*

Josh and Gus were once again in charge of the Jacob's-ladder as the Maryborough pilot climbed on board the *Northern Orchid*. The ship danced around her anchor cable as restless as the crew. They had waited and watched while the schooner, *The Blue Bell*, made her way through the bar and out into the open sea. A sigh of relief blew through the crew like a whispering wind when the pilot vessel approached their ship. Waiting too long anchored outside the Wide Bay Bar until they might gain access to the Maryborough port meant an irritable captain.

Josh nudged Gus as they heard Mister Evans greet the new arrival.

"G'day Jack. You still at it, I see."

"Can't keep an old dog down." The pilot laughed. "And what about you, Noel? I thought you must have gone to visit Davey Jones's locker; it's so long since you came by this way."

"We've had a fancy new engine put in. Didn't you see the funnel?" Evans pointed to where a lazy stream of smoke drifted out behind them like a pennant. "Anyway, the captain'll be sure glad to see you. I hope you're going to tell him it's only a three-seas running over the bar and not a four."

"At the moment, it is only a three-seas. The wind will be getting up soon and the tide will change in another couple of hours. The bar will be closed later today. Getting a bit impatient is he then,

Billy Sloan?" The pilot was still laughing as he made his way up to the wheel-house.

Josh looked at his brother. "Do you know what he was talking about?"

Gus shrugged. Once the ladder was rolled and stashed securely, they both went to where Evans was checking the longboat and the jolly-boat stored in the davits above the first-class cabins. He looked up as they called him.

"Mister Evans, what did the pilot mean when he was talking about the three-seas and four-seas?"

Evans scratched his head for a bit before he began to explain that was the way the danger of the bar was measured.

"No one in their right mind crosses the bar if it is running more than three-seas. Four-seas means that the breakers are visible on the bar. It is all influenced by the tides."

When the captain called for them to weigh anchor, excitement throbbed through the men along with the vibrations of the engine below. All hands put their backs into their efforts at the capstan. Josh and Gus were careful they did not end up on the same horizontal bar of the capstan as Sykes. As far as they knew Bony was still down in the engine room shovelling coal for Mister Winston. The welcome rumble of the anchor cable all but drowned out Sykes threats.

"The cap'n's bastards better be careful yer don't end up over the side and into the whirlpool of the bar or we'll never see yers again. It's so easy to topple overboard."

With the anchor on board, most of the crew stood at the rail watching their progress through the bar. The sands and mud driven down through the Sandy Straits on the strong currents had been deposited on a shallow bank that seemed to have blocked the entire entry between the Points. It appeared inevitable that the ship was going to beach on this sandy shoal. At the last minute, the bow curved around into a narrow deep channel which crossed the bar at an angle. When the rough turbulence was left behind and the ship sailed into the calmer waters of the straits, a cheer erupted from the spectators on deck.

"This water, between Great Sandy Island there on our starboard side and the mainland on our port side, is called the Sandy Straits. We're not in the clear yet; not by a long shot. The channels around here are fickler than a gold-digger's heart. Every time we pass through this way, the sandy shoals have shifted." The voice of Mister Evans at their side made the boys jump. "You boys seem a bit jumpy. Is everything okay?"

The boys did not hesitate. "Yes, Sir." They could not meet Noel Evans' eyes. Their gaze shifted towards the mainland which was lined with mangrove trees.

Evans watched the boys as they looked out over the water.

"Hmm; that Sykes has not been giving you a hard time, has he?"

"Nothing we can't handle, Sir," Josh spoke for the two of them. "We have to go do some work." Josh gave his brother a meaningful nod of his head.

They moved into the alley between the chartroom and Mister Winston's cabin and made their way to The Captain's Cupboard.

"What work?" Gus whispered.

"Sleep, brother. I barely shut my eyes after watch this morning before we were dragged out again. You can be sure that when we arrive at the harbour it will be all work. I need to get a bit of shut-eye."

The stack of new sails made comfortable recliners after a little rearranging. Just a few yards away, in the wheel-house, Captain Sloan and the pilot caught up with the latest news of the Maryborough district. Ewan MacGregor had the helm.

"You'll find the dredge working near the north bank as you enter the river-mouth." The pilot offered this piece of information as they approached the entrance to the Mary River. "They started work there after we sent the *Mary Smith* off through the northern channel yesterday afternoon. She'd brought in the first batch of kanakas to this area."

"Have they started the work on the western railway yet?" Mac did not take his eyes from the channel he was following.

"Working on it now. This place here is going ahead in leaps and bounds," the pilot said, as he guided Mac to where he wanted them to anchor the *Northern Orchid.* Mac noticed that the new townsite had indeed developed considerably since their last visit. William Sloan shook the pilot's hand and thanked him. Mac was saying his farewells to the pilot when the captain left the wheel-house to fetch the manifest sheets from his cabin. It was the captain's voice outside their door that brought the boys to wakefulness.

"What business have you in this area, Sykes?" There was only a mumbled reply before the captain spoke again. "Be off with you. I'm sure Mister Evans has something for you to do as we settle at our new mooring."

When the captain opened The Cupboard door, he found the Dougall boys with their noses buried in navigation and seamanship books. He closed the door with its attending scrape on the wooden deck. Josh chuckled softly.

"That door, scraping on the floor like that, is a good warning signal, Gus. Maybe we should not file it back as we'd planned."

"Yeah, I reckon. Come on then, you heard the man, we're ready to drop anchor. Let's see what this town of Maryborough is all about."

Unnoticed; or so they thought, the boys slipped into the group of men about the capstan preparing for the order to drop the anchor. A sibilant whisper in Josh's ear made his blood curdle.

"The cap'n's bastards can't hide behind the cap'n's coat-tails forever. My friend Bony wants the juicy Gus and he'll have him."

Josh barely noticed the mangroves growing thickly on the banks, nor the township that had been fashioned out between tall timber forests. Cattle grazed by the side of dirt tracks on which several drays pulled by draught-horses were making their way to the business area. If he was not so preoccupied, he may have noticed the lack of high ground in the district. As the *Northern Orchid* secured her anchorage, two barges from upstream came into view carrying wool bales and sugar cane. Another barge towed floating timber. Engrossed in his thoughts as he was Josh did not see the pilot's boat collect its principle passenger as the sun dipped behind the village.

"The captain wants to see you Dougall boys." Bosun Evans caught the boys just as they were heading to the galley for a feed.

They about-faced and headed to the wheel-house.

"You wanted to see us, Cap'n?"

"Er, yes. After breakfast tomorrow, I want you pair to row me to the shore in the jolly-boat. I will need your promise first. Can I trust you not to get sucked into one of the opium dens or one of the many public houses or brothels in this area?"

"Yes, Cap'n" Their eyes shone as bright as the smiles on their faces.

"Well, off you go then. Be ready at first light."

"Yes, Cap'n." Their feet thudded down the companion-way and into the galley.

"You looking to wash the dishes, are you? Don't come here like a pair of wild horses. You kill my dumplings."

"Yeah, China, we'll wash the dishes for you. What's happened to Bellyache Basil, I thought he was on galley duty today?"

"Humph." was China's only reply besides the face that could sink a ship with one glance.

On Thursday morning, a dismal sun barely penetrated the crew's quarters. Lying in his hammock at the end of the row, Josh snored peacefully. It was Gus shaking his arm that caught his attention.

"Come on, Josh. What's the matter with you? The captain wants us to row him to the shore in the jolly-boat."

The boys raced down the deck to where several of the crew were waiting to lower the boat over the side. Sykes stepped up.

"'Urry up then, lads; don't want to keep the cap'n waiting now, do we?" A slimy smirk hung on his face.

Gus scrambled into the boat. Josh was about to do the same when he stopped and dropped back onto the deck. His head swivelled around in all directions.

"Come on, Josh." Gus urged his brother. "What's the matter with you? The captain'll not be happy if this boat isn't in the water waiting for him. What are you looking for?"

At that moment, Josh saw what he was looking for. He ran to where the second oar blade was visible amongst the timber lying along the edge of the bulwark. He pulled it out and tossed it to Gus before throwing himself into the boat, just as it was being lowered over the side.

Josh held the boat steady against the hull of the *Northern Orchid* as the captain climbed down the Jacob's-ladder and settled himself in the seat at the stern. With a little more finesse than on their first outing with the oars, Josh and Gus rowed to the shore. Without so much as bumping into it, they even managed to navigate their way around a ship pulled in at the wharf. They did nudge the wooden ladder leading up to the jetty floor. Captain Sloan jumped out of the jolly-boat and while hanging on to a rung of the ladder he dug into his pocket and dragged out a piece of paper. He reached down and gave it to Josh.

"I want you to find this place and speak to someone called Lee. He is one of China's many relatives. Tell him China wants to buy fresh supplies. I'm off to see the shipping agent. Meet me at the harbourmaster's office when you have finished, and don't take all day."

"Yes, Cap'n." Josh read the note before tucking it deep into his pocket. In the captain's writing was the address *Fresh Vegetables Farm, River Road.* That should not be too difficult to find. Gus and Josh took the boat along the side of the wharf until it came to a stop on the muddy river bank. They jumped out and pulled the boat up above the tide mark before tying it to a mangrove tree.

At the top of the river bank, the boys broke off handfuls of grass and began to scrape the mud from their feet and legs. While doing this they looked about them. Two large warehouses stood out a short distance along the river bank. Several government buildings, with their unmistakable design, were scattered between other simpler wooden structures. Dirt roads dissected the business district. People, horses and drays stirred within the town centre. The boys moved towards the General Store across the road. The unpainted slab-timber walled structure comprised of one long room with a shingle roof. A horse-hitching rail stood at the front of the building. A sign hanging skew-whiff above the door was unreadable.

"Don't you bring that mud in here. I just swept the floor." A female voice berated them before they got as far as the door.

The boys came to a full stop allowing only their heads to move past the hessian-bagging doormat. They peered through the opening but they could not see who had been speaking.

"What do you want?" A grey-haired woman unwound herself from behind the long counter at the back of the room. The material of her long black dress covered a stout body. The gullies and ridges of her forehead said that her frown was most likely permanent.

Gus nudged his brother. Josh swallowed twice.

"We're looking for a place called Fresh Vegetables Farm, River Road, Missus."

"Oh, the Chinese gardeners. Just follow this road upriver a tad." She waved her hand vaguely to the outside. "You can't miss it."

Together the boys offered their thanks before retreating. They set out along a narrow track following the river upstream. Clustered together near the river's edge were several ramshackle huts made of corrugated iron.

"What's that smell?" Gus lifted his nose up into the air.

Josh answered smugly. "Opium, brother."

Mumbling voices came from within one of the buildings. Skin hung loosely over the gaunt frame of an unwashed man wearing threadbare trousers who stepped outside. The man faced the shrubs and proceeded to relieve himself. A fish-wife voice shrieked from the furthest dwelling along. A short sharp slap silenced the sound. The boys put their heads down and moved along at a quick pace.

After a short distance, a long-roofed shelter could be seen through the trees. The sound of loud voices and the screech of saw blades being pulled back and forth through timber logs came to them before they noticed the saw pits. The morning clouds had passed to be replaced by a vindictive sun. Dust rose up about their feet. The further they travelled the thicker the forest and the shadier their path.

A quietness had fallen between the boys for some time when suddenly Gus burst out laughing.

"Is that your belly rumbling or is that a croc in the mangroves?" Gus swung a leafy branch in front of his face. Flies lifted then settled as soon as the branch was still.

"I'm starving and perishing with thirst. Why didn't you wake me for breakfast?" Josh grumbled.

"I did try, but you wouldn't budge."

"How much further is a 'tad up the road' do you think?" He sniffed the air. "Is that a boiling-down plant that I smell?"

Gus sniffed several times. "It sure smells like they've been rendering sheep. If we follow our noses, we can find the place and you can get a drink, there."

"Next farm we come to; I'm going in to get a drink." Josh spun about seeking to get a look through the trees. "Gus, have you noticed. We've changed direction. This river has almost turned right back on itself."

As they rounded the next corner, both boys stopped in surprise.

"What's that?" Gus whispered.

Coming towards them was a small man, or was it a big boy? The face was almost completely covered with a coolie's hat. Baggy shirt and pants flapped in the breeze made by his movements. Walking beside him was a white goat harnessed to a small cart loaded with plants and vegetables. A long stick in the small man's hand guided the goat when it showed any sign of losing concentration.

"This fellow has got to be from the Fresh Vegetables Farm, surely." Gus nudged his brother.

"Do you think he can speak English?" Josh looked askance in return.

Gus stepped forward to stand in front of the man and his goat. The animal did not look like stopping. It went to walk around the intrusion. A grunt from the guide and the goat came to a standstill.

"I speak perfect English, yes?"

Gus and Josh stood with their mouth's wide open. It was Gus who collected his wits first and asked their question.

"Do you know a place called Fresh Vegetables Farm?"

"Who wants to know?"

"Our cook, China, on the ship the *Northern Orchid*, he wants to see Lee from the Fresh Vegetables Farm."

"Uncle China, he is here; in Maryborough? On his ship?"

Josh smiled at the man's enthusiasm. "Yes, he wants to buy supplies from a man called Lee."

"That's me. I'm China's nephew, Lee. You will take me to his ship right now, yes?"

Josh noticed the canvas water bag hanging on the side of the cart. His eyes spoke of his desperate thirst.

"You want a drink, yes?"

Josh was barely able to interrupt his drinking to offer his thanks. It was some moments before he became aware of the goat chewing on his shirt tails. Neither Gus nor Lee had noticed as they chattered away while examining the produce. Josh finished drinking and turned.

"Oih!" He complained as he retrieved his shirt which was now slimy with the goat's saliva. Gus laughed heartily while Lee offered profuse apologies. Josh shrugged his shoulders as he returned the bag to its hook. Once again, the dust rose as the procession began the walk back to the town.

Without any explanation, the man began to lead his goat off into the grass at the side of the track. Josh opened his mouth to ask why Lee did this, but then he noticed a grey horse and dray approaching. On the seat of the dray, a whiskered man appeared to be nodding off to sleep. A felt hat wet with sweat was pulled down tight on his head. Rough tanned hands held the reins in slack fingers. With a start, he sat up straight. Piercing eyes glared at the group with the goat. The whiskered man spat out over the side of his dray sending a thick stream of phlegm onto the ground near Gus's feet.

"Bloody Chinese. They can all go back to where they come from and you along with 'em."

Josh and Gus were embarrassed for their new friend. It was their turn to offer Lee profuse apologies.

"Please, it is not your fault. Not everyone is like that; only the few."

When they reached the outskirts of town, a further example of this unpleasantness emerged. Three young lads, no more than eight-year-old, came running out of the trees and began to throw stones at the Chinese man and his goat. The goat threw up its head and bleated when one of the rocks hit the target. Josh and Gus took off after the boys.

"Get back here you young scrags. I'll give you throw stones." But the lads had disappeared into the scrubby bush.

"Sorry, Lee. They've disappeared; like little rodents."

"Please don't worry on my account."

As they neared the spot where the jolly-boat was moored, Josh told Gus to wait with Lee.

"I'll go and see if I can find the captain at the harbourmaster's office." Josh had not gone three steps when the captain came striding down the street.

"You two took long enough. Any longer and they'd start calling me a landlubber. Who's this you have here?"

"I'm Lee, from Fresh Vegetables Farm. If you take me over to China's ship, I'll trade him some fresh vegetables." The man pointed to his goat and loaded cart. "See I have much with me here."

The captain's eyebrows rose. "China's ship now, is it? What does that make me, do you think?"

The boys grinned. William Sloan tapped them both lightly on the back of the heads.

"Keep those stupid grins up and I'll box your ears. Well, come on then what are you all waiting for. Load up." He turned to Lee. "How much do I owe you for this lot?"

While the bartering continued Gus and Josh emptied the cart, placing the produce in the bow of the boat.

THE MARINER'S REST

"Sarah, have you seen Miss Millie?" Jacko rushed into the dining room where Sarah was clearing away the dishes. The midday heat had produced sweat stains around the underarms and down the middle of the back of his shirt. "I've looked in her office and I've knocked on the door of her rooms."

"If you take that pile of plates into the kitchen, while I take this tray of cups, I'll tell all that I know."

The plates landed with a thud on the kitchen table. Jacko stood back hopping from one foot to the other while Sarah began filling the sink with water and soap suds.

"Well, Sarah?"

"Well what, Jacko?" Sarah turned back to the sink.

"Miss Millie; you said you'd tell me where she is."

"Actually, Jacko, I said I'd tell you all that I know. I don't know where Miss Millie went to. Sorry, Jacko, I just wanted a hand with the dishes."

The back door crashed against the wall as Jacko stormed out mumbling long and loud. Sarah ran to the doorway and called to him as he disappeared around the corner of the stables.

"Jacko, Ned brought her a message about midmorning. Miss Millie was dressed and left within minutes. Ned took her off in the sulky, but I don't know where they were going."

The afternoon sun lay low in the sky as Sarah and Blossom folded the last sheet of the day. Sarah heard the crunch of the sulky wheels on the gravel outside. She went out to see if Miss Millie needed assistance with any shopping.

"Sarah, find Jacko, then I want the three of us to meet in my rooms. Be a dear and bring up a tray with tea and biscuits when you come."

Sarah held the door open as Jacko squeezed the tray in sideways. Millie shut the door behind them and pointed to the table and chairs. Jacko lay the heavy tray down and Sarah poured the tea.

"You're flushed, what is going on, Miss Millie?" Jacko asked as he pulled in the chair to sit.

Sarah drank thirstily. She waved at the front of her mouth when the tea burnt going down.

"Miss Millie is everything alright?"

"Yes, dear, well it will be, I guess." Millie drank her first cup of the beverage without taking a breath. She reached over and poured another from which she took two sips before continuing. "Now, what was I saying? Oh, yes, I had a message from my friend, the Police Magistrate. He invited me to his office. An invitation I couldn't refuse." Millie stopped speaking and sipped again at her cup.

"Well, what did he want?" Jacko encouraged her.

"In two weeks, Brisbane is going to be overrun with dignitaries of all shapes and sizes; including two toffee-noses from London. They are inspecting all the towns that are on the itinerary of H.R.H the Duke of Edinburgh's Australian visit next year. The Magistrate wants to ensure that all prostitution has been cleared from the area before this inspection. Our ladies-of-the-night are to be moved on until these inspectors and their ship taking them back to Sydney return down the Brisbane River. He also made it clear that during the Duke's visit next year we remove all evidence of the ladies' presence once again."

"Hypocrite." Jacko would have said more but Millie interrupted.

"Hush, Jacko. There's no point getting upset about things that we can't change. Hypocrisy has been around for just as long as the professional ladies. One must learn to bend with the wind, like the willow; not snap in two like the oak tree."

Sarah stood up and refreshed the teacups. "Miss Millie, what will you do with our top-floor ladies?"

"I will suggest they take a short holiday either out west to Warwick or Toowoomba on the Cobb and Co or to Sydney on the *Diamantina* which leaves at the end of this week." Millie reached over and took another biscuit from the tray. She dipped it briefly in her tea before popping it into her mouth. After a few moments, she looked up at her two visitors and smiled. "I saw Doctor George Goldfinch today. He has accepted my invitation to dinner here after their morning church service this Sunday."

THE *NORTHERN ORCHID*

The *Northern Orchid* spent Friday at the Maryborough wharf where they took on board timber for transport to Rockhampton. Mister Evans had the Dougall boys, with Adams and Andrews, screwing large cleats in rows at the edge of both sides of the top deck. Cables were attached to secure this cargo. In return, supplies for the Maryborough hospital, the new school and the customs house were unloaded onto a dray pulled by a grey horse driven by the unpleasant man Josh and Gus had encountered the day before.

"Make sure China stays out of sight. We don't want a barney starting here. I can't see China remaining as patient as young Lee," Gus said with a wry grin.

Another dray load of general freight was unloaded and sent to J.E. Brown Warehouse in Richmond Street.

When the coal-lighter delivered several bags of coal on Saturday, The *Northern Orchid* was again anchored out in the river. The pulleys squealed, the ropes strained and coal dust drifted in the light breeze as the bags were lifted, one at a time, from the barge before being lowered into the hold. It was late in the afternoon of that day, when the two first-class passengers made their way on board the ship, in preparation for departure on the morning tide. Gus was down in the engine room working with Mister Winston servicing the engine and restocking the coal bins. Josh swung in the bosun's chair hanging outside the vessel scrubbing the grime from the kitchen portholes to the water level.

Out of the corner of his eyes, he watched as the ship's mate, accompanied by Bandy and Rollins as oarsmen, escorted the two gentlemen in the jolly-boat from the jetty. Both the passengers wore dark suits with stiff white collars. Their faces were flushed. One of the strangers kept running his fat finger around the inside of his collar. It was such a hot day that Josh, in his loose trousers, did not envy them one little bit. The taller of the two men had a face that looked as if his mouth was full of sour lemons. Josh heard him chunter away to himself as he climbed the unstable Jacob's-ladder. The short fat man struggled to lift his feet from one rung of the ladder to the next. Josh nearly fell out of his bosun's seat when Evans roared out over the side just above where he was working.

"Are you gawking or working out there, Dougall? The captain wants to see you when you've finished."

Later, in the galley, as Josh and Gus ate their meal, Josh told Gus of his new job, as steward to the first-class passengers.

"Miss Millie and Sarah will be pleased. You'll get to wear the new clothes they insisted we bring with us. What are the passengers like?"

"I'm not too sure yet. I've only met them the once; when I took in their meals. The tall one seems to be forever grumbling but the fat man seems cheery enough."

Josh shoved a lump of coarse bread and syrup into his mouth and stood.

"I'd better go and collect their meal trays. I'll see you later."

At last the passengers were settled for the night. Josh rubbed his heels as he removed his new canvas shoes. The moonlight fell on his face when he threw his head back and savoured the fresh breeze coming in off the river. He wondered if all ship's passengers might be so time-consuming. He hoped they wouldn't all be such a misery as Mister Renshaw.

Josh was just about to step over the coaming at the companion-way on his way down to the crew's quarters when the voice of Captain Sloan halted his steps.

"So, how's our Mister Renshaw and Mister Applethorpe; settled in then, Dougall?"

"They are just retiring now, Cap'n."

"What a shame, it will be too late for me to meet them; maybe tomorrow." The gleam of mischief in the captain's eyes was impossible to see in the moonlight. "Goodnight, lad."

"Goodnight, Cap'n." But Captain Sloan was well on his way back to his cabin and did not hear.

Morning fog reduced visibility to less than a mile. The pilot stood at the wheel-house window watching the river closely. Tension hung in the air like the sound of a doomsday bell. William Sloan's hand eased the wheel to port while below his feet the engine rumbled reassuringly. The ship idled down the Mary River until they came in sight of the twin lighthouses recently built at Woody Island to mark the channel entrance into the river. As the bay opened out before them, the south-east sea breezes dissipated the fog and tempted William Sloan to open his sails; but he resisted. Let Guthrie give his engine a bit of a workout, he decided, at least until the crew has eaten and Evans comes on deck at eight bells.

The smell of cooked toast and strong tea heralded the arrival of his bosun who entered through the port-side doorway of the wheel-house.

"Thought you'd be looking for this by now, Captain."

William Sloan's eyes lit up. "Thanks, Noel. Here, do you want to take the helm for a moment while I do it justice?" He stepped back and drank thirstily from the pannikin before taking a large bite of the thick toast and lard.

The bosun jumped forward catching the helm just as it was beginning to wobble.

"We have a perfect day to be sailing past the Breaksea Spit. The sandy shoals there shouldn't give us any problems. When you're ready we'll give the sails an airing."

With the helm back under his hands, Sloan gave Evans the thumbs up. The bosun's voice roared above the rattle of the rigging and the creaking of timbers. The crew jumped into action. Adams and Andrews slithered up to release the sails while the crew below manned the halyards ready to release the spars. William spoke into the voice tube leading to the engine room.

"Guthrie, you can cease the engines. We shouldn't need the pressure in the boiler until late today when we reach the Burnett River. It's a flawless sky up here."

As the wind caught the sails, the *Northern Orchid* jumped forward like the thoroughbred she was. The captain felt it in the helm and through his whole body. His face lit up in a smile. The sun had not reached its zenith before that smile disappeared like salt poured into a cup of water.

EIGHT

THE MARINER'S REST

Meg Hamilton looked up from the scrubbing board to where her mother was adding firewood to the stove on which the flat irons were heating.

"Why isn't Blossom here doing the wash today, Ma?"

Mrs. Hamilton picked up one of the hot irons, licked her finger and flicked the tip onto its base. Not happy with the result of the heat test she placed it back on the stove.

"Blossom and her tribe have gone walkabout. She'll not be back for several weeks, according to Billy Toe-bite."

"Well, I do hope Miss Millie gets someone to do her work. My hands are red and swollen and I think the skin is going soggy around my fingernails."

"Toughen you up a bit, girl. When you've finished what you're doing, you'd best go inside and give Peggy and Lizzie a hand with the linen change upstairs."

Meg could not get out of the wash-house quick enough. It was a beautiful day. She turned her face up to the sun. A soft voice calling from the stable doorway drew her attention.

"Hey, Miss." Billy Toe-bite was holding out a small hessian bag which wriggled and twisted as it dangled from his hand.

"What on earth have you got there, Billy?"

"Miss, you tell Mister Boris I got his eels. You cook 'em up for him. He likes his eels."

Meg's top lip was curled up in disgust as she held out her hands to take the proffered bag. The jiggling bag was held well away from her body as she entered the hotel via the back door. With a thud and a wiggle, the bag landed in the kitchen sink. Meg wiped her hands vigorously on her skirt.

"How am I supposed to cook these?" She mumbled, slipping out through the dining room and down the hallway to knock on Mister Boris's door.

"Enter!"

Meg partially opened the door. She always found this man and his room of books that covered every wall to every ceiling quite daunting.

"Yes, what do you want?"

"Billy Toe-bite just left the eels here for you. How shall I cook them?"

Mister Boris rubbed his hands together. A grin revealed his crooked nicotine-stained teeth.

"Good, good; that is good. Just put them in water and boil them maybe ten or fifteen minutes."

A shiver ran down her spine as she raced back to the kitchen. The pots on the shelf near the stove clanged as she shuffled among them to select a large pot to place on the stove top. She filled the boiler pot with water. Using only her fingertips, she undid the string at the neck of the bag and upended the slithering slimy eels into the boiler. Water spat as the overflow hit the hot stove top. Meg wasted no time sitting the lid lightly in place. She ran upstairs to collect the bed-change linen. After wrapping the sheets and towels into one big pile tied up in one of the sheets, she struggled down the stairs on her way to deliver it to her mother in the wash-house. By this time, she had forgotten all about the heating boiler on the stove.

Sarah came into the kitchen to prepare a drink. She and Miss Millie had been working in the office all morning. She opened the crockery dresser against the back wall and took down two china cups with matching saucers and one small plate. She paused in what she was doing. With her head cocked, she stood trying to place the sound of an unfamiliar noise. Never before had she seen eels placed into cold water and then brought to the boil. Therefore, she had never witnessed the contortions they get up to as the water begins to heat. Not being able to place the sound, she continued to collect two spoons from the dresser drawer. At the very moment, when she turned to lay the items on the table, the uncomfortable eels forced the lid off the pot and exploded over the edge. Scorching eels landed firstly onto the stove-top before bouncing off across the kitchen floor. One lone, muddled eel landed on the table beside her hand that was still holding the cup.

Her scream filled the air. The cup hit the ceiling. She screamed again and stepped back to the door that led into the bar room just as Jacko came tearing in through that doorway. He gathered her up in his arms to prevent running clean over the top of her.

"Sarah, what's wrong? What's the matter?" He did not release his grip.

The dining room doors slammed open and Millie appeared.

"Whatever's the matter?" She looked at the dark wiggling eels scattered across the table and floor. "What's happened here?"

Mrs. Hamilton and Meg burst through the back doorway. Meg wailed.

"I forgot; I'm sorry, I forgot all about them. They're Mister Boris' eels. I was cooking them for him."

Millie's frown quickly lifted. The situation tickled her sense of humour.

"Clean up the mess, Meg. Then have another go and wait until the water is boiling before you put the eels into the pot."

As Meg tentatively tried to catch the slippery eels, Millie's focus turned to Jacko and Sarah. Millie raised her eyebrows when she noticed Jacko's arms still wrapped about Sarah's waist. Sarah's face reddened. Her hands grabbed at his thick arms in an attempt to unravel herself from his grasp.

"Oh, I was just getting to enjoy that too."

Sarah frantically slapped at his arm. "Jacko, let me go."

The moonlight found Millie peering through her front windows as she was wont to do each evening before retiring. Having little history with a church of any denomination, she still felt no guilt praying for the safety of the *Northern Orchid* and all who sailed in her. Usually, it was the tall captain who captured her thoughts but tonight her mind was full of the scene she had witnessed earlier in the day. Jacko looked so happy with his arms wrapped around Sarah. She would not like to see him end up with a broken heart though. Sarah had a great sense of humour but her reaction today could mean that her experiences with that opportunist, Mister Dingle were not forgotten. Hopefully, time would soften her poor impression of men.

THE *NORTHERN ORCHID*

"What are you saying, Mac?" Captain Sloan swung his head around to stare at the ship's mate.

Mac ran hardened fingers through his hair revealing the fine hairline scar. His frown dragged his eyebrows down to where they sat over his eyes, like a pair of red unripe mulberries.

"I dropped by to check the passengers on my way here. The thin man, Mister Renshaw, says young Josh has stolen his wallet."

Sloan looked up, startled. A frown fell across his face shutting his mouth with a snap.

"What! Josh Dougall, I find that hard to swallow. What are your thoughts?"

"Renshaw says that the wallet was in his coat hanging over the chair before his breakfast. It was not in his pocket later. After breakfast, he did go for a walk around the deck." Ewan MacGregor rested his butt on the chart bench. "I've only known the boys this past week or so but a thief is not how I would have described either of them."

The captain took a moment to ease the helm to port while he gathered his thoughts.

"Like you, I have only been in contact with them recently but I put full faith in several people who have known them for a long time. They come with excellent references. Jimmy was always saying how his missus was bringing the kids up well. I met Mrs. Dougall, the once. I found her to be a very proud and honest woman; of that I am sure."

Sloan's mind drifted to a red-haired beauty with soft lips and fiery eyes who would make his life a misery if he were to accuse either of the Dougall boys of stealing. He did have total faith in her assessment of a person's character. A smile teased his lips. He stood tall.

"Well, we must get to the bottom of this. Have you spoken to the other passenger, Applethorpe?"

"Yes, I spoke to Applethorpe after Renshaw made his accusation. He, Applethorpe, said the man had his wallet out in the lounge last night but he did not see it at all this morning."

"It seems odd to me that if you were going to steal the man's wallet you would do so in the bright light of morning and not in the dark of night."

Mac scratched his arms where the salt had dried the skin.

"You know, William, there is the possibility that someone may be trying to cause Josh trouble. We must consider that."

"You're meaning Sykes or Bony, I take it. Those two have been hounding the boys since they arrived on board. I don't want to interfere. The boys have to work out their own problems. I don't think they'd thank me if I did step in. Sykes has the brains to stir something like this but I'm not sure Bony would instigate such an action."

"No, Bony does whatever Sykes tells him."

Sloan kicked the base of the helm stand.

"Blasted passengers, now I know why I hate having them on board. They are just trouble, with a capital T. You had best send Josh up to me and I'll talk to him. Meanwhile, you and Evans are to question the remainder of the crew, separately, and find out who was where at the time the wallet is supposed to have disappeared. Once you have done that, I want the pair of you to search this ship from top to bottom. The remainder of the crew are to be kept out of their quarters while this is all going on. Mister Winston should be able to guard that area, it being just next to his engine room. Geez, I thought our only problem today was to ensure we did not end up on the shoals near Sandy Cape."

Josh tapped at the wheel-house door. "You wanted to see me, Cap'n."

"Yes, Dougall, come on in." Captain Sloan watched the lad closely as he moved inside and stood respectfully in the corner. He found it impossible to believe that this boy was responsible for theft; but how to prove it. On the other hand, he did not think that rogue, Sykes, would thieve on board this ship either. But then again, he might go to any length to get Josh into strife. For some reason, he really had it in for the Dougall boys. William did not know why. Neither Sykes nor Bony had been with the *Northern Orchid* in the era of the boy's father, Jimmy Dougall. It seemed unlikely there'd be some long-term grudge going on there.

Concern filled Josh's face as Sloan's mind wandered.

"You alright, sir? You wanted to see me?"

Captain Sloan could not help but notice the growing protuberance at the boy's throat and the dark fluff on his top lip. What a tragedy if this incident ruined the future for this promising boy/man. Daffy Harris had such high hopes for him. Sloan dragged his focus back to the issue.

"Oh, yes. How are you getting on with the passengers?"

Josh shrugged. "They're no trouble, Sir. Mister Applethorpe is very polite. The other man, Mister Renshaw, must have a lot of worries, I think. He never smiles or says thanks."

"Josh tell me everything that happened when you served them this morning; every step."

Josh's eyes opened wide. "This morning? Nothing much. I took them breakfast at six bells of the morning watch like they asked."

"Where did you serve them?"

"They were both waiting in the lounge room. I went immediately in there with the tray."

"Were they both sitting at the table at the time?"

"Yes, Cap'n. Mister Applethorpe said he was ravenous. He hardly waited for me to place the plates around. He spilt some milk on his coat but I wiped that off with a damp cloth."

"What about Mister Renshaw, did he have his coat on as he ate breakfast?"

Lines furrowed the boy's forehead as Josh thought.

"Come to think of it, no, Cap'n he didn't. I think it was hanging over the back of his chair."

"So, what happened then, lad?"

"Well, I asked them if they wanted me to make their beds or would they prefer to do that themselves; like you said yesterday. They both chose to make their own. I went down to breakfast myself. After that, I went and collected their tray and tidied the lounge. We were just about at the river-mouth at the time."

"Were both men still in the lounge when you did that?"

"Yes, Mister Applethorpe was reading a book. Mister Renshaw was putting on his coat. Oh, he thought he'd lost his pipe. He patted his pockets and then realized it was on the window ledge. He said he'd go for a walk on the deck and have a smoke."

"He never said anything about losing anything else at that time?"

"No, sir, only his pipe. What's going on, sir?"

"The gentleman has lost his wallet. He is saying that you took it when he was having breakfast."

Josh threw his head up. “I’ve never stolen anything in me life and I sure didn’t steal his miserable wallet. I didn’t even go into his cabin this morning and he was in the cabin with me last night giving orders when I was there turning his bed down.”

“Don’t get all a fluster. I believe you, lad, but we have to find out what is going on. Now, I want you to make yourself scarce; in The Cupboard. I want you to write down every single thing that has happened with the passengers and yourself since their arrival; word for word. And I want you to stay there until I have solved this riddle.” William Sloan did not speak out loud, his curses upon all passengers, that filled his head.

“Yes, Sir.” With his fallen face and head hanging, Josh made his way down to The Cupboard.

Captain Sloan readjusted the ship’s heading two points east. The sound of pounding feet on the walkway announced the arrival of Gus to the wheel-house. He skated to a full stop. His chest expanded as he took a steadying breath. The tap on the doorway was firm.

“Permission to speak, Cap’n, Sir.”

The captain turned to face his next visitor. “Yes, Dougall.”

“It’s about my brother, Sir.”

“Now, why am I not surprised. Go on lad.”

“I just heard they’re accusing him of pinching the fellow’s wallet. Sir, my brother never stole nothing in his life, Sir. Our dad would have scalped us alive if either of us ever did. Whatever they’re saying, it’s a lie.”

“Your father always said you boys were honest and good kids. Jimmy Dougall never told me a lie in all the time I knew him. I don’t think he has been wrong in that belief. We just have to work out what has happened to the man’s blasted wallet. Go join your brother in The Cupboard. Can I take it that you were with Mister Winston all morning?”

"Yes, Sir. Oh no, Sir, I went to the galley early, to get something to eat for Mister Winston. I was only gone for a few minutes and I didn't go up onto the top deck."

Gus turned to retreat and almost bumped into the ship's mate as he entered the wheel-house.

"Sorry, Sir."

Sloan's voice called his friend inside.

"So, Mac, what have you got for us; good news I hope." He spun the helm one degree west.

"We finished talking to the crew; all except Rollins that is. He's been up in the crow's nest all morning. He should be in the clear. I'll see him when he comes down shortly. Bandy is going up to relieve him after he's finished eating. Sykes and Bony were in the aft area this morning early. They were splicing that anchor cable that frayed when we left Brisbane. It's unlikely that either of them could have taken the wallet as Bandy was working with them most of the time. Adams, Andrews, Bellyache Basil and China all saw Renshaw for brief periods at different times when they passed the stacked timber where he sat smoking his pipe. None of them saw the man's wallet. Evans has begun the search. I'll go down and join him now. How did you go with young Josh?"

"Sounds innocent to me. I don't think he's trying to pull the wool over my eyes. Keep at it, Mac. There has to be a logical explanation. Take Renshaw with you and search his room also."

Mac left the wheel-house, his face was grim. When, about an hour later, he was searching Renshaw's room while the man ranted, raved and threatened all types of legal action, he was seriously thinking that Billy Sloan may have been right all along. Who needs passengers? Lucky for Renshaw that the wallet was not in the cabin or he would have been tempted to ram it down his scrawny whinging throat like a shot down the barrel of a cannon.

It was mid-afternoon when Mac dragged his feet into the wheel-house from the port side walkway. Evans, with Rollins in tow, and a huge smile across his face, entered from the starboard doorway.

"I'll take the smiling face first. Mac, you look like you're full of bad news. Evans, what have you got for us?" William Sloan rubbed his reddened eyes. Mac shrugged and raised his hands; palms up.

Evans grabbed Rollins by the shoulders pulling him through the wheel-house doorway. The man only reached Evans' chin but the tubby body was almost as wide. Rollins pale eyes looked down at the deck.

"Come on, man. Tell them what you told me." Evans urged the man but he could not wait for the shy man to speak.

"From the crow's nest, Rollins saw Renshaw when he went for his walk this morning. He saw him stop for a pipe at the timber stacks. Renshaw had his wallet out. He was taking what looked like bits of paper out and then putting them back in again. Rollins was not looking when the man got up to move on."

Fearing a reprimand for watching the ship instead of the horizon the man spoke up.

"I wasn't watching him all the time you know. I was watching the sea too."

Captain Sloan was more interested in the ship, at that moment, rather than the sea upon which she sailed.

"That's alright, man. Was there anything else you saw?"

"No, Cap'n. I told Mister Evans. I went with Mister Evans and showed him exactly where the man sat."

Not to have the climax of his story stolen from right under his nose, Noel Evans took up the tale.

"We searched amongst the timber in that area and guess what we found?" He held a tattered brown wallet aloft like a flag above a face hidden by a very wide smile.

All in the wheel-house began laughing and slapping each other on the back. Even Rollins spoke up, albeit very quietly.

"I knew that boy didn't steal the thing. He's just not the type."

Sloan heard the man. He slapped him on the back and said, "Amen to that."

THE MARINER'S REST

Mrs. Hamilton rolled her eyes as Millie fluttered about redoing everything that she had already done; three times over. This was the first time she could recall Millie inviting friends as guests for a Sunday lunch since old Mister Carson had passed on. The woman was going to make herself ill with worry.

"I'm sorry, Mrs. Hamilton. I know you're doing a magnificent job here in the kitchen but I really want things to go smoothly." Millie stood at the kitchen-dining room doorway with her index finger across her lips. "Should I sit Eve, Jane and Thomas at the same table as the doctor and Miss Abigail. They are staff after all. That would never happen in old England I shouldn't imagine. When she was here yesterday, Abigail did say they usually eat together."

"I'm sure one big table is what they will enjoy most."

Sarah glanced up from where she was giving the glasses one last polish. "You did say you wanted Jacko and me to join you at the table, Miss Millie. We are staff. It might be rude not to have Eve, Jane and Thomas included too, don't you think?"

"Rubbish, you're my family. Now, can we join four of these tables into one big table." Millie once more had Jacko and Sarah rearranging the tables of the private dining room.

Jacko's whisper had Sarah stifling a giggle. "If Miss Millie has us moving these tables one more time, I'm going to put them on wheels."

"I heard that Jacko, my boyo. Do you want to be polishing the silver this week? Now let's have the table cloths out, Sarah."

The pink and red flowers that Millie placed in small vases along the length of the now, one long table contrasted attractively with the white linen cloth and her best silver cutlery. With her polish rag, she inspected each item of silver. A frown marred her forehead as she picked up a soup spoon. She rubbed it until it squeaked.

"Mister Carson gave me this silver when we wed."

Sarah returned to the kitchen, where she placed out the trays for Mister Boris, who wished to eat in his room, and Mrs. Keppel, who planned on eating upstairs. There were to be four hotel guests eating in the other dining room.

As midday approached, Millie began fidgeting. She ran to ensure all the windows were open to catch the little breeze that was drifting up from the river. The aromas from the roast lamb and vegetables tantalized her nostrils. What if the minister drones on for hours and they are late back from church? What if the meal becomes overcooked and dry? Millie's head swung up. She listened intently.

"Is that the sulky I can hear?"

Thomas and Doctor George were at the rear of the sulky untying the perambulator which hung from the back of the vehicle. Millie, Sarah and Jacko rushed out to receive their visitors. Millie held out her arms for baby Henry.

"God, I hope Miss Millie is not getting clucky," Jacko whispered in Sarah's ear.

She replied with a sharp jab in his ribs and smiled at Millie who now rested her face against that of the baby. Jacko helped the ladies to alight.

"I do declare this child has grown since I held him yesterday." Millie smiled as she ran her finger across the soft down on his head. She straightened up and directed everyone with a nod.

"Come, come in all of you. This sun is dreadfully hot for this time of the year. Come in where it is cooler."

It took a few moments for the group to settle around the table. Jacko sat Doctor George at one end with Thomas and himself on either side. Abigail was seated at the other end with Millie and Jane on either side of her. Sarah and Eve sat in the middle section of the table on opposite sides. Baby Henry was ensconced in his pram which Millie pushed gently back and forth while the baby sucked his thumb and watched her in deep concentration.

"Can I get everybody a drink?" Jacko stood to take the orders before disappearing into the private bar. It was here that Sarah had placed a large jug of lemon water to complement the selection of refreshments.

Sarah rose to help him pour the drinks and place the glasses on a tray.

When they returned, Mrs. Hamilton was serving up the dinners.

"Oh, Mrs. Hamilton, that smells absolutely wonderful." George breathed in the aromatic steam rising from the roast lamb with rosemary, roast vegetables and lashings of gravy.

"Miss Abigail, will you say grace for us, please?" Millie asked her guest.

Laughter rang out from the dining room during the meal. Sarah helped Mrs. Hamilton collect the dirty plates and to deliver a large silver tea-pot with matching milk jug and sugar bowls. The very best china cups were lined up for filling.

As Millie sat quietly watching her friends, she smiled contentedly. It had been a very successful day and one which she wanted to have repeated when the time permitted. Her gaze softened as it fell upon Sarah who knelt to fondle baby Henry in his pram. Her thoughts turned to her friend, Lucy. How proud she would have been to see how her daughter had matured.

NINE

THE *NORTHERN ORCHID*

Gus rubbed his bloodshot eyes. The first light of day creeping into the east was a welcome sight. To remain awake in the crow's-nest as it rocked gently back and forth during the middle-watch, while the ship was at anchor, he discovered, took a monumental effort. There was little he could do to stimulate himself but stand up and stretch. He noticed the two men on watch below head down to check the lower decks and the level of the bilge water. A faint glow of a lantern shone out from the men's sleeping quarters. Someone down there was stirring. A piercing whistle vibrated his eardrums.

"You awake up there, Dougall?" Mister Winston's voice floated up from the wheel-house below.

Gus coughed, twice, in an attempt to clear his throat that would have liked to remain at rest.

"Yes, Sir. There are scattered clouds in the east and the sea swell has increased a tad."

"Stay watchful. It may only be morning fog."

"Yes, Sir." All he really wanted to do was curl up and sleep on his sou'wester lying on the floor of the crow's-nest barrel. He stretched his arms above his head and hung out over one side and then the other side of the lookout cage. Only another ten minutes or so until Rollins was due to relieve him. He spun around on one foot then on the other until he began to feel dizzy. His feet danced in the limited confines as he began to shadow box. Sipping from the waterbag only made him want to pee. He had heard the tales of those who had peed out over the deck but he really didn't want his name added to the list. When next he looked towards the east, the glare from the imminent sunrise almost blinded him. He swivelled and peered into the north where they were to travel to Gladstone through the Curtis Channel, later today. From their current position at the mouth of the Burnett River, he could only imagine the Lady Elliott Island off to the north-east. An inspection south of their position assured him that there was no sign of any shipping traffic from that quarter. The channel leading into the river-mouth was easily seen against the paler waters of the shallows. Even though he knew there were timber cutters and a squatter's camp hidden somewhere upriver, it was impossible to see them through the mangroves; even from this height.

The single mast supporting a sulky sail was all that he first noticed of the vessel. A barge, with four oarsmen helping to propel it, gradually appeared through the river mist. The vessel made its way on the ebbing tide out towards the *Northern Orchid.* This must be the boat the captain had been waiting for. It was here to collect a load of dry food and chandlery supplies stashed away in the hold of the *Northern Orchid.*

"Boat ahoy, from the river-mouth," Gus called down to the wheel-house.

It was Captain Sloan's head that peered out of the doorway. He was up on deck early today. His voice drifted up to Gus.

"Where, exactly, am I looking?"

Gus pointed with his arm. Captain Sloan took up his telescope and examined the new arrival.

Gus sat with his head bowed over the bowl of porridge that China had served up to him in the galley. He barely had the energy to lift the spoon to eat. The loud voices and rattle of lines through the pullies on the impromptu crane drifted into the galley from the other side of the ship where they were loading the barge. The noises did not penetrate through his somnolent state. It was not until a heavy hand patted his salt-encrusted hair that he knew Bony was standing at his side. He sucked in a sharp breath and slipped along the wooden form, away from the unwelcome touch. Bony grunted loudly and followed the boy. Gus moved again but came up against the bulkhead. The heavy hand came down upon his head again; just patting; firmly. Gus slithered under the table and out over the second table with its wooden forms down each side. He skipped out the doorway nearly colliding with China as he did so. As Bony attempted to follow the lad, China stood with his feet planted. The small Chinaman crossed his eyes. They looked as welcoming and as cold as black-ice. A long-nailed forefinger was pointed at the burly giant. The big man whimpered and cringed backward hugging the bulkhead until China was able to move past him into the galley.

With the little time China bought him, Gus made himself scarce. He raced up the companion-way and into The Captain's Cupboard. The door scraped and slammed behind him. He stood with his hands on his knees gasping for air until his breathing and heartbeat returned to normal. The bed of sails welcomed his tired body and he slept. Intermittent groans accompanied by the twitching of his limbs interrupted his rest.

Josh gathered the breakfast dishes from the table in the passenger's lounge and packed them onto his tray. Mister Applethorpe settled deep in the lounge chair with his arms resting on his ample stomach.

"Josh, you can send my compliments to the cook; his food is superb."

Mister Renshaw sat up to the table reading an old newspaper that he had found in the drawer of the sideboard against the wall. He sniffed.

"You do know he is only a Chinaman, Applethorpe? Are you saying the Chinese can cook better than our own people?"

"It never hurts to offer a compliment wherever it is earned." Mister Applethorpe shut his eyes to draw a line under the discussion.

Not wanting to become involved in any way, Josh took up his tray and escaped out through the open doorway. After pushing the door shut with his foot, he leant back against the cabin wall savouring the salt air. Noise from the loading of the barge drew him forward. He stood watching the process until China's voice stirred him.

"You plan on standing there with the dishes waiting for rain to come and wash them clean, funny boy?"

The tray nearly came to grief against the bulwark when Josh spun about.

"No, China, sorry. I'm going now."

"And when you're finished, you can clean the hen cages and change the water too. And after that, you will need to change the cat sandbox. Next opportunity I want you to get fresh sand for the cat too; maybe in Gladstone in a couple of days."

"Yes, China, Sir."

China grinned at the 'Sir'. He liked that. A smile hovered at his lips as he paused to watch the action at the barge where Mister Evans and Mister MacGregor supervised the transfer of several large crates. After a few minutes, he continued on his way to the wheel-house. He tapped on the door when he arrived. Inside, Captain Sloan was deep in thought over a chart he had lying out across the front bench.

"Did you have enough to eat, Cap'n?"

Sloan rubbed his face and pushed his hair back off his forehead. The scar stood out white. He smiled at the cook.

"Yes, China, superb as usual. What brings you up here? You're not planning on steering the old girl, are you?"

China giggled. His crooked white teeth flashed.

"No, Cap'n. I just want you to know that Bony man bullying Gus Dougall. He chasing the boy out of the galley this morning. I don't know what he up to. He's not a nice man, that one."

"Well, I cannot argue with that. We have been keeping an eye on him and his mate Sykes. Let me know if you witness anything else. China, don't get caught in the middle of anything. You're not as young as you were once, remember. Besides, I don't want to lose my cook."

"Age and strength are in the mind of the warrior, Captain." China bowed as he made his way out into the sunshine.

When the ship's mate entered the wheel-house a short time later, the captain took him to the starboard side door and pointed to the east.

"What do you make of those clouds? They're building up. Can you feel the extra swell beneath us?"

Mac nodded his head. "During the time it took us to load the barge, the swell became quite noticeable. It made things difficult in the end."

"It will be no fun making our way through the Curtis Channel if we encounter stormy weather later today. I was hoping we'd make anchor off Lady Elliott Island."

"Captain, if the bad weather does hang about, it'll be no fun trying to load those cattle at Gladstone." The ship's mate was talking about a cargo of a stud bull and three cows that were to be collected at the Gladstone harbour and delivered to the Rockhampton port.

"You are a cheery fellow, aren't you, Mac? I just had China up here a minute ago reporting on a bit of a kerfuffle between Gus Dougall and Bony. If you get a minute can you see the kid's alright? Now, are we ready to put some wind into the sails and be on our way."

"Aye, aye, Captain."

Mac's voice rattled around the deck as he issued orders to weigh anchor, prepare to release the sails from their bondage and set the ship on its way.

THE MARINER'S REST

Millie sat at the kitchen table opposite Sarah. The polish-rags squeaked as they rubbed the silverware vigorously.

"I think dinner went off well enough yesterday, don't you, Sarah?"

As she reached over to take another knife to polish, Sarah smiled at her friend. "Miss Millie, it was a wonderful afternoon."

The continual banging of a sheet of iron flapping in the increasing wind irritated Millie. There was a storm brewing, she just knew it. She hated to think of her sailor out in bad weather. Too many ships had been lost on the reefs, while negotiating the narrow inner-channel along the Queensland coast, over the years. Why, in the paper every week there was an announcement of a memorial for some ship or other that had disappeared along that route in bad weather. She could hardly talk to Sarah about it and have the girl worrying for her brothers. She walked to the back door to peer out into the yard. After a minute or so she returned to her polishing but her thoughts were elsewhere. How long will it be before Jacko and Ned return from delivering the four girls to the Cobb and Co station? She wished that she had gone with them to Toowoomba. Having heard so many great reports on the town, she would have liked to visit.

Sarah looked up startled when Millie pushed her chair back and jumped up. "There they are now. I'll get them to fix that damn sheet of iron before this storm hits. They can check everything else is secure while they're at it." She tied a scarf around her head and opened the door before stepping out into the wind.

Whirlpools of dust danced across the back yard. Jacko and Ned were in the process of backing the two very nervous horses into the stable. Millie spat dust from her mouth and brushed at her dress. After talking to Jacko, she put her head down and ran to the wash-house. Mrs. Hamilton was instructing young Maureen Ryan on how to fold the towels and pillowcases.

"Mrs. Hamilton, I think you may call an end to the laundering today. It looks like we are in for a nasty storm." She turned to the young girl. "Maureen, you had best run home before it catches you on the street, lass. If you prefer, you can stay here until it blows over."

"No, thanks, Miss Millie. I must get on 'ome to help Ma with the kids."

"Well, don't dawdle child. Thanks for helping out. Can you come again tomorrow?"

"Yes, Miss Millie."

Millie's smile eased the tension lines on her face. It was a boon having Maureen help in the wash-house. It was a blessing to both her and Maureen that Abigail had recommended the young girl.

While Millie was busy outside, Sarah began an inspection inside the hotel building. She closed all the doors and windows. Wooden shutters were latched. Leaves and twigs swirled across the verandahs. Mister Boris was sound asleep, totally undisturbed by the rising wind.

The bar was empty. She shut all the windows of both dining rooms. Neither of the two gentlemen from the downstairs rooms of the B-wing was in. Sarah found Mrs. Keppel sitting in the corner of the upstairs lounge room knitting. The speedy needles sounded like a drummer on his kettle drum.

"I do hate storms, you know, Miss Sarah. I do hope your brothers, in their ship, miss this bad weather."

"I'm sure they'll be fine, Mrs. Keppel. They are sailing with a good captain."

A shiver ran down her spine as she walked through the working girl's wing which was now empty of tenants. All the doors and windows had been shut and bolted when they left for their enforced holiday a few hours previously. As she ran down the stairs, she could not hear her own footsteps above the sudden clap of thunder which accompanied the drumming of rain on the roof. The skies opened up with a vengeance.

The back door crashed behind Millie as she stumbled inside. She looked up woefully at Sarah who stopped on the bottom step.

"That rain has come out of nowhere. I'm drenched. If you have everything under control here, I am going upstairs to change into some dry clothing."

Sarah grinned. "As my Da would say; 'You look like something the cat dragged in.'"

"Cheeky little Miss"

Sarah called to Millie as she made her way up the stairs.

"Miss Millie don't worry about the *Northern Orchid*. My Da said that Captain Sloan is a top rate sailor. They'll be fine."

Millie retreated down the stairs and dragged Sarah into her arms. Tears stood out in her eyes.

"Oh, Sarah, I should be the one comforting you; not the other way around, but thank you, dear."

Again, the back door slammed; behind Jacko this time. He arrived with water dripping from his hair and clothes.

"Is everything okay, here?" He looked curiously at the two women with their arms wrapped around each other.

"Yes, Jacko, all is well." Millie made her way up the stairs with a slow step.

Sarah turned to Jacko.

"You look like you could do with a dry towel and a hot drink." She jumped back with a squeal as he shook his head like a dog shaking a shaggy coat. Water splattered all over her.

"Jacko!"

Jacko's eyes twinkled as he grinned.

"Thanks, lass, that would be wonderful." He reached over and patted her hand.

At the touch of his fingers, a shiver ran through her body. Sarah felt herself go cold. A vision of a sweating Mister Dingle pounding into her body with that piece of oily hair tapping her cheeks appeared in her mind. She could not breathe; if she could, she might scream. It was her turn to shake her head. With a gasp, she moved quickly into the kitchen where she selected a towel from the drawer. Her hands trembled as she threw it to Jacko. The whirlpool that was her head confused her.

With the towel in his hand, Jacko began to rub his head furiously and to pat down his clothes. He looked askance at Sarah.

Sarah moved the kettle over the heat on the stove. After preparing the trays with soup and sandwiches, she left the kitchen to deliver lunch to Mrs. Keppel and Mister Boris.

Jacko poured his second cup as Sarah returned. He filled her cup also. Sarah nodded gratefully. They both looked up as Millie's footsteps were heard descending the stairs.

"I could sure finish off a bowl of soup, Sarah." Millie pulled out her chair. "I do hope this is only a passing storm. Lucky for us, it did not happen yesterday afternoon and spoil our dinner party. Did you see that baby smile at me, Sarah?"

Jacko laughed. “Heaven preserve us. What about you, Miss Sarah, are you hankering for bawling babies?”

A frown edged over her brow as Sarah sat thoughtfully for some time.

“Maybe one day, but not any time soon, Jacko.”

THE *NORTHERN ORCHID*

Captain Sloan was at the helm for most of the day as the sea swell deepened and the wind strengthened. Mister Winston poked his head in through the doorway just before noon.

"Do you want me to start a fire under the boiler and build up the pressure just in case we need the engine before the day is out?"

The captain scratched his head and thought for a few moments.

"It certainly looks suspicious out there to the east. I think we might be glad to add the engine to our sails before the day is done. Take Josh Dougall with you to help shovel the coal. You'll find him in The Cupboard, working."

Both Mister Winston and Josh took a drenching as a rogue wave sent an avalanche of sea water rolling over the starboard bulwark. They disappeared down the companion-way pulling the hatch down tight over the opening after themselves. Both men braced their legs and feet against the roll of the *Northern Orchid* in the building sea. Mister Winston started the fire while Josh added the coal as necessary.

Rubbing his eyes, Gus wandered out onto the deck where he found China struggling to drape the covers over the hen cages. He took hold of one side of the canvas while China held the other. The wind ballooned it up and then, as the wind shifted, it settled down into place. With nimble fingers, China and Gus secured the ties before the next wind gust struck.

"You're awake then, are you, Dougall? Good, you can slip up the mainmast with Rollins and Bandy. We'll take three hitches in the mainsail." Evans shouted to Gus from where he was hauling in the rigging alongside Sykes and Bony. Several sails were being hauled in while others were being reduced. Seamen lined the yardarms, their legs held loosely to accommodate the tug and flow of the footropes. Others pulled on the web of rigging lines on the deck.

Water rumbled down the scuppers as it rushed in over the dipping bow. The ship's hull twisted and tossed like an unbroken horse. A cloudburst of rain hit the men stinging their faces and saturating them. Like the drumming of the feet of stampeding cattle, the rain thundered over the timber deck. Up on the yardarm, it made the task of hanging on and securing sails at the same time, quite precarious.

Captain Sloan glanced sideways when Mac walked into the wheel-house rubbing water from his eyes. He nodded a greeting and commented.

"This is going to be a miserable day, I'd say."

Mac smiled. "I'll go along with that; it will be slow going. Can I get you a hot drink in the meantime?"

"I won't say no to that. Did you want to kip out, Mac? This does not look like it's going to develop into anything too much. You've got the first night-watch later."

"Thanks for reminding me."

TEN

THE *NORTHERN ORCHID*

The ocean rolled over the bow flooding the decks before tumbling down through the scuppers. Seamen responded to Evans' shouted instructions to reef more sail. From his perch on the yardarm, Gus watched the crew scrambling about the deck hauling on the halyards. He shivered as the rainwater ran into the neck of his sou'wester. His hands were chilled to the bone. He did envy Josh who was down in the engine room loading coal onto a warm fire. He clenched the spar as the wind gusted over the starboard beam. His toes curled around the footrope. The ship heeled over. Captain Sloan's voice was heard calling further instructions to the bosun. A scream rose up from the deck. Andrews lost his footing. His arms flailed the air as he was being whisked away toward the stern of the ship on the avalanche of sea water. Evans threw out his arm and caught the sorry lad by the scruff of his coat pulling him to his knees and then to his feet.

"Easy on, boyo; don't go wandering off. There's still more work to be done up here."

At that point, the vibrations of the awoken engine shuddered through the decks. It was a comforting sound. Even in his high tower, Gus felt its reassuring flutter.

In the wheel-house, Captain Sloan looked up as Mac blew in with the wind through the doorway.

"So, how can a man sleep with all this going on?" Mac laughed as he handed his captain a pannikin of tea. "Sorry, I think it may be part sea water and part rainwater by now."

The captain took the proffered cup. "Thanks, Mac. This squall has almost blown itself out. If you look out to the east there, you can just see a lightening of the sky. It will all be over before dark, I'm thinking."

"I heard the engine start. Will you keep it going until we're ready to anchor up for the night?"

With a shrug, the captain answered. "May as well make up some of the lost time. We can get ourselves back on course easier too, once we get a positional reading; if the sun comes out. There'll be little moon up there to help us for a few nights yet."

"If the weather does clear, we should get past Lady Elliot Island tomorrow. All going well we'll be into the Curtis Channel proper when we anchor up tomorrow night. From there it will be a quick run into the anchorage near Facing Island at Gladstone."

Captain Sloan grinned. "You are forever the optimist. One day, you'll tempt fate once too often."

"What, you want me to run around with the long face of a pessimist?"

"Saints preserve us."

That night was spent anchored up south-west of Lady Elliott Island. The journey the following day was uneventful. As Mac had predicted they anchored north-west off Lady Elliott Island at dark with the distant glow of the Bustard Head lighthouse reflected in the light cloud cover. After a wet anchorage, the men were busy in the early hours adjusting cargo in the hold. The ship made a late start on the last leg of their journey to Gladstone. Josh took celestial readings late in the day, with Mac standing at his shoulder. The *Northern*

Orchid, with Captain Sloan at the helm, managed to limp into this refuge towards nine o'clock with engine power and the main and mizzen sails and by the light of a quartering moon. Adams and Tanner were out with the weighted line checking the depth of water beneath their hull as they rounded the southern tip of Facing Island. William Sloan did not want to be another sailor to take his ship onto the shoals just waiting to catch unwary travellers.

A watery sunrise found the *Northern Orchid* secure in the lea of Facing Island. Most of the crew were in the galley early, having their breakfast before the bosun called them to action. Today they were to prepare temporary cattle enclosures on the fore' deck for the stock expected to be loaded in Gladstone. Depending on the state of the wind today, the remainder of the seamen were under instruction to hang the sails for drying in the sun. Sykes stood behind Gus for a few moments before leaning in close to his ear.

"Yer be nice to Bony, boy." Sykes pinned Gus's left hand to the tabletop with the prongs of his fork. The man's eyes narrowed. A grimace accompanied his words. "Yer ever seen what 'appens when a kid falls into the bullpen?"

"Piss off, scum," Josh shoved Sykes aside as he climbed in beside his brother. Sykes stumbled away.

"Yer'll pay for that, shit'ead. Don't think the Cap'n can be watching out for you every hour of the day."

Josh and Gus were in the small dinghy boat that usually lay upside down in the bow of the ship. They were on their way over to a sandy bay on Facing Island. Three large sacks lay in the bottom of the boat along with two shovels.

"Run away to sea to shovel sand for a cat to shit in? We must be mad." Josh laughed.

Gus gave one last hard pull on the oars as they skimmed into the shallows.

"Oh, I don't know. It's nice to get off the ship and away from everyone for a bit; especially that creep Sykes and his companion, Bony. How are your two passengers doing? Has that Mister Renshaw been accusing you of anything else lately?"

"Nah; I don't know what the captain said to him but he hardly ever complains to me now. Mister Applethorpe's a great fellow."

"I guess that makes up for the other one, then."

They pulled the boat above the tide mark, took up the shovels and sacks and began to fill the bags with dry sand.

"Have you read that note the Captain left on the desk in The Cupboard this morning?" Josh stopped to pull off his cap and wipe the sweat from his forehead.

Gus grunted in the negative.

"We're to sketch, in detail, the fore topmast and the topsail yard as it is on the *Northern Orchid.* We are to identify all the parts, attachments and the rigging."

Gus looked up from his shovelling. "We did one like that for Captain Harris last year; that was the mainmast. We had to copy one out of his books. Do you remember how fiddly that was?"

"I'm not likely to forget. It took us days." Josh held one of the bags open. Gus emptied his shovel full of sand into it.

With the three full sacks of sand, there was little room for the two boys in the boat. Gus sat in the bow on one of the sandbags. It was Josh's turn to row.

Due to factors beyond their control, the boys were not able to begin their assignment until late in the day. On their return from shovelling sand, they were allocated the joyous tasks of cleaning the deck beneath the hen cages and washing the windows of the wheel-house and the cabins. When Evans saw their faces fall, he grinned.

"Just be grateful you're not cleaning the decks after the cattle are loaded. No doubt you'll get your turn at that too."

With haste, the boys gathered up the buckets on their lanyards and the scrub brushes.

Josh began laughing until water poured from his eyes.

"First shovelling sand for a cat's shit and now sweeping up chook shit; the adventurous life of a sailor."

They both laughed out loud.

"Good to hear the crew happy in their work."

"Damn." Gus bumped his head on the bottom of the cage when he heard his captain's voice. He rubbed the spot vigorously.

With fresh water and wash rags, they applied themselves to the not-so-easy task of removing all the salt, clouding the windows. One washed and the other attempted to remove all smudges with the dry cloth.

As they worked their way towards the bow, the crew building the cattle enclosures came into their view. Rollins and Bony were manhandling timber railings while Sykes and Bandy were bolting them onto corner posts secured to the decking. Three small enclosures began to develop. Mister Evans' voice was heard explaining the structural plans to Mister Winston, who had wandered up to watch the activity. One for the bull, one for the cow and calf and one for the single cow. There was very little room between the milled timber cargo already stored on the deck and the rails of the cattle pens. That timber was due to be unloaded before the cattle were loaded.

Overhead, Adams, Tanner and Andrews were manhandling the sails to hasten the drying process before the sea breezes lifted and made the task impossible. Mister Evans' attention was drawn back to the window cleaners.

"When you have stopped gaping about, you fellows can finish up there and go help haul on the halyards and get them sails shipshape."

Captain Sloan stood on one leg with his other foot up on a rail. His elbows rested on his knee. He peered into the waters off the stern of the *Northern Orchid*. This was a night that made up for all the hardships and privations of sailing. Moonlight danced on the surface of the calm sea. The calls of the gulls on Facing Island floated across to him on a light sea breeze. His thoughts were on his sweet Millie when a voice nearby had him swallow his displeasure at the disturbance.

"Captain Sloan; I hope you don't mind my interrupting your thoughts?"

"No, Mister Applethorpe, not at all. It's a lovely night out. Better than being closed up in your cabin, I should think."

"I just wanted to tell you that I've had a wonderful journey on the *Northern Orchid;* short though it may have been. I also wanted to say that I found that young lad, Josh, an excellent steward. It would be a shame if Mister Renshaw's false accusations affected his career in any way."

"Thank you, Mister Applethorpe. I'm glad that we were able to be of service." Captain Sloan stood straight. "What brings you to the Gladstone area?"

Mister Applethorpe rested his body against the bulwark.

"Investment really. The pastoralists and agriculturalists have made a lot of progress up through the interior here. Mind you, at the moment, they're struggling with this infernal drought and the financial crisis that's affecting the whole country. Good times will return and they'll be wanting services for supply and distribution of products. I'm looking for opportunities."

At that moment, China shuffled past. He was on his way to check his fishing lines that were set out over the stern. Mister Applethorpe continued his conversation.

"You know, Captain, I also dabble in the restaurant business in Brisbane. If ever that cook of yours wants a job in the city, send him my way. His cuisine is memorable; in a good way."

Captain Sloan laughed. "China is one of the best but like most of us on the ship, he is damned with his love for the sea. This is my good fortune. Numerable ships' captains and others have tried to steal him away but for some reason, China is held to the *Northern Orchid* by invisible bonds. I am not planning on cutting those any time soon."

"I can understand why the *Northern Orchid* is the envy of the other crews."

The moon bathed Josh and Gus as they climbed out onto the deck after a tea of damper and syrup. They stood for some moments admiring a sea that had long forgotten its anger of seventy-two hours previously.

Josh sighed. "You don't see nights like this in the town."

Gus offered his brother another of the biscuits that he held in his hand. China had slipped the boys a few of the biscuits destined for the captain's table. His reward for their having collected the sand for his cat and cleaning under the hen cages. The boys breathed in the briny breeze as they nibbled on these treats.

"Well, come on Gus, this isn't getting the job done." Josh led off to The Captain's Cupboard where they settled down to search through all the books and papers that they could find on the shelves behind the door. In the flickering lamplight, they sought sketches that might help them make a start on their project. Tomorrow they planned on climbing the rigging to confirm everything that they discovered tonight.

Startled, they both looked up at the screech of the door on the timber floor. They watched frozen as the heavy door opened slowly. Both breathed easily again when the ship's mate, Mister Macgregor, entered.

"How's it going, lads? That door could do with the attention of a file; or do you like to be warned of visitors?"

Both boys looked up guiltily.

"Er, yes," Josh mumbled.

The mate did not push the issue further. Instead, he took a look at what Josh and Gus were working on.

"Whew, what are you up to? I never realized we had so many books on board. Is there anything here you haven't opened?"

Josh handed over the note that the captain had left earlier in the day.

Mac rubbed his forehead. He sighed. "Ah, yes, I remember doing this half a dozen times in one month when I was a midshipman. No doubt, Captain Sloan has done the same in his career a few times too. Do you want a hand?"

"Sir, thanks, but we really have to learn this stuff so we'd best do it ourselves."

"That's probably a good attitude. Remember though, sometimes you must take a break to clear your head. Come with me to the galley. We'll get a cup of cocoa then go out onto the deck. I'll point out some of the areas that you may find have modifications here on the *Northern Orchid*. You should be able to see well enough in the moonlight tonight."

Gus stoked the boiler before the sun presented itself above the horizon. Overhead he heard feet pounding on the deck as the crew prepared the ship to weigh anchor. The creaking of the cable and the capstan resonated through to the lower deck as the anchor rattled its way on board.

A piercing whistle issued from the speaking tube. Mister Winston received the instruction from Captain Sloan for slow-ahead. The engine pulse deepened and a shudder ran through the ship as the gear was engaged. It was difficult to feel the movement of the ship from deep in the bowels of the vessel. Only when Gus had the chance to peer through the porthole near Mister Evans' cubbyhole, was he entirely sure that they were moving. An innocent sea presented itself to the world.

When next he had an opportunity to glance outside, Gus noticed that they were within the confines of a river. The mangroves were thick on the bank. Once again, the whistle preceded the orders via the speaking tube. At dead-slow, the engine propelled the ship forward for a few moments. The whistle sounded again and the engine, with a loud clunk, swung into reverse. The last whistle preceded the call for neutral. A bump bounced Gus into the edge of the coal bin. The bosun's voice reverberated through the timbers followed immediately by the crew's running feet. The order was issued for lines to be secured to the bollards on the Auckland Creek wharf.

"You can dampen down the boilers, Gus. We'll be here at Henry Friend's wharf until tomorrow. They're going to off-load the timber here later this afternoon. Apparently, the bullock wagon is nearby and will collect it for transportation to the hinterland. Tomorrow we move up to the cattle wharf where we are to load the stud bull and his harem."

The two passengers, ready to disembark, shook the captain's hand and then the hand of the ship's mate.

"Thank you both for a safe passage." Mister Applethorpe's eyes glinted as he smiled.

Mister Renshaw nodded his head and mumbled a few indecipherable words as he gave a perfunctory handshake to the two seamen before moving out across the gangplank with his suitcase in his hand. Mister Applethorpe followed in a more sedate manner.

Mac leant towards William Sloan's ear. "I guess you'll be glad to see the end of at least one of those chaps."

"Shame that Renshaw doesn't fall into the drink. Preserve me from passengers for a bit." Captain Sloan and the ship's mate turned at the sound of a voice behind them.

"Cap'n, Sir." China stood politely with his coolie hat held by his side.

Captain Sloan sighed. "Ah, China; don't tell me. You have good relatives here who have fresh vegetable for you, yes?"

"Yes, Cap'n. Can Mister Josh and Mister Gus take me to the farm?"

Sloan rolled his eyes. He looked askance at Ewan MacGregor.

"Did you have work for those pair today, Mac?"

"Not really; there's only the stock feed and bedding hay to be loaded later and Evans has plans to teach Adams and Tanner how to cooper more water barrels together this morning. He needs them for the extra water for the stock. The lads are up to their eyeballs in books working on that project you gave them to do. Takes one back to the old days when you and I had to do that sort of stuff."

Captain Sloan hid a smile and turned to the cook. "China, you can have them until mid-afternoon and then they have to be back here to help unload the timber; and I don't want you leading them astray."

China giggled as he donned his hat and almost disappeared in the process.

"How can I? You don't pay me enough money." He retreated to the galley laughing aloud leaving the captain scratching his head and Mac slapping his thigh and hooting with laughter.

"We'll have our breakfast in the chartroom thanks, China." Captain Sloan's voice followed the Chinaman down the companion-way.

THE MARINER'S REST

Jacko stood in the shadows at the stable door. He watched Sarah as she stretched up and down hanging the sheets out onto the wire clothes-line strung between the corner posts of the stable and the wash-house. In the middle section of the line, that was not too far from the ground, young Maureen Ryan was hanging some of the smaller items for drying. He sighed at the sight of Sarah's fine young body and pondered at her odd behaviour on the two occasions when he had come into the briefest of physical contact with her recently. He still recalled his surprise at her sudden change of temperament. Had he repulsed her? Was it the age difference? He was only thirty years old; well, okay, almost thirty-one. Sarah must be going on seventeen soon. That was only about fourteen year's difference. What's so wrong with that? Look at Miss Millie and Mister Christopher. They had nearly thirty years difference between them and that was a very successful relationship. He was hardly what one could call a womanizer but the few women he had known never complained. He'd never led them on; not like that darn Arthur Rankine. Now there was a chap who showed little respect for a woman or for her feelings. There was something very special about Sarah. She was not like any other woman he had known. At that point in Jacko's meandering thoughts, Sarah took up the strong pole that was hooked onto the middle of the clothesline. The tight bodice of her dress rippled in tune with the muscles of her back and shoulders when she lifted the line and its wet washing into the air. He felt the heat expanding in his loins.

Jacko sighed. “A fine piece of womanhood, that girl.”

From the top floor of the back verandah, a pair of hazel eyes watched the watcher. Even though he stood in the shadows, Jacko’s stance revealed to Millie most of what was churning in his head. She could see where his gaze was directed. A clasped hand covered the pain in her heart. Sarah was like a daughter to her. It was not difficult for her to understand what was bothering the girl. Of course, Jacko must be confused. It was doubtful if Sarah had ever come to terms with her encounters with Mister Dingle the previous year. Millie knew also that Sarah had never accepted her young sister’s rape by that deviate, Mister Bland. Sarah blamed herself. Millie fervently hoped that time might heal Sarah but, in her experience, many girls, in similar situations, were never the same again.

Jacko was the son whom she never had. She wanted a happy and contented life for him, with a woman of his choice. One who could look after his needs and produce his children. Was Sarah the woman to do this? Could Jacko help Sarah to heal? Would she allow him to do so? She twirled a stray tendril of hair.

THE *NORTHERN ORCHID*

Gus held up the small cup in his hand and grinned at his brother as they sat on their haunches around the low table beside China and his four cousins. Giggles drifted in from the room next door from where several women and small children peeped through the bamboo curtains at their Uncle China and the visitors. Gus smiled. This stuff they called green tea was rather good. Maybe the captain should get some on board the *Northern Orchid.*

China's family spoke in a language that sounded not unlike the crickets in the trees outside Millie's hotel in Brisbane. Gus watched fascinated as they each used their little sticks to pick up the food from the bowls on the table and deliver it to their open mouths without breaking into their conversation. He bit off a laugh when Josh lost every morsel from his chopsticks after laboriously loading them. Lucky the ship provided spoons in the galley or the crew might starve to death.

"Excuse me, Mister China. Should we be getting ready to leave? Don't forget that Josh and I have to be back at the *Northern Orchid* early to help unload the timber?"

China sighed. "Always busy, busy. Come on then; we will go."

After having said that, it was still quite some time before a donkey was harnessed to a cart and the cart laden with China's purchases of fresh vegetables. Farewells were a drawn-out process also. Gus and Josh threw worried glances at each other and set off at a sharp pace when eventually China and his cousin Chang were ready to move.

At the wharf, all was hustle and bustle. Standing on an angle, the spare yardarm was already secured with a strong cable part-way up the mainmast. Ropes had already been threaded through the pulleys. On the wharf, a teamster, accompanied by loud grunts and a few curses, worked at harnessing two strong bullocks. They were to provide the bulk of the muscle required to raise the bundles of milled timber from their storage on the deck, up into the air, over the bulwark and onto the wagon standing on the wharf ready to receive its load.

"What, the cap'n's bastards doin' the woman's work, are yer boys?" Sykes passed a spiteful comment, that went unheeded, as Josh and Gus, with loaded baskets on their shoulders, ran up the gangplank and down to the galley. China followed closely to ensure not one leaf was lost from his precious purchases. The boys returned to the top deck without delay where they found Mister Evans shouting orders to the crew. Without a pause to catch their breath, they were assigned to the tail ends of two lines and instructed to put a bit of heart into it. Out on the wharf, the teamster flicked his whip lightly over the bullocks' backs in encouragement as they took the weight. One by one, ten bundles of timber were removed from the starboard deck. The crew was then sent scurrying up the yards to reorganize the pulley system to enable the unloading of that timber stored on the port side of the ship.

With all the timber unloaded, Josh and Gus stood watching the teamster working on the wharf. He slotted the two bullocks, that had been used to unload the ship, into the team amidst bellows and grumbles from the other beasts. He then harnessed the lot up to the wagon of timber. Standing at the rear of the wagon he sent off a loud crack of the whip that tickled the ears of the leaders. This was received with a twitch of the muscled shoulders and a bellow. The bovines leant into the traces causing them to creak and groan. At first, it looked like the wagon was not going to shift, then inch by inch the wheels began to rotate.

"I could do with that whip in my hand right now to get a couple of boyos up and doing. We've got to move this ship to the cattle wharf before dark so your presence would be greatly appreciated lads, thank you; MOVE IT."

Josh and Gus scrambled out to release the lines from the bollards of the wharf. They only then noticed the sound of the engine whoosh whooshing below decks.

After an early breakfast, the crew manned the yards seeking the most advantageous viewing point from which to see the arrival of the next cargo. Josh, Gus and Andrews were leaning against the engineer's cabin when Sykes sidled past.

"Yer boys ever seen a man trampled by a bull? You be careful young Gus. You wouldn't be a pretty boy then."

"Maybe you should fall into the pen with the bull, it might improve your ugly mug," Josh retorted in return.

First to be loaded were the two cows and the calf. One cattleman with an armful of green grass led the group while the other man ushered the animals from behind. They made their way down the fenced jetty lane, across the specially designed fenced gangplank provided for the purpose and onto the top deck. Extra water barrels required for the stock were now lined up forming a lane leading to the new enclosures at the bow of the ship. The calf stopped and started as its curiosity overwhelmed it while its mother fussed and bothered over her offspring. The other cow was happy to chew on the tasty morsel of green grass the man was dealing out in dribs and drabs. Without any trouble, the animals were soon ensconced in the two pens allocated.

Next to be loaded was the bull. A huge muscled beast that ambled along with its stiff rear-legged gait and a waddle like a duck. A large ring was embedded through its nose to which a lead rope was attached. The cattleman talked softly to the animal and intermittently scratched his shoulder with the whip handle.

The bull stopped as his feet hit the deck. He raised his wide nose and sniffed the strange odours. The scrape of his front hoof on the timber as he dragged his foot back in an act of defiance sent a shiver down the spines of the observers. A drawn-out bellow ending in a seesawing of noisy inhalations and exhalations filled the air. He swung his head left and right. The cattleman gave a small tug at the lead accompanied by a reassuring scratch with the whip handle. The animal roared. He swung his head again knocking aside one of the water barrels behind which Andrews had been hiding. Andrews scrambled to a new cover. The barrel rolled over and rumbled off down the deck scaring the bull further. He swung his rump around pulling the cattleman off his feet. Another barrel went sailing across the deck. This one split asunder. Water gushed across the beast's front feet. The animal dropped his head and sniffed at this unexpected flood. He slurped until the water had disappeared; some into his belly and the remainder across the deck. The animal again sniffed the air and bellowed. A return lowing from the cows up front had the bull about-face. Once again on his feet, the cattleman tugged at the lead and without further complaint, the bull followed obediently into the pen. He began inspecting the railings while the cattleman slipped behind him and secured the wooden gate.

"Geez, did you see his eyes? I swear he looked right at me." Josh ran his hands through his hair.

"Poor Andrews; I bet he shit his pants. Imagine a herd of them rushing down on you." Gus laughed; a nervous laugh.

The boys jumped when their captain spoke beside them.

"Those railings look so fragile beside that beast. One wonders if they can really hold such an animal but the farmer assures me that they will be secure enough."

"Will that fellow be travelling with us to Rockhampton, Cap'n?" Josh pointed to the cowhand.

Captain Sloan gave a short laugh.

"What, are you volunteering to look after that bull, Dougall?"

"Gosh no, Sir. I would not know where to start." Josh was aghast.

"Yes; the pair of station hands that brought them on board will be travelling with us. That bull and his harem are worth more than the *Northern Orchid* and the rest of the cargo put together. I certainly don't want to be responsible for their comfort. Those two blokes are going to camp with their charges."

It was the crack of stockwhips and the whistles of the stockmen to their dogs that turned everyone's attention to the shore. Dust rose like a cloud around a large herd of cattle coming through the township towards the cattle yards near the jetty.

"Looks like we got our cargo loaded just in time before this lot upset the works."

It was Evans' voice echoing across the waterfront and bouncing off the walls of the several buildings along the riverbank that stirred the crew.

"What yer all standing around there like dummies for? The show's over. Let's have a bit of action. Secure these barrels. Prepare the ship. We'd like to leave this wharf before that new herd wants passage with us too."

Gus turned and raced down to the engine room. Mister Winston's voice greeted him as he stepped over the coaming at the doorway.

"I thought you'd given up on your engines and decided to become a stockman."

"No, Sir; never. I'd rather face this big brute here when it's contrary than that bull out there when it's having a bad day."

"Well, come on, we've got enough steam pressure to sneak us out into the middle of the river. Captain Sloan says we are to anchor up there and await the coal barge and another load of hay. We should get away on the tide tomorrow morning."

ELEVEN

THE MARINER'S REST

Sarah peered through the slats in the wall of the hotel wash-house. Slowly her arms propelled the smooth whitened stick around and around in the boiling water of the copper. The latest batch of sheets gradually sank below the sudsy surface. She barely glanced at what she was doing. Her gaze was on Jacko and Ned who were on their knees repairing the hen-house fence where a dog had forced its way in last night. Already Ned had plucked the two dead hens that had been left behind. He delivered them to Mrs. Hamilton in the kitchen for cleaning and cooking. They were still six fowl short in their numbers. The raider did not access the remainder of the hens that had been perched high in the branches of the mulberry tree. Neither had it been able to break into the duck or chicken enclosure. As she watched his agile hands at work, she mused on how Jacko was quite competent at every job he put his mind to. She smiled at the sound of laughter between the two men as they shared some amusing tale. From where she stood, she could see the flash of the younger man's white teeth. In her mind, she conjured up the laughter wrinkles at the corners of his eyes, which she knew to be there. He was a good-looking man with his thick curly hair and the dignified moustache and trimmed beard with its sprinkling of grey.

Just at that moment, the relieving cleaner, Mrs. Waterman, came strutting across the yard. A frown touched Sarah's face as she watched the woman's hips swing from side to side. If the *Northern Orchid* were to rock like that her brothers might have trouble with mal de mer. Miss Millie had called the woman a bit of a doxy but did concede Mrs. Waterman worked well. Their usual cleaner, Mrs. Lawson, was off for three weeks. Mrs. Randall, the other regular cleaner, said that Mister Lawson had been busy with his fists again.

Mrs. Waterman held a large bundle of washing in her arms but instead of walking towards the wash-house she headed to where Jacko and Ned worked. The woman walked straight up to Jacko and ruffled his hair with her hands. Hidden within the wash-house, Sarah drew a sudden deep breath. Jacko looked up at Mrs. Waterman and grinned. He said something. Mrs. Waterman said something in return and they both laughed out loud. The relief cleaner then swung on her heel and moved towards the wash-house.

Behind Sarah, Maureen Ryan was busy sorting the next load of washing to be attended. She looked up and gasped, then she squealed.

"Miss! Miss! Miss Sarah. Your dress is on fire."

Smoke was rising from the hem of Sarah's skirt and petticoat which were hanging too close to the wood fire under the copper.

"Ooh." Sarah gathered up the lower skirt and petticoat and dunked them into the rinsing tub on the bench near where she stood. Steam rose up across the water. "Now young Maureen, let that be a lesson to you. Be careful around open flames. Don't let yourself be distracted."

Feet stamped at the doorway. Mrs. Waterman's gaze drifted around the room. It fell upon Sarah who was retrieving her skirt ends from the water.

"Good morning, you must be Sarah." Mrs. Waterman unloaded her bundle onto the central table. "Are you all right there? Don't tell me. You've burnt your dress on the copper fire. That's so easy to do. I've lost two good dresses that way, over the years." Her wide dark eyes turned towards Maureen. "And who is this little helper?"

Maureen kept her eyes lowered and spoke quietly. "Maureen, Missus."

"Well, I'll leave you two ladies to your labours then and get back to my own work. I see Jacko is still working here at The Rest. How he has not been snatched up by a woman before now, is really a mystery. That is one very good-looking man going to waste. I wonder who he is saving himself for?" She went off laughing.

Sarah swirled the clothes vigorously in the rinsing tubs before squeezing them out.

"Maureen, can you push these sheets through the mangle while I turn the handle?"

It was nearly tea time when a dray pulled up in the yard with the rattle of wheels and flurry of dust. Sarah and Maureen had just folded the last of the day's washing into the baskets. Ned, Miss Millie and Jacko came out of the back door of the kitchen to see what was happening.

"These five ladies belong to you, Miss Millie, I believe." The driver of the dray jumped down from the seat and began to unload boxes, bags and other paraphernalia.

"You're all back; at last. It has been so quiet without you." Millie greeted her working ladies. There were lots of smiles and laughter.

Maggie with the black glossy hair and pinkened lips moaned.

"Miss Millie, I really must find a rich man to keep me. Holidays quite suit me. I could do it all the time without any trouble at all; except it costs money."

"So, you enjoyed Toowoomba, then?" Millie asked.

"It had its moments. A very respectable country town but we discovered they did have some surprising entertainment; we'd tell you all about it but you're too young to hear it all."

Everyone present burst into squeals of laughter. Millie flicked her fingers at Maggie.

"Cheeky, Madam." More merriment erupted.

"We are starving. I do hope we are not too late for tea." Cissy the blond gathered her small case and made her way inside.

THE *NORTHERN ORCHID*

An occasional cloud rolled across the almost full moon. Josh and Rollins were on the last round of their watch. Rollins had gone below to check that area for any disturbances, signs of smoke or rising water in the bilges. Josh patrolled the top deck. As he passed the cattle pens, he stood with his head through the rails of the bullpen. The big animal was fast asleep on the thick mat of hay laid down by the stockmen earlier. Josh smiled when he heard the snores coming from under the canvas awning set up outside the pen. The two stockmen were curled up on the store of hay.

Like a shadow, a man crept up behind Josh. The first Josh knew of his presence was the flash of pain through a body being crushed up against the pen. Head, shoulders and arms were secured between two rails. One foot kicked backward in an attempt to reach the attacker while he strived to maintain his balance with the other. Josh was not kept in the dark about his attacker's identity for too long. Sykes foul breath overwhelmed the odour of the cattle as his voice hissed in Josh's ears.

"I told yer yer'd pay for touching me in the galley the other day. Now, let's see what this bull makes of you." Another rough shove caught Josh's kidneys. Both feet flailed the air uselessly.

On the opposite side of the pen, the bull lifted its head. It snorted its anger at the disturbance. Josh twisted to his limits but there was no escape. The bull rose awkwardly from its straw bedding. He stood with a baleful glare aimed towards the tossing head at the far rail. The animal snorted again. The bull took several steps in the direction of the captive boy.

"Easy, Samson." A soft whisper near the beast.

Sykes pushed harder into Josh's back forcing the lad to protrude further through the rails squirming as he did so. Josh gasped at the pain tearing through his spine. The bull ambled closer. Sykes drew back to kick the lad further when something dropped around his neck. The whip end was drawn tight. Sykes grabbed at the leather strip. He endeavoured to release its hold. Strident breaths escaped his throat as he struggled to draw in some air. Leather tightened on his neck and another whip wrapped around his wrists.

"That'll hold yer for the moment." The harsh whisper of the stockman froze Sykes in his tracks.

Josh cringed at first when he felt hands at him again. It did not take him long to realize these were not the vicious hands of Sykes. He slipped back out of the rails and landed with a thud on the deck.

Sykes' voice was heard demanding. "Release me; yer -- yer -- yer -- dust-eater. This was just a bit of fun. I'd never 'av let the boy be 'urt."

"Well, me old salt-muggins, I reckon it's time Samson had a bit more fun. It's been a few weeks since he's had a chance to rough a man up. I'm for tossing yer in there with him."

The arrogance turned to pleading. "Please mister, don't do that. It was only some 'armless fun." Sykes gasped out as he twisted and turned in an attempt to release the pressure of the ties.

The stockman gave the whips another pull as he turned towards Josh who struggled to regain his feet.

"So, lad, whatcha think? Whatcha want done with him?"

The voice of Captain Sloan drew them all to face mid-ships.

"I rather like the idea of putting him in with the bull but I don't think it fair to make such a majestic animal share accommodation with such a snake of a man. I'll have him put in the brig for a couple of days to help him remember to look after the crew; particularly the new members."

Under Captain Sloan's direction, Josh secured a set of chains on each of Sykes' ankles. The cattleman released the whip securing the prisoner's wrists allowing it to be interchanged for a set of handcuffs.

He looked up at the captain.

"Do yer want me to leave the neck hold on him until you have this creep where you want him, Sir?"

"All these tempting offers of a solution but no; Dougall and I'll manage. Thanks again for your help." The two men shook hands.

Josh reached over and shook the cowman's hand too.

"Thanks, mate."

"Anytime; happy to oblige. Try to keep yer nose out of the bullpen in the future." They both laughed. Captain Sloan managed a grin.

Half the crew was lined up along the footropes of the yards unfurling the sails while the other half was down on the deck hauling on the halyards as they trimmed the sails. The ship's mate called the orders. Of the bosun, there was no sign. The final filaments of smoke from the funnel dissipated into the fresh morning breeze. The *Northern Orchid* glided past the shoals on the southern tip of Facing Island before heading north through the Curtis Channel on the way to her next port of call; Rockhampton. The early morning sun spoke of a hot day to come as the south-south-east breeze billowed the sails.

The hot tea spilt unnoticed over his hand when Gus ducked back in through the galley doorway. It was the voice of Sykes as he descended the companion-way that caused the one hundred and eighty degrees turn around. What was Sykes doing out of the brig? The sound of another in booted feet accompanied the man.

"So, Bosun, 'ow long's the Cap'n gonna keep me in the brig? Yer know I'm the best sailor on board this floating flea-'ouse."

It was the acrid smell of the slops' bucket, in spite of having been rinsed in sea water, that explained Sykes' presence outside the locked door of the brig. He had been out, under guard, on the morning round of emptying the slops' buckets. Having himself experienced the cleaning of these buckets, Gus recognized that undeniable smell.

The bosun's response drifted towards him as the two men made their way past the galley back to the small brig at the stern of the lower deck.

"You'll be there until Captain Sloan thinks to release you. And don't be too sure of yourself being the best sailor on board. You are one of the crew; no more. I don't know why you want to keep pissing the Captain off. What have you got against Jimmy Dougall's boys?"

The clunk of the lock accompanied the man's answer.

"Just a pair of spoilt kids is what they are, those two; bleeding upstarts."

"Just shows you how little you know. Those boys and their sisters were little more than wee bairns when they lost their dad. He died while saving the lives of Captain Sloan and Mister MacGregor. Their father taught me all I know. He was a good teacher; a tough but fair man. This ship is a good ship run by a good man. Not too many would say any different. You may like to remember that boyo. You're doing yourself no favours upsetting our captain."

Gus moved across to the engine room and handed the mug to Mister Winston who sat at the bench writing in his ledger. As Gus handed the hot drink over, Mister Winston looked into the half-empty tin mug.

"Have we run out of water on board lad; or did you think to share with me."

Horror crept across Gus's face as he also peered into the mug.

"No, Sir. Sorry, Sir. I must have spilt some. I didn't look. I'll just go and get you another."

Before Guthrie Winston could say another word, the boy took off to bring a fresh drink.

William Sloan and Ewan MacGregor were both in the wheel-house when Josh and Gus knocked at the door.

"You wanted to see us, Captain?" Josh took the lead.

"Ah, yes, the Dougall boys." Captain Sloan turned towards the ship's mate. "Mister Mate our course through this Curtis Channel is to be plotted by these two young whelps. In fact, I think one of these lads should steer our trusty vessel and the other can plot the course; what do you think?"

Awe and terror chased each other over the boys' features as Mister MacGregor answered.

"I think that a splendid idea. Should we go for a feed in the galley while they get on with it then, Captain?"

"Bbbut … Sir, Captain." Josh started to say then he stood tall and passed a glance at his brother. "Yes, Captain, we'll get right onto that."

Gus rolled his eyes. The Captain grinned at the ship's mate.

"They're a chip off the old block, aren't they; nothing phases them. Mac, if you're brave enough, you go have a feed. I'll get this pair started."

For two hours, Gus's hands remained glued to the helm while Josh ran out on deck to take the sightings before he returned to plot their course on the new maps. Captain Sloan rested back in the seat with his feet up on the front bench. At first, his eye seldom left the compass floating in its binnacle, but after seeing the boy's focus and determination the older man's tension abated.

"Sailor, if you hold that wheel any tighter those spokes will start to snap off and take an eye out; relax."

Gus took a deep breath and eased his grip. Colour returned to the whitened fingers. Mister MacGregor returned at eleven in the morning just as the Captain called for Josh to take the helm. Gus was instructed to check all the readings and confirm his brother's plotted course. When Josh's hands touched the wheel, his fingers stroked the timber and caressed the spokes. Captain Sloan glanced up to see if the ship's mate had noticed a natural helmsman in the making. Their eyes met; they smiled.

Every step was checked by Gus three times before he was confident in his work and in the writings on the map. His heart thundered in his chest when he nodded to the Captain. He intended his career to be within the engine room not up here with this responsibility.

"It's all correct, Captain."

"You're sure we are not going to end up on the reef at Masthead Island then, young Gus?"

"No, Sir. We'll be ready to anchor five nautical miles off the reef." Gus crossed his fingers.

"Well done, the pair of you. You're a credit to Captain Harris's tutoring. I will write and tell him so. Now, when we've finished here, I want you to write a letter to your sister. There's sure to be a ship's captain at the Rockhampton wharves who will deliver it for me. Miss Millie will see Sarah gets it."

With their epistles in their hands, they knocked on the captain's cabin. The man was writing at his desk.

"Ah, you've finished. Good, I'll see these get away. It's nearly time to anchor up. We should not be too far off Masthead Reef. All going well we'll be moored off Rockhampton late tomorrow."

At the sound of the bosun's roar, the boys took off to line up at the capstan ready to drop anchor.

Faint morning light in the east competed with the moon on its way to the western horizon as Josh scrambled up the rigging to the crow's nest. He popped his head over the barrel to find the midnight-to-four-shift standing with his head sagging onto his chest. Soft snuffling breaths spouted puffs of mist into the air.

"Wakey, wakey, Andrews. If the captain finds you asleep on watch, you'll be riding the grey mare; probably for the whole day.

"You won't tell him will ya, Josh? I'd never survive standing on the topsail yard for the rest of the shift, let alone the rest of the day. If I didn't crash down onto the deck, I'd land in the briny and I can't swim."

"It's not my place to say anything but this is the second time I've found you asleep on watch. What would happen if it was one of the officers? Think yourself lucky to get away with it this time; particularly with the bosun on watch."

Andrews shook himself like a dog before dragging his weary body over the side and making his way down the long climb to the deck below. Josh jumped nimbly in the crow's nest. He peered to the horizon and to all quarters of the compass.

Below, Gus and Adams were drawing straws. The one picking the long straw got to make the rounds on the upper deck and the other with the short straw had to patrol the lower deck. Captain Sloan grunted as he passed them. Steam rose from the pannikin in his hand; a drink for his bosun.

Gus punched the air when he came up trumps. It was always more pleasant wandering around the upper deck at night. The sea was an ever-changing canvas and usually, a light breeze delivered fragrant salt air to inhale. This was always preferred to creeping around the dark lower deck with the many ghost stories of the older tars rattling around in one's skull. The burst of foul fumes spewing up into the watchman's face, when the below-hatch was opened to check the bilge waters, did little to make this area the most popular to those on watch.

The faint light of the captain's lamp stretched out onto the foredeck. The aft areas were sharpening into shadows and light as the dawn crept in. The cattle in the bow were stirring. The young calf fed hungrily on its mother's bulging udder. The second cow concentrated on the bundle of hay that the stockman had placed at her front feet.

"G'day mate; great morning."

Gus looked up from where he leant on the rails watching the animals.

"Hello. How's your night?"

"Yeah, they've taken to the life at sea like a crew of old tars. When's grub? I'm starving."

"About five, the galley opens for breakfast. Usually porridge; and that will be stodgy if Bellyache Basil is the morning cook."

"I don't think you blokes have anything to complain about. The meals we had yesterday were one hundred times improvement on what we get from our station cook. Killer, he's called. We recite the last rites, not grace before we eat out there."

"Our head cook is called China; he's a Chinaman. He puts on some good food, not just the tinned or salted meat every meal."

"I sure noticed that. When do you think we'll get into Rockhampton?"

Exuding the demeanour of an old salt, Gus looked up at the skies before peering into the sea.

"Yeah, it should be a good day for sailing. We'll make it there late today, I'd think."

And Gus was right. All day, the *Northern Orchid* skimmed across the waves as she made her way through the Curtis Channel. Most of the crew, when not trimming the sails to please the winds, were huddled in the shade under the awning of the poop deck over the passenger cabins. The mate had Sykes carry up several large sacks of old ropes as his first job on his release from the brig at first light. Accompanied by many mumbled complaints and painful and bloody fingers the men teased the old ropes apart producing what looked like handfuls of dirty, coarse fibrous balls. This was the oakum which was needed to caulk up the timber seams and waterproof the ship. China had reported water running down between the top deck timbers during the last squall. The bosun's plan for occupying the crew at quiet times was to seal the seams of the deck timbers throughout the ship.

The ship's anchor dropped with a rattle at their mooring between Mackenzie Island and the top of Curtis Island. Evening chased the day's heat. A river pilot would guide the ship into the Rockhampton harbour, thirty nautical miles up-river. Despite almost continual dredging, many shoals and mud banks lay across the mouth of this river waiting to lure an unsuspecting ship.

The sun had not broken above the horizon on the following day when the pilot climbed aboard the *Northern Orchid*.

"You're up and about early, Sir." Captain Sloan greeted the man in the wheel-house. "Wet the bed, did you?"

"Didn't get the chance. The fellow, waiting for these cattle you have on board, has been at my boss for two days. He's been fussing around like a hen with chickens. He wants them unloaded and safe and secure in the wharf cattle yards first thing today. I'm to take you straight to the cattle loading ramp."

Anticipating the need for the engine early, Mister Winston had dragged Gus from his slumbers two bells short of the morning watch. After stumbling to the engine room, Gus started the fire under the boiler. The pair sipped at their first tea of the day while waiting for the steam pressure to rise. Once the gauge sat at the green mark, the engineer relayed the information through to the Captain. The bosun's orders bounced across the deck above, as the crew weighed anchor. Captain Sloan had the topsails unfurled to assist the engine as it powered the vessel up the river.

As the ship made a winding course along the Fitzroy River, the rumble of the full water barrels echoed off the river banks. The crew, once more, set up the alleyway of barrels from the cattle pens to where the gangplank would be attached.

TWELVE

THE MARINER'S REST

"Mrs. Hamilton, I was thinking of going for a walk down to the river this morning. Will you be all right on your own? Miss Millie has business in town today." Sarah dropped her breakfast plate in the kitchen sink as she greeted the cook on Monday morning.

Mrs. Hamilton smiled as she hung her jumper on the hook in the wall near the back door.

"Go on, dear. You need a break. It's a lovely morning out there."

Jacko's head was bent to his porridge but his ears did not miss a word. Miss Millie did not like Sarah going down to the river on her own. Not only because the girl tended to spend too much time blaming herself for her sister's suicide but because of the increasing numbers of undesirables to be found there. He gulped his last bit of porridge and followed Sarah out of the back door. She was half-way across the yard.

"Hold on a bit, Sarah."

"What's up Jacko, can I help you?"

"Sarah, do you mind if I tag along? I need to check my crab pots this morning."

Sarah stopped. Her eyes dropped towards the ground. She brushed imaginary crumbs from her long dark skirt. Her hands trembled as she secured the tapes of her bonnet.

Fearing a rebuttal, Jacko continued rapidly. "I promise I won't intrude on your privacy while you pay your respects to your sister. Besides, I'll be too busy gathering up the bounty from my traps. Who knows, I may need an extra pair of hands to carry it all home again."

Sarah's smile was slow coming but developed into a wide grin.

"Fat chance, Jacko. I don't know what you do differently to Billie Toe-bite but he produces lovely fat crabs, shrimps and large fish. I'm still waiting for a feed from your traps."

"That's a bit harsh, Sarah. I usually catch enough for one sandwich; sometimes two." Jacko's spirits lifted at the sound of Sarah's laughter.

"Come on then, Jacko. There have been a few strangers down on the riverbanks lately. It'll be nice to have a big strong man to call on."

The crisp spring air and clear sunny sky encouraged a brisk step from them both. They walked in silence for some distance; contented with their individual thoughts. Jacko was surprised and gratified when Sarah confided in him.

"You know, Jacko, as long as I live, I'll never forget that day when Josh, Gus and I made our way down to the river looking for her. I had the strongest premonition. It made me sick in the stomach. Daisy was always fragile; you know; in the head. That's why, when she knew she was dying, Mum made me promise to take care of her." Sarah's breath caught in her throat. Her hands twined about each other. "Yet, within a few hours, she'd been raped and not long after that committed suicide." Her eyes glistened with unshed tears. "If there is a Heaven, what must my mother be thinking of me as she looks down and sees what a poor job I've done."

"Whoa right there, Sarah. There's only one person responsible for raping young Daisy and that was that mongrel, Bland; not you. And, who of us understands suicide? Who knows what goes through the heads of those tormented people? Daisy was not only fragile; she was just a little girl. Within a few days, she'd been raped and then she lost her mother. Is it any wonder the child did what she did? I'm sure if there is a God and that Heaven you're talking about; Daisy will be up there with her mother right now."

Tears rolled down Sarah's cheeks. She reached out and held Jacko's hand.

"Thank you, Jacko." She gave a watery smile and let go of his hand. "Hadn't you better go recover that monster catch of yours?"

Jacko would have been just as happy to stay right where he was with Sarah holding his hand and damn the crabs but he did not want to frighten her off.

"Yeah; Miss Millie will love a seafood meal when she gets back from town today. You just yell out if you want me back here in a hurry."

Sarah walked over to where a large limb of a paperbark tree stretched out parallel to and only a few feet above the ground. She sat staring out over the waters. When Jacko was out of sight and there was no sign of any other company, Sarah hitched her skirts up, nearly to her knees. She reached down and removed her shoes. Her stockinged feet wiggled back and forth, savouring their freedom.

It was the sound of laughter echoing across the river that drew her out of her reverie later. Jacko, Billy Toe-bite and three young piccaninnies approached her retreat. Mud covered the lower legs of them all. Sarah slid her feet back into her shoes before slipping the hem of her skirts down to her ankles. The children squealed with delight as Jacko pretended to chase them. Jacko held a sizable crab out in front of him. The two huge claws stretched out seeking to grab at whatever they could. Sarah stood up and joined the small group.

"So, Jacko; did you catch that or did Billie?"

Jacko rolled his eyes and looked to Billie for support.

"Mark my words, Billie; the women of today have no faith."

Billie Toe-bite grinned but said nothing.

"Poor Jacko, I take that to mean Billie caught the crab then; do I?" Sarah smiled indulgently before jumping backward as the claw stretched out in her direction. "I hope you've got a good hold on that thing, Jacko."

He pretended to drop the prize. The youngsters squealed in delight.

"Let's get back to The Mariner's Rest and cook that up; before you lose it or lose a finger; will we?"

THE *NORTHERN ORCHID*

The overhanging branches of the mangrove trees lining the riverbanks floated on the waters of the high tide as the *Northern Orchid* eased her way up to the cattle wharf at the Rockhampton harbour. The crew rushed about securing mooring lines and furling sails. Barely had the gap in the ship's bulwark been opened to await the railed gangplank, when a heavily built man in blue shirt, trousers, brown leather shoes and a large dusty hat jumped across the gap between the wharf and the deck with an agility that belied his size. He walked straight towards the cattle pens.

Up in the wheel-house, the pilot grinned at Captain Sloan.

"That's him; that's the fellow who has been on our backs every day this week looking for his cattle."

"A bit short on courtesy, I see, but on the other hand, at the value of that stock, I really don't blame him, I guess."

The two men shook hands as the pilot made his departure. The captain then climbed down to the deck and walked towards the visitor.

"Good morning, I'm Captain Sloan. Good looking cattle you've got there. Is everything to your satisfaction?"

"Yes, yes of course. They are looking well. I thought if they got seasick, they might not travel too good; and of course, there's always the worry of a storm." The man climbed out of the pen and shook the captain's hand. "Simon Halstead, I'm now the owner of these cattle. Pleased to meet you."

The two men leant on the rail of the bullpen admiring the bovine flesh.

"We had an uneventful trip. Hardly a cloud in the sky. My family, in the old country, have cattle. They'd be impressed with this animal as a sire for their herds." The captain pointed to the bull that was chewing his cud as if content with the world.

The cattleman gazed in rapture at the new addition to his herd.

"Hopefully he can deliver on the promise of his breeding. How long until we get him onto solid ground again?"

As if on cue, the bosun's voice was heard issuing instructions to the crew. The special cattle-loading gangplank rattled as it was lifted by the pulley ropes and levers. With the guiding hands of the crew, it then clattered into place bridging the space between the wharf and the deck.

Ramming his hat further onto his greying head, Simon Halstead shook the captain's hand once again.

"I'll go and give my men a hand to lead this lot out, then."

As requested by the stockman who had saved his life at the beginning of this trip, Josh stood by the bullpen ready to undo the rope holding the gate. The sibilant whisper of Sykes sounded in his ear.

"'Ow'd yer like a donger like that up yer arse, boyo? Just reminds me of Bony. That's what yer brother's got coming to 'im, one day soon."

Josh swung around but the voice of the stockman in the pen drew his attention back to the job at hand.

The newly arrived Mister Halstead called to have the gates into the cow-pens opened first.

"If we get those girls moving this fellow'll follow like a lamb."

Josh opened the first gate as instructed and stepped back ready to open the bullpen gate when told. The one stockman, with his arms full of hay, led the cows out as he had done the day they were loaded. When the bull got a whiff of the passing cows, its nose lifted into the air. He sniffed appreciatively. His mouth spread from one ear to the other. The bull liked what he smelt and produced repetitive mewling sounds, not unlike an exaggerated mewling of a cat. Mister Halstead cursed.

"That blasted agent promised me both these cows were in calf. The last thing we need is a cow on heat and a lecherous bull on the rampage."

The cows made their way out of the gate and along the laneway of water barrels. The bull expressed his frustrations with more urgency. The second stockman and Mister Halstead endeavoured to control the animal as it pushed repeatedly at the gate. The crack of the collapsing timbers sent a shiver down everyone's spine. Josh jumped aside. The stockman was having trouble keeping ahead of the beast and holding onto the lead from the bull's nose-ring. The bull twisted his rear end left and right even managing to kick his back legs into the air and sending three water barrels flying. Splintered timber and water sprayed the deck and the onlookers. The boss-cattleman and the first stockman were doing their best to rush the cows and calf along the deck and over the gangplank to the relative safety of the railed wharf. Where the deck met the gangplank, the calf stopped to sniff at the jump-up from the deck to the plank. It baulked. The mother who had already entered the narrow-railed gangplank fussed and mooed. The cow strived to turn around on the narrow passageway in an attempt to attend her offspring. The plank rattled and bounced threatening to become undone. Mister Halstead ran forward and lifted the young animal in his two arms, grunting as he took the weight. He hustled it and the mother and the other cow down the gangplank and onto the jetty. He placed the calf at the mother's feet and scrambled out of the way just as the bull rumbled ponderously up to the cow offering her his attentions.

Mac, the captain and the bosun stood on the deck near the gangplank. Mac wiped his sweaty forehead with the back of his arm.

"Whew, I thought he was a gonna then; or at the very least they were all going to end up in the drink."

"Jimmy Dougall always said that you never knew what animals might take it into their heads to do next. He'd have laughed if he was here now." Bosun Evans grinned.

"He would have, at that." Mac laughed at the thought of the infectious laughter of their long-gone friend.

William Sloan chuckled and shook his head as he looked about him.

"This ship looks like a mad woman's boudoir. It will take a couple of hours to get things ship-shape. I'll leave that in your capable hands, Mac. I'm off to call on the harbourmaster and our agent. See what other exciting cargos they might have for us."

"Will there be any shore leave for the men tonight, Captain?" Evans asked.

The captain lifted the cap from his head and ran his fingers through his dripping hair.

"I guess that will depend on how long we are going to be here. I won't know that until I know what cargo awaits us. If we're here a couple of nights, we'll let them have some shore leave." He turned to the ship's mate. "Mac, it might be a good idea to shift the *Northern Orchid* out to a mooring in the river while Guthrie still has pressure in the boiler. They won't want us hanging about their cattle wharf for no reason."

It was the bosun, Noel Evans, along with Guthrie Winston, Sykes, Bony, Adams, Tanner and Bellyache Basil who were the lucky ones to have shore leave at the end of the day. As the sun delivered its last farewell before disappearing over the horizon, the envious crew hung over the ship's rail watching the jolly-boat as the oarsmen pulled for the shore. Those in the small vessel laughed and catcalled at their not-so-lucky crewmates.

Josh and Gus were huddled over their assignments in The Cupboard when the scraping door announced the arrival of the ship's mate. They jumped to attention.

"Still at it then, are you? How's it going?"

Josh turned his writing book towards Mister MacGregor.

"We're just about to take it to the captain now. Will you have a look at it and see if you think it will pass muster, Sir?"

Mac held the pages up to the fading light that struggled through the window. The boys' hearts plummeted as the minutes ticked away and not a word was spoken. They looked glumly at each other.

"You know boys, this is very good. I think the captain will be suitably impressed."

The sigh of relief from both lads was audible. The ship's mate went on speaking.

"You lads have been given the first watch with me tonight. Rollins and Bandy will take the next watch with Captain Sloan. You'd best go and have yourself something to eat."

As they packed up their paperwork, Gus grinned.

"At least we don't have to worry about that weird Sykes and his offsider Bony. They'll be otherwise occupied on shore tonight."

In the moonlight, they barely needed the lantern swinging from Gus's hand. The Dougall brothers took a turn around the top deck to ensure all was as it should be. Music and song floated across the river from the tavern on the waterfront.

After the first inspection of the ship, their next chore was to ensure the cabins on the top deck were in a fit state for passengers. Later, in their watch, they were to prepare the steerage class dormitories in the stern section of the lower deck. The captain was expecting three businessmen for the top deck and two families and four single men in steerage to travel from Rockhampton to Mackay.

Josh punched his brother playfully on the arm. Their laughter was as bright as the full moon above. They came to a sudden halt as China's voice came at them from the shadows at the stern.

"How I catch fish with all the noise around here?"

The boys fell quiet as they made their way to join China who now hung over the stern pulling in a fishing line. The phosphorescence sparkled on the water as a reluctant fish struggled in its attempt to escape the inevitable. They jumped back as it was flung on deck along with a spray of salt water. The fish flipped and flapped on the deck for some time before coming to rest alongside three other similar specimens.

"Fish for morning, boys?" He spoke as he baited the line and tossed the hook overboard.

"What do you use for bait, China?" Gus asked.

"Bellyache Basil made flat-cakes today. They were hardly touched but at least fish like them."

Josh pulled at his brother's arm. "This won't get those dormitories ready, Gus; come on."

Slivers of cloud drifted across the moon as it rode high in the sky, casting intermittent shadows over the two figures. With stealth, they shoved the jolly-boat into the inky water. After having padded the oarlocks with scrap sacking, the movement of the oars made little more than a faint groan. The water dripping from their elevated blades blended with the gentle lapping of the wavelets on the river bank. With the larger man standing to push the oars, the boat edged towards the hull of *The Northern Orchid*. The second man waited in silence with his arms outstretched to cushion the noise of their arrival. In one hand, he held the line attached to the bow of their boat. As the little boat nudged up to the ship's hull, his other hand grabbed the cable dangling from the deck. This cable was intended to secure the smaller boat while the ship lay at anchor. With a practised twist, the knot was secured. Neither of the men moved to climb the Jacob's-ladder hanging over the ship's side. Even the larger man had no difficulty swinging up nimbly onto the cable that now secured their vessel. One after the other, they used their bare feet on the hull to push themselves up the ship's side as they climbed hand over hand to the bulwark. Those bare feet emitted a soft whisper as they landed on the timbers of the deck.

"They must be below deck; there's only the wheel-house lantern on up here. The ship's mate must be in there." The sibilant hiss reached the ear of the larger man. "They're probably asleep. Follow me."

In the soft glow of the moonlight that squeezed through the porthole, Gus swept the floor of the steerage class port-side dormitory. Josh had taken the lantern to check the level of the bilge water. A movement on the river seen through the porthole drew his attention from the broom. He peered out into the night. Why would the jolly-boat be sneaking back to *The Orchid* without a sound, like that? The oarlocks must be padded with something. A shiver ran down his spine as he recognized the large body-shape of the rower. He spun about and went in search of his brother.

"You can bet your life they are up to no good and I'll bet they've got something planned for us two." Josh took up his lantern and motioned with his other hand for Gus to follow his lead.

"Pity they don't fall into the river with the crocs," Gus mumbled at Josh's back.

The boys slipped around the bulkhead, separating the aft cargo hold, to the starboard steerage dormitory. The wick of the lantern was lowered until there was just a dull glow. With care, they hung the handle over a spike just inside the doorway. In darkness, they hastened back to the opposite dormitory from where the lantern now hung. They peered through the porthole.

"Why are they climbing up the cable? It'd be easier to climb up the Jacob's-ladder surely." Gus whispered to his brother while at the same time admiring the skill of the poisonous pair.

"They don't want the wooden slats of the ladder banging against the hull; they'd soon be discovered. That pair don't want to be discovered tonight; it seems. Let's make ourselves scarce."

The boys hastened back to the other side of the lower deck. Josh stood in the doorway of the starboard dormitory where he had left the lantern. In the dull light, he glanced around himself. A wedge-shaped piece of timber set into a slot of the door frame caught his attention. An idea was beginning to form in his mind. He slipped the wedge down his shirt before leading Gus to where spare bags of coal were secured against the wall near the engine room. From there, it was easy to watch the doorway into the dormitory. Josh pulled aside two bags and pushed his brother into the space before slipping in beside him. They juggled the coal bags back in front of their bodies and settled in silence to wait.

China and Mac sat in companionable silence at the stern while China waited for another promise of a fish on the end of his line. China's head snapped up.

"What that?" He spoke softly.

"What? I don't hear anything." The ship's mate cocked his head, listening. The music from the tavern had ceased and only occasionally a few voices floated on the light breeze. Waves lapped at the shore and jetty. An owl called from a tree near the waterside. The *Northern Orchid's* cable and timbers creaked a little at her anchor but nothing seemed out of place.

"Listen."

And then he noticed. The trickle of water that was not wavelets on the riverbank. A faint groan that sounded like oarlocks when they are padded. A shuffle of timber rubbing on timber. Creaking of a hemp-line under strain.

"We have company," Mac whispered.

China nodded. As one, the two rose and moved quietly to where they could see the Jacob's-ladder hanging over the side. It was the figures of two men climbing the cable that surprised them; two figures which they recognized immediately.

"They up to no good, those two."

Mac nodded at China's whispered remark and added. "You can bet they've got the Dougall boys on their minds."

They retreated back into the shadows to wait and watch.

Sykes led the way down the companion-way to the lower deck. Their bare feet did not make a sound but the ladder produced a soft complaint at Bony's weight.

The pair traced the glow of light around past the engine room and stopped when they saw that it was coming from the starboard dormitory.

"Like I said, Bony; asleep, the slackers. We won't need these vials of opium after all." The words were heard by more than one pair of ears.

They moved closer to the light. Sykes peered into the room.

"They're not 'ere. Where the devil are those sods?" The hiss was loud and clear.

Like surprised deer, Sykes and Bony spun around at the sound of Mister MacGregor's voice close behind them.

"You two volunteering for extra duty on watch, are you?"

Bony stood with his head down. Sykes looked back with defiance.

"No, Mister Mate. We just returned to get an early night and noticed the watch not present. Just looking to see everything's alright."

"Thank you, very much. Now you can leave it to me."

"Yes, Sir, going, Sir."

Mac watched the pair return to the companion-way ladder. He turned to China who had stayed back in the shadows near the coal bags.

"I'd best go make sure those lads are not asleep somewhere and finish my report; goodnight China."

"Wherever the Dougall boys are, I bet they not sleep, Mister Mate. Goodnight." China raised a hand in farewell. He moved as if to make his way to the galley.

Gus stirred to disclose his presence but Josh held his brother's arm tight.

Mister MacGregor headed along the same route as Sykes and Bony. China stood quiet for some time in the shadows.

"You come out now, funny boy. Why you not tell Mister Mac where you are?"

With blackened arms and faces the boys rose from their concealment. Gus turned to his brother.

"Yes, Josh, why didn't we tell Mister Mac where we were?"

Josh sighed. "Didn't you hear what Sykes said to Bony about not needing the opium anymore? If we follow them, we may find where they hide it. We can chuck it overboard. If we don't, we'll be looking over our shoulder every minute of every day and every night."

"Not just a laughing boy, then. Come on, hurry up." China turned as he spoke and hurried off. The boys had to run to catch up.

As they climbed over the coaming, onto the top deck, they heard the mate's footsteps on the walkway outside the wheel-house. China pointed his long finger towards where he could see Sykes and Bony hiding in the shadows made by the halyard lines at mid-ship. The three slipped into deep shadows of the officers' cabins and watched.

It was impossible to see exactly what Sykes and Bony were up to but they were quite some time fiddling with something at the bitt-head. With surreptitious glances around the deck, they moved off towards the bow of the ship where they liked to sleep at night.

"I keep eye on that pair. You boys find out what they doing at bitt-head." China's sandaled feet made little sound as he moved forward.

It took quite some time for the secret of the bitt-head to be revealed. Eventually, they worked out how to screw the top off. Inside they discovered a hollowed-out cache. From this space, two rubber-corked glass vials were removed. With a soft clink of the glass, Josh slipped them into his pocket. He waved to China before tapping Gus's elbow to follow.

At the stern of the ship, China watched as Josh tossed the vials far out into the water. A ring of phosphorescence and a soft splash signalled their trip to the bottom of the river.

Mac looked up from his writing. He was hard put not to burst out laughing at the pair of lads standing at the entrance to the wheel-house. It was only the whites of the eyes that stood out in the coal-dusted faces beneath black hair spiked with dirt. Their darkened arms and legs poked out of clothes smudged with the black dust.

"Mister Mate, Sir, we just came to tell you that we weren't asleep as Sykes said." White teeth flashed as Josh explained. "We were hiding behind the coal bags. We did not expect you and Mister China to turn up when you did."

"Now, why does that not surprise me?" Mac could not stop the grin that split his face. "What were you planning on doing?"

Dust fell to the deck as Josh reached into his shirt and retrieved the wooden wedge that he had stowed there earlier.

"When he was sweeping the port-side dormitory, Gus saw Sykes and Bony sneaking on board. We figured they'd be after us. I was hoping they'd go inside the dormitory where I'd left the lantern turned down low. Once they were inside, we were going to wedge the door shut behind them."

Mac could not contain himself any longer. He burst out laughing. Eventually, he became serious. He pointed to the wedge in Josh's hand.

"You see that wedge, lad. Your father made that. He made one for all the doorways on the ship; you'll see them if you look. They are stored in slots made specifically for that purpose. If China and I had not turned up that one there may have saved your bacon tonight. Your dad would be glad about that." Mac stared off into the night remembering a friend before swinging back to face the boys.

"Now, for goodness sake go clean up and then wake up Bandy and Rollins. It's time for them to start the watch."

As the boys left, the Captain arrived. He gave them a curious look and raised his eyebrow to the ship's mate.

"Do I really want to know?"

THIRTEEN

THE *NORTHERN ORCHID*

Neither Josh nor Gus had been invited to the discussion in the wheelhouse between Captain Sloan, Ewan MacGregor and Bosun Evans. They were the subject of the discussion.

"Mac, what on earth does a fourteen and fifteen-year-old do on shore leave? Millie Carson and no doubt, their sister, would ensure that I never lived to see another sunrise if I let the Dougall boys into the grog houses or gambling rooms and don't even mention the opium dens. Probably ditto for the brothels." Captain Sloan's imagination threatened to explode. "I'd probably have Jimmy Dougall's spirit haunting me at nights, too."

Mac smiled at the frustrations of his captain and friend. "Are you saying that our activities as fifteen-year-old midshipmen-on-leave were unacceptable?"

"What else; few of those stories could ever be told in mixed company. How about you?" William Sloan's eyes crinkled at the corners as a boyish grin twisted the scar at the side of his face.

"Let's put it this way; I could never have told my parents the half of what we got up to; definitely not my mother." Mac gave a rueful smile.

The captain's attention turned to the bosun.

"Evans, what about you; any ideas? You were on shore last night, was there anything going on that these boys could take part in?"

Noel Evans ran his fingers through his hair.

"Can't say that there's a lot of last night I remember, Cap'n." He shut his eyes and attempted to dredge up memories of events after he had entered the river-side pub. The gutters in his forehead smoothed and he looked up with a smile. "Do they know how to play Irish football?"

"How should I know? Why?"

"All the talk in the pub was about a football match on tonight. The Rockhampton Community Women's Group, run by a Mrs. O'Leary, with the sponsorship of Liam O'Farrell, who runs the pub, have combined to put on a football match. The women are raising money for the new community hall. Surely that sort of do will be above reproach."

A sigh of relief floated above the three men in the wheel-house; a solution. Evans then went on to relate more of the information as it came to mind.

"The pub's team is short two players. The boys'll get a game if they turn up before three in the afternoon. After the game's over, the ladies are putting on a feed for the players."

"That should keep them out of mischief for a while, then. Now we only have to teach them how to play football."

"Geez, don't look at me," said Evans. "The closest I ever came to the game was the brief glimpse we had of the players in the park, on a Saturday afternoon when us kids from the orphanage were marched off, to clean the church before the Sunday services."

"Mac, how about you? I know you played at school. I'll drop into O'Farrell's pub this morning, on my way to see the agent. They'll be glad to hear that we have two players for their team. In the meantime, you can teach the boys the basics; not too many of the dirty tricks either." Captain Sloan's face wore a cheeky grin usually found on a face much younger than his. "I knew you'd come in handy one day."

Mac only rolled his eyes at the captain's tease and asked, "What about the boys? Will they want to play football?"

"Of course, they will. All boys want to play football, don't they? Now, I'll be off to sort out the cargo for Mackay and points further north. Evans, you'd best start unloading the stuff for here. And Mac, you get to play football."

The mish-mash team was lined up in the shade at the back of the pub. Two pair of blue eyes, almost hidden under the straggly black hair, sparkled with excitement. Even though all except the Dougall boys were grown men, the pair of youngsters were not that much smaller than the others in the team. Beside them, a tall skinny man calling himself Lanky sucked on a sagging smoke, that had been rolled in a piece of newspaper. He instructed Josh not to worry and to just keep an eye on him. Gus was told never to leave the side of the short muscly man called Mo.

Horses of all breeds were arriving. Some were being ridden by farm-boys while others pulled wagons filled with families from the local agricultural community. Dust rose into the air along with the squeals and laughter of the mingling crowd. Josh raised his eyebrows at his brother when they noted that the opposition team gathering nearby was much bigger built than the men of their own team.

"Take heart, brother. At least we're both quick on our feet." Josh's teeth flashed in a rueful grin. "We could take up knitting."

The Reverend Gorman stood in the middle of the paddock. He had been allocated the unenviable position of the umpire. The wind tugged at his dark coat and a brown scarf wrapped his hat securely on his head. In one hand, he held the white flag to be raised when the ball passed over the crossbar, signalling one point for that team. In the other hand, he held the green flag, which would be raised when the ball went under the crossbar and into the net, signalling a goal. Several times, he blew on the whistle attached to a piece of string hanging around his thick neck. A foot, inside a well-worn shoe, rested upon a spherical leather ball. Lined up on his either side were the two teams of fifteen men.

At the sound of the starting whistle, the crowd roared for their respective teams. The pub crowd stood at one end of the shade, many of them with a drink in their hand. The community team supporters were at the other end of the shade with the men yelling encouragement and punching the air. Their ladies sat on the chairs brought out by the publican. Some kept their hands busy with sewing and knitting while others twitched with contained excitement.

After the first twenty minutes of the game, Josh and Gus began to feel more at ease. Every time they received the ball they tossed or kicked it off onto Lanky or Mo as they had been instructed. Gradually they became more confident and began interacting more with the game. The result of this dribbled blood from Gus's nose and opened up the old scar on Josh's right eyebrow. The tally pendulum swung back and forth between the two teams neither holding the lead over the other for too long. At the rest-breaks, the ladies handed out pannikins of lemon water and dabbed at wounds with scraps of cloth that quickly became saturated in muddy blood. A brute of a man, from the community team, barrelled down the grounds repeatedly, dropping the ball onto his foot and reclaiming it in calloused hands. It was he, who, in the final second sent the ball through the nets with a magnificent kick. Someone, in the near future, would need to repair the damage to the nets and possibly even to the seams of the ball.

In the fading light, voices rose and fell like the sounds of beaching waves as the game was verbally played over and over while everyone enjoyed the sandwiches and cakes provided by the ladies. Three large tubs of fruit drink stood at the end of the trestle table.

Friendly, after-game banter, flew back and forth between the teams. Several lanterns were lit and hung from the rafters. Gus and Josh glowed in the praise of the locals, especially a pair of young ladies, who had recently been promoted to long dresses, serving at the punch bowls under the watchful eye of a diligent mother.

Around the small table, holding a bottle of whisky and four glasses, sat Captain Sloan and his companions enjoying a few quiet drinks in a secluded corner of the hotel. The captain lifted his head after listening to the whispered message delivered into his left ear by the barman.

"What! Impossible! It's supposed to be a church function for heaven's sake."

Opposite him, between the agent and the harbourmaster, Mac looked up.

"Everything okay, William?"

"No, it's not. After the football match, some smart-aleck spiked the fruit drink with a fermented spirit. I'm told there are bodies lying about everywhere over at the church; including our latest crew-members. I might need a hand to get them back on board."

A cold mist drifted in from the river to blend with the lantern light that spread out over the detritus on the tables. Ladies were clearing things away with admirable efficiency. The captain and the ship's mate stood with their caps in their hands as Mrs. O'Leary bore down upon them, with a force that may have been a useful addition to the football team. Her nose was turned so far up into the air that her nostrils looked like a pair of miniature dark eyes peering out between a pair of brilliant blue eyes. Trotting along at her side waddled Mister O'Leary with a face full of worry lines.

"Now Esme, dear, perhaps we should get all the facts, first."

But Esme was not listening.

"Mister O'Farrell should have vetoed the character of his team members more closely. This can only be the work of the hotel's team, or those sailors they added at the last minute. It's all a disgrace. I will speak to him, right now."

Like a fish out of water, the captain's mouth flapped open and shut. Before any sound was forthcoming, the long wide skirts had swept onwards to the hotel.

"Glad I'm not in O'Farrell's shoes right this minute." Mac's laugh deepened when one of the team members, with his body and clothes covered in sweat and mud, spoke beside them.

"Poor Mrs. O'Leary; she'll have a stroke if she ever learns that it was her own darling son, Cuthbert, who made the additional brew out of their own pumpkins. She did say she wanted fruit juice, after all. A vegetable's nearly a fruit; isn't it? Her lad has a scary sense of humour and you can rest assured he did not get that from his mother."

Eventually, after falling over more than a dozen bodies lying in the dark, Mac and the captain discovered their errant crew members near the water tank.

"They stink like a pig pen. It's all that mixing with these lands-people." Mac complained. "Couldn't we leave them here until morning? They'll be able to walk back then."

Captain Sloan's grin was tight. With the aid of the moonlight and the flickering beams of the lanterns, he took up the empty pail lying on its side under the tank tap. This he filled with water before throwing the contents over the vomit-covered body of the younger brother. The boy made no response. The process was repeated several times. Once he was a little cleaner, the buckets of water were aimed at the older brother who sat with his back against the tank wearing a stupid grin on his face.

The boy sucked in deeply as the cold water hit his body. A gravelly voice slurred as he spoke.

"Cap'n Sloan, Sir and Mister Mate, Sir. I think I could get to like that game of football."

Captain Sloan sighed as he put down the bucket.

"This will be one of those tales that's never repeated, I think, Mac." The captain helped Josh to his feet and passed him on to the ship's mate.

Deep groans rolled out of Gus's throat as he was dragged unceremoniously to his feet. The captain drew one of Gus's arms over his shoulder. The other arm sagged, alongside the body, with fingertips almost dragging on the ground. Sloan wrapped his arm around the boy's waist providing additional support.

"Right sailor, start marching back to the ship; and don't even think of vomiting over me."

The mumbled answer was scarcely understandable.

"No, Cap'n, Sir, I have nothing left in my guts to bring up. It must have been something I ate that made me sick."

The morning sun beat down upon their heads. Gus groaned. His head felt as if it was going to explode. Why did the crane winches and pulleys squeal louder today than they ever had before? Sweat poured down his pale face and his knees trembled, like Sarah's custards.

At his side, Josh was not looking too healthy himself but he did his best to help Gus secure the cargo in the slings ready to be winched on board. He had a rag tied at four corners on his head but it seemed to do little to reduce the effects of the punishing heat. If only he had not lost his cap at the game yesterday.

"Chin up brother, this is the last load. After lunch, we can look forward to loading the bags of coal." Josh slapped Gus on the back.

Gus was sure the hair on his head was about to fly off into the river. He groaned once again.

On the deck near the hen cages, China and Mac were relaying, to Captain Sloan, the events of Sykes' and Bony's escapade two nights ago.

"The Dougall's never told me anything about the opium," Mac commented when China told of the boy's solution to the drug threat. "They're an independent pair, I'll give them that."

Captain Sloan had been watching the Dougall boys for most of the morning.

"Make that independent and determined. The pair of them must have a blacksmith's hammer thumping between their ears this morning but they won't give in. The storekeeper was telling me, five of the team members ended up needing the doctor's treatment. I dread to think what was in that rot-gut."

Mac pointed to the jetty, where the hooves of two Clydesdale horses in harness clattered on the timber. A cloud of black soot hovered above the dray they were pulling.

"That will be our coal supplies, I'm betting. This will be the last coal we can access until we return to Rockhampton from the north. There is talk of a coal supply inland from Bowen but it's still only that; just talk. If we do run out, we'll be back to either using the sails exclusively or chopping wood at every port."

Captain Sloan rubbed his face. "It shouldn't be a problem. If the weather holds, it will be all sails to Mackay harbour and the same again to Port Dennison. We'll use the engine for entering and leaving harbours only. Did I tell you that the passengers are loading in the morning? The pilot will be ready to guide us out into the channel tomorrow at two in the afternoon." He turned to Mac who was tying his shoelace. "You'd best send the Dougalls up to see me later, I'll have them both as stewards on this trip. They've got the top deck passengers and the steerage class to contend with." The captain put an arm on China's shoulder. "How about you, China? Will you be able to manage in the galley with just Bellyache Basil? Perhaps the stewards can help clean the dishes after their passengers."

"Good, Captain. They always willing to help."

"What about your fresh vegetables? Will you want help to collect more? I doubt if either of the Dougalls will be in any fit state to be of much use to you today."

"My cousin be here tonight with much vegetables. He has three sons to help."

Mac was the first to leave the group. He was on his way to run an eye over the loading and to collect the manifests from the bosun. Captain Sloan headed off across the gangplank to confer with the driver of the coal wagon. China fussed at his hens and collected the eggs.

THE MARINER'S REST

Sarah yawned as she pulled the knitted jumper close about her body. The spring morning held a chill in the air. She stumbled across the still-dark back-yard to the hotel's kitchen entrance. At the door, she stomped her feet while her numb fingers dug into her pocket for the key. She squealed as a small body materialized beside her.

"Morning, Miss Sarah. I forgot to ask Miss Millie yesterday, what time she wanted me to start this morning, so I came early." Maureen Ryan had been sitting on the verandah.

Sarah's body may have been up and about but her brain was still snug asleep in her bed. She was having trouble working out what the child was talking about. Suddenly comprehension dawned. It had slipped her mind that Miss Millie had asked Maureen to help in the kitchen. Neither Mrs. Hamilton nor her daughter, Meg, would be in today.

"That's good, Maureen." Sarah opened the door.

After lighting the lantern, Sarah huffed and puffed in her attempts to resuscitate the fire in the wood stove. Between her breaths, she told Maureen to shut the door to keep out the cold.

"Would you like me to do that, Miss Sarah. I'm the best stove-starter in our house."

With a dubious look at the girl, Sarah stood aside and invited her to take over.

"Dad says you've got to woo a fire, like an alluring woman. Treat it nice and whisper sweet nothings to it." Maureen paused for a moment while she did just that to the fire. She then asked, "Miss Sarah, what is an alluring woman and what are sweet nothings?"

With the breakfast plates in her hands, Sarah paused to consider the question.

"As far as I know, an alluring woman is a good-looking woman. As far as sweet nothings go, I can't say that I've ever heard any of those." A pensive expression held her features for a moment, then cleared. "Oh look, you've got the fire going a treat. Let me pull the kettle over to the heat. In the meantime, I'll show you how to prepare the breakfast oats and set up the tables."

While the porridge was cooking, Sarah carried the heavy trays out to the two dining rooms where Maureen set the tables. It was time to prepare the tray for Miss Millie.

To the background of shuffling feet and the banging of doors, breakfast was served. Sarah worked over the hot stove cooking the bacon, eggs and toast while Maureen ran the meals out to the guests.

At the sound of the chairs being scraped back, Sarah sent Maureen to the dining room to begin clearing the tables. She savoured the last swallow of her tea before helping to stack the dirty dishes. It was Maureen who set to the washing up. After delivering Miss Millie's tray, it was time to start preparing the shepherd's pie for their midday meal.

The tea towel dripped with moisture as Maureen dried the last of the pots and pans. Out of the corner of her eye, she watched Miss Sarah working at the table. She liked Miss Sarah. Miss Sarah reminded her of Mrs. Schollick who lived in the street up past her house. Mrs. Schollick had those same eyes. Her mother called Mrs. Schollick's eyes, *haunted*. Her mother said that the poor woman saw the ghosts of her murdered husband and kids every day. She said that it was a miracle the poor woman was not dead and buried with them, having received a terrible blow to her skull during the attack on their homestead. What ghosts did Miss Sarah see every day?

Sarah looked up from slicing the carrots.

“Maureen, it’s nine o’clock. Miss Millie said she’d start you with your lessons after the breakfast dishes were done. You’d best be on your way. You’ll find her in the office.”

“Thank you, Miss Sarah. It’s kind of Miss Millie to do this for me. I really want to be able to read and to learn me numbers too. Will she teach me to speak proper too?”

“You’ll find Miss Millie a great teacher. She taught Jacko his lessons when he was a boy and she helped me a lot when I was learning the office work. I don’t know how many other kids she’s helped over the years.”

THE *NORTHERN ORCHID*

Rollins stood back while Bandy hooked up the sling onto the cable leading to the pulleys. Ten bags of coal were enmeshed in the rope netting waiting for the word from Bosun Evans to the crew at the smaller windlass at the stern of the ship. The pulley cable tautened as the six men threw their weight into the work.

"Come on now fellows; put some muscle into it. What have we here; a bunch of sissies?" Evans harangued the men.

Slowly the netted coal-bags rose into the air and inched across from the jetty to the ship. Using the tail rope, Andrews and Bellyache Basil guided the bundle until it hung over the aft hold. Mister Evans called for the chock to be secured while the windlass crew prepared their bodies to hold the reverse pull. The coal sunk slowly below decks. Josh and Gus were among those sent to remove and stack the coal bags on the lower deck; so also, were Sykes and Bony.

"I knew a smart aleck once who was the captain's pet. The crew got sick of 'is telling tales. They loaded 'im into these nets." The foul breath accompanied the sibilant hiss.

Gus and Josh continued their work without acknowledging the words of Sykes. Gus helped Josh swing a coal bag onto his back. Doubled over, the young man carried it to the storage area near the engine room.

"I'm talking to yer; shark bait," Sykes directed his comment to Josh. "The bloke wasn't so up 'imself when the crew 'auled the net over the ship's stern and dunked it into the water a few times. Squealed like a baby 'e did." Sykes spoke louder.

Josh and Gus ignored the taunts. This time Josh loaded Gus up with the next coal sack. Beside them, Bony picked up coal bag after coal bag like they were no more than feather pillows.

"Yer two don't want to go on thinking yer're any better than the rest of us, yer know. Men 'ave disappeared overboard when at sea." Sykes wasn't finished yet.

Bony waited until Josh was close by before he swung his body sideways in the process of removing the sack from his back. The load caught Josh off balance. Down he went; his body splattered across the deck. His bag of coal and that of Bony's crashed across his back. Mister Winston's voice rang out from the engine room.

"You looking for a permanent job shovelling coal into this boiler, are you, Bony?"

Venom hung in the air along with the cloying coal dust.

With shiny faces, clean clothes and hair combed with the fingers of one hand, Josh and Gus stood behind Captain Sloan and Mate MacGregor at the gangplank ready to receive the passengers headed for the next port of call, Mackay. Gus's feet twitched inside his seldom-worn canvas shoes. The first to arrive were the businessmen booked into the cabins on the top deck. Mister Wright in cabin one, Mister Harrigan in cabin two and Mister Field in cabin three. The gentlemen were handed on to Josh who assisted them to their quarters.

At their heels, followed the Bateman families; brothers Jack and Simon Bateman, along with their wives, Gladys and Joyce respectively, and their children. The captain's heart quailed at the sight of the six youngsters. The ship's mate helped with the introductions before Captain Sloan hastily passed them on to Gus.

Along with dusty swags, tattered clothing, boots tied together and with canvas bags hanging over their shoulders, six men were directed to follow Gus to the lower deck.

Captain Sloan let out a sigh as the passengers disappeared down the companion-way.

“Hell’s teeth, Mac, this is going to be one long three-day-trip to Mackay.”

A grin tweaked at the corners of Mac’s lips as he listened to his captain’s exaggeration; he expected no less.

“Oh well, Cap’n, the pilot will have us out of the river before nightfall. We can anchor up north of Curtis Island. Tomorrow we’ll be on our way at first light.”

FOURTEEN

THE *NORTHERN ORCHID*

After delivering his charges, with their luggage, to the top deck cabins and serving a bottle of ale and glasses on a wooden tray from the galley, Josh found that his passengers had no need of his services. Sliding down the companion-way ladder with his hands and feet touching the narrow rails only, he went to offer his brother a hand. Everything was chaos. Three young children ran about squealing with excitement. The sound of the engine's clinkity-clanking in his ears indicated that the boiler had reached its required pressure. Mister Winston and his offsider, Andrews, were prepared for the *Northern Orchid's* trip to the Fitzroy River mouth. At the engine doorway, two curious lads peered in at the activity. Mister Winston did not sound too happy at his audience.

"You boys, shove off now. This is a dangerous machine. Get back to your dormitory."

"I'll take this pair up top, Mister Winston," Josh called. He gathered up the boys, one about ten years of age and the other thirteen, perhaps.

As they moved away from the engine room the two Bateman brothers arrived accompanied by the sisters and cousins of the boys Josh had in tow.

"Can we take these kids up to the top deck, Josh, before they drive their mothers mad?"

"Yes, Mister Bateman, follow us. We were just heading that way. I'll show you from where you can watch all the activity without getting in the way." Josh led the group up the companion-way ladder.

"Ain't yer got any proper steps, Mister?" One of the younger children asked.

"These are proper steps, for a sailing ship." The older Mister Bateman stepped into the breach left by his daughter's bad manners.

Josh settled the family in the shade of the poop deck and warned them they must keep out of the way of the crew preparing the ship. Gus arrived with the wives of the Bateman brothers just as the bosun's voice hailed them from where he stood on the hatch covering the fore hold.

"Hey, you Dougall boys; don't feel left out there. Bring in the stern lines when the wharfie releases them from the bollard."

The loud splash of the heavy ropes hitting the water sent Josh and Gus running to the stern of the ship where they began hauling the lines inboard while rolling them neatly on the deck. Beneath their feet, they felt the tide gathering up their ship and gently nudging it out from the jetty. They grinned at each other as the vibrations of the engine set their hearts pounding. It was good to be on the move again. Several of the crew were on the halyards while others unfurled the main topsail to assist in powering the ship. The wind cracked in the canvas as it took charge. The salt of the sea on the late afternoon air strengthened as the *Northern Orchid* made her way down the Fitzroy River.

The squeal of the young passengers sent Gus searching for his charges.

"Yours, I believe, brother," Josh laughed as he made his way to check on his own passengers, calling back as he did so. "You'd best make sure the kids keep out of China's way. He's just as likely to screw their necks, like a chook, and drop them in a pot."

Gus had only just finished delivering, firstly a tray with plates and cutlery to both dormitories followed by a large pot of salt-beef stew to both areas when the call came for the crew to line up at the capstan. The captain was ready to drop anchor. Looking out of the porthole he could see Port Curtis about ten miles off their starboard bow.

The odour of the burning oil in the galley lantern competed with the aromas of the evening meal. In the dim light, Gus and Josh shared the chore of cleaning up the galley. Only three of the crew were sitting at the table, finishing off their meal: Sykes, Rollins and Bandy.

"'Ey, yer ladies at the wash tub, do yer know what I 'ave 'ere?" As he addressed the boys, Sykes held up in the air, what looked like, a small leather bag.

Josh had his hands in the tub of water while Gus wiped the pots with a not too white cloth which may have had a previous life as Captain Sloan's best shirt. Neither boy answered but both turned to see what he was talking about.

"I picked this up in Rockhampton." A jingling sound reached their ears as he waved the small bag from side to side.

Bandy and Rollins did not deign to lift their heads and Sykes never commented on this. He knew better than to bother them with his torments.

"This is me new coin bag; nice, ain't it. It's a ball-bag from a black fellow who didn't do as 'e was told. Old sod can't do much of anything, now. We don't want that to 'appen to yer boys now, do we?

I could add a paler version of this coin bag to my collection." Sykes burst into a husky laugh.

Gus swung back to the bench in disgust. It was China who approached Sykes at the table. The slippers on his feet did not even whisper on the timber deck. He sat on the stool at the table, opposite Sykes. Without haste, he slid along the wooden form until he was directly facing the man holding up the coin bag. China's face remained impassive as he reached into his tunic. His hand returned holding a small sack still attached to a string around his neck. Once the purse-string was released the Chinaman gently poured the contents out onto the table in front of him. Ten pieces of differently shaped leathery items lay on the table at his fingertips. Hooded dark eyes bore into the pale eyes of Sykes. The one long fingernail stroked each item before it was gently placed in a particular pattern in front of him. Five of the dehydrated pieces, each about the shape of a bean-pod, were placed parallel before the tips were pulled to an arrow point, aimed directly at Sykes's heart. The gaze of the dark eyes never wavered. The other five lumps, in a variety of shapes, were placed at the base of each of the bean-pod pieces.

Josh, Gus, Bandy and Rollins were now interested observers. Sykes slowly withdrew his hand, with its coin purse. He held it under the table. His eyes watched the Chinaman's every move, warily. Imaginations soared in the heads of the group as they attempted to recognize these grotesque pieces.

"The things we collect, eh, Sykes?" China's usually piping voice had sunk to little more than a whisper. All in the galley leaned in closer to hear as the Chinaman continued to stroke the aged and wrinkled items that could have been anything from small human appendages to rejects from a slop bucket. "One thing I learn treasures most valuable when process of collecting them is most challenging." Once more the small hand delved inside his tunic. From the folds of material covering his chest, the hand reappeared dangling another string bag. With great care, the fingers reached inside this bag and came out holding a larger, almost round, object. It was placed at the tip of the arrowhead pointing towards Sykes. This wrinkled leathery substance was about the size of the knob of a gentleman's cane. Silence held as everyone moved in even closer to examine this strange item. It took several seconds for his audience to realize that they were looking at a shrunken head.

"Hell's breath!" Rollins was the first to twig. He crossed himself in the way of the papists.

"Wow! I'd heard of those things in the islands north of Australia, but this is the first time I've laid my eyes on one." Bandy's eyes widened in amazement.

China let the surprise settle before he spoke. During this whole process, his stare never left the eyes of Sykes.

"That was a night never forgotten. It all about the powers of the mind." China explained himself no further. He began to collect his souvenirs and return them to their place of concealment.

Opposite China, Sykes jumped up throwing his hands across the table as he did so. China was way too quick for him and the bags had disappeared inside the folds of his gown before any harm was done.

"Bloody Chinese and yer curses. You're all mad bastards." He stomped out of the galley.

China bent down and picked up the black cat that had been walking up and down the wooden seat beside him. He placed the animal on his lap and stroked the soft fur while the noise of its purring filled the galley.

The voices of the captain and the mate drifted in through the open window of the Captain's Cupboard as Josh and Gus made themselves comfortable on the heap of unused sails. They prepared to complete their daily journal. In hushed voices, they spoke more of the incident in the galley than the events of the day.

"Did you see Sykes' eyes? They bulged from his head like they were planning on moving out, I swear." Gus's grin split his face. "China soon sent him on his way, didn't he?"

Josh looked thoughtful. "What do you suppose those other things were, in his little bag; besides the shrunken head?"

"How should I know? The things like sticks may have been fingers, perhaps. It's anyone's guess, what the lumpy things were. Maybe other parts of the body of the man who once owned that head."

"And another thing, how do they shrink a head like that? What happens to the bone of the skull?"

Gus did not hesitate in his reply. "Black magic, no doubt. Maybe China knows about black magic. Maybe he can cast Chinese spells like Andrews says."

"One thing's for sure, I don't think I'd like to get on the wrong side of him."

The morning sun did not present itself the next day. A blustery wind blew in from the east bringing with it grey cloud cover. Choppy waves made the *Northern Orchid* impatient at the anchor. Captain Sloan had his crew up and about when there was only a hint of light in the sky. No sooner had they weighed anchor than several of the crew were climbing the rigging to unfurl the sails. Others were hauling on the halyards and lines to bring the yards around to capture the breeze. The captain had set fore and aft lateen staysails at the foremast and at the mizzen mast to act as aerofoils on the square sails of the mainmast. Like a racehorse released from its stable, the *Northern Orchid* bolted across the sea, her sails savouring the winds. A fine spray of seawater burst over the bow as the ship crashed into each large swell. Curtis Island fell away to starboard as they headed nor'-nor'-east towards the Capricorn Channel.

Once released from his sailing duties, Gus served breakfast to his steerage class passengers. While they ate, he collected the slop bucket from each dormitory. One by one these were taken up to the top deck. Two wooden piggins with clean fresh sea water stood on the deck beside a coarse brush and a lump of tallow soap. Having provided amusement to the rest of the crew on his first day cleaning slop buckets, Gus knew to assess the wind direction before tossing the contents overboard. He unclamped the lid of the first bucket. While holding the container as far out as he could, Gus emptied it into the sea, trying not to breathe in as he did so. Once both slop buckets were scrubbed and the clean water buckets refilled, Gus prepared to make his way back to the lower deck. At that moment, Josh arrived with a slop bucket in each of his hands.

"I hope you left clean water for me, Gus."

"Nah, forgot."

"It's all right for you; you've only two buckets to empty. I've got three."

"Yeah, but you only got one person pissing and shitting in each bucket I've got ten using one bucket and six using the other. Want to swap?" Gus smiled as Josh shook his head vehemently. "Course the clean water's been refilled."

Gus knocked on the door of the starboard dormitory. A female voice called for him to enter. He walked through the doorway and in behind the canvas drape hanging across the corner near the door. The clean slop bucket clunked against the edge of the stabilizing frame as it was settled into place. It was time to clean up the room. Like the port dormitory, this room held eight narrow double bunks against the perimeter. A thin mattress lay rolled up on each of the unused bunks.

A table was secured to the floor in the centre of the room. Two portholes allowed fresh air entry and the twelve-inch gap above the bulkhead allowed this air to circulate below decks; albeit sluggishly.

The younger Mrs. Bateman lay upon her bunk. Her little girl lay in her arms; both their faces white. A pail sat on the floor in easy reaching distance. In the middle of the narrow room, the two older girls and the youngest boy sat playing with coloured strings and several pegs. The older Mrs. Bateman had the breakfast trays loaded up on the table ready for Gus to collect.

"Gus, can I help you with the washing up, lad? It'll be no bother."

"Oh, no thanks, Mrs. Bateman." Gus almost laughed at the thought of China's face if he found a lady washing up in his domain. "The cook don't like strangers in the galley. Anyway, it only takes a few minutes."

"I'll be thinking I'm Queen Muck, with nothing to do." She smiled a wide infectious smile. "It's pleasant today, without that engine going all the time. How do you get used to those fumes of the burning coal?"

Gus shrugged. "Will you be going up to the top deck this morning, Mrs. Bateman? It is a bit blustery and cold up there, at the moment. We may even get a rain squall later."

"Maybe, the children will need a bit of exercise."

"What are you going to do when you get to Mackay, Mrs. Bateman?"

"Our husbands were up this way recently. They bought a large farm near the town which they want to develop into a sugar plantation."

Mate MacGregor was in deep conversation with Mister Wright, Mister Harrigan and Mister Field. He stood with his back against the door frame of the first-class lounge room while the three passengers enjoyed the comfort of the padded chairs. Large sheets of paper covered in pencil drawings of machinery and building plans lay across the table.

"You see, Mister MacGregor, a farmer named Spiller, on Pioneer Plantation, has already set up a crushing plant on his cane land. He is using wooden rollers. When we arrive at Mackay, we plan to talk to other cane farmers about setting up a larger, commercial, enterprise for milling the cane. Now that they're bringing in the Kanakas to this area, the cane farms will be able to expand rapidly." Mister Harrigan explained their presence on the *Northern Orchid.*

"We have the know-how and the financial backing to set this up." Mister Wright spoke while pouring another cup of tea for himself and collecting two of China's biscuits that sat on the tray on the sideboard.

At that point, Mac poked his head out of the doorway. He listened. The ripple of sails flapping in the breeze was borne to him on the wind. They were in need of suitable trimming. As the thought passed through Mac's head, the bosun's voice was heard above the increasing breezes and the start of light rain, shouting for the crew.

"Sorry gentlemen, I've got work to do." He ran to the forward section of the *Northern Orchid.*

The midday sun remained hidden behind the miserable sky. Tears had fallen from the heavens already this morning. Josh and Gus were on the poop deck removing the cover from the longboat. They had just rolled up the sheet of canvas when a small voice called up to them.

"Why'd you take the blanket off the boat? Now it'll fill with water and sink." It was the youngest girl belonging to the older Bateman woman.

Gus jumped down to the top deck and explained.

"That boat has not been used for a long while and the timbers have become very dry. When they dry, they shrink, leaving gaps. If we put it into the water like that the boat will leak. The captain wants the rain to fill the boat with water. This will saturate and swell the timbers and close the gaps. When we row you and your family to shore, in a couple of days, the boat won't sink."

"I'm not going in no leaky old boat, Gus."

Gus rubbed his head. "No, of course not. We won't put you in a leaky old boat. Now I'd best get down to the galley and see what the cook has for your dinner."

The single blokes were hunched up around the card game being played on the floor of the dormitory. Gus had to nudge his way around their bodies as he delivered the tray with the noon meal. He jumped when a yell rang out from several players.

"That can't be right. How can he win again?"

"Be damned; I can hardly believe it."

The winner of the day rose to his feet, smiling broadly.

"It's about time I had a win, anyway. Now let's eat; me stomach thinks me throat's been cut."

While the men ate with gusto, Gus learned more of their travel plans. The six of them had recently given up on their gold fossicking north of Rockhampton. They were on their way to try their luck working in the developing cane industry at Mackay. One man had spent most of his life in the wool industry. He was also a creditable saddler. Two amongst them were brothers. They had come off a small mixed farm in Victoria. The number of sons had outgrown their father's farm and these two young men had moved on, firstly, to the Victoria goldfields and then on to Queensland. The three remaining men had worked cattle most of their lives but had been sucked in with the gold fever. There was little that they couldn't do, or at least weren't willing to have a go at.

Today, Gus was the one with his arms up to the elbows in the suds. China supervised Bellyache Basil while he prepared a damper for the evening meal.

"China, have you ever been digging for gold?"

"Gold comes in many disguises, young Gus. What exactly do you mean?"

"Those blokes in steerage, they've been searching for gold. As far as I can see they have little to show for their efforts."

"Ah, you mean on goldfields. My observation, it not men up to necks in dirt and sweat, living in hovels fit for dogs, who make fortune. Most these walk away broken men; that's if they live to walk away at all. The people supply equipment, food, entertainment and other services are winners. Them ones dressed in warm coats when winter comes."

THE MARINER'S REST

Millie stood, looking through her front window, into the night. From where she sat at the small table, Sarah could see the recently acquired streaks of grey reflected in the moonlight that highlighted her mentor's reddened hair. She marvelled at the smoothness of Millie's skin and the scarcity of lines on her face.

"Miss Millie, how do you keep your skin looking so young? I've got more lines on my face and I'm not even seventeen yet."

"Why, thank you, dear. That's a lovely thing to say, even though I think you exaggerate. A woman I once worked for, told me, to never let the sun near my skin and to always use creams on my face." Millie proudly ran her fingers lightly over her forehead, under her eyes and down her cheeks. "Not too bad, I guess, considering it won't be too long before I'm closer to fifty than forty." Millie looked sharply at Sarah. Was the girl taking an interest in her looks at last? "What brought this on? This need to improve on your complexion? Is it anyone I know?"

The shadows hid the blush that rushed across the pleasant landscape of Sarah's face. She pulled several errant strands of hair behind her ears.

"Oh, Miss Millie there's no-one who'd want to take a second look at me and anyway it's years before I'll want to be getting married."

Millie hitched her hip up onto the window ledge and leaned back against the window frame. She hid her smile behind the muslin curtain. If she knew anything, the glances of Jacko's, that she'd intercepted, were not from a man without interest. The smile vanished at Sarah's next words.

"Miss Millie," Sarah paused here, picking at her fingernails, "Are all men going to be just like Mister Dingle?"

It was Millie's turn to pause and consider her next words.

"Sarah, my dear, all men have their needs and will seek out women to satisfy those needs. Sadly, you have experienced the emptiness of this act when it occurs between a man and a woman, just as a business arrangement. There is never any fanfare in that. This act may also occur with no other feeling but lust on the part of one or of both parties. One must say that, on the part of the women, any lust is often doused under the weight of everyday survival or fear of pregnancy. Lust lasts only as long as the sweat raised in the effort of satisfying the urge. When the act occurs between a man and woman who love each other, then you have the whole orchestra in full throat. Love fills the act, not only with sexual satisfaction but with a deeper and more meaningful gratification." Millie paused while staring out at the river, before continuing. "The difficulty is in knowing, what is love and what is lust."

Silence filled the room as both women pondered on these words. The clatter of a horseman passing the front of the hotel broke into the calming whisper of the wind in the trees outside.

"Miss Millie, how will I know what is love and what is lust?"

Millie took quite some time to consider her answer to this question. The moonlight picked up the frown lying like a judge's gavel above her eyes.

"Sarah, that is not easy. I could say, to just follow your heart. In my experience, you may know what your heart is telling you but that is not necessarily what may be in the heart of the other person. I will offer the advice of an old employer of mine who had a world of common sense. Ethel always said, 'Lust is like a sheen of polish. Scratch it and you will find a core of solid self-interest within a vast expanse of nothingness. Love, on the other hand, runs very deep. One can drill down to any depth and the only thing to be revealed is a softness, a world of respect, consideration, caring, understanding, protectiveness all enveloped in the courage and confidence that will allow freedom.' I have been fortunate in my life to have had two men love me as I have loved them. Mind you, I sometimes think that my William loves his ship more than his woman. I have not yet been invited aboard the *Northern Orchid*, you know. Apparently, sailors are a superstitious lot and redheads on board ship herald impending doom." Millie laughed at such nonsense. "Sarah, when you do find that magic called love, it is truly something to be captured and treasured, my dear."

"I hope that one day I'll be so lucky. For now, though, I had best go and sleep; tomorrow's another busy day. Are you sure you have everything you want for the night, Miss Millie?"

"Thank you, my girl, I have. Good night, dear."

Millie was still staring over the river with dreamy eyes when she noticed a rider approaching the front of the hotel. His seat in the saddle was none too steady. From below her, the rattle and clang of Jacko cleaning in the bar drifted up to the top floor. At the hotel steps, the rider slid to the ground landing in an awkward heap just in time to be greeted with the bucket of dirty water which Jacko tossed out into the garden.

The man coughed and spluttered. Millie held a soft hand over her mouth to muffle the laughter.

"Geesh, Jacko, whatcha doing?"

Millie immediately recognized the voice as that of Arthur Rankine; as did Jacko.

"Hell's teeth, Arthur. What on earth are you doing hanging around here, in that state, at this time of night? If Miss Millie hears you, she'll tear a strip off you. She won't want you waking the guests."

"Aah, our saviour, Miss Millie. It's not her I've come to see."

"Arthur, you know better than to come bothering the girls upstairs in that condition. Miss Millie will not allow it."

Arthur Rankine attempted to tap the side of his nose with his forefinger but missed hopelessly, nearly taking off his receding chin in the process.

"No, I don't want your top floor ladies, I've come to collect the biggest prize of all. I've come to claim little prissy Miss Sarah. Don't tell me she's all innocent. I'm sure Miss Millie won't mind if the girl wants to make a few dollars on the side."

Millie felt her blood boil. She hissed through the window when she saw Jacko's arm raise up in the air.

"No, Jacko. Take him into the kitchen."

On her way out of the bedroom, Millie reached into the top of her cupboard and took a small brown bottle with a dirty stopper in the narrow neck. This she slipped into the pocket of her dressing gown before moving quickly down the stairs.

Jacko had Arthur draped in a chair. The man's head drooped onto the tabletop. Jacko was in the process of pulling the kettle over the heat of the shallow fire when Millie came in with her face drawn taut. She lifted down the teapot and three cups from the cupboard as well as the tea canister.

Jacko's eyebrows reached his hairline as he watched Millie pour several drops of the mixture from her brown bottle into one of the cups; the one she had placed in front of Arthur. He did not say a word.

Millie had to almost pour the tea down Arthur's throat. He was incapable of holding the cup in his unsteady hands. She was determined to ensure he drank the lot. As the last drop of the brew gurgled down his throat, Arthur's upper body slumped again onto the table. Millie looked up with a grin at Jacko.

"That should quieten him down for the night. Can you drag him out to the stable? He can sleep on the hay. I doubt he'll feel the cold."

"It will be my pleasure, Miss Millie. Tonight, I'll sleep on the old stretcher on the verandah just to make sure that reprobate doesn't wake in the night. We don't want him bothering young Sarah."

"That's a good idea, Jacko. The girl would be mortified if she knew what had happened here tonight."

THE *NORTHERN ORCHID*

After a night anchored just south of Broad Sound Channel, the *Northern Orchid* greeted the new day of sunshine and brisk breezes. Once the ship was underway, the crew were set packing the oakum, gathered previously, into the joints of the deck timbers of the ship. Adams and Gus worked together near the stern. The raking hook screeched against the timber as Adams scraped out the old worn packing between the planks. An odorous mixture of damp musty hemp and old tar hung on the air. Gus stood up to roll teased chunks of their collected oakum against his thigh to form a loosely rolled cord. The stale smell of stored hemp added to the malodorous atmosphere. He then laid it in the cleaned gap between the planks and packed it in firmly by belting the grooved wedge with the double horned mallet. Adams followed up behind him, slapping on the pitch with a weary bristled brush, sealing off the packing, making it water resistant.

"You know," one of the passengers, the saddle-maker, said in his slow drawl, "I can see that is not as easy as it looks. Do you need a hand?"

Gus stood up straight and stretched his aching back.

"Believe you me, you really don't want to do this; but thanks for offering, anyway." Gus turned to Adams. "I'm sorry, Adams, but I must go and serve the morning tea."

"Geez, why didn't the captain make me a steward. Even tea making'd be easier than this." Adams grumbled at Gus's disappearing back.

The saddle-maker bent to his knees and took up where Gus had left off. He turned to Adams working on the next timber joint.

"Whereabouts are we now?" The landsman asked.

"Just nor'-nor'-east of Broad Sound Channel." Adams slapped on another dollop of the pitch to the newly laid oakum. He looked up for a moment and pointed to starboard. "If you look out there, you can see the Swain Reefs. By this afternoon, we'll be in amongst the Northumberland Islands. You'll see them on the other side. With any luck, we'll anchor north off Percy Isles on dark tonight."

FIFTEEN

THE *NORTHERN ORCHID*

Shadows danced around the chartroom as Sloan and the mate poured over the map spread out on the table. The remnants of the evening meal lay scattered across seats of the chairs pulled back against the wall. Feeble light flickered from the lantern sitting on the map just west of the name Northumberland Islands.

Sloan's finger traced the inner channel through the multitude of islands off the Queensland coast.

"Sailing through these islands and reefs is like trying to navigate one's way safely through the whims of the fairer sex. One false move or slip of the tongue can bring down an avalanche of calamity."

Mac chuckled. "Stay safe, William; stick to the sailing ships. At least one has a map from which to plot a course."

"Maintain shorter periods for the lookout in the crow's nest again tomorrow, Mac. We don't want them losing concentration. You can utilize the Dougall boys too. Surely those passengers don't keep them busy all the time."

Knowing how prickly his friend could get over the subject of passengers, Mac chose to return the subject to safer waters.

"We made good time today. I didn't think we'd get to anchor-up so far north of Percy Isles this evening."

"If we continue like this, we'll be cooling our heels off Mackay by mid-afternoon tomorrow." Captain Sloan stood erect as a set of knuckles beat a tattoo on the open timber door.

"Excuse me, Cap'n. I've just come to collect the tray." Josh's glance took in the map on display. His hungry eyes did not shift when the captain invited him in.

"Come in, young Dougall. When you and your brother have finished with your passengers and in the galley, you'd best come up here and inspect this channel map. Perhaps you might like to plot us a course north of Mackay."

Suddenly the weariness brought on by the drudgery of the day, playing nursemaid to his charges, as well as to those energetic kids that Gus had running all over the deck, fell like a weight from his shoulders.

"Yes, Sir." With alacrity, he loaded the used dishes onto the tray and almost ran out of the doorway.

"You've made that boy's day, William."

"So, it seems and now I must finish off my own day."

"The look on your face tells me that you are going to make your obligatory visit to our passengers." Mac tried to keep the grin from his own expression as he went on. "Hoping the parents have their little tear-a-ways all tucked up asleep in their bunks, are you?"

"Pox on you, Mac." William Sloan did not bother to take a lantern. He knew every nook and cranny, timber and splinter on his ship.

The mid-morning sun beat down upon Gus's back as he shuffled on his knees caulking between the timbers at the stern, behind the passenger cabins. This was the last area left to be caulked. For the moment, he was working on his own. The raking hook, the grooved wedge and the mallet were lined up in order of use beside the pitch pot and brush. He pulled at a pile of oakum, preparing the next cord for packing. Gus felt the shadow, rather than saw Sykes approaching. The man sank to his haunches holding his marlin-spike out in front of him. Sykes' hand stroked the twelve-inch-long tool, used when splicing the cable ropes, in a repetitive sensuous manner.

"Aah, sweet Gus Dougall. Back 'ere, all on yer own."

The sibilant voice raised the hairs on the back of Gus's neck. He jumped to his feet. His heart thumped in his chest. The breath died in his throat. He stared into Sykes' eyes and looked into the frozen land of the south pole. His throat felt as dry as a discarded fish scale. He tried to swallow but no spit was forthcoming. Like a snake, the man opposite Gus arose swaying from side to side. Gus held the wooden mallet tightly in his hand; a poor defence against a marlin-spike.

"Bony is becoming impatient, boy. Yer can come willingly or on the end of this 'ere serving fork. Now, that would be an entertaining sight to see, you squirming on the point of this." Sun glinted off the tip of the spike, where it had been recently sharpened. Sykes' fingers continued stroking.

Gus glanced left and right. He was fleet of foot, he should be able to outrun the older Sykes, but the way was blocked by two cargo crates stored behind the cabins.

"Don't even think of it, boyo. Dunno what's so special about yer, myself. A bit of an upstart, as far as I can see; but yer what Bony wants and I like to make my friend 'appy."

Gus dragged in a strident breath. Despite his attempts to sound normal, his voice came across scratchy.

"Piss off, to the two of you."

A new voice surprised the two sailors locked in their glaring combat.

"Oh Gus, this's where yer 'idin'. We were 'opin' yer could bring us a pot of tea. This 'eat 'as me throat parched. Besides, I'm losin' all the money I won yesterday so I needed an excuse to interrupt the game and give me luck a chance to find me again."

Three of the steerage passengers stood shoulder to shoulder behind Sykes. The marlin-spike disappeared down the inside of Sykes' trousers so fast, Gus was left wondering if he had only imagined what had just occurred. Sykes slinked off giving the passengers a wide berth.

Gus was grateful to have been called by the bosun to take a turn in the crow's nest. Ever since his altercation with Sykes that morning, he had felt as if he were covered in a film of foul scum. His skin crawled. Every breath he took filled his nostrils with the memory of the smell of the man. As he climbed higher and higher up the rigging the breeze cleared his mind and freshened his skin.

Gus greeted his brother who was preparing to exit the barrel and return to the deck. Josh listened to the story Gus told of the morning events.

"Brother, you have to make sure that you are never alone."

"I will from now on." Gus peered out over the waters. "Oh look, the dolphins are back." Six of the sleek mammals frolicked near the bow keeping pace with the vessel.

Josh reached around his brother in the confined space and pointed sou'-sou'-west. "You can just see the Percy Islands disappearing over the horizon there. The captain will start to veer nor'-nor'-west shortly to bring us onto the Twin Islands outside Mackay."

After Josh had returned to the deck below, Gus stretched out his arms and breathed deeply. The salty breeze captured the faint odour of tar on the rigging lines along with the musty smell of the canvas. A laugh of pleasure exploded into the sunny afternoon. He watched as the twin islands, Flat Top and Round Top Islands, grew from distant grey blobs, larger and clearer until individual trees were identified on their surfaces. The waters around the islands' shorelines were a much darker blue than the shallow waters covering the sand bars at the mouth of the Pioneer River nearby. Here, thick mangroves reached out onto the mudflats disguising the entrance of the river-mouth. As the *Northern Orchid* nosed her way into the lee of the Round Top Island, a piercing cooee from the bosun down below had Gus joining the sailors who were at that moment racing up the rigging to the yards where they were to furl the sails.

The splash of the bow anchor on its way to the bottom of the sea still lingered in the ears as the bosun gave the order to have the stern anchor lowered as well.

An evening breeze robbed the tropical sun of much of its heat. Captain Sloan and Mate MacGregor stood with their arms outstretched leaning into the port side bulwark.

"Mac, I don't like that bit of a smudge on the southern horizon. I've been watching it most of the day. I think we'll be in for, at least, a squall, within a day or two."

Mac screwed up his eyes in an attempt to see what the captain had seen. "Well, I can't say I can see anything but I've already lost a fortune to your gut instinct so I'm not arguing with you."

Captain Sloan grinned. "Want me to get the telescope for you?"

"I believe you; I believe you." Mac threw up his hands and laughed.

Deep lines appeared across his forehead as Sloan rubbed his lower chin considering his options. "I'm hoping, whatever it is, doesn't arrive before tomorrow when we boat these passengers onto Flat Top Island to await pickup by the barge. If things aren't too dismal, I'll take the three first-class passengers with me, in the jolly-boat, all the way into Mackay. I want to see the agent there anyway. They may have some cargo for us now or, if not, maybe on our return from further north. We could also do with some fresh newspapers to read. The half a dozen books in the chartroom can become a little tiresome."

The grey skies of the next morning hung heavy above them. Choppy wavelets stirred by a light wind had the longboat and the jolly-boat jigging on the end of the umbilical cords securing them to the ship. Mac and the captain cast concerned gazes to the skies as they waited for the last of the passengers to arrive at the disembarkation point.

"I'll take the two Dougall boys in the jolly-boat, as oarsmen, with myself and the first-class passengers." Captain Sloan began. "That will leave you to transfer the remainder to Flat Top Island."

"No trouble, Cap'n. The sooner they start dredging this river to take the larger vessels, the better. You'll organize the barges to come out to collect the passengers and to take our cargo, then?"

"Yes, I'll do that as soon as we get to Mackay. Make sure the passengers only take the minimum of baggage. The rest will go ashore, on the barge, with the cargo. Geez, that reminds me; have you talked with China this morning?"

Mac shook his head in the negative. Captain Sloan went on to explain.

"I'd better go and see if China wants anything brought back. No doubt he'll know someone here who can sell him something."

Evans had the bosun's chair, the hoist sling and the Jacob's-ladder ready at the port side of the ship with the attached coils of rope lying tidily on the deck. Rollins stood in the bow of the longboat below and Josh stood in the bow of the jolly-boat. Both were there to receive each passenger as they arrived from the deck and to assist them into the boats. Gus was up top with Mac and Evans helping to load the passengers. The youngest child set up a wail that sent the seagulls screeching up from the yardarms. She wanted Gus to go with her. Eventually, the youngster was seated on her mother's lap in the bosun's chair and lowered to the longboat. Rollins took a small wooden ball from his pocket and gave it to her. The tears soon dried on her face; replaced with a wide grin.

Mister Winston stood to the side of this activity talking with the group of ex-gold prospectors. He left them in a huddle discussing their future after learning of the first arrival in Mackay, only a month before, of seventy south-sea islanders. This group had come in on the *Prima Donna;* all destined as cheap labour on the sugar plantations.

"That puts a different light on our plans then. Looks like we may have to go over the ranges to see what the cattle industry has to offer." One of the men walked to the edge of the ship and spat a dollop of tobacco into the sea.

The three men who had previously worked cattle looked at each other. The tall, skinny one, the one who was also a leather-worker, named Stretch, took off his hat and rubbed the sweat from his hair.

"Whatdayer blokes think? Should we go further north? There's supposed to be plenty of cattle work up in the Bowen area."

Dave, the short muscly man at his right side, shrugged his shoulders. "All the same with me. What do you reckon, Reg?"

The third man, wearing the droopy felt hat that covered his bald head grinned setting his piercing blue eyes sparkling. "Yeah, why not. Trouble is, with the country flat broke as it is, the cow cockies ain't spending as much on workers as they used to. What the heck, have we got enough for our fare?"

The trio dug within their pockets. There were many copper coins, a rattle of threepenny bits and sixpences as well as a few ten-shilling notes, several one-pound notes, a few five-pound notes but no ten-pound notes.

"Yeah, this should just about do it. I'll ask the ship's mate if we can get a berth on the *Northern Orchid*." Reg walked over to where Mac stood watching the process of disembarkation.

The captain slung himself over the side holding onto the rope secured to the jolly-boat below. Just before he slithered down its length, he called to the bosun.

"Evans, get the men working on that aft mizzen sail. I want it replaced today. It won't take much of a blow to split it from end to end."

His answer floated on the breeze over the side of the hull.

"Yes, Cap'n"

China and Mister Winston stood at the rail watching as the boats of the *Northern Orchid* headed off; one to the Flat Top Island and one to the mouth of the Pioneer River. Several other smaller boats from the two adjacent coastal traders bobbed upon the choppy seas, busy with their own business.

THE MARINER'S REST

She could not be sure if it was a dream or if she really had heard the tapping on the door of her little shack. Sarah struggled to bring her mind to focus. She held her breath as she strained to listen but all she could hear were heartbeats thudding in her ears. There it was again. It really was a knock on her door. Her mouth felt dry. Who would be knocking at her door in the middle of the night? Did she remember to bolt it, when she came in? Was Miss Millie alright? No; if anyone from the hotel wanted her, they'd call out and let her know who they were. The knock sounded, almost insidious.

Struggling to rise as quietly as possible, and that was no mean feat with the squeaky wires in the bed frame, Sarah made her way to the door. The koala bear that lived in the tree outside her window grunted, making her jump. With shaky legs, she avoided the board near the table that she knew, from experience, creaked loud enough to rattle the windows. Pain screamed in her foot as a splinter penetrated the sole. She clenched her teeth in an attempt to remain silent. With light fingers, she pulled aside the curtain next to the door, ever so slightly. She nearly fell backward at the sound of a man's slurred voice.

"Open up, Lady Sarah, I've come to pleasure you. I know you've been pining for me all this long while. Now I'm here. Open this door, woman, it's cold outside. Take me into your warm bed."

Sarah froze. She held a hand over her mouth to contain a threatened scream. In the moonlight, she recognized Arthur Rankine standing on her stoop. As soft as a butterfly's touch, her fingers checked the door bolt was drawn across. Curled up into a ball, she cringed in the corner of the room.

The knocking became louder, along with the voice.

"Open up, Miss High and Mighty, many women would be grateful for the opportunity I'm offering here."

Outside, the man leaned with his arms against the doorframe. He shifted his lower body in an attempt to support the wobbly legs. Just as Rankine drew his arm back with its fist balled ready to knock again, another hand took hold of his loosened collar. Rankine was pulled back and around to meet the fist of Jacko. Down Rankine went like a beast at the meatworks. As smooth as any dance step on any high-class dance floor, Jacko slipped the man over his shoulder and strode off to drop him, once more, on the hay in the stable.

Jacko then stood at the stable doorway in two minds whether to call on Sarah or not. Had she been awoken with the fool's goings-on? Was she at this very minute in fear of what was happening? He headed back to her shack and gave a solid knock on the door.

"Are you awake, Sarah? It's Jacko."

In her corner, Sarah attempted to reply but her throat would not operate. She stood shakily and made her way to the door before she could gather up enough saliva to moisten her mouth.

"Oh, Jacko, is Mister Rankine still out there?"

"Not anymore. I've shut him away in the stable, Sarah. He'll be out of it for some time. Are you alright?"

"Yes, Jacko. I'm fine."

"Well, you try to go back to sleep and if you have any more trouble with lover-boy tonight, give a yell. I'm on the spare stretcher on the verandah. I'll be able to hear you."

Sarah pulled the nightgown close about her chilled body and crept back to her bed. She reached over and secured the window near her pillow. She did not need that open on a cool night like this. It was quite some time before slumber gathered her up. The secure feeling of having Jacko not too far away was something new for her to analyse.

Mrs. Hamilton was already in the kitchen preparing the breakfasts when Sarah, rubbing at her eyes, ran in through the back doorway. Jacko was seated in front of the warm stove with his jacket pulled tight around him. His eyes and nose were red. He kept sneezing, sniffling, blowing his nose and coughing.

"Ooh, my throat is red raw," he groaned.

"Silly man, sleeping out in the cold like that," Mrs. Hamilton grumbled. "I'll have this hot lemon and garlic gargle ready for you in a moment. Men; they're like little babies."

Sarah felt aghast. Was she to blame for Jacko's affliction? If it wasn't for Rankine annoying her, Jacko would not have been sleeping out in the weather.

"Oh, Jacko, I'm so sorry." She looked across to see if Mrs. Hamilton was listening, then leant in closer. "Has he gone?" She whispered as she rolled her eyes.

Jacko nodded as he winked. "Don't bother yourself, lass. Just a bit of the sniffles. They'll be all gone before lunchtime." A bout of coughing took hold of him once again.

Sarah threw aside her jumper and began stirring the lemon drink on the stove. Mrs. Hamilton added a generous dollop of medicinal whisky from the bottle kept at the back of the kitchen cupboard behind the plates. She poured a good measure of the heated brew into a tin pannikin before handing it to Sarah.

"Make him sip on this, Miss Sarah. It'll do him the world of good."

Jacko was not any better by lunchtime. In fact, he looked and sounded grimmer. His face was flushed. Sweat poured in rivulets down his body. The sheet and mattress below him were damp. Miss Millie visited him in his room. She flew out of there and called loudly, through the back door, for Ned.

"Throw a bridle on one of the horses and fetch Doctor Goldfinch; straightaway, Ned." She explained when he had come running to see what was amiss. "It's Jacko, he's not well; not well at all."

Both Miss Millie and Sarah stood outside the door of the room while Doctor George Goldfinch was busy inside examining Jacko.

"Miss Millie, I am so sorry. This is all my fault. I must have misled Mister Rankine somehow and now he has caused such trouble. I'll never forgive myself if anything happens to Jacko."

"Hush, child. There is only one person responsible for all the hullabaloo and that is Mister Rankine himself. I'll have a few words to say when I see him next. Don't you go blaming yourself; do you hear me? Nothing is going to happen to my boy. He's as strong as an ox. Gosh, I remember when he was a nipper, he had a dose of whooping cough. He was up and about in no time."

At that point, the doctor came outside and pulled the door shut behind him.

"How is he, Doctor George?" Both Millie and Sarah spoke together.

George took both ladies by their elbows and directed them into the kitchen, next door.

"Now, if you make me a cup of tea, I'll tell you all." He said with a gentle smile.

Both women bustled about in the well-practised routine of tea making. Millie asked George if he would prefer to drink his in the dining room but he chose the cosy kitchen.

"Jacko seems to have a touch of influenza. His chest is rather moist. I have left some medicine there for him to take four times a day. I'll send Thomas around shortly with a poultice. You'll only need to heat it up on the stove. Thomas will apply it when he arrives. Change the bed-linen regularly. Try not to leave him lying in a wet bed and keep him out of air draughts. He'll need plenty to drink. You'll find he'll bounce back in time. Can you manage that Miss Millie or would you like him to go to the hospital?"

"Never! You'll never need to put my Jacko in hospital. We'll care for him right here, won't we Sarah?" Millie looked over at Sarah standing by the stove. The younger woman nodded her pale face.

The women stood at the door while Doctor George mounted his horse.

"Thanks again for coming so promptly, Doctor George. Give our regards to Abigail and the others, and a kiss for little Henry." Millie called.

"Will do that. Bye now, both of you." He called as he turned the horse's head towards the back gate of the hotel.

Jacko sat on the chair by the bed while Millie and Sarah stripped the damp linen. His hands trembled so much that the drink of lemon water threatened to spill over. Sarah placed it on the small cupboard.

"I'll help you with that when we've finished."

Once the clean sheets were in place, Millie turned to the man she regarded as her son and gave a wicked grin.

"Now lad, it's time we stripped those strides off you and replaced them with some clean ones."

Jacko's mouth dropped open. His eyebrows rose to his hairline. The flush of his fever turned to a bright red of embarrassment.

"Not likely, Miss Millie. I'll change my own pants, thanks."

Standing on the other side of the bed, Sarah's face flushed as red as Jacko's. She scrambled to the door.

"Call me when you have changed and I'll come back and help you with the drink."

Millie was unfazed. Chuckling she dug around in the drawers looking for clean pyjama pants. She held up two pair of striped cotton items of clothing that may have been pyjama pants at one time but now, were candidates as floor-polish rags.

"Is this all that you have here, Jacko?" She did not wait for a reply. "I'll send Ned over to Mrs. Coates to have three pairs made up urgently. In the meantime, you'll have to wear the better one of these two, I guess."

"When you go out the room, I'll change."

"No nonsense now Jacko, you're so feeble you'll fall over and break your fool neck. Throw this old sheet over yourself and we'll do it all under cover."

Millie tried very hard not to grin. Jacko wore a frown she had not seen on his face since the time she took him in off the streets of Sydney and demanded he have a tub bath. That must have been all of twenty-something years ago.

"Come on dear, I won't bite you."

By the time the two women had assisted his return to the bed and poured a cup of the drink down his throat, Jacko was exhausted. He coughed repeatedly. Millie tore off one leg of the old trousers and told him to use that as a snot rag. She took the remains of those trousers with her to send with Ned as a pattern for Mrs. Coates.

As they walked out of the room, Millie took Sarah's hand.

"Sarah, I want you to rest as much as you can today. Tonight, you and I will need to keep a close eye on Jacko. I'll ask Mrs. Hamilton if her daughter can come in and help in the kitchen."

THE *NORTHERN ORCHID*

Josh and Gus worked in the chartroom plotting a course between Mackay and their next destination, Bowen. Everybody was giving Captain Sloan a wide berth this evening. In the late afternoon, the weather had begun to deteriorate and no barge was willing to attempt a transfer of cargo waiting in the hold of the *Northern Orchid* for delivery to Mackay. Several large crates awaited collection. At least the passengers had been transported from Flat Top Island to the fledgling town. Re-ensconced in the steerage dormitory were the three passengers, Stretch, Dave and Reg, who were now planning to travel on to Bowen. Gus looked up from his calculations that covered a whole page of his book.

"Hopefully the weather tomorrow will be fine again and we can unload and be on our way."

Josh put down his pencil and rubbed his red eyes.

"There's cargo to be loaded also, don't forget. We may be here another night yet."

Captain Sloan's high spirits were restored as the *Northern Orchid* with sails unfurled gathered up the winds and put them to work. The delay of one day, due to Sunday's weather, was forgotten after yesterday proved to be a perfect day for loading and unloading cargo. Now they must manoeuvrer their way, through the Cumberland Islands and reefs, north.

"Did you see the map-plotting the Dougall boys completed, Cap'n?" Like a ball of flames on his head, MacGregor's hair tossed about in the wind. He stood at the wheel-house doorway holding his cap in the hand by his side. With a curse, he jumped back swiping at a grey sludge stripe dripping down his cheek. "Blasted seagulls."

Sloan roared with laughter before settling to answer Mac's question.

"Yes, I looked at their work last night before I turned in; not bad really. They missed a couple of points but I'll discuss that with them today." With one hand firmly on the helm, he reached over and took a sip from the pannikin on the bench. "Who have you got on watch tonight, Mac?"

"Gus and Andrews are on the first watch from eight until twelve. Josh and Rollins will come on then for the middle watch with you."

"That sounds like it should go smoothly. All going well, we'll be only about six or seven hours out from Bowen when we anchor up at dark today."

Gus fell into his hammock after waking his brother who was to take over the watch. He did not need any rocking to sleep. Even the unseasonal heat failed to keep him awake. This same heat had driven several of the crew out of the quarters to sleep on the open deck. His soft snores rose into the stale air before the single bell indicating the first half an hour into the middle watch had rung.

The rhythmic stroke of the brown fingers back and forth across Gus's forehead did not register in the lad's conscious thought for some long moments. The perception of his sub-conscious was the soft fingers of his mother soothing his brow as she settled her younger son to sleep. Peace and bliss overwhelmed him until he drifted upwards from the depths of his sleep enough to realize his mother was dead this past year. Through eyes parted ever so slightly he knew the moon had passed over the yardarm. The moonbeam, shining through the two portholes, produced a glow within the crew's quarters. His conscious thoughts now raced in upon him. He was a young man working on a ship, not a small boy sleeping in his own cot. He froze. The little he could see of the hand on his forehead fired alarm bells inside his skull. One name flashed across his brain; Bony. The strange man who lived in the shadow of the bullyboy of the ship, Sykes. The man who never spoke a word but stared right through a person. The man built like a tugboat. The man who now purred like a cat. Gus had difficulty drawing air into his tight chest.

When these things fully registered, Gus threw himself out of the hammock landing on the opposite side from where the big man stood. A muscled arm reached across the swinging hammock. The thick fingers grabbed the webbed bedding and tore it from the cleats in the supporting strut. Gus jumped back. He felt the wind of the falling hand flash past his face. The man's feet slapped on the timber deck as he moved around one of the struts. A ferocious growl rumbled deep within his belly. The sound sent Gus searching for a retreat. Three rows of the struts, each reaching from the under beams of the upper deck to the floor of the lower deck, held metal cleats from which the hammocks of the crew swung in two rows down the length of the quarters.

The few crewmen left within the quarters awoke, grumbling about the noise. Once they realized what was happening, their feet thudded on the floorboards like the beat of a sharp drum roll. The dim light in the room revealed an exodus led by a terrified Andrews. Gus swung around the next strut, putting another hammock between himself and Bony. This bed too went the way of the first. Gus dodged in and out of the struts. He kicked and threw seabags and any other items he found towards his pursuer. Bony batted them away like he might turn aside irritating mosquitoes. Size slowed down the older man. Gus knew that it was imperative he kept moving and moving fast. If just once, he came within reach of those arms it was going to be the end of him. This man could snap his neck like one might break a chip of wood for the fireplace. He knew if those arms reached around his chest, his rib cage would splinter into a thousand shards of bone.

Josh arrived on the run. Andrews followed close behind but held back as Josh rushed through the doorway. From the shadows, Sykes stepped out in front of the older brother.

"I think not, boyo. Let Bony have his fun. He likes the young ones. He won't want you."

Josh spun to face the new danger. He was ready to close in and use his fists but the flash of moonlight on the long knife held in Sykes' hand pulled him up short. He moved to the left, then to the right, searching for an opening. Sykes swung the knife between either hand with a practised skill. Hate seared across the space between the opponents' eyes. Josh feinted to the left but danced back sharply as the knife swung past his face. He tried again from the right. The man seemed confident on both fronts.

Josh risked a glance in the direction of Gus and Bony. His brother hung from his throat with his feet twelve inches above the floor. Gus's fingers clawed ineffectually at the thick hands of his attacker. Even in the pale moonlight, the changes could be seen as the young face darkened and the veins in his forehead and temple stood out like thick ropes.

Josh swung his eyes back to his own opponent. Sykes' eyes narrowed; an attack was imminent. The knife arm lifted high before beginning its descent. Josh took evasive action just as another long arm reached from behind Sykes and held the attacker's knife-arm in a vice-like grip. A second arm dragged Sykes' other hand up his back to way past the shoulder. Sykes squealed. The knife flew out of the nerveless fingers onto the floor.

"Go, Josh, look after your brother." Josh did not need a second telling from Evans.

Bony was so engrossed in his own activity that he had not noticed the squeal of pain from Sykes. Josh approached Bony from behind. From there he could see just how mottled his brother's colour had become. Only the whites of Gus's eyes showed. The clawing hands had fallen to hang like limp rags at his sides. Josh used every ounce of his strength to place a left and right fist into each on the big man's kidneys. They went unnoticed. Josh did not waste any time thinking of the rights or wrongs of things when he stumbled over a torn-out strut on the floor. He grabbed it up in both hands. He swung it as high and as hard as he could. It struck the back of the giant's head. Blood and bone spurted in all directions splattering Josh before flowing down the muscled back of the man. The cleat in the strut of timber cleaved the skull open. For what seemed a lifetime, Bony's body remained standing upright before it crumpled to the floor as a forest tree may drop after it is felled. Josh slipped past the falling body to catch his brother and drag him to safety.

Captain Sloan arrived to find his bosun holding a screaming Sykes in a bear hug. The captive's feet kicked out in all directions. Across the room, under the porthole, Bony lay spreadeagled on the floor. His head rested in an ever-increasing pool of blood. Near the giant, Josh Dougall knelt at his brother's side. His hands touched the unmoving chest lightly. The ribcage remained at rest. The boy's tongue sagged from a slack mouth. Blood-stained spittle dripped onto the floor. Josh's words were heard by all the crew frozen at the doorway.

"Come on, Gus. Don't you dare die. Breathe, damn you."

Josh shook his brother's shoulders. The limp head nodded with each shake. He reached his arms under Gus's upper body. The head now rolled to the side. Josh hugged his brother. He slapped the unresponsive face. The haemorrhaging within the corneas stood out before the eyes rolled back.

"Wake up, Gus. Come on, fella, wake up."

He lay his brother flat. Tears ran down his cheeks. As the body rested on the timber deck, a rasping breath whistled through the damaged airway. The inspiration was interrupted by a fit of coughing. A thin spray of blood covered Josh's already bloodied body. Again, a raucous breath struggled to the surface. Again, the coughing followed it.

"Come on, Gus. Wake up. Keep trying, brother. Sarah'll kill me if anything happens to you."

"Evans, clap that man in irons and lock him in the brig." Captain Sloan's order broke the deathly silence. His finger pointed directly at Sykes. This set the man off on another kicking, biting and screaming struggle that even the well-muscled Evans was at his limit to control. The captain then spun around to cast his eyes over the group of men standing at the doorway straining to see what was going on.

"Rollins, go and do another watch-round. Make sure all is well with the remainder of the ship. You might like to wake Mister Winston and ask him to take charge of the watch." Just at that moment, Mac appeared with China on his heels. "Mac, can we have someone to help us carry the boy up to The Cupboard. Put him in there where I can keep an eye on him. Adams and Tanner can help me to wrap Bony's body and clean up this mess." Captain Sloan turned to China. "Can we have breakfast for the officers, in the chartroom, in an hour China; that will include Evans. We'll need to discuss these events."

"Can we 'elp with anything?" Stretch, Dave and Reg, the only passengers on board at the moment, rubbed their tired eyes.

Mac did not waste time looking any further for his extra hands.

"Yes, if you don't mind. Can you help us carry Gus to the top deck?" He turned to Bandy at his side. "Go fetch a sail that we can use to lay the boy on," Mac spoke again to the three volunteers. "By the way, I'll speak to the captain and suggest he cancel your fare in return for your filling in as crew, as far as Bowen at least, if you're interested."

Three heads nodded in unison.

The dawn struggled as a bleary-eyed William Sloan entered the small room. He felt filthy after handling the body of Bony. It was not just the volume of blood spread over the floor of the crew's quarters but the depravity of the man. An immediate wash with a scrub brush tempted him but first, he wanted to see how young Gus was. The lad lay stretched out on the store of new canvas. Through the window above his feet, dark clouds were to be seen filling the sky. Josh lay on the floor beside Gus with his head resting near his brother's knee. When the door scraped on the floor he did not stir. It was Gus, whose body jerked. Swelling and mottled black bruises engulfed his face and neck.

"Good morning, boy. I doubt you'll be able to talk for several days yet."

The door scratched at the floor once more as China entered the room. In his hand, he held a basket containing several jars. The Chinaman threw his long pigtail over his shoulder to hang down his back as he knelt beside Gus's head. Light fingers barely touched the skin as he examined the damage to the boy's body; particularly the face and neck. From one jar, he removed strips of cloth thick with grey sludge. The foul smell sent Captain Sloan back a step. He may have chosen to go further but the room was too small. Even Josh's nostrils twitched as he awoke with a start.

"What's going on?" His voice croaked.

Captain Sloan placed a steadying hand on Josh's shoulder.

"It's alright lad, China is trying to reduce the bruising and swelling in your brother's neck. We don't want the airway to be cut off."

While the captain explained, China bound the pasted linen around the bruised neck and chest. He then wiped his hands on the corner of his robe. Next to be retrieved from the basket was another jar with a dark green liquid mixture.

"Drink, Gus, drink. This not nice but will fix inside your throat." Gently, China slid one arm under Gus's shoulders, raising the boy's head enough so he could swallow.

Even through the swelling of his face, the boy's nostrils twisted in distaste.

"Drink, boy." China continued his firm hold.

Gus was sleeping before the captain and China made their way out of the room. Captain Sloan poked his head back through the doorway to give Josh instructions.

"You stay with your brother, Josh. Someone will bring you breakfast. Don't worry about the ship, we have three new sailors to help out today. And if there's any change for the worse, you give me a call immediately, right."

Josh nodded his head. He could not speak.

William Sloan, Ewan MacGregor, Mister Winston and Evans spoke around mouthfuls of oatmeal, egg and steaming tea.

"I don't know if you've had a chance to notice, Cap'n but bad weather is building up again; quite fast." Mister Winston put his pannikin down on the table.

"Yes, Guthrie, I felt it when we delivered Bony's body to the stern recess behind the hold. The deck bounced around like a whore in a brothel."

"So, what's the plan today? It will be no picnic trying to run the ship, in a storm, with four good crew down and only three landsmen to help," Mac gave a rueful smile when he spoke.

"You're right, Mac, it would be foolhardy to shift the *Northern Orchid* in the face of a possible storm with such a skeleton crew." He looked over at the bosun, who sat with egg on his chin. "Evans, drop the second bow anchor along with the stern anchor. Set a man in the crow's nest at all times unless it becomes too unsafe to do so. Have the sea anchor available; in case it's needed." After draining his tea, Sloan spoke again. "If the bad weather hangs about, it could be days before we can make our way on to Bowen. We'll need to have a sea burial for Bony's body first thing this morning. I don't want a putrefying body in our hold, Mac. Line the men up for a short funeral service at two bells into the forenoon watch. Today will be spent gathering statements from all the crew who were witnesses. The judge at Bowen will want to see those. Guthrie, can you help with that too?"

Guthrie Winston nodded his head in acknowledgment of his instructions as he gathered up the breakfast dishes and stacked them on the tray.

"I didn't realize that Bowen was now a District Court area supporting a judge," He commented.

It was the captain's turn to nod his head.

"Yes, Guthrie. The Judge's been there for a couple of years now."

"Do you want me to tell China about the change in travel plans. He may need to review his supplies."

"Thanks, Guthrie, no. I'll pop down and see him myself. I'll need to ask him if there's anything further he can do for young Gus."

Light precipitation fell from the grey skies as the crew gathered on the upper deck. Despite the extra anchors utilized, the *Northern Orchid* tossed about on the choppy sea. The white navy uniforms of Captain Sloan and the ship's mate stood in startling contrast to the dark suit worn by Mister Winston who stood a little behind them and to the side. Wrinkles in the material along with the musty odour that was snapped up on the strengthening breeze suggested a considerable period of storage.

The body of Bony, in its cocoon of canvas, rested on two wide planks bolted together on the underside. The feet-end was balanced on the rail on the starboard side of the ship while the other end, beneath the deceased's head, was supported by Evans and Bandy on one side and Rollins and Tanner on the other.

The pages of the bible in Captain Sloan's hand ruffled in the breeze despite his attempt to secure them with his rough fingers. He scanned the group of crew members lined up near the main mast. At least the bosun had managed to convince them to wear trousers and shirts for the event. Several even wore canvas shoes. He was surprised to notice the three passengers also present.

Since Bony's death in the early hours of this morning, Sloan had struggled to choose words of respect for the chap. Below, lay an innocent young man whose prognosis still teetered in the balance while beside him another innocent young man had blood on his hands defending his brother. A distorted sense of humour crept up on his thoughts; here he was, going to saturate this body in time for the devil to make cinders of his soul. Mentally he shook himself. It was not his place to judge. The voice of Reverend Prendergast, from long ago, roared in his ears, delivering instructions from the pulpit. 'It is not for us mere humans to judge a man's soul. That is for God alone.' He, again, felt the clip of his father's hand under his ear as he shared a grin with his brothers. Regrets drifted into his mind further distracting his concentration. Should he have got rid of Bony and Sykes long ago? On a social level, they had always been trouble. Yet their work as sailors on the ship could not be faulted.

Mac spoke twice before he caught the captain's attention.

"Ready when you are, Cap'n"

As one side of his brain delivered the standard burial-at-sea service, another part of William Sloan's brain catalogued the number of times he had performed this service; too many. His deep, modulated voice finished with the usual ending.

"Unto Almighty God we commend the soul of this departed sailor and we commit his body to the deep. Through our Lord Jesus Christ; amen."

The four sailors began lifting the one end of the twin planks holding the body. Captain Sloan began to worry. What if the old sail he had chosen was not strong enough to hold such a large body plus the added weights of the old cannon balls placed there to ensure it went straight to the bottom of the ocean. What if the coarse stitches he had used to sew the joins did not hold and the body and cannon balls disappeared leaving the sail behind? On the planks, the body made no indication it planned on leaving the ship. Evans and Rollins stepped up onto the blocks placed near their feet allowing them to raise the planks higher. With a dull sucking sound, gravity and height overcame the dead weight and the body stuttered its way along and off the end of the plank. To Sloan's relief, it remained contained inside the packaging. A brief silence, then a loud splash. The body landed into a restless sea that threatened to return the offering. Rain burst from the heavy clouds above and the swell of the waters beneath the ship rose higher.

Above the thrumming of the rain on the deck and slap of waves on the hull, a howl rose into the air. All heads turned, listening. Still chained in the brig, Sykes set up a keening for his friend.

Sarah's heart stopped. Had something happened in the night? Jacko was gone. His bed was stripped of linen. The window was open and the curtains pulled aside.

"Oh, no." She groaned. Tears pressed against her eyelids. She jumped as a voice spoke near her shoulder.

"Sarah dear, you're not going to believe this." Millie took her hand and led Sarah out to the front of the hotel where Jacko sat on the stairs savouring the warmth of the dawn.

Sarah's smile shamed the morning sun. Her hands went to her stomach where she felt a strange trembling in her belly; a bit like a flock of miniature birds fluttering around inside. Hopefully, she was not coming down with anything. That would be the last straw.

"What are you doing out here? Are you trying to catch another dose of influenza?"

Jacko grinned his boyish smile.

"Good morning, Miss Sarah." His grin widened even further. "I'm certainly not trying to attract another dose of influenza. I've had enough of women bossing me about."

Millie rolled her eyes. Sarah struggled to hide the tears of relief. Jacko reached up and took her hand gently in his own.

"Are you telling me you care for me; maybe just a little bit?"

Sarah's initial reaction was to pull her hand away. She looked up into the deep dark eyes and fought that urge. She patted the large hand and wondered if it wasn't her own trembling, she was soothing.

"Now Jacko, we'll have no nonsense. It's time we got you inside. The breeze will be getting up shortly."

When Jacko stood up, his knees felt weak. He did not say a word but he did enjoy the one small hand in his own and the other under his elbow, leading him back to the room. He drew the freshness of her skin into his lungs.

THE *NORTHERN ORCHID*

The mango tree above him swayed in a wind that tossed the branches viciously. What was he doing here? Blackness swept over him once more as an ocean wave sweeps over the shoreline sucking up all in its path before dragging it back into the hungry depths.

He felt his body moving back and forth. The black fog retreated a shade. Pain rushed into the vacuum it left, seeping into every muscle. There was nothing that did not ache. What was he doing here? Why did his body hurt so much? Where was here? Is that the smell of the sea? The unending questions were tiring. He welcomed the arrival of the blackness when it oozed once more into his brain. A voice called to him but he did not have the energy to climb back up to it.

A continuous swishing sound held his attention. The black curtain slowly opened. Who was that groaning? A bushfire of pain rolled in. His arms and legs burnt with the aching of it. Where was he? Who was he? Pain held his throat tight. Each breath was a struggle of concentration. Had he ever felt so dry? Something lifted his shoulders. The cool fluid on his lips was received with a gratitude of short duration. A foul smell drifted into his nostrils. He clamped his lips; or thought he did. The smell and fluid remained at his mouth. He tried to open his eyes but nothing visible showed itself. A firm hand touched his shoulder. A voice that was vaguely familiar drifted into his mind.

"Drink, young Gus. You must drink."

Gus; am I Gus? He was well past resisting the persistent pressure of the sips of fluid forced into his mouth. Again, the voice spoke.

"Whatever you do, Josh, hold his shoulders up. Only give sips of drink each time. With the swelling in his throat, it could just as easily flow into the lungs."

Whose throat's swollen? That name, Josh; that sounds familiar. Was that his name? Oh, not too fast, it hurts so much to cough like this. Let me sleep.

The blackness dissipated slowly. His companion, pain, remained the fire within. A rocking motion, like that of a boat, filtered into his consciousness. There was only the creaking of timbers and splashing of waves to be heard. No, he heard another sound. Someone was snoring. Fear stirred his heart beats to a quick tattoo when the snoring turned to snorts and grunts. What was it? Why was he unable to see? Then a voice spoke close by.

"Gus, Gus, are you awake, brother? You surely gave us a fright. I thought you was going to die."

Brother? Josh, brother Josh. Memories burst into his head. Fearful memories. Running, fighting, running, pain, a band of steel around his throat. A sinking, hopeless feeling in his guts.

"Gus, can you hear me? I know you can't talk, just yet. Can you wriggle your fingers at all? You probably won't be able to open your eyes for a couple of days. Your whole face, neck and arms are black and blue with bruises. They're all swollen up to twice the normal size."

Swollen bruises. Did he look like Mister Campbell, the blacksmith, after the horse kicked him that day? He had never seen so many shades of blue, black, red and yellow. Mister Campbell displayed the bruises to the boys every afternoon they went to the smithy to help out. He reminded them never to take an animal too lightly. Even the quietest ones can give you something to remember them by. As Gus drifted down again into welcome pain-free oblivion, the name, Bony, was the last thing that his mind grabbed a hold of.

Voices again dragged him back to the surface. He recognized that of his brother, Josh. The other voice belonged to someone he knew; he should know; who was it? Like a picture inside his head, the image of Captain Sloan standing on the deck of the *Northern Orchid* presented itself.

"Josh, is there any change with your brother today?"

"I think he's a little better this morning, Cap'n. He drinks his tonic better and listen to his breathing. He's not straining near so much. I can't tell if he can open his eyes or not, they are still too swollen but I think his hands moved when I rubbed the ointment into them."

"That sounds like good news, Josh. I'll be going ashore this morning to talk to the District Court Judge in Bowen. There should be little for you to worry about as there were witnesses to the attack and to your defence of your brother. You remain with Gus here and let Mister MacGregor know if there's any change."

"Yes, Cap'n."

Gus Dougall; his name returned to his mind like an errant schoolboy. The attack by Bony returned in all its harsh reality. He tried to force his eyes open but still, the lids could not be parted. How long had he been lying here? He remembered Bony in the crew's quarters chasing him. When was that? Was it last night? Was it a week ago? In his mind's eye, the enormous hands reached out for him, again. Did he really see Sykes standing in the corner, watching? It had been the reflection of moonlight on the end of a knife in Sykes' hand that caught his eye, briefly. That was when he heard his brother's yell. He wanted to scream to warn him of the knife but he could not make a noise with the large hands tight about his neck. He saw the flash of the knife swinging downwards. Was his brother dead? No, of course not. He was just talking to the captain.

His brother is safe. He welcomed the envelope of sleep.

The rhythmic creak of the oarlocks and the light splash of the oars in the water relaxed Captain Sloan as he went through, in his head, all that he wished to discuss with the Judge and the police today. Within the oilskin wrappings in the satchel over his shoulder he carried all the written and signed statements from the relevant crew members on events of the morning, two days previously. He knew that he'd been lucky the storm had only delayed the *Northern Orchid* for twenty-four hours. Yesterday had been a smooth trip into Port Dennison Harbour. He planned to leave the ship anchored in the lee of Stone Island until they were ready to load and unload cargo. When that time arrived, he'd take her into the harbour jetty. He feared this legal business might drag out. A frown rippled his forehead. Sykes still remained locked in the brig. The fellow could stay there until the police worked out what they wanted to do with him. At least the man had stopped that infernal wailing. This morning, Evans reported that Sykes had not touched his food since the burial of his friend Bony. No doubt when he was hungry enough, he would eat. The frown softened at the thought of Gus Dougall's improved condition. At least he appeared to be on the mend even though he was unable to open his eyes when spoken to. The boy was still unable to talk. Sloan's face split in a grin as he recalled Mac's comment yesterday. Mac said that the brew China poured down the boy's throat would take anyone's speech away as well as their breath. At this stage, the boy had no muscle power in his arms but China seemed confident that would be temporary only. Three times a day, Josh rubbed a brown coloured greasy mixture, prepared by China, into the muscles of his brother's arms and legs. The captain scratched his head at the thought of what might be in some of China's mixtures but he could not deny the man was a great healer.

"You men stay within sight of the boat," Captain Sloan told his oarsmen, Tanner and Adams as they glided smoothly up onto the sands. He turned to the three landsmen who had assisted as crewmen these past two days. "If you fellows decide you want to continue as sailors make sure you meet us here later today. Give the ship a yell if this boat is not here. If you want information on employment on the land hereabouts, the agent is up that street on the left." He waved his hand in the general direction of the main street.

William Sloan drew himself up tall, hitched the satchel further onto his shoulder and strode off in the direction of the courthouse. He expected the judge to be busy and that an appointment would need to be made. At least he could make his call on the harbourmaster while waiting.

It eventuated that the judge was available. The man greeted him profusely at the door to his office. He wore a white shirt and dark pants but no coat or tie. The top buttons of his shirt were undone. Perspiration glistened on his forehead and stained the underarms of the shirt.

"William Sloan, as I live and breathe. It's an age since we saw you up this way. I thought you must have changed the name of your canoe to the *Southern Orchid* or some such thing." The judge gave the captain's hand a vigorous shake.

"Good to see you again, Richard. I expected you'd be working at this hour of the morning. What; don't tell me you've tamed this town?" Sloan looked about him before going on, "And they still have you in this slab hut, I see."

Richard Masterson burst out laughing. A cheerful sound that echoed through the gum trees standing tall behind the slab hut courthouse with its shingle roof. His rotund stomach shook with the effort. Bright coloured birds erupted from the branches in a burst of noise before settling.

"Just because I'm not sitting with a whip in my hand does not mean I'm not busy. There's a mountain of paperwork that keeps glaring at me every day. Since the telegraph arrived in Bowen, I find it can be a curse as much as a blessing. Telegrams from Brisbane bring more work to my desk. It's alright for you sailing around on a continual sea holiday." Once more the belly-laugh and the squawking birds. "Now, it's time for a break. I'll just ask my housekeeper to bring us morning tea. I'd add something a little stronger but that would be the end of the day's work for me. What about you? Can I offer you a wee dram?"

Sloan smiled. "No thanks, Richard. There'd be two of us sitting out here getting nothing done. This verandah is new. When did that happen?"

"I did it myself. It's the only bit of the place that doesn't leak and there is always a breeze out here. It's stifling in the office. Go on, you make yourself comfortable. I'll only be a few minutes."

The morning tea extended to a light lunch as Captain Sloan and the judge discussed the recent events on board the *Northern Orchid*. Subjects covered were the witness statements provided, the confinement of Sykes, the burial of Bony, the medical condition of Gus Dougall and the legal position of his brother Josh.

"It seems straight forward to me, William. This Josh saved the life of a victim of an assault. The fact that he killed the assaulter in the process does not make him a murderer. It seems a simple case of self-defence. The fact that the co-conspirator of the assaulter tried to do serious harm to Josh when he was attempting to save the assaulted boy clearly convicts him."

William Sloan relaxed as a long-held breath eased out of his nostrils.

"Thanks, Richard. That is a load off my mind. Now, as you can imagine, I don't want to be held up for months waiting for all the legal processes. What will it all entail?"

Richard Masterson explained that a hearing could be held before him on the very next day.

"There's nothing of great importance on the calendar that cannot wait a day or two. I will come out to the ship with the police officers this afternoon. They'll need to bring the fellow, Sykes, here to the jail. I'd like to talk to the two boys and your Mister Evans the bosun today; to form an impression of these people. Also, I presume, from what you say, that the victim will be unable to attend the court."

"Yes, that's right. Gus will not be up and about for some time, it seems. It could be a week or more before he can speak again. I thought I might get the town doctor to come out with me today to review the lad's medical condition. Mind you, I think I have the best physician on board as it is, but sadly he has no medical degree."

The judge's housekeeper wasted little time loading her tray with the mid-day meal dishes. She left the makings of a fresh pot of tea and crockery behind as she waddled off to the house next door.

"His evidence will be required tomorrow, anyway. Once that is all over if there are no complications, I'll expedite my judgement. I foresee no problem. After that, you will be free to get on about your business."

He then reached over and filled the two teacups and added ample sugar and fresh milk before going on.

"You seem to have an attachment to the Dougall boys. Are they family?"

The captain leaned back and thought for some time.

"In a sense, they are, I guess." He then went on to tell the tale of how their father, Jimmy, had died saving his and Ewan MacGregor's lives. William told of his own involvement in the boys' education since that time and the immense satisfaction he experienced each day watching them succeed in their endeavours.

SEVENTEEN

THE *NORTHERN ORCHID*

Voices, many loud voices, dragged him up from the abyss. Who were they? How long had he slept? He tried to filter the voices. Occasionally the captain spoke in short sentences as if answering questions. An unfamiliar deep voice droned on for some time. Josh answered several questions put to him. Gus recognized the nervousness in his brother's speech, like when they'd been in trouble with their father. Strange hands began touching him; his face, his neck, poking fingers into his mouth and pulling at his eyes. A knife of pain struck as the lids were pulled apart allowing the light to enter. A softer voice accompanied the pain-stirring fingers. It asked him if he was awake. He could not answer, even if he had wanted to.

"From the little I can see, there appears to have been quite a bit of damage inside the mouth and throat. The lacerations are healing nicely. There are considerable ruptured blood vessels in the corneas of both eyes. The boy does not appear to be feverish. I don't think bleeding would benefit him." There was a pause for a moment, then, "You say his hands and feet are starting to move again?"

It was Josh's voice that answered.

"Yes, Doctor. Gus has improved a lot, since this morning, even."

"Well, Richard, I think you can be assured this boy has been the victim of a serious assault that, if not for the Grace of God, and his brother, would have surely killed him."

This time the deep voice reverberated on Gus's eardrums.

"So, Josh, it looks like you have risked your own life to save that of your brother. This should be a simple case of assault and defence. Captain Sloan will bring you to the courthouse tomorrow morning for a preliminary hearing. There is no reason that I can see why you should not be returned to the ship before the evening."

"Thank you, Sir."

Josh's guts were in turmoil. The sight of breakfast on the tray that Andrews delivered did little to help. He pushed the tray with the oatmeal, damper and jam that China had prepared to the side of the room against the wall. He took up the jar of grease and began massaging Gus's limbs once more. Every time he touched the fingers they curled around his own hand. He took courage from the touch even though no words were forthcoming. Josh did think that his brother's eyelids were not so blown-up this morning. He jumped at the voice of China from the doorway.

"You eat that food, funny man. You have a big day ahead of you. What, you think I nothing better to do than cook food you throw out. Eat. How is Gus today?"

Josh pulled the tray back towards himself and prepared to make an attempt to please China.

"He is definitely improving, thanks to you, China. I can never repay what you have done for him."

"Phish. Who else I got to get the sand for cat shit and feed my chooks without dropping the eggs? I need the boy back on his feet."

China dug into one of the many big pockets tucked away in his loose clothing. He drew out an almost-transparent orange coloured stone. The perfectly smooth surface told of handling by countless fingers.

"Josh, you put this in safe place close to you. It has much good luck. You not be charged for murder, you see. I set a place at the table for tonight's meal." He folded the stone into Josh's hand.

Josh bit his lip. Muscles contracted and bulged in his jaw as he struggled to keep his face impassive.

"Thank you, China, thank you very much."

"Now, you not waste that food." China fired as he headed off down the corridor.

THE MARINER'S REST

"Miss Millie, Miss Millie." Sarah's skirts swirled around her legs as she ran up the front steps of the hotel. Gone was all decorum and any concern for loud voices around the hotel precinct by staff. Her feet clattered across the front foyer and up the staircase. She hammered on the front door of Miss Millie's apartment.

"Miss Millie, Miss Millie, are you there?"

The door was flung open from within and Millie stood with a frown on her face.

"Sarah, whatever's the matter? Why are you screaming around the place like that? Have you taken leave of your senses? This had better be important. I was just taking a tub."

Millie stood with water dripping from the tendrils of hair framing her face, A gown had been thrown around her body.

Sarah waved two envelopes in front of Millie's face.

"Is this important enough? The letter carrier has just delivered a letter to each of us from the *Northern Orchid*." Her eyes sparkled. A smile lit up her face.

Millie's face reflected Sarah's excitement.

"Oh, which is mine? Thank you, thank you." She made to grab the envelopes but Sarah flicked them back and held them close to her chest.

"Now Miss Millie, I don't think you should be getting so excited. Perhaps you had best finish your tub before I give you the letter." Sarah laughed as she skipped back a few steps.

They were laughing like little children as they wrestled for the epistles. When Millie eventually rescued her mail, she jumped inside her room and slammed the door.

"And don't disturb me for two hours, at least." The heavy timber door muffled her laughing voice.

Sarah's laughter bounced down the staircase as she descended in a more sedate manner to that which she had made the climb. Light hands crushed the envelope from her brothers close to her heart as she made her way over to her small shack. With great care, she opened the letter. This was the very first letter that she had received from her brothers. Her chair scraped on the floor as she moved it closer to the window to access the light. She flattened the paper out carefully on her lap. Two individual styles of penmanship were immediately obvious to her discerning eye. The first and briefest section had been written in Josh's scrawl. The rounded and more tidy work was in Gus's hand and contained more information. Hunger for news of them both sparkled in her blue eyes.

To our dear sister,

Here we are on the Northern Orchid heading towards Rockhampton. Tonight Captain Sloan plans to anchor near Masthead Reef and tomorrow we should make it to the mouth of the Fitzroy River on which Rockhampton is built. On board at the moment are two cows and a calf and a bull going to Rockhampton. That was pretty exciting getting them on board. Now we will have to get them off again. We have had a good trip and except for a couple of squalls it has been ideal weather. The Captain and Mister MacGregor the Mate have been very helpful and always ready to teach us stuff. The other officers are the engineer Mister Winston and Evans the bosun. The crew are good chaps except for a couple that we avoid as much as we can. Hope you are well. Say hello to Miss Millie, Jacko and Ned for me. And don't forget Mrs. Hamilton or she'll never make me anymore of her fruitcakes. Hope you are well. Your brother Josh.

At this point, the penmanship changed. Sarah smiled.

Sarah. It's good of the captain to get our letters delivered for us in Rockhampton. He is going to ask a friend of his on another ship going south to pass it on. It has been a great adventure and I really enjoy working in the engine room with Mister Winston. The engine is a Maudslay Oscillating Steam Engine with a screw propeller. I could go into more detail of its power and parts and things but I don't think you would be interested. The older crew members say it has made things easier for them when they are making their way into and out of a harbour. Also for manoeuvring within the harbours. The captain likes it that he does not have to hang about for the wind. He does prefer to use the sails when out at sea though. The cook is a Chinaman called China. Evans said he is the best ship's cook on the east coast. He (China) does not say a lot and is sort of mysterious but I like the old fellow. Josh and I had to dig for clean sand for his cat to shit into. He keeps chooks and the officers get eggs for breakfast.

Sometimes he does a special treat for the crew with the eggs too. He uses lots of vegetables to make his meals. They are very different to what we are used to but very good. He puts some dried leaves that he calls herbs into the food. I suppose that is what the Chinese eat. Josh and I went with him to buy more vegetables and fresh herbs from his cousins in Maryborough. Did you find the map that Josh and I left on our bed for you so you can follow our journey?

We stopped at Maryborough then at the mouth of the river at Bundaberg. Bundaberg doesn't have a harbour. It is only a very new town. We did not get to see that. They sent a barge out to the ship. The cargo was then loaded from our hold onto their barge. The next stop was at Gladstone where we took the cattle on board that Josh told you about. Lucky for Josh and me they sent two stockmen with the cattle or we may have got the job of looking after them. I did not fancy that. The bull was enormous. Cleaning up the mess after them was bad enough.

I will finish now and say hello to everyone at the Mariner's Rest for me. Also, send our regards to Doctor Goldfinch and his family. I'll take this to the captain now.

Your brother Gus.

Sarah swiped at the tears running down her face. How could she feel so happy for her brothers and yet so sad? She did miss their lively chatter, even the pranks they pulled on her sometimes. An inner peace descended upon her, knowing they were contented in their jobs.

Upstairs in her apartment, Millie dabbed at the tears trickling down her cheeks. She tried to wipe some of the moisture up before the ink ran all over the page as she placed her letter back on the table. The paper was rather crinkled after being read six times. Now she let the words run by memory through her head.

My dear lady love,

As I usually do, weather permitting, I am sitting down the day before we reach Rockhampton to send off a quick note to the caretaker of my heart. I do hope this finds you in good health. Yours is the last face I see before sleep snatches away my conscious state and the first that greets me in the morning when I awake. I see the red of your hair in the sunsets and the hazel of your eyes in the colours of the morning seas. Your smile is a clear horizon. The beauty of your body is found in the stars on a clear night. The touch of your kisses can only be compared to the kiss of the winds in the unfurled sails on a clear day.

My other lady love, and I speak of the Northern Orchid, has outshone herself so far, this trip. I cannot say that I am not pleased with the new engine. I do think the engineer is not too pleased that I insist on sails once we are clear of the various rivers and ports.

The whoosh of the wind captured by the sails and the whistle of it through the rigging, along with the rattle of the pulleys combined with the sound of her timbers creaking, as she flies over the crest of the waves, is far superior to the smell of burning coal and the noise of a thumping engine through the decks.

So far this trip, things have been pretty straight forward. Your two protégées have done well. If you are talking to Daffy Harris, please pass on my compliments of a job well done.

I cannot even estimate a date for our arrival back in Brisbane. I am still not too sure if I will or will not proceed on to Townsville this trip. We have nothing in the holds for that port at this time but that could change further up the coast.

I do hope all is well at The Mariner's Rest and that you are not working too hard. God bless you, my little seagull. With all my love from your sailor.

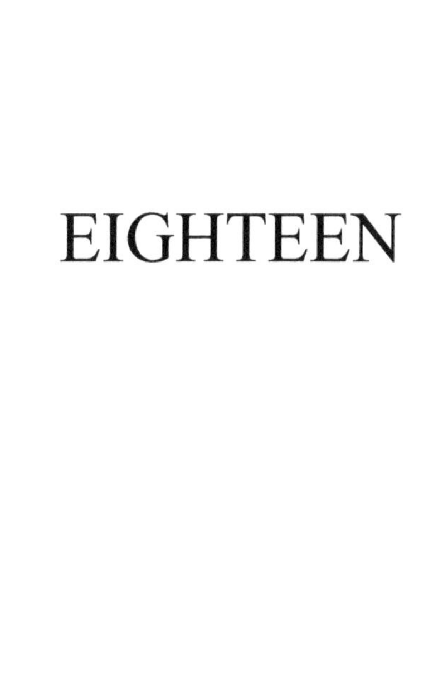

EIGHTEEN

THE *NORTHERN ORCHID*

Josh chewed at his lip as he waited. Fingers twitched where they rested on the seat. The captain and mate seemed to be taking such a long time to ascend the Jacob's-ladder from the jolly-boat. His had been the first oar brought on board and secured. Andrews, Tanner and Rollins were not in that much of a hurry either. When it was his turn to board the ship, his feet, in their canvas shoes, flew up the slats of the ladder. He swung his two legs over the bulwark in one swoop and did not stop until he reached the door of The Captain's Cupboard. He came to an abrupt halt staring uncomprehendingly at this brother who sat on the side of the makeshift bed of sails.

Gus's face was still a bloated picture of dark colours. The eyes were the same short, sharp lines on either side of his nostrils. The mouth was the twisted slit below. But Gus was sitting up. Mild swelling could still be seen to stretch the skin of his brother's feet that were placed on the floor. Hands and fingers looked like hands and fingers and not like lumps of stewed dumplings resting within his lap. On the floor beside Gus, with his back against the bulkhead, sat Mister Winston. The engineer was reading from a book; a book on engines according to the picture on the cover. The reading stopped at the sound of Josh's arrival.

"Ah, young Gus, we have company. It's your brother returned. By the look upon his face, he may have good news. Is that so, Josh?"

"Er, yes, Mister Winston. How come Gus is sitting up? Is he alright?"

"Your brother is very much alright. We've been catching up on his studies. As you can see, we've devised a communication channel." He held up his hand from which a small piece of string led to Gus's fingers. "When Gus wants more explanation of an issue, he pulls the string and we go back in our reading to clarify. He is probably due to rest now though, having been at it for half an hour. You may like to help him lie back." He removed the string from Gus's finger. Mister Winston used the bulkhead to assist his climb to the perpendicular. "I'll leave you two boys to it."

Josh stood to the side as Guthrie Winston made his exit before moving over to his brother. Gently, he took Gus's hands in his own.

"Are you sure you're alright?" His heart soared at the slight nod of the head by his brother. "This is great news. Come on then, I'll help you lift those feet and lay you back again for a bit." Josh was almost light-headed with relief as he felt Gus taking some of the weight of his legs. China had been right. Gus's legs would regain their strength. He'd been filled with fear of Gus never being able to move his hands or feet again.

"My news seems so insignificant in comparison to the news of your improved health. Will your face return to its normal ugly mug or do I have the pleasure of looking at this purple pufferfish for the rest of my life?" A weak grip held Josh's wrist as he continued. "Looks like I'm going to have to do the smiling for the both of us for a while yet." The grip tightened a fraction. "Oh, you want to hear what happened at the court-house today." Josh sat down near his brother and told of his day which had started, for him, in terror. "I could have shit my pants when the judge cleared me of any charge to be answered."

Josh collected a bowl of soup from the galley and was ladling the contents into his brother's mouth when Captain Sloan entered.

"Good evening, young Gus. I hear tell that you have made great strides of recovery today."

Gus gave a slight nod of his head.

"That is indeed an improvement, lad. Will you be confident on your own, for intermittent periods, if I took Josh from you tomorrow?"

Again, Gus's head moved a fraction.

"Good. We have three businessmen looking for a first-class berth to Townsville. They'll come on board when we make dock tomorrow morning. We have cargo to load and offload while we're at the jetty. Josh, you can keep an eye on Gus in between running after those three."

"Yes, Cap'n."

The smooth silver waters lit by the sliver of moon fractured when an occasional fish jumped through the surface. The stars stood out above like diamonds on dark velvet. From the shore, the music of a honky-tonk piano echoed across the bay. No doubt, several of his crew were kicking up their heels on their leave. Captain Sloan sat against the outside wall of the wheel-house breathing in the sea breezes. He had only to deliver the three passengers and the cargo destined for Townsville and then the *Northern Orchid* would be returning to his southern seagull. He leant his head back and closed his eyes. Her face filled his mind only to be splintered at the sound of a voice at his elbow. Silently he cursed China's timing.

"This where you are, Cap'n."

"Ah, China? That was another good meal you put on tonight. We were all starving after a day at the courthouse. It was more exhausting than a week of stormy weather. What can I do for you?"

China dug into one of his pockets and extracted two hard sugared sweets that he had made that afternoon. He offered one to his captain.

"Where the devil have you been hiding the sugar for these, China?" The captain sucked the lolly. "No, don't tell me. This is not bad, not bad at all."

"This very last of our sugar. Tomorrow I'd like to take someone with me to replenish our stores. Josh cannot come as he has his brother to look after but maybe Adams could help. Bellyache Basil can do the dinner at noon."

Captain Sloan rolled the sweet within his mouth savouring the rich flavour.

"One could become used to these lollies, China." He sucked noisily. "Yes, talk to Evans, but I cannot see a problem with that. We have three first-class passengers boarding tomorrow. No doubt they'll not be too happy with burgoo and burnt-bread-coffee. Mind you, after your cooking, I'd hate going back to that myself."

China grinned and savoured the praise as the captain savoured the sweet.

"Young Gus show improvement today, Cap'n."

"He certainly has, thanks to you, China."

China nodded his head and continued to grin.

"He not talk for at least a week. He lucky his voice box not smashed altogether."

"I'll leave you to give the boys your medical instructions, China." Captain Sloan stared out to sea in silence for several moments before he spoke again. "China, you've been a sailor on many seas. You know just how superstitious seamen can get."

"That is so, Cap'n. I see many strange things happen at sea."

"You remember Jimmy Dougall, don't you?"

"You mean Josh and Gus' father?"

"The very same. You were on the *Northern Orchid* the day he died, weren't you?"

"I was."

Sloan shifted his rump into a more comfortable position before going on.

"Since then, there's been more than one occasion when I could have sworn that his spirit, or whatever, has been wandering around these decks; especially after all this business with Bony and Gus. That lad should have died after the hiding he took, yet here he is on the mend. You try and tell me something or someone is not looking out for the lad."

"Sometimes Cap'n, it easier to accept calmly that which we cannot understand."

"Maybe you're right, China. One thing I do know; if Jimmy's spirit is hanging about, he'll look after the *Northern Orchid*."

The two men sat back in companionable silence.

At the stern of the ship, the three latest crew members leant on the bulwark looking over the jetty towards the few lights of Bowen town. Stretch drew on his thin rolled smoke, sucking the fumes deep into his lungs.

"Whatdayer fellas think we should do when we get to Townsville?"

Reg rolled his eyes when Dave made an admission.

"To be honest, I could handle this life as a sailor for a few months yet, I think."

"Dave, old friend, you're only attracted by the thought of a woman in every port. What about the rope burns and stench of slop buckets, not to mention the continuous rolling of the deck and occasional seasickness?" Reg rubbed his shiny scalp while listing his woes. Stretch laughed.

Dave grimaced when he replied. "That's better than a broken back digging rocks for gold that's not there or being tossed from a cranky horse that don't want to be ridden and limping about for weeks on end. Besides, China's always ready with his brew to stop seasickness. It's pretty good stuff too."

"You did hear what that fellow in the Bowen bar said yesterday."

"What was that?"

"The one that was telling us about some Townsville businessmen who've offered a reward for the first gold found within their area. He reckons there's some promising country inland from there."

"Yeah well, why isn't he out there digging, I say?"

Stretch flicked the butt of his smoke into the water and stood straight.

"I'm ready to turn in for a bit. I'm on the middle watch so I'll 'ave to be bright eyed and bushy tailed at midnight. Whatareyer chaps doing?"

"I'll call it a night too." Dave yawned.

Reg grunted. "I'll sit here for a bit longer."

The last rumble of the engine throbbed through the ship as she moved nor'-nor'-east out from Gloucester Island and into the channel. The old tars danced along the foot ropes of the yards unfurling the sails while the three greenhorns, under the directions of the bosun, manipulated the halyards. His voice was heard from bow to stern.

"Can you blokes pull on those halyards in unison? Yer like three washerwomen fighting over the clothesline."

The sails welcomed the thrust of the south-east winds. White waters rushed down either side of the ship's hull.

"Whales to starboard." Andrews excited call drifted down from the crows-nest.

Everyone's gaze turned to the east to watch the graceful giants. The three passengers from the top-deck cabins ran out to lean over the side.

Up in the wheel-house, the captain grumbled to the mate.

"Mac, I hope Andrews pays as much attention looking for the shoals, reefs and other ships as he does looking for the whales. He'll have us sitting on top of Nares Rock or Cape Upstart before he ever sees them, I'd reckon."

"Don't be too hard on him, Cap'n. He's still not much more than a boy yet. Besides hitting a whale can be a bit uncomfortable too, remember."

William Sloan burst out laughing at the memory of a navy ship that they had been on together. The ship had come very close to sailing on the back of a huge whale when south of Tasmania. Mac went on.

"All going well, and not ending upside down on Nares Rock, we should make it off the mouth of the Burdekin River by tonight, don't you think?"

"I was hoping maybe as far as Cape Bowling Green."

Mac frowned. "Maybe."

"Have the three new chaps spoken to you of their plans in Townsville. Will we need to take on new crew members there?"

Mac scratched his head. "They're still conferring between themselves. They have promised to let me know before we arrive off Townsville."

"At least I can then get straight onto the harbourmaster and see if he has some seasoned sailors looking for work."

"Yeah, well, that's never a guaranteed thing either."

Gus sat on the chair that Josh had set up in the morning shade on the port side of the ship outside the mate's cabin. Even though the size of his face had receded to the point where he was able to open his eyelids a fraction, his brother had tied a bandana around them to reduce the sun's glare which caused him excruciating pain. He luxuriated in the ability to wiggle his toes and fingers and turn his head almost forty-five degrees. A fine salt spray cooled his body each time the bow broke through the increasing swell of the ocean. He rested back against the bulkhead; his body soothed by the rhythmic whistle of the wind in the rigging. Nostalgia teased his mind when the vibration of the engines, felt in the soles of his feet, ceased. His vision may still be an issue but his hearing was acute. Somewhere on his left, three voices he did not recognize, caught his attention. These must be the three new passengers Josh had spoken of. According to his brother, one was a government official preparing a report on the progress of the development of the northern settlements. The second was a bank official reporting on similar issues and the third was a private investor.

As their conversation bounced back and forth, Gus drifted off into a somnolent state from which he recovered with a start when Josh touched his shoulder.

"Come on brother, I'll take you back inside now. China gave me strict instructions that you are not to do too much today."

With stiff limbs that did not seem to belong to him, Gus stood up and leant heavily on his brother's arm. His feet shuffled their way back to the sail-bed. Josh removed the bandana from his brother's face before turning to go.

"I'm on my way to take my turn on the bilge pump. I'll be back in time to bring you a feed at noon."

Gus squeezed Josh's hand in acknowledgement.

The stench of bilge water tormented his senses right from the top of the companion-way steps. The sound of men at the open hatchway below floated up to Josh as he climbed down to the lower deck. Mister Evans' distinctive language encouraged the sailor's efforts. As he approached the group, the miasma became more pronounced. The noises from the busy bilge pump became clearer. The creak of the cross-bar sounded in unison with the deep grunts of the four men taking their turn at the pump. The rhythm was underlined by the frequent harsh cough from those having difficulty coping with the foul air. Josh joined Bandy, Andrews and Stretch who the bosun had lined up ready to take over the next shift in the bilge.

As Josh, along with his fellow shift members, slipped in to replace the previous men at the pump handles, he felt the choking odour hit the back of his throat like the kick of a horse. He struggled to inhale as little as he could but as his body began to push and pull at the pump it demanded more and more oxygen. Josh's breaths deepened. The fits of coughing increased; as did those of the remainder of the team. Sweat ran down his body like malodorous rain. Relief gushed through every aching muscle at the sound of Evans' voice calling time. The bosun was satisfied that the little of the bilge waters remaining were not of any consequence and called a cessation to the pumping.

THE MARINER'S REST

The afternoon sun was high in the sky when Spud made several trips from the stable to the back verandah. The bicep muscles in his wiry arms knotted at the weight of the timber planks that Jacko planned to use to build the bookshelves in Mister Boris' room. Years of handling racehorses followed by years of carrying barrels of ale up and down cellar steps contributed to the well-toned muscles in his short body. He was not quite sure how he'd come to be roped into helping with this chore. Jacko managed to convince him he'd enjoy the experience. Jacko had a compelling argument. It was the only time in the foreseeable future that Miss Millie was going to be a way for the whole afternoon. Spud knew the reason for the anxious frown which distorted the usual laughter lines on Jacko's face. Miss Millie had told Jacko not to do anything strenuous for at least a week but Jacko was fretting at the idleness. If Miss Millie found out, when she returned from her meeting in town, she'd be furious. Jacko came out from the room carrying a comfortable chair for Mister Boris to rest in while they worked.

It was not too long before their hammering echoed throughout the building. Mrs. Waterman who was relieving Mrs. Randal, the cleaner today, poked her head in to see what was going on. Her dark eyes sparkled when she found Jacko alone in the room. She slipped up behind him and ran her fingernails down shoulder muscles hidden under a cotton shirt moist with perspiration. She whispered hoarsely.

"Oooh Jacko, I do love to see a man's rippling muscles."

Jacko felt her breath warm on his skin. It was unfortunate that at the very moment, Sarah entered the room via the verandah doorway. Jacko's head swung her way. He did not miss the disappointment swimming near the surface of her deep blue eyes nor in the paleness of her face. Her look took him in the stomach like an unexpected punch. He opened his mouth to speak; he was not sure what he wanted to say. But there was only the back of her head, held high and a swish of her skirts to receive any message he might offer. Why he should feel so guilty he did not know. In fact, he was rather angry that she had made him feel that way. He snapped at Mrs. Waterman telling her to get on with her work. This only made him feel guilty all over again. He shook his head before resting his forehead against the wall. Women were not worth all the trouble.

"You alright, Jacko?" Spud asked when he came in to see Jacko slumped against the wall. "Geez, if Miss Millie comes in here, she'll tear a strip off me for letting you work like this. Why don't you go lie down for a bit?"

A low growl was his only answer.

Millie hauled on the reins to guide Emperor and the sulky into the side-street. The ratchet of the brake handle grated as she pulled it into position. Her gloved hand adjusted the frilled bonnet more firmly atop the hair roll on her head before she twirled the tendrils of hair on either side of her face. With surprising agility, she climbed down to the street. She flounced her skirts into place and stepped out towards the building from which Arthur Rankine conducted his business. Her heart quailed. Arthur had been a likeable lad but the man was not so appealing. Was it her fault? Had she spoilt the child? He wasn't a bad person really. Sadly, he had not learnt that he could not have everything he wanted. Nor had he learnt to have any respect for others; unless he was trying to weasel his way into someone's good graces. There had been many times she had been called on to reprimand Arthur and every time she felt sick to her stomach. Over the years, she had often pondered on the reports that filtered back to her of how the boy had suffered far too many unreasonable reprimands from his father. Today was no different. Today though, she knew that she must be strong. Arthur had well and truly overstepped the mark. She'd have to tell him, in no uncertain terms. She took a deep breath and reached up to take the door knocker in her hand.

It was some moments before Arthur opened the door. He was in the process of shaking the hand of a departing client. He had not turned yet to see who was waiting on the outside of his door. When he did, the narrow features closed. Wariness swam in the depths of his pale eyes. His thin lips struggled to smile a welcome.

"Aren't you going to invite me in, Arthur?"

He dragged the door open further. Her skirts swished against the door and the door frame as she made her way through into the cramped space. In his office, he guided her to a seat on the faded couch against the wall.

"Can I get you something to drink, Miss Millie?"

"Thanks, Arthur, a glass of sherry will be lovely."

Arthur opened a door to his right. He instructed someone inside to bring the drink for their guest. By the time he settled himself on the chair beside Miss Millie, his aplomb had returned somewhat. His smile was wider and more relaxed.

"You're here to speak to me about my abominable behaviour last week; is that not so, Miss Millie?"

"Then you agree, it was abominable behaviour?"

Arthur hung his head. Shame may have been in the body language but not in the suppressed sneer in his hidden eyes.

"Miss Millie, I do not know what came over me. I know that I had too much to drink that day. It's just, I get so unbelievably lonely here sometimes." With his eyes downcast, Arthur continued. "You don't think I'm becoming like my father, do you? Please, don't say that. I so much want to please you. I appreciate all that you have done for me over the years; especially your support when Mother died."

The familiar tragic eyes looked up at Millie. She felt her heart teeter.

"Arthur, don't try to soft soap me with those woebegone eyes. You know very well I have spoilt you. How many times I should have handed you over to your father for a thrashing when you were a boy? I blame myself and my soft heart for your selfishness now. BUT, there will be changes. Sarah is as a daughter to me and I will not have you treating her like a common doxy. Do you understand? If you cannot remain sober and act as a gentleman should, you are to keep away from The Mariner's Rest. Is that clear?"

Arthur's mouth dropped open. He sat back in his chair. He had never seen Miss Millie so angry at him before. Maybe he had gone a little too far. That was a nuisance because her ladies were lots of fun to be with. He'd have to patronize Mrs. Lacrosse's boudoir for the next few weeks until she cooled down.

"Yes, Miss Millie, of course. I do humbly apologize."

As she walked back to her carriage, Millie did not feel contented with the way things had gone, despite Arthur's apology. He was becoming a sneaky cove just like his father had been years ago. She recalled how that man could be as trustworthy as a snake at mating season.

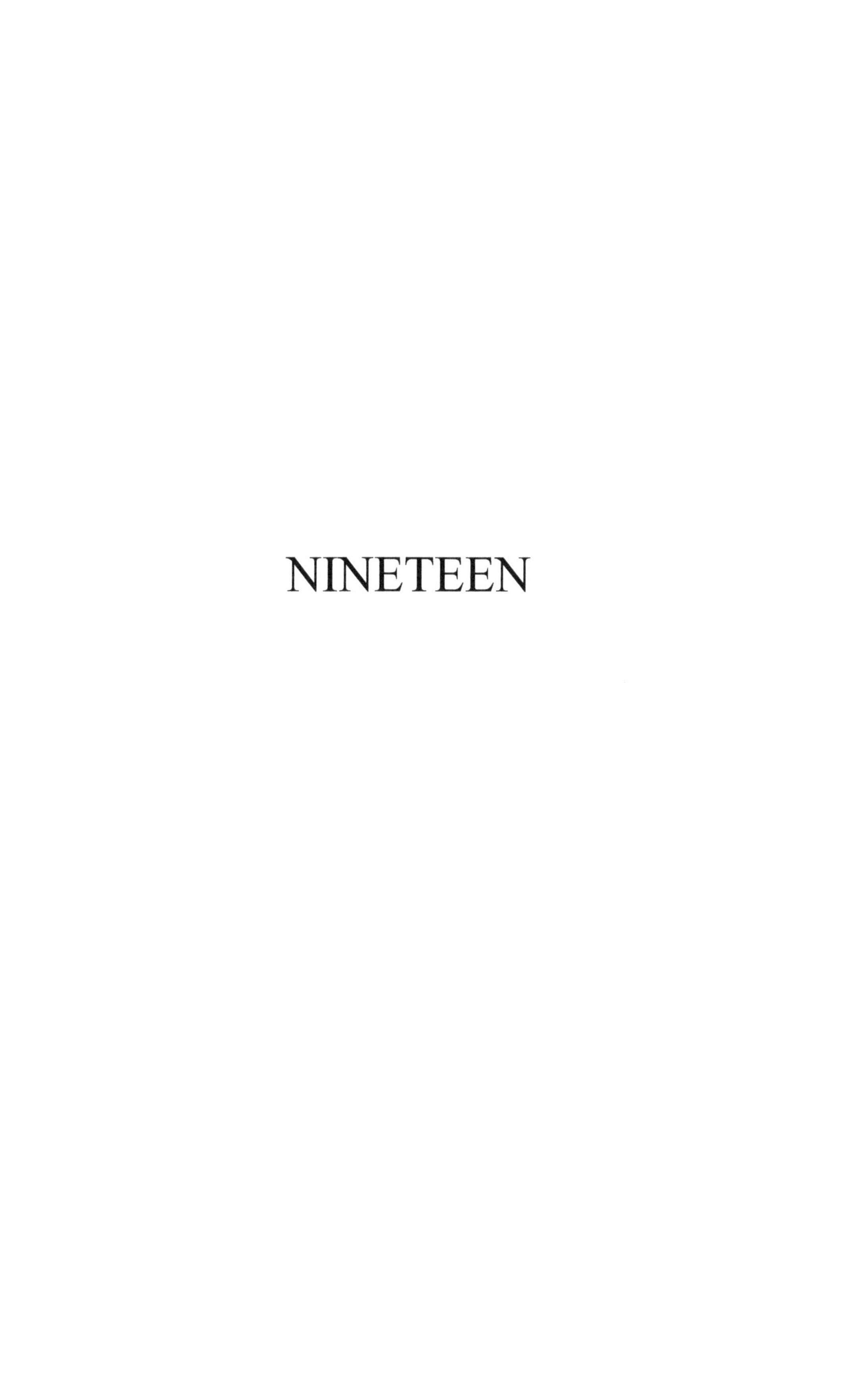

NINETEEN

THE *NORTHERN ORCHID*

Josh and Andrews worked at the yardarms. They were in the process of using mutton fat to lubricate the pulleys for the rigging. Their toes hooked onto the footropes below the yards. They both knew the risk of getting the grease all over their hands. It was a frequent occurrence that sailors on this job ended up slithering down the lines struggling to secure a hold with slippery hands. Most ended up with rope burns that hurt for days. The bosun issued strong bristled brushes to access the fat in their individual cans in the hope of preventing this happening.

Josh's one arm clenched firmly over the portside gallant yardarm. From his fingers swung the fat-can, in rhythm with the rolling of the ship. His other hand utilized the brush to dip and dollop, dip and dollop. After each pulley was given a dollop of fat and a rub with the bristles, he tugged the rope back and forth a couple of times to ensure a free flow before moving on to the next pulley. Sometimes he'd rest his arms and relax all his weight on calloused feet with toes clinging to the foot ropes. The views on all sides of the ship took his breath away. Having spent so much time watching Cape Upstart as they sailed by, he'd invited a sharp reprimand from the bosun who had come out onto the deck below.

Barely had that shout dissipated on the breeze when a screech filled the air that was not caused by any feathered wildlife. Andrews' feet flapped around below the yard while his one arm clung by the elbow in desperation as he endeavoured to regain his hold on the footropes. Josh watched horrified. It looked as though his fellow sailor was about to make a fast trip back to the deck, over fifty feet below. From his position, nearly twenty feet away on the opposite yardarm, there was no way he could do anything to help. Josh's sigh of relief almost equalled that of Andrews when the toes of the boy's right foot brought the footropes under control. Gradually Andrews resettled his position. With an ashen face, he draped himself over the pole struggling to breathe.

From the deck below, Evans watched the near miss and Andrews' recovery. He gave the boy several moments to gather his wits then called up the main mast.

"You on holidays up there, Andrews? We'll be ready to drop anchor shortly. Will you be joining us?"

A scratchy voice, barely recognizable, floated back down.

"Yes, Mister Evans. Be right down."

After a peaceful night at anchor just north-east of Cape Upstart, the *Northern Orchid* sailed on without incident, to end this northern journey on the lee side of Magnetic Island just off the fledgling port of Townsville. With only a small amount of cargo to be transferred, Captain Sloan opted to anchor offshore rather than be a slave to the tides, shallow waters and one not overlarge wharf at Townsville. Dredging was very much needed to make this port more accessible.

With the early morning sun at their backs, Stretch, Dave and Reg stood at the ship's side waving off the three businessmen who were sitting in the rear of the jolly-boat with Captain Sloan standing at the bow. Bandy, Rollins, Andrews and Adams manned the oars.

"Do yer think the captain didn't choose us to row them fellas ashore because 'e thought we'd change our minds once our feet 'it dry land?" Stretch laughed.

"More likely he didn't want to have you upturn the boat with your attempts at manipulating a pair of oars," Reg grunted. He was still not totally convinced he wanted to be a sailor, even if only for a few weeks.

"It looks easy enough. I bet we'd manage no trouble at all. Can't be harder than riding a young horse, surely. It's all a matter of balance I reckon." Envy filled Dave's eyes as he watched the boat move off.

It was four bells into the afternoon watch when the jolly-boat, with the captain on board, returned. Since then the ship was in an uproar. Mister Evans had everyone clearing the decks and setting up the cleats ready for the loading of timber on Saturday morning. Tomorrow, Friday, a lighterman skiff was expected to arrive with a load of wool and cotton bales. Several crates and the last of the farming implements in the hold would be ferried ashore on that vessel.

Gus limped along beside Josh as they made their way to the galley for the evening meal. His uncovered eyes blinked rapidly and watered a lot but the pain was barely noticeable; even with the light of the lanterns on the tables. Climbing down the companion-way ladder had been an effort. Even though his vision was blurred and he had China's strict instructions not to try to talk just yet, he still enjoyed listening as the crew talked, laughed, joked and whinged. It was good to be alive.

"You be good to get cat-shit-sand soon and clean hen shit I think, young Gus," China laughed.

Gus was able to nod his head a little and give a twisted grin.

Saturday a faint mist clung determinedly to the sea as the early morning sun worked hard to absorb it within its warmth. Two barges approached the *Northern Orchid* from the direction of Magnetic Island. From their bows to their sterns, freshly sawn hoop pine timbers were stacked high along their lengths. The fresh smell of the cut timber blended with the briny smell of the sea water. The *Northern Orchid* was charged with delivering this timber to Bowen on her return journey.

Like huge stick insects, the makeshift cranes were again secured to the three masts, under Mister Evans' supervision. The largest pulleys carrying the ship's heaviest chains and hemp lines had been employed. When all was ready, Mister Evans called orders to the sailors on the ship. The barge captain ensured his crew attached the lines securely to the slabs of timbers before they were hauled up with the muscle of the men behind the spokes of the ship's capstan. Nobody was free of sweat, grime and short tempers when the job was completed. The load from the first barge lined the port side bulwark and that of the second barge lined the bulwark of the starboard side of the ship. Everyone was ready to eat by the time the last bracing line was secured.

The bosun removed his cap and rubbed his wet forehead with a grubby rag as he entered the chartroom where Captain Sloan and the mate poured over the new map obtained from the Townsville harbourmaster.

"All's loaded and secured, Cap'n."

"Good work, Evans. Did all the men get a turn of shore leave in the last two days?"

"Yes, Sir. Oh, except the Dougall boys. One is still not well enough and the other won't leave his brother. And before you ask, our three landlubbers did return." He grinned. "We'll make tars out of them yet."

"Thanks, let the men relax a bit this afternoon. We'll make an early start south, tomorrow."

Evans turned to go, paused, then swung back.

"Before I forget, Cap'n. We'll need a load of wood for the galley and boiler fires. If you can do without me. I thought I'd take Josh Dougal and one of the new fellows with me in the jolly-boat before we return it to its davit. There'll be plenty of old fallen timber on the shores of the island. No doubt China will be nagging me for more sand for his mouse-catcher while we're there, too."

The captain looked to Mac for his opinion. Mac shrugged his indifference.

"Good idea, Evans. I think Mac and I can manage on our own for an hour or so. You're right; whatever you do, don't forget China's sand or I'll never hear the end of it."

When the jolly-boat with Josh and Stretch matching oars and Evans pulling on two oars together left for their work detail, the remainder of the sailors lined the *Northern Orchid's* rails. Not particularly to see the shipmates on their way but to admire and cheer on the two vessels full of day-visitors returning from their picnic on the beaches of the island.

THE MARINER'S REST

Pedestrians, on the road outside, shivered in the cool morning breeze. The women pulled their shawls a little tighter around their bodies. The men tucked their hands inside the pockets of their coats. Inside, perspiration trickled down her face. Dark curls lay damp against the side of her temples. Her knees, her back and her shoulders burnt with the pain of it but she did not pause. Back and forth, back and forth the soft cloth in her hands rubbed over the freshly placed polish. Section by section she worked her way over the floor of the upper-story lounge.

Sarah may have presented a calm exterior to the world but inside she was sick to her stomach. The memory of Mrs. Waterman's long fingers running down Jacko's arms played over and over in her head. It was nearly driving her mad. No amount of rational thought seemed to have any impact. She knew that what Jacko did was none of her business. She knew he was a man with a man's needs. She knew that Mrs. Waterman was a bit of a doxy. They were both adults. What right did she have to be getting into a tizz? It wasn't as if Jacko belonged to her.

As she worked on her hands and knees, the routine daily noises faded into the background of her churning mind. The clamour of the wharves on the riverside, the screech of Birley's sawmill all faded into the distance. Each firm stroke of her reddened hands underlined the irritation, the anger, the fury, the jealousy that pervaded her mind. In her vision, the woman's fingers became exaggerated in their slenderness and their attractiveness while her own fingers seemed mere stubby bulbs at the end of her hands.

‘Strong, all-purpose hands, just like mine,’ her mother had told her as she lay their two hands side by side. ‘A great asset to the likes of us, dear Sarah.’

But Sarah did not want all-purpose hands; strong or otherwise. She wanted long slender fingers just like Mrs. Waterman. Fingers that she might walk down the length of Jacko’s muscled shoulders. The floor received another good rub. It gleamed in the morning light breaking through between the wind-blown curtains at the open windows. The smell of floor polish filled her nostrils, removing all trace of the fragrance of the early spring blooms drifting up from the garden below.

Even Miss Millie had noticed something was amiss. Why, it was only this morning when she had taken in breakfast, Miss Millie commented.

“Sarah, have you noticed that Jacko’s been walking around like a Scotsman who’s lost his last penny? Do you have any idea what’s up his nose?”

“Why should I know anything? Maybe you should ask that Mrs. Waterman with her slender fingers.” Sarah had thrown her hands over her mouth. Where had that come from?

Miss Millie’s eyebrows had lifted in surprise. Sarah thought, at the time, that for some reason, a faint grin twitched at her lips but she couldn’t be sure. At that moment, Miss Millie had turned her head to view the passing boats on the river. It was all so confusing. She apologized to her best friend.

“Oh, Miss Millie, I’m sorry I snapped. I really don’t know why I said that.”

Then to make it all the more embarrassing she had burst into tears. Just the memory of it all had her rubbing her leaking eyes against her sleeve. She doubled her efforts at the floor polish as she cringed at the memory of what she had said next.

"I don't know what's the matter with me. Jacko's just a friend, after all. What he does is none of my business."

She could still see the quiet calmness in Miss Millie as she had sat her down and poured a cup of tea from the breakfast tray.

"Drink this," Miss Millie said softly.

Again, the floor received several rough swipes with the polish rag. She felt her stomach curdle inside at the thought of the whole thing.

"Sarah, as you know, Jacko has been like a son to me. I'm going to tell you something that I don't want repeated; ever. Can you give me your word on that?"

Sarah had sniffled a little more, before nodding her head.

"Yes, of course, Miss Millie."

"Jacko's father was killed on the Sydney wharves. His mother died of typhoid a short time later. Jacko was only about eight or nine at the time. He made enough money to sustain himself by running messages and doing odd jobs for all the folk who lived in his street. Most of the mothers kept an eye out for the lad. I met him one night when I was on my way to meet a gentleman. A drunk came out of an ale-house and began abusing then assaulting me. This skinny lad flew out of nowhere with his fists flailing. He shinnied up the fellow's back and boxed his ears." At this point, Millie had given a chuckle. No doubt at the vision re-playing in her mind. "The lad became a daily visitor at my residence. He'd fetch and carry for me between his other chores. I ensured we were both fed reasonably well. The client of that night became my husband and he was more than willing to take on this boy who had saved my life. Jacko thought the world of my Chris and the feeling was reciprocated. We brought him to Brisbane with us when we moved here nearly twenty years ago."

The arms wielding the polish rag relaxed somewhat. The strokes on the floor became almost sensual. After some moments, Sarah's thoughts returned to that conversation earlier in the day.

"Jacko has always been a very private person and a discreet person. He has never satisfied his man's needs at my hotel. I presume he does satisfy them somewhere, but never on his own doorstep." Again, there was a long pause. "As for our Mrs. Waterman, it was only a week after she first started working at The Rest that Jacko came to me begging to know what he should do about the woman. She was always pestering him. The poor man was flummoxed. My advice to him that day was to keep out of her way and don't let her get the chance to catch him on his own. I couldn't really afford to get rid of her because whatever else she might be, she's a good worker and she's content with just the casual work. If you take notice, you'll see that it is always her who does the chasing; never him. In fact, he is quite embarrassed at her forwardness."

The physical exertion of the polishing along with the commotion of her thoughts and visions absorbed Sarah's attention. She did not hear his footstep or notice his arrival. A squeal escaped her lips when he tapped her shoulder. The turning of her head to look up almost sent her toppling over onto her side.

"Oooh, Jacko. I didn't hear you; sorry."

"You've worked through your morning break. I see you have that floor looking a treat." After placing the tray he carried on the table, he reached his hand out to help her to her feet.

With only the slightest hesitation she took the offer of assistance. She groaned as her muscles complained, or was it for something else? She dropped his hand and stumbled back onto the chair in the corner.

The cup rattled against the saucer. Milky tea spilt over the side. Jacko stepped forward to assist. She replied, more sharply than she had intended.

"Please, don't bother. It's just the sudden change of position that has given me the trembles." Still, he did take the cup from her hand and sat it on the table at her side.

"I'll leave you in peace then."

With her balance restored, she sipped at the welcome drink. Try as she might, her thoughts refused to let go of her memories of the early morning conversation. She digested every word that Miss Millie said. Was Miss Millie, right? Did Jacko have no interest in that trollop whatsoever?

"You know, Jacko is the type to be more interested in an invitation to a cup of tea and a biscuit than some frivolous night out. He likes a quiet life."

Now here, as she sat admiring her morning's handiwork, Sarah felt a lightness fill her chest. Gone was the heavy stone that had weighed down her stomach. She remembered her ungratefulness when Jacko had brought her the cup of tea. Maybe she should return the favour.

Her heart pounded in her chest. Her hands shook so badly she nearly dropped her mother's precious teapot when she drew it out of the little cupboard above the sink in the shack. Sarah stifled a squeal as she rescued the cream china teapot with its lavender flowered pattern. Perhaps she had better not pour the water over the leaves until Jacko arrived. After all, he might change his mind. Although he did seem pleased when she offered the invitation for him to take afternoon tea at the shack. She'd opened all the doors and windows. One must maintain some sort of propriety; don't want people getting the wrong idea. What if it became too cold? The weather still had a chill in the evening air. What if he thought she was just a silly young girl? He might be laughing at her right now, with no intention of turning up.

The soft tap on the door drew her attention. She smiled. Her breath caught in her throat as she looked upon his familiar face. The dark curls were brushed back. The beard and moustache recently trimmed. She could not speak. Her tongue felt thick in her mouth. It took all of her power to pull out a chair with one hand while pointing to its seat with the other.

TWENTY

THE *NORTHERN ORCHID*

Josh's feet felt light as he scaled the rigging to the crow's-nest. It felt good to return to normal duties especially knowing his brother was making a fast recovery. Andrews hung over the side of the barrel watching his approach.

"Bejesus, it's good to see you this morning. I swear that's the longest four hours of my life."

Josh laughed.

"Andrews, you say that every time you're on middle watch. Anyway, be off with you. The dawn and I have come to take over your darkest hours."

Andrews needed no second bidding. His hands must have been hot by the time he landed on the deck. Josh's eyes quartered the compass to familiarise himself with the current situation related to their anchorage. At least two nautical miles to the east he could see what appeared to be a brig, anchored; its two masts with all sails furled. Over on the north-west, Cape Upstart was almost totally hidden in cloud. In the faint light of early dawn, the sullen seas rose and fell, dark and brooding. Fish jumped near the bow of the boat

Pensively, his finger stroked the immature stubble growing on his chin and above his lip. Sometime today he should take out his father's blade and shave the fine growth. It had not gone unnoticed that Gus was already showing signs of early beard growth. How embarrassing if his younger brother became a man before he did. For all his day-dreaming, he did not miss the grey clouds forming on the horizon. The little breeze that drifted in haphazardly from the east, had shifted a couple of points to the south if he was not mistaken. He peered towards the deck to see if Mister Winston or Bandy, the other two on the morning watch with him, were in sight. Bandy with his lantern was just disappearing through the hatch on his way to check the lower deck. Mister Winston must be in the wheel-house if the glow of the yellow light spilling out onto the deck was anything to go by.

Later today, all going well, the ship should be back in Port Denison. Josh's stomach swirled. Just the thought of entering Bowen sent a shiver through his body even though Cap'n Sloan said he did not need him on this visit to the Judge. The captain only wanted to follow-up on any unexpected outcomes related to the Bony incident.

Four bells into Josh's watch and the familiar bellow from the bosun was followed by the pad of feet on the wooden decks. Within minutes the clinking of the pawls in the capstan, the rattle of the chains and the creaking of the blocks drifted up the mast as the men on the capstan weighed anchor. Shortly after, like large clouds unfolding beneath him, the sails were unfurled. The *Northern Orchid* caught the reticent wind and turned her bow for Gloucester Island and the entrance to Port Denison.

A large tub of hot soapy water had been set up on the end of one of the eating tables. Gus sat on the form, washing the dirty dishes. He relished the movement of his hands and fingers. His vision may have been too blurry to attempt cutting up the contents for the mid-day burgoo with China's razor-sharp chopping knife but he could see well enough to clean the breakfast dishes. He threw a grin at his brother who dragged his feet and rubbed his red eyes when he arrived looking for a feed after his early morning watch in the crow's-nest.

"There's still some oatmeal left on the stove, Josh. Mister MacGregor did not want his extra egg this morning so I've put it away for you. It's under that tin plate on the edge of the stove."

"Thanks," Josh grunted. "Is China about?"

A familiar piping voice called from the little inner room.

"I here, funny man. What you want?"

Josh went to the entrance of China's cubby hole.

"Mister China, I've come to return your lucky orange stone. It certainly seems to have bought me good luck; just like you said it would."

"Aah, Josh. The luck in the stone can only continue if it passed on to another deserving person. You must keep it safe until that day arrives."

"Oh, I see. Right then, I'll tuck it away with my things."

Josh returned to sit at the long table and eat his breakfast. Gus clattered away with the dishes and questioned his brother on the events of his morning on watch. Josh's answers were delivered in monosyllables.

Captain Sloan had chosen not to use the engine to enter Port Denison this trip. He told Mac, Evans and Guthrie Winston that it was time the crew was given a bit of practice in manipulating the sails to manoeuvre the ship into the jetty. By the time the *Northern Orchid's* portside lines were secured to the Bowen harbour bollards, the sun hung low in the sky.

The men grumbled, more from habit than from any real reason, when Evans had them on deck at first light. They were set the task of re-building their giant insect cranes of spars, masts, pulleys and strong lines. At Mac's suggestion, it was decided to unload the timber before the cargo awaiting in the hold. While the ship's crew were occupied with this task, the land crew harnessed a horse team to a line of three flatbed rail carriages. Evans was in the process of doing a final check on the outcome of his makeshift cranes when the rail flatbeds, being hauled along the jetty behind the working horses, rattled to a stop beside the *Northern Orchid.*

During the time Evans and Mac discussed the shore-bound cargo with the wharf foreman, the horse-handler unharnessed the team of four horses. Amidst the creaking of the leather and clinking of the chains, he walked them to the wide end of the jetty where he turned them around. Once they were about-face, he led them back passing to the side of the carriages. He then began to re-harness them to the opposite end of the flatbed carriages in a position enabling them to drag the load back to the shore.

On deck, the ship's crew secured the chains around several long planks of the timber before attaching them with the steel hooks to the lines from the makeshift cranes. Men positioned themselves around the capstan and at Evans' call, pushed their muscles to the limit. Each lift began slowly until the weight was absorbed in the lines when it became a little easier. Smaller lines, hanging freely, in the hands of two shore-men guided the direction of the loads aloft to their new position on the flatbed carriages. The wharf foreman yelled an all-clear signal after the hooks and chains were released. Everything went smoothly until the very last load was delivered to the rail carriage. The foreman's premature call had the bosun direct the ship's crew to rewind the lines; one of which had not been disconnected properly. On the wharf, at the flatbed carriage, the timber still attached, lifted three feet into the air again before it dropped when the hook fell off the line. The slab crashed down onto the top of the other timber. In the process, it caught a wharf worker in the middle of his back. The man was sent flying into the ocean ten feet below the jetty. His scream reverberated in the air along with the screech of the seagulls that had been picking at leftovers on the wharf.

With a large splash, the man hit the water and sank. His body could be seen twisting and turning in the deep clear water. His head and arms broke the surface. He screamed again.

"I can't swim."

Everyone stood stunned trying to comprehend what had happened.

"Shark." This scream came from the bow of the ship. Andrews' thin arms pointed.

It was one of the new landlubber crewmembers who dove straight into the water. His hand was already reaching for the knife he kept in its scabbard at the side of his boot. Those on the deck and on the wharf stared with mouths and eyes open wide. Hardly a breath was taken and not a word was spoken except for Captain Sloan's mumbled curse as he ran to peer over the bulwark.

"What the devil does that man thinks he's doing?"

Stretch could be seen just below the water holding the knife in his hand. He twisted left and right, searching. The shark sliced through the water directly towards the leather-maker. At the last minute, Stretch dived. He came up under the shark's belly. The water clouded over, shrouding the spectator's view, as blood spilt out into the sea.

The body of the shark arched. It flipped left and right. It twisted and rolled until eventually, it floated to the surface with its open belly facing the sun. The waters around it became more obscured with the pouring out of blood.

It was Mac, Sloan and Evans who had two lines over the side of the ship. Evans shinnied down one ready to assist Stretch and the wharfie to safety.

"Come on mate, hold onto the rope; tight. We'll be up to our eyes in sharks once they all get a smell of that lot." Evans encouraged the trembling wharfie.

When Stretch eventually got to throw his long legs onboard the *Northern Orchid*, a cheer rang out from both the crew on the jetty and his shipmates. Captain Sloan grumbled as he shook the man's hand.

"Bloody fool, trying to feed the sharks? What the devil did you think you were doing?"

"Nothing to worry about, Cap'n. Years ago, when I was a bit younger, I'll admit, me and me mates used to dive in and gut the crocs for fun. I figured a shark was little different to a crocodile; both out to eat you." He laughed as he took off his boots and began to empty the water.

"Raving lunatic." Captain Sloan shook his head and went back to the wheel-house.

China's jacket flapped around his knees as he rushed out onto the deck. He reached out and grasped Stretch's arm.

"Where it is? Where it is?" He asked breathlessly.

"What, China; where's what?" Stretch attempted to pull his boots back onto his feet but China was holding tightly to his arm.

"The shark; where the shark? I cook it for tonight's meal."

Stretch eased his arm free and led China to the bow of the ship. He pointed to where the bloody corpse drifted on the outgoing tide. As they stood looking out over the sea, they witnessed the first attack by other sharks. The corpse lifted out of the water with sharp-toothed snouts attached to its sides. The water swirled and writhed in a mass of froth, blood and hungry grey sharks. China's wide sleeves dropped down to his shoulders as he threw up his arms.

"What use are you? Such a waste."

"China, how was I supposed to know you'd want the wretched thing? Even if I did, there was little chance of carrying it up onto the deck with me."

"Bah!" China stomped off back to his galley.

THE MARINER'S REST

His breath caught in his throat as he stood at the doorway watching her fuss over her afternoon tea table. She had changed her frock and her hair had been brushed. The loop of dark plaits pinned behind her ears gleamed. How many times lately had he found himself admiring this fine-looking young woman.

She looked up. Her faint smile captured his breath once more. One hand pulled out a chair while the other invited him to sit. She did not speak a word. Her brilliant blue gaze bored into his own. He felt himself drawn along its pathway. He was unaware of his feet in their spit-polished boots touching the wooden floorboards. He had never experienced this flutter in his chest like a flag at the top of a flagpole in the middle of a gale. Hot and cold waves raced through his body. Hopefully, he was not going to have a relapse of his recent bout of influenza. Through partially parted lips she whispered.

"Jacko ..." The muscles in her lovely throat stirred as she swallowed. "I ..."

Suddenly all the advice that he had offered himself on the need for caution flew out the open window on the light afternoon breeze. He reached for the pointing hand and enveloped it within his own. The quiver he felt in her fingers, was matched ten-fold in the shaking of his own knees. He lifted the hand to his chest. Her gaze still ensnared him with gossamer threads. He felt his body tremble. She had not withdrawn her hand. He took a deep breath.

"Sarah, you look lovely."

"Why Jacko, you are shaking; are you unwell?"

"I don't know. I feel like a runaway bullock wagon is barrelling towards me but I do not wish to move out of its way." His heart dropped to the floor. What a gaffe thing to say.

For a brief moment, her gaze faulted and then changed. A hint of amusement lurked in the depths of her eyes. He knew it. He'd blown it. What did he expect? He was a man of nearly thirty-one years of age. She was not yet seventeen. He must seem like an old fool to her.

A chuckle, like waters running through the downpipes into the water tanks, brought fear into his heart. She disengaged her fingers from his own. If his feet could move, he'd turn to go. He gasped when she moved close to him and set her hands on either side of his waist.

"Jacko, I hope you're not saying I'm nothing but a runaway bullock wagon." Again, the chuckle played on his ears but this time the sound filled his heart. "Did you know, I too have been terrified. I worried that you'd be thinking it forward of me to invite you to tea. I nearly called it all off."

His voice returned, although rather scratchy.

"Sarah, of course, I didn't think you forward. After all, we've been friends for nearly a year. And I'd have been most cross to miss out on that splendid looking tea cake you have there. But most of all, I'd kill for a cup of tea. All this nervousness has made me as dry as dust."

They were both chuckling as Jacko sat up to the table with a gentle nudge on the back from Sarah. He noticed that Sarah's hand still trembled a little as she lifted the kettle from the stove and poured the boiling water into the cream coloured teapot at the end of the table.

"I made this teacake myself. I'm still a long way from being as good a cook as Mrs. Hamilton but I have improved since that first one I made. Do you remember that day, Jacko?"

He burst out laughing. The vision of a blackened, flattened offering that even the residents in the hen house turned their noses up at, flashed through his mind.

"Lass, we all have to start at the beginning. This looks very tempting. I shall endeavour not to leave a crumb on the plate."

He was pleased to see that both their hands were steady as he held his plate up while Sarah placed a slice thereupon.

They soon relaxed in familiar conversations on the happenings at the hotel, the council projects on the south side of the river and the expected entertainment that was to coincide with the anticipated itinerary of the Prince's visit next year. Both had read much of this in the newspapers.

It was the voice of Mrs. Hamilton calling farewell to Miss Millie that brought them back to earth.

"The soup is on the back of the stove and the sandwiches are in the pantry, Miss Millie. I'll see you first thing in the morning." Her voice echoed around the back yard.

Jacko smiled when Sarah jumped up as if bitten by a wasp.

"Jacko, is it that time already? I must fly. Miss Millie will wonder where I am."

Jacko reached over and took up her hand. He savoured the feel of it in his clasp. It felt like a small bird at peace in its nest. His confidence soared.

"Somehow, I don't think Miss Millie will be wondering where you are at all. In fact, I would not be at all surprised if she is as pleased as punch that you and I are here having tea."

A shy smile flittered over Sarah's face.

"You could very well be right, Jacko."

"Will we please her some more? Will you come with me to the church fete next Saturday afternoon? The brass band will be playing."

His heart rolled over as her eyes dropped shyly to the floor.

"I would like that very much, Jacko."

He made to turn, then stopped; thinking.

"Should I ask Miss Millie to come with us? You may like to have a chaperone?"

"Jacko, that is a lovely thought. I don't think I'll ever be frightened to be alone with you but Miss Millie may enjoy the day out."

He held both her hands in his own again and looked deep into those blue seas.

"Sarah, may God strike me dead if I ever give you cause to be frightened of me."

He nearly fell down the step after Sarah had released his two hands, reached up to take his shoulders and dropped a light kiss on the side of his cheek. With his heart pounding in his chest, he followed her lead as she firmly spun him about giving him a gentle nudge towards the door.

TWENTY-ONE

NORTHERN ORCHID

On the second day at the Bowen Jetty, the horse-drawn flatbed rail carriages returned. The few crates of cargo still in the holds, destined for Bowen, were unloaded. Late in the morning, Stretch accompanied the captain into the town where the shark-killer was hailed as a hero. Captain Sloan left him at the hotel bar while he took the opportunity to visit his friend, Judge Masterson. He sighed as he walked out of the hotel into the street, reconciled to the probability of having to carry the new sailor back to the ship.

Richard offered no sympathy for his plight but did offer the use of his horse and buggy, if the need arose. As they sat in the garden enjoying a mid-day repast and a glass of excellent ale, Richard commented.

"There are many things to moan about in the north but a glorious spring day like today is not one of them. A person could not wish for better. How's the weather been holding out on this trip of yours, William?"

"So far, it's been quite placid. We've been watching a smudge on the horizon; it's been keeping pace with us for a couple of days. It might turn into something." Sloan shrugged.

"Surely, it's a bit early in the season for anything significant, isn't it?" The judge wiped the froth from his lips.

"More than likely but I have known the seasons to throw surprises our way. It could mean nothing or it could mean a great deal. We'll keep our eyes peeled."

After the pair shook hands and promised to catch up next trip, William Sloan made his way back to the hotel where he'd left his sailor. He found it hard to keep a straight face on finding his latest crew member sitting at the table in the corner with a buxom beauty hanging off each arm and both of them hanging onto his every word. Empty glasses and bottles covered every inch of the table.

Fearing a riot from the locals for removing their hero, Captain Sloan approached the situation cautiously. Relief flowed through him when his target dropped his booted feet from where they rested on a chair and stood up without a wobble.

"Captain our Captain, you've come to rescue me from these wicked women, I 'ope. I'm way too young to know what they're suggesting I do. Please take me away."

Captain Sloan was amazed that the fellow's speech did not contain a hint of a slur. If those empties on the table were anything to go by, he did not understand how the man's tongue twisted around the words without a fault. Other than a half stumble on the doorstep, Stretch's step was no less straight than his captain's own.

When they reached the bottom of the gangplank, Stretch drew himself up tall, took a big breath, turned to his guide and declared.

"Please, excuse me if I 'urry past this point. I really don't think I'm in any state to go swimming with the sharks this afternoon." He then ran the length of the gangplank before falling flat on his face onto the ship's deck at Mister Evans' feet.

Several willing hands were there to take him to the crew's quarters where he passed out on his hammock. Meanwhile, the captain's voice gave instruction to his bosun.

"We'll weigh anchor at first light, thanks, Evans."

The bow sliced through the waves. Fresh winds filled the sails of the *Northern Orchid.* As she rounded Gloucester Island the new course took the ship south. The Captain and his ship's mate spent their breakfast time arguing over the projected site for that night's anchor. Out on the deck, Stretch and Reg worked on the port side while Josh and Bellyache Basil scrubbed the decks on the starboard side of the ship. Stretch's tenor voice rang out over the sea. The men's brushes moved in rhythm with the music. In the galley, Gus assisted China in the preparation of the day's meals. His fingers, having returned almost to normal, handled the sharp knives without a problem. Even though he was happy to learn new skills and enjoyed China's amusing tales, he could not wait for tomorrow. Mister Winston had promised that he had been assigned to the engine room.

Mac had been right. the *Northern Orchid* did make it to the southern area of the Cumberland Islands when the sun, low on the horizon, witnessed the splash of the anchor as they settled for the night. The ship's mate and the captain discussed the persistence of that smudge on the eastern horizon which seemed to be dogging their every move.

The following night found the ship and crew anchored in the lee of Round Top Island off Mackay. Again, the day's sailing had been uneventful. The breeze was crisp and a slight swell lifted the bow but nothing untoward. Even though the services of the engine had not been called on during the day, Gus thoroughly enjoyed examining and servicing every moving part of the machine. He'd even managed to unload a bag of coal into the bin and top up the wood-chip bucket. Mister Winston left the lad to his own devices. That evening at tea, the subject of the grey skies to the east dominated the conversation. There was little that could be done but watch and wait.

"Mac, do you want to take the jolly-boat into Mackay tomorrow? You haven't been ashore for some time."

"Yes, Cap'n, I'd enjoy the feel of dry land under my feet for a bit." Mac took a swallow of tea from the large tin cup.

"You'll need to see the harbourmaster and organize a collection for the freight from Townsville and hopefully pick up a consignment going further south. And while you're there, will you arrange for the water hoy to deliver a load." Captain Sloan turned his head towards the bosun. "Noel, you did say that the ship's tanks were getting a bit low, did you not?"

Evans looked up from the stew and flour cakes on his plate. "Yes, Cap'n. It might be advisable to fill up here because Rockhampton can sometimes be short of water. Particularly in such a drought as the whole state is struggling with at the moment."

Mac spoke to the captain while he took up his next mouthful. "Have you any particular choice of oarsmen you want me to take in the morning then, Captain?"

"What do you think, Evans? Perhaps Josh Dougall might like a change and we need to see how our new crewmen manage rowing a boat. Can we spare the three of them as well?"

"Yes, Cap'n, that's no trouble."

The sun was still weak in the sky when the good-hearted banter rang out across the waters. The crew lining the ship's rail watched and ragged the three new sailors as they took up the oars in the jolly-boat. Laughter and ludicrous suggestions rained down upon their heads as the boat wiggled and waggled across the waves. Sitting beside them, Josh did little to hide the grin on his face. He recalled the trip his brother and he had made with Captain Harris up the Brisbane River, over nine months previously. He had learnt so much since that day.

It was deflating for these oarsmen on their return when nobody was lined up to witness the considerable improvement in their rowing skills. They did not have time to dwell on their poor audience. After Mac delivered his news to the captain, the whole crew were out on the deck preparing for the arrival of the water-hoy, within the hour. Once Evans was satisfied with that preparation, he then had the men resetting up the temporary stockyards on the bow to receive a small herd of ewes the following morning.

Mac chewed on several dry ship's biscuits and drank his strong tea as he told the captain about the sheep travelling to Rockhampton. Sloan listened with interest.

"You do realize, Mac, the fun and games we'll have trying to load these woolly monkeys from a barge. Always a tricky business."

"I've no doubt that Noel Evans will cope quite well. There's not much he hasn't done; Jimmy Dougall made sure of that."

"He did, Mac. He certainly did, at that."

Mac was in the process of collecting the pannikins lined up in the chartroom when he slapped his forehead with the palm of his hand.

"Captain, I nearly forgot to mention, there'll be several barrels of sugar cane extract and bales of wool and cotton going to Brisbane too."

"If we keep going like this, we'll end up with two full holds when we sail into Brisbane. Who knows, we may even make a profit."

Evans' voice was heard above all others as he communicated with the captain of the water hoy. The vessel rose and fell on the swell alongside the *Northern Orchid.* The ship's crew used lines to drag the canvas hoses, through which the water was to be pumped, up onto the deck. Smoke drifted up out of the hoy's small funnel to be carried away on the freshening breeze. As soon as the ends of the water hoses were placed into the water tanks the order was given to begin pumping. All in all, it proved a smooth operation despite the increased motion of both vessels. The wind almost howled through the rigging by the time the job was complete and the hoses rolled up onto the deck of the water hoy.

"Going to get a rockin' to sleep tonight, Evans," The hoy's captain called as he turned his vessel for the return journey through the sandbars and mangroves of the Pioneer River.

The man's prophecy came true. The winds strengthened during the night. Gus, on his first night back in the crow's-nest, wrapped the southwester close about his body. The morning dawned clear and the winds had abated somewhat much to the relief of Evans. Loading stock was always a challenge but to load from a barge was likely to add further excitement to the day. He was pleased to see that he did not have a gale force wind to increase his problems. He gulped his breakfast and strode out to examine the finishing touches that had been applied to the stockyards late yesterday. One makeshift crane hung over the port side of the ship attached to the mainmast. When the two barges carrying the twenty sheep did arrive all the crew was on deck ready to assist as needed. The animals lay on the barge's deck, each with three ankles tied. Their bleating filled the air. Large hessian bags of feed accompanied the animals.

Evans sent two large hemp nets down on the line from the crane. The barge-master with the help of the farmer himself and the barge crew lifted a sheep into each net. One at a time, the nets were secured to the hook on the line from the crane and then winched up to the ship. Noisy protests expressed the sheep's terror. It was Stretch and Dave who took charge of each animal as it arrived. They placed the sheep in the enclosure provided before releasing the leg ties. Each animal hastened to gather closely with its fellow sheep endeavouring to seek succour in their numbers. The crew of both vessels soon set up a rhythm with the job in hand. It looked like all was going to be done by the time the sun stood overhead.

It was as they attempted to load the last animal into the net that everything became undone. After hours of the animal's struggles, the tie on its legs loosened. The sheep struck out with four feet and the tie flew up and over the side of the barge. The animal struggled to find its balance on the moving deck of the vessel. Its frantic calls were returned from the animals in the enclosure on the ship's deck above. The farmer threw himself onto the sheep in an attempt to restrain the animal but the sheep was having none of that. Its patience was at an end. The rattling clack of its hooves on the barge deck defied the three other men who chased the terrified animal from stern to bow. It was the farmer who took the final dive as the sheep leapt over the side. He caught the nearside hind leg. The animal twisted and turned determined to escape. Amidst the yells and shouts of encouragement from the ship's crew above and the yells of the barge crew themselves and the bleating of the sheep, everyone heard the unmistakable snap of the leg as the bone broke.

"Tinker's cuss upon you." The farmer cried as he grabbed the animal by its hide and dragged it back on board.

The bleating stopped. The sheep lay still. Its pale eyes rolled backward in the eye sockets. The animal's chest fluttered up and down as it sucked in the air. The tongue hung out of the side of its mouth. The farmer knelt on his haunches.

"Stupid blighter. I may as well feed you to the sharks."

Stretch remembered China's disgust at the wasted shark at Bowen. He called out to the farmer in the barge. "Please Sir, don't chuck it overboard. There's a lot of mutton-starved men on this ship'd love a good feed."

"Do you know how to butcher the thing?"

"Done more than I can count," Stretch called back.

Captain Sloan, Mac and Evans were in the wheel-house recapping on the sheep-loading earlier in the day.

"Tell me again, how come we have a sheep hanging from the mast with its throat cut and bleeding into a tub?"

Evans chuckle threatened to explode.

"It was Stretch, Cap'n. Once the animal broke its leg, the farmer was all for hoisting it into the sea in disgust. Stretch told such a sob story of the need of our crew to be fed mutton that he had the farmer forgetting his own troubles and almost crying with compassion for us. He sent the thing up on the net for us to butcher."

Mac took up the tale.

"China has Bellyache Basil firing up the stove as we speak. He has roasts and stews planned for the next few days. He either thinks the thing is a large as a horse or he forgets how many there are here to feed."

"I'll have Stretch hanging from the yardarm for telling everyone we can't feed our crew. On the other hand, a nice fresh roast of mutton sounds quite palatable." The captain joined Mac and Evans in laughter. "Now, when can we expect the remainder of the cargo to arrive?"

"That should be here shortly," Mac replied, "Early afternoon according to the barge-master. The men are setting up a second crane, as we speak. One to load the barrels of sugar extract and one for the bales of cotton and wool."

Captain Sloan nodded his head in agreeance then turned again to his bosun.

"Evans, it might be an idea to get the three new fellows up into that high rigging for a bit of practice while the weather is mild. If there is a storm in our future, we may need them to be able to work up in the heights without falling into the sea."

"Aye, Cap'n." Evans skipped a little jig as he exited the chartroom. "Roast mutton for tea, without the mould and weevils; hurrah."

The mood was echoed by everyone as they worked with gusto during the remainder of the day receiving the cargo into their holds.

Gus felt the hands on his shoulder. He dived out of his hammock twisting to land on his back on the deck. Using his hands and heels he scuttled along on his rear end until he came up against the bulkhead. He pushed himself upright. One hand clutched at his chest where his heart pounded, almost deafening him. Nothing registered in his mind only the hands that had touched him. Air passages in spasm allowed only short gasping breaths. It felt like hours but was only moments until a voice repeating over and over entered his conscious thought.

"I'm sorry, lad. I'm sorry, Dougall. I'm sorry. Are you all right? Are you all right?"

His eyes opened and in the dim light, he recognized the shape of Mister McGregor. Gus nodded his head feebly. He could not get enough air to speak.

"Lad, I'm sorry. I for one should have known better than to startle you like that; especially after recent events."

As Gus began to relax, the mate continued with his calm deep brogue.

"You know, I remember when I was not much older than yourself. I had a terrifying experience. I was in the crow's-nest when a storm blew up out of nowhere. It was on a four-master, square-rigged vessel. The crow's-nest was very high in the air; higher than the *Northern Orchid*. It spun around and spat me out like a dog will spit out a lemon. I fell over one hundred feet, it felt like one hundred miles, down into the wilful sea. I remember distinctly how it took such a long time. All the while my head was telling me, in that storm, there was no way the ship was going to be able to find me. I was off to Davey Jones's locker and there was not a thing I was able to do about it. I was going to end my days in a stormy sea. To this day, I can remember the pain as I hit the water. Then I sank, like a large stone; down, down, down. The pressure was almost too much for my rib cage. My body desperately wanted to breathe but my mind kept telling me there was no air to breathe only water.

Gus gradually began to take in the mate's story. He stood straight and moved back to take a hold of the strut supporting the end of his hammock.

"How did you get out, Sir?"

"That was the strangest thing, lad. The whim of the sea did it. That particular wave, with me inside of it, was tossed over the bow of the ship. I was sent hurtling down towards the stern along with all the other debris. My arm hit something solid. I didn't know what it was at that moment, but I curled my elbow around it and held on like a vice. It was Captain Sloan who actually saved me. He wasn't a captain then. We were midshipmen together. He was not much older than I. He'd seen the events unfold. Without hesitating, Sloan made his way through the avalanche of water to help me. Thankfully, he had the safety line hitched to his waist. When he tried to lift me to my feet, my hold on the mast was such that I could not release my grip. He had to forcibly unwind my arms."

Mac smiled in the dim light as he noticed the change in his listener. They both stood quiet for a moment as three pairs and a single bell rang through the ship. Half an hour until the end of the middle watch. Not long before the morning shift would take over.

Gus felt his breath flowing along his air passages with ease. No longer did his heart beat threaten to burst through his chest wall. He looked up as the mate spoke again.

"Anyway, you don't want to hear me rambling on. I just wanted to reassure you that you will have nightmares for some time after your experience. It does become easier as you learn to take control again. In fact, there is the odd time that I still wake feeling the pressure on my chest but my mind immediately knows it is only a dream and I relax."

"Thank you, Sir."

"Dougall, I came to tell you to put a fire under the engine boiler. There's a drizzle of rain outside and not a breath of wind. The captain will not be wanting to sit around here all day. He'll be looking to the engine to get us on our way."

"Aye, aye, Sir; right away."

The rumble of the engine beside where he sat, comforted Gus. The captain had manoeuvred the *Northern Orchid* from between Round Top Island and Flat Top Island. The forenoon watch had just ended when a watery sun filtered through the clouds heralding the arrival of a stiff breeze. Gus jumped up when he heard the men running on the top deck in response to Evans' call to unfurl the sails. He turned to Mister Winston who dozed on the bench against the wall.

"Do you mind if I go and give a hand to set the sails, Mister Winston."

"Yes, lad. You may as well. That's a fine wind out there by the sound of it. No doubt, the captain will be calling for cease engines very shortly."

Later in the afternoon, having dampened the boiler down and with the sails humming in his ear, Gus was thrilled to be setting a course for the ship through the Capricorn Channel under Mate MacGregor's tutelage. He felt his heart swell with pride when he overheard the two men talking inside the wheel-house. The captain ordered Josh be rostered in the crow's-nest as they worked their way through the trickier areas of the Northumberland Reef. The captain said Josh had the sharpest eyes he'd known and a wisdom beyond his years. Once Gus had finished with the course plotting, he went to assist Stretch feed the now resigned sheep. He watched with interest, the way Stretch, the one they called the leather-man, calm the animals with his soft murmurings and low humming of a tune. If he hadn't been so drawn to the sea, he might have enjoyed working with animals.

That night, the Percy Islands unseen in the distance, lay south-west of their position when they dropped anchor. So far, everything pointed to an easy trip.

THE MARINER'S REST

Jacko rolled his eyes as he walked out through the back door from the kitchen. He ran his hands through his hair. Why should simply going to a church fete cause such a hullabaloo? Miss Millie had Sarah in such a dither. When told of their plans, Miss Millie turned into a whirlwind.

"Jacko, you'll have to look after the hotel tomorrow. Sarah will need a new dress. We'll go to the dressmaker first thing in the morning. She must look her best at the church fete."

Sarah had looked quite shocked. She protested.

"Miss Millie, I can't afford such a luxury. I'll launder one of my day-dresses. It will be perfectly suitable to wear to a fete; won't it?"

But when Miss Millie took the bit between her teeth there was no stopping her. Jacko recalled how Mister Christopher took the newspaper and disappeared into the dunny when she was in full flight over some cause or other. He thought he might be best advised to do the same thing.

When the next Sunday arrived and Sarah came out of her little shack dressed for their outing, Jacko admitted that Miss Millie had been right. Sarah looked an absolute picture. A full skirt of pale blue flared out from her waist. Jacko did not want to contemplate on how many petticoats may have been hidden underneath. A small matching bolero provided modesty over a long-sleeved white blouse scattered with blue flowers. On her head perched a small straw hat with long blue ribbons trailing out behind. Her dark tresses were neatly settled in rolls behind her ears. His heart pounded in a very disturbing manner. He stood gaping. Silence filled his mouth but his mind swirled. If he wasn't mistaken, Miss Millie used to have a dress of that very same colour and possibly the same texture. In fact, he'd put his shirt on it, that this may be a renovation of that same outfit. A grin slipped over his face but was quickly retrieved. Maybe, Miss Millie did not have everything her own way.

Miss Millie slammed the back door as she walked out to join the pair. Her long green well-supported frock blended perfectly with her eyes. Ecru lace decorated the bottom of her sleeves. Tendrils of her hair lay upon her face at the edge of her matching lace cap. Sensible black shoes poked out from under her hem as she walked.

"I take that stunned look as one of acceptance, Jacko," Miss Millie quipped. "Now, where's the carriage or do you plan on making us walk, my boy?"

Jacko hastened to bring Prince, who was already harnessed to the buggy, from the shed. Firstly, he assisted Miss Millie up into her seat. Before he moved Sarah towards the step, he held her hand close to his chest. He could have bit his lip when his words came out almost with a stutter.

"Sarah, you look beautiful."

Again, his heart did somersaults in a very appealing manner as the girl dropped her eyes and whispered.

"Thank you, Jacko."

As the horse's hooves clip-clopped on the roadway, Jacko sat up tall. He kept turning his gaze to the ladies behind him; particularly the younger.

"I'm going to be the most envied man at this fancy do this afternoon." Awe filled his voice.

Sarah turned and whispered to Miss Millie. "Are you sure Mrs. Hamilton will be alright on her own until we return?"

Reaching out to pat the girl's hand, Miss Millie reassured her.

"Everything's under control. You have nothing to worry about. Young Maureen Ryan turned up just before I left. She'll stay and give a hand with the afternoon teas and with preparing the evening meals."

After they found a suitable place to park the horse and buggy, Jacko double checked to ensure that the brake was pulled up tight. With gallantry, he assisted the ladies to the lawn. His heart quailed as he looked about him at the crowd of visitors all dressed in their finery. The noise of the brass band playing at full strength assaulted his ears. He questioned his common sense in bringing Sarah here. Maybe she would have preferred somewhere quieter; maybe a walk by the river bank or through a park. He knew that he would have. But when he looked into her eyes, he knew that he had done the right thing. Blue eyes sparkled like precious stones. Her face glowed with excitement. Her head swung back and forth as she endeavoured to capture every single piece of action happening here this afternoon. Jacko proudly lifted her hand onto his elbow. He offered his other elbow to Miss Millie who laughed.

"Jacko, is it the rose between the thorns or the thorn between the roses?"

"Miss Millie, looking at my two ladies here, I'm sure it's you pair who are the roses today."

Miss Millie leaned forward to catch Sarah's eye. "This man has a silver tongue, Sarah. What do you think?"

Sarah smiled then returned her gaze to where a tall man in brightly coloured shirt and trousers threw five red balls around in circles in front of his face; keeping them all in the air together.

The first stall that they came to was selling home-made sweeties. Miss Millie peeled aside and drifted over.

"I did promise Mrs. Keppel to bring her back some lollies if I found any today." She opened her little bag and paid for a large packet of the assorted sweets.

Jacko bent his head towards Sarah. "Would you like a bag of lollies, Sarah?"

Sarah shook her head and flushed. "Jacko, I've never eaten lollies before. I'm not too sure if I'd like them."

Jacko dug several pennies from the pocket of his trousers and claimed a bag of sweets for his lady.

"Look, look, Jacko, a Punch and Judy show. Goodness me, I don't think I've seen one of those since Christopher took me to a garden party in Sydney, a lifetime ago." Millie grasped his spare arm and pointed.

Sarah had already spotted the little stage with the dolls bouncing back and forth. She watched enthralled.

When they eventually began to move on, Jacko could not help but notice how the numbers of people had increased. All the ladies had their parasols up to protect their complexions against the harsh sunshine. These formed a writhing aerial carpet of a multitude of pastels. A voice caught their attention.

"Miss Millie, Sarah, how lovely to find you here."

Abigail Baldwin, flanked by Jane and Eve, pushing the perambulator, approached.

"Abigail, this is wonderful. I didn't know you were coming this afternoon." Miss Millie took up Abigail's hand and squeezed it gently.

"We didn't know we were coming until it dawned such a glorious day."

Sarah deserted Jacko's arm and joined Miss Millie who was now peering into the pram at a sleeping baby Henry.

"I do believe that lad has grown twice the size since I last saw him." Like a butterfly wing, Millie's finger caressed the baby's cheek. "He is so beautiful, dear. And you; are you well?"

"I'm feeling grand. It is Jane and Eve that I have been worried about. They've been locked away inside for days. I think this outing has already brought colour to their cheeks. What do you think, Miss Millie?"

Jane blushed at the attention. Eve rolled her eyes at Sarah and laughed.

"We were commandeered for this trip but I'm so glad. What a wonderful event."

Abigail touched Millie's shoulder. "You did get that bottle of carbolic acid that you wanted for your sea captain's medical kit? I sent it with Ned last week."

"Yes, thank you, Abigail. I'm so sorry. I've been meaning to drop in to say thank you, but the chance never presented itself, this week. The hotel has been all but full most days. It was remiss of me though. I packed the bottle into a small box and sent it, with your instructions, in the care of another ship's captain, who will deliver it to the Rockhampton harbourmaster's office. Captain Sloan will collect his mail there on his return trip." Millie touched the baby's cheeks once again before looking up at the young mother's face. "How's Doctor George getting on? He's not here with you today, I see."

"No, Miss Millie, he and Thomas will be playing cribbage all afternoon."

Jane moved forward to touch the edge of Sarah's gown.

"That material is a delightful colour. It suits you perfectly, Sarah." She looked over at Jacko and asked, "How did these two ladies cajole you into escorting them to a garden fete, Jacko? I see you are the envy of many men here this afternoon."

It was Jacko's turn to blush. Sarah intervened.

"Miss Millie, we really must make a move to go home. Mrs. Hamilton will be wondering where we are."

Farewells were shared and Jacko took up his ladies' hands on his elbows once again and led the way to where Prince had scratched a large bare patch in the grass with his impatient hooves. Jacko spoke soothing words and offered a carrot from his pocket.

As Jacko assisted Sarah into the buggy he whispered in her ear. "I have had a very enjoyable afternoon. I hope you did too."

Sarah grinned.

"It was lovely, Jacko, to play ladies for one afternoon, but to be honest with you, I'll be happy to return to the hotel and the little shack out the back."

TWENTY-TWO

THE *NORTHERN ORCHID*

While on morning lookout in the crow's-nest, Josh welcomed the diversion of watching Dave and Stretch feed and water the sheep. The sunrise appeared unhindered by the smudgy horizon of previous days. A cool breeze rippled through his hair and his shirt, sending goose-bumps along his arms. Within the hour, the bosun had the crew on deck weighing anchor and unfurling the sails. Unimpeded by his recent wounds, his brother scrambled up to relieve him.

The *Northern Orchid* may have been said to have developed some of the captain's impatience to swallow up the miles between their current position and Brisbane. The brisk breezes of the day sent her flying over the waves. That evening the anchor entered the water several nautical miles east of Broad Sound Channel.

During that night, with the moon almost full, the watch reported the return of the clouds to the eastern horizon. The winds shrilled through the rigging as the strained sunrays struggled to dispel the night's shadows. The ship was underway when the sound of a couplet followed by a single bell drifted up through the shrouds; five thirty in the morning.

Later, in the chartroom, after routine duties were completed, the ship's mate explained to Josh and Gus some of the finer points in manipulating sails to make a ship do more than just sail before a wind. Large sheets of paper were spread out on the table and pencil marks underscored the important points that he was making with his diagrams. The sun had given up on competing with the cloud cover and a lantern was called on to make the diagrams more easily seen. At the sound of the captain's voice calling for the sails to be furled and the anchor to be dropped, the boys raced outside to assist. The ship lay south-east of Cape Clinton.

"You know, I think those sheep will be sad to say goodbye to you, Stretch." Gus gave a cheeky grin to the man doling out hay the next morning.

"We should be at the mouth of the Fitzroy River by noon, or so Mister Evans was saying last night. I think they'll be glad to put their feet on solid ground once again." Stretch nodded his head towards the small herd in the pens. "Can yer fill another bucket of water for that other lot, Gus?"

Gus wandered over to the water barrel secured against the bulwark where he began ladling the fluid into a wooden piggin'. It was at that moment the bosun stepped out of the wheel-house and called for the capstan to be manned. The time had come to weigh anchor.

During the day, the wind was as reliable as a holed vessel. For much of the morning, the sails hung limp on the yards. Frustration etched across his face, each time the captain prepared to call to have the fire started under the engine boiler. As if on cue, a vigorous wind billowed the sails causing him to change his mind. It was after noon before they dropped anchor in Keppel Bay, north of Curtis Island; within easy distance of the Fitzroy River mouth.

The captain's next decision was to choose whether to wait here, on the off chance of a pilot's vessel exiting the river-mouth or to row the twenty-eight miles into the harbour and request one. He and Mac were just settling to a pannikin of tea when the watch in the crow's-nest called a sighting of a vessel nosing its way through the mangrove-lined banks at the mouth of the river. Mac retrieved the flags from the ledge in the wheel-house and produced a signal to alert the pilot on board that vessel, of their needs.

Dark shadows mingled with the remnant light of the sun hidden behind the horizon, when they dropped anchor, for the second time that day. They settled for the night in the river opposite the wharf, where they were to await permission before approaching the stock-loading jetty. The pilot shared a small rum with Captain Sloan and Mate MacGregor before he disappeared over the side of the *Northern Orchid* via the bosun's chair.

Mac and half the crew were given shore leave that evening with instructions to return before the middle watch began at midnight.

The crew kept out of the captain's way as he paced the upper deck, constantly watching for the arrival of news to prepare for unloading the sheep. Their bleating never faulted. At mid-morning, Mac's smile was contained as he listened to Captain Sloan's impatient grumbling.

"Mac, how's a man supposed to keep the engine's steam up indefinitely. For all I know, it could be today or even a week's time before we're told to unload." He grimaced when Mac pointed out that the boiler's fires were not alight; as per his orders. "That's not the point. They don't know that."

The sun was high in the sky before a man from the harbourmaster's office signalled them to move up to the stock-loading ramp. The captain chose to use the sails to manoeuvre the *Northern Orchid* the short distance. As soon as the ship was secured, Captain Sloan strode ashore heading towards the harbourmaster's office. Left on board, Mac supervised while Evans had the crew line up the water barrels to produce a laneway for the sheep to move across the top deck and onto the animal loading gangplank. The crew was out in force to say goodbye to their four-legged passengers. Stretch slid in beside China and spoke.

"China, you're not up 'ere putting a curse on the sheep in the 'ope that another may break a leg, are yer?"

"Aah, Mister Sheepman. I think everyone enjoyed their lamb dinners, don't you?"

Both stood silent watching as the small cloven hooves clattered across the timber deck encouraged by their new shepherds.

Mac joined China and Stretch.

"Don't tell me you're feeling homesick, Stretch?"

"No, Mister MacGregor; I've 'ad my fill of looking after sheep."

"Well, we'll need to clear up this deck and prepare to move up to the number three wharf this afternoon. Gus has a head of steam in the boiler now so we'll use the engine. Apparently, tomorrow morning they'll be ready to load the cargo of hides. After that we have to hang about until the bullock team arrives carrying the wool-clip and grain, going through to Brisbane. It's expected here either late tomorrow or the next morning. I'll have Evans set the men catching the rats in the holds. We don't want to land in Brisbane with holes chewed in all the sacks of grain." Mac went to walk away then turned, suddenly. "I guess you've heard that the crew who did not have shore leave last night are free from four bells into the dog-watch, until midnight."

When the captain returned to the ship, he called the Dougall boys to his cabin. Their eyes lit up at the sight of a letter from their sister.

Early though it was, the heat of the day was already building when the loading of the hides began. Two of the crew members peered through red and bleary eyes. This did not evoke any sympathy from the bosun.

"Self-inflicted injuries," he mumbled when he listened to the groans from those with the painful heads.

Captain Sloan spent the following day in his cabin, having received word that the bullock wagon, with its cargo of wool and grain, was not now expected to arrive at Rockhampton until the morrow. He did not take kindly to a day's delay.

"Keep those men busy, Evans," was his parting remark as he retreated to his domain.

Men were set to scrubbing decks as well as outside the hull where the sludge from the galley stained the sides of the ship. Others inspected the rigging lines to ensure all were in top condition. Sails that had been stored awaiting mending were retrieved and needles set to work. Tins of paint and brushes were allotted to anyone who dared to look idle for a few moments.

Everyone was pleased when the loading of the wool bales and sacks of grain commenced the next morning. With the cargo holds full and secured, Captain Sloan's humour was restored; as was that of the crew. Everyone cheered when a pilot was made available to take the *Northern Orchid* out into the bay on the afternoon tide.

The sun sulked behind the grey clouds all morning. With each passing hour, the wind progressively increased its ferocity and its wailing. The crew fought to furl the reluctant main and gallant sails leaving only the reefed topsails to thrust the ship forward. These, the wind attacked savagely. They resonated like whips cracking. The noise competed with the frequent claps of thunder in the skies above. Down in the engine room, Gus stood with his legs braced apart as he shovelled coal from the bin and into the fire. Grim determination was written in the frown on his face. He knew the boiler pressure must be maintained. With the rising storm and the ship confined in the narrow channel, the engine could be required at a moment's notice to propel the *Northern Orchid* out of a dangerous situation.

"We are nearing the Capricorn Island Group area where there is little room to manoeuvre. This is not the best time to have a storm hit us." Gus had heard the captain tell Mister Winston.

High above the deck, in the crow's-nest, Josh hung on for dear life as his eyrie swayed back and forth, around and around. For the third time, he checked the safety line attaching him and the barrel to the mast. What use were his eagle eyes when the sheets of rain covered their ship like night's blanket? He had little hope of seeing any threatening reefs or an approaching vessel through this. Icy rain lashed the decks which were lit up intermittently by streaks of lightning. He wrapped the borrowed sou'wester tight about his shivering body and pulled the cap down firmly on his head. Still, water managed to trickle down his neck to wet his flannel shirt underneath. With cold hands, he rubbed vigorously at his frozen arms. A brief lapse of envy ran through him when a vision of his brother snug and warm in the engine room filled his mind.

"Lucky sod."

Spitefully the waves tossed the vessel up and down, bow to stern, then sideways from port beam to starboard beam without showing favouritism. At times, the *Northern Orchid* balanced on the crest of a wave like a javelin in the hands of an Olympian. The pointed bow aimed directly at the ocean floor. With a jaw-cracking thud, the ship landed in the trough of the waves. Tons of water rolled over the bows leaving the deck awash. Dislodged equipment became missiles in the knee-deep water covering the deck while awaiting drainage through the flooded scuppers. With creaks and groans of her timbers, the *Northern Orchid* crept up the crest of the following wave only to be smacked down into the next trough.

In the wheel-house, Captain Sloan and the mate struggled together to control the recalcitrant helm. The order roared out above the storm's din for the bilge pumps to be manned.

"The last thing we want now, Mac, is for the boiler fires to be flooded and we lose our engine."

Ewan MacGregor's red hair hung wet around his head as he leant out of the wheel-house door to ensure the message was received by the bosun. When he moved back to help his friend, he mumbled.

"The crew are probably safer down below working the pumps than hanging around the deck waiting to get washed overboard."

"Oh, Heavens; I forgot China. I do hope he has the sense to stay in the galley. I would not put it past him to take it into his head to come out and check on his hens."

"I'll tell Evans to look in on the old fella; when he has a moment."

"Thanks."

But it was Dave who came to China's rescue as he struggled to cover his drowning fowls. It took the combined strength of them both to hold the canvas down against the gusting winds long enough to tie it tightly. The short muscular man almost picked the Chinaman off his feet as he escorted him back to the companion-way leading to the lower deck. They both slipped through as quickly as they were able but it was frightening to see how much water flowed down around them before they could secure the hatch at their backs.

Then, as if someone had pulled aside a huge curtain, the wind scattered the clouds and the sun shone out triumphant, banishing the rain. Only a few stubborn clouds were left to spit at the world. The swell of the sea lessened but was not so ready to call a truce. An occasional large twisting wave gave the ship a surprise toss. The rush of the water drumming down the overloaded scuppers remained the only evidence of the short-lived storm; that and the torn foremast top sail flapping in the now moderate winds.

Josh jumped up to hang out over the side of the lookout. His eyes narrowed. He shut his eyes tight and looked again.

"Breakers to port," he yelled to the wheel-house below. He pointed his arm in the direction of his find. "Looks to be a sail in trouble, Captain."

"Mac, take the scope and tell me what you can see," Captain Sloan held firmly to the helm as the ship's mate took up the telescope and stepped on to the walkway outside the wheel-house. He stood for some time peering through the lens at the situation on the reef five or six miles portside of the *Northern Orchid.*

Ewan MacGregor moved back into the wheel-house. "Certainly, breakers out there; most probably the Masthead Reef by the look of it. There's definitely a ship. Looks like it may be a small schooner in trouble over there."

The captain stroked his chin. "It could be the *Fleur.* According to the harbourmaster in Rockhampton, she's supposed to be in these waters at the moment. Can you see any activity going on?"

"The ship's taking a pounding in the surf on the rocks. The mainmast has snapped in half and there's no sign of the other masts. I think the crew are trying to launch the boats."

The helm came around in Captain Sloan's hand.

"Tell young Josh to keep his eyes peeled up there for the reef and tell the men to begin the soundings as we make an approach." As the captain picked up the speaking piece, he blew down the tube sending a piercing whistle into the engine room. "Guthrie, give me very slow ahead. We may have a rescue." He turned back to Mac.

"Bring up the relief crew from the bilge pump. We'll need a few hands on the deck and send someone up top to clew up those topsails ready to furl."

Once the instructions were relayed to the bosun, Mac stood with his eye at the telescope watching the flailing craft. He acknowledged and passed on to the captain each snippet of information that came down to him from the crow's-nest. He listened and repeated aloud the calls from the men taking the depth readings as they walked with the submerged weighted line from the bow towards the stern.

From up in the crow's-nest, Josh had a splendid view as they drew closer to the reef and the stricken vessel. He waved to Andrews and Tanner who slipped lightly through the rigging like spiders in their webs securing the earing on the sails above as the crew below hauled on the halyards.

Mac held the telescope tighter into his eye.

"Oh, God save them," he cried. "Their jolly-boat has been overturned and all are in the water."

At the same time, Josh called down from the lookout with a similar update. Mac strained to see if he could identify, through his scope, the individual bodies in the seas and froth of the breakers.

"Prepare both our jolly-boat and the longboat, Mac. If possible, put our most seasoned crewmen on board. I don't want unnecessary lives lost from the *Northern Orchid*. Make sure they have extra lines on board and the medical box. If I anchor the ship out in the deep, will we get a line across do you think?"

"Looking at their position, I'd say we'd be better placed if we can find a break in the reef for our smaller boats. Once into the lagoon, we can work from the shore."

"Ask Josh if he can find a gap."

A frown creased the captain's brow as he edged closer to the reef. It was the frantic call from Josh above, as he told of rocks ahead three hundred yards combined with the warning from those taking the depth readings that had William Sloan spinning the wheel to angle away from the reef.

From his bird's-eye view, Josh watched the dark shadows of the rocks become clearer as the ship edged closer and closer. He began calling the distances. Seventy-five yards. Fifty yards. Would the ship never respond to the rudder? It seemed to be taking forever to turn away. Then it happened.

THE MARINER'S REST

In an effort to remove the dangling tendrils from her face, Sarah poked her bottom lip out further than her top lip and blew. Her flour-covered hands thumped, twisted and folded the dough as she prepared the day's bread loaves for the oven. So engrossed was she in her work, that she did not hear the man slip in through the back door. When a smiling Arthur Rankine pulled out a chair at the table and seated himself opposite her, she froze. The large ball of dough dropped from her nerveless fingers into the refreshed heap of flour sending it spraying out in all directions before falling like a white cloud over his dark suit. It was Arthur's turn to jump. He quickly contained the frown of anger that distorted his features.

"Miss Sarah, I have come to apologize and this is how you greet me; with a dusting of flour."

Flustered, Sarah rushed to the sink to clean her hands before taking a laundered cloth from the drawer and brushing down Arthur's jacket. The next man to enter the kitchen wore a frown to match Arthur's own earlier look of displeasure.

Jacko asked, "Is everything alright here, Sarah?"

Sarah stood back, her face flushed and her hands trembling.

"Jacko, I'm so sorry. The flour fluffed up onto Mister Rankine's good clothes. Do you think it's all out now?"

"Shouldn't you be apologizing to me, Sarah? It is my suit that has been destroyed."

Jacko moved a step towards the visitor. Fury fanned across his face. Sarah held up her hand towards him. Her stuttering reply was interrupted by another's voice carrying much more weight.

"You have a reason to be here, have you, Arthur?" Miss Millie stood at the dining room doorway with her hands on her hips. The glare from her eyes streaked across the room.

"Aah, Miss Millie, it is you I have come to see; after I've apologized to Miss Sarah for my behavior recently. Can we talk privately?"

Millie led her visitor out through the dining room towards her office. Jacko's unspoken reply to her retreating glance reassured Millie that he would be within calling distance if required.

Millie moved in behind her desk and indicated a chair in the corner of her small office. Arthur sat, still brushing at the flour on his clothes.

"Now, Arthur, what is it that you have to tell me?"

"Miss Millie, I pondered on your words of wisdom recently. That is why I've come here today; to apologize to Sarah. I also wanted to tell you that I have decided to leave Brisbane and move on to Maryborough. An established legal firm there has offered me a partnership. This might be what I need. You know, to get out of the city. I was hoping for your blessing."

Millie's heart softened. She stood up and walked around to the front of the desk. She took Arthur's hands in her own before kissing the cheek of this man who was once a lonely badly treated young boy.

"Arthur, I think that's wonderful for you. You'll write often and tell me all that you are doing, won't you?"

"Yes, Miss Millie, of course. Now, if it's all right with you, I'll slip out of the front door. I prefer not to get too close to Jacko. He seems very protective of Sarah."

"Yes, he is, rather."

Later that day, as Sarah sat on the log at the sandy spit by the river, Jacko left her to her own thoughts. He wandered down to where he kept a fish trap in the mangroves but it was empty. Whether because no fish had been tempted to enter or because someone may have helped themselves, he could not be sure. On his return to Sarah's side, Jacko scrounged around picking wildflowers to make a small posy. He watched surreptitiously as he gathered. The shadow of her wide-brimmed bonnet half hid her face but he was sure she was not as sad as she usually appeared when visiting the river that had taken her sister from her. He approached the young woman who, in recent times seemed to fill his every thought. With a smile, he pointed to the space on the log.

"Do you mind if I sit beside you, Sarah?"

It took a moment before she focused on what Jacko said. Her mind was not on the here and now. Looking up, she smiled as she tucked her dress closer about her and moved aside a little.

"Of course, Jacko. What have you got there?" She pointed to the small straggly flowers in his work-hardened hands.

"These, my lady, are for you." A grin spread to his eyes.

A flush brightened her features.

"Oh, Jacko, they are lovely." Sarah took the flowers and cradled them in her hands. "What have I done to earn this sweet surprise?"

"Sarah, I think you know that you only have to smile to bring joy to my heart. If I could, I'd buy you jewels and castles and everything you could want but these flowers are all I can afford, I'm afraid."

The flush infused her face once more. She lay her hand over Jacko's hand resting on his lap. Even above the pounding of his heart, he heard her whispered words.

"Jacko, this posy of flowers is of more treasure to me than all the castles and jewels in the world. What on earth would I do with jewels and castles? I'd just worry and think of all the cleaning they'd need."

Jacko relaxed. He chuckled then went quiet for some time. When he looked up, he found Sarah's blue eyes staring at his face. He dragged in a deep breath.

"Sarah, I don't want you to feel pressure and I don't want to hurry your decision. I just want to tell you that, one day, I would very much like to take you for my bride."

Sarah sprung up. Her hands including the posy flew to her face.

"Ooh."

Jacko stood also and tentatively reached out his own hand.

"Sarah, Sarah, I'm sorry if I've frightened you. I know you are only young and I must seem like an old man to you. Please, at least think about it."

Her eyes sparkled. The posy of flowers ended up stragglier than ever as they were wrapped about his neck in her hands.

"Jacko, I think that would be the most wonderful thing that could ever happen to me."

Cautiously he folded his arms about her waist. He felt himself swallow the unmanly tears in his throat.

"You do?"

"But what will Miss Millie say? What will she do? I mean, we don't have to be married immediately, do we? I can still go on working at the hotel for her." Sarah stepped back; her face aflame. "What a shameful hussy you must think me. I'm being too forward, aren't I?"

Jacko laughed aloud.

"I think you're perfect. And I don't think Miss Millie will have too many complaints either."

Miss Millie wore a smile when she noticed Jacko and Sarah returning from their riverside walk, hand in hand. As the three of them enjoyed their nightly cup of cocoa, Jacko and Sarah told her most of what she had already gathered. Millie reassured Sarah neither she nor Jacko was to leave the Mariner's Rest. After they marry, they would be accommodated in the shack.

Before Sarah could ask, Millie went on to say, "After you are married my dears, Josh and Gus will share what was Jacko's room in the hotel; that is when they are not on the *Northern Orchid*."

Silence fell around the table while the young couple gazed into each other's eyes and Millie's head filled with plans for a betrothal party.

TWENTY-THREE

THE *NORTHERN ORCHID*

Overhead a rainbow arched across the sky above the *Northern Orchid*. From the crow's-nest, Josh held his breath as he watched the bow swing aside missing the reef by a matter of feet. He whistled his relief.

At a more positive report from Josh and those with the soundings, the captain whistled down the voice pipe telling Mister Winston to cease engines but keep the boiler pressure up until further notice. He ordered the anchor away.

Without pausing to inhale, the captain then rattled out further orders. "We'll have the stern anchor out too, Mac. Has Josh found a gap in the reef yet? Let's have those two boats in the water. Mac, I want you to go in the first. You may be able to pluck a few souls from the sea."

Evans had the boats in the water by the time Mac had received directions from Josh on the most likely spot to attempt the reef crossing. The jolly-boat rose up and down with the ocean swell about a chain out from the side of the ship. Evans stood at the bow. Bandy worked with an oar in each hand while Andrews shared the next pair of oars with Dave. At the ship, the mate shinnied down the line over the port side and into the longboat where Tanner, Adams, Rollins and Basil waited for their orders to row.

The remaining crew, including Guthrie and Gus from the engine room and China from the galley, lined the starboard side of the ship watching the drama unfolding on the nearby reef. Josh had the best seat of all. From his position at the top of the mast, he watched as Mister MacGregor and Rollins struggled to lift three lifeless bodies into the larger boat. The oarsmen bent their backs to the oars straining to keep outside the reef until they came to where he was sure they'd find an opening into the lagoon. A wide grin split Josh's face as the two vessels rode a wave into the more placid waters beyond.

Mac jumped out of the longboat, up to his thighs in the water. He began pulling the boat up onto the sand. Dave was doing the same with the second boat. Blood ran down the arms and legs of a man running along the sand towards them. Torn clothing flapped around his body. He had come from near where the wrecked vessel was breaking up on the reef about thirty yards out from shore. In a spray of sand, he pulled up beside them.

"Thanks for stopping. Jacobson, bosun from the *Fleur*. That's 'er on the rocks. The captain's still on board. I've two men setting up a cable to the beach. We still have two women and a child on board."

"Ewan MacGregor, mate, *Northern Orchid*. Glad to help." Mac swung back to his men. "Bring the extra cables, lads; hurry now. It won't be too long before there's nothing left of the vessel." He was just about to move off when he called Rollins back. "Might be a good idea to cover those bodies in the bottom of the boat with the sail before you come with us, lad." He ran after the group heading to the rescue point.

An old man with blood running down the side of his face scrambled amongst the rocks in the shallow water attempting to reach the end of a cable that had been thrown with a very strong arm from the man at the bow of the *Fleur*.

"Go and sit down, man. We'll take it from here." Mac led the man into the shade of the only palm tree on the miniature island.

"Make that cable secure around this rock." He ordered Dave and Bandy pointing to a large boulder that looked like an earthquake would not move it. "I'm going out to see if I can help some of the passengers to the land."

He turned to Tanner who wrapped the safety lanyard around his waist, attaching him to the thick cable. A makeshift rope seat was also looped around that cable. A smaller line was attached to the seat and held on shore by the *Fleu*r's bosun, Jacobson.

"Let that line follow me and the seat, slowly. We don't want it snagged. You can use it to pull the seat in later." A similar line was secured to the other side of the seat. This line, Mac held rolled over his shoulder.

"Keep the cable taut, Tanner, will you? I don't want to be bashed senseless on the rocks."

"Aye, Sir."

With one hand on the safety cable and the other pulling the seat along with him, he made his way through the rocks and out to the deeper waters.

"Aaah," Mac sucked in his breath as the cold water hit his chest. His booted feet slipped on rocks slimy with sea moss. Those boots protected him when scrambling over rocks treacherous with sharp-edged oyster shells. Along the journey, there were several gaps of deep water where he had to kick with his legs to help propel himself forward. As he neared the ship, the cable rose high into the air to reach the bow pointing to the sky. The aft was nothing but splintered timbers wrapped around the rocks.

Mac steadied himself on a flat rock just below the surface. He threw the other end of the line, attached to the seat, towards a man clinging to the bulwark at the bow of the ship. He assumed this man to be the captain of the *Fleur*. Beside this man stood two women with dresses saturated and their hair askew. They also struggled to maintain their position at the bow of a deck on a steep incline. A pair of eyes peeped out of the folds of one skirt like a baby kangaroo peering out of its mother's pouch. The two women were politely arguing about who should go first. The younger one insisted the woman attached to the child should lead off.

"Jeez, just move will you," Mac mumbled to himself. "This water is freezing me bits off."

The man at the bow settled the mother and child in the rope seat and with quiet words of advice, he eased them on their way. The weight swung the pair down to where Mac waited on the rock below.

"Ma'am, give me the child. You'll need both your hands. I'll swim with the child beside you. You'll go into the water in the lower area but I'll do my best to ensure your head remains clear. Whatever you do, don't panic."

"I have never seen the sense in panic, Sir, but thank you for your help and advice." As she handed her son over, she assured Mac, "My son won't give you any trouble."

Mac was relieved at the common sense of the woman. They began their journey to the shore. The small lad clung to Mac's neck like he was bent on strangling him. His large eyes bored into those of the strange man. At times Mac assisted the seat along while paying attention to the perilous rocks under his feet. One rogue wave surprised them both. He called a late warning but the lady's head disappeared under the surface. Mac was able to lift himself and the boy up on the passing wave. As soon as his feet returned to the rocks, he pulled at the rope seat to help bring it to the surface. The lady came up spitting and coughing.

"You alright, Ma'am?"

After taking a deep rasping breath, her reply was a strained whisper.

"Thank you, yes."

Bandy and Rollins waded out to assist the pair to shore while Mac left on the second trip to the stricken vessel. The man at the bow was loading the lady when Mac arrived at the large flat rock. It was this fellow at the bow who called to Mac above the noise of the crashing waves.

"Our captain has a broken leg. The bone's sticking out. I've wrapped the leg in sailcloth. We've built a stretcher with spars and a sail spread over a cabin door and three float rings. I'll need a couple of men to help lift him on the stretcher out over the side before guiding the float along the cable."

Mac waved his hand in acknowledgement of the message. So, that fellow is not the captain, he pondered. The captain is out of sight with a compound fracture of a leg. That does not sound good; certainly, not in this situation.

"I'll bring men out after delivering this lady to shore." Mac turned around to do that only to find the young woman had already set off on her journey in a very capable manner. Mac struggled to catch up.

"Dave!" he called. "And Rollins! Come with me."

At the wreck, Mac directed Dave around to where he could climb onto the deck showing above the water. Like an ape, he clung to whatever ropes, rails and cleats were available to him as he climbed up to the bow of the boat. Using the lanyards attached to the four corners of the stretcher, the men at the bow were able to lower the wounded captain over the side and down to where Mac and Rollins waited. When it reached the water surface, the make-shift stretcher floated admirably. The wounded man lay with his ashen face distorted in a grimace of pain. Utilizing the safety cable, they floated the raft as gently as possible through the waters and rocks to the sandy beach. Mac looked back to see Dave and the bow-man right behind. They stood on a rock; transfixed. Their bodies were turned facing back out to sea. Then he saw it; a large grey fin.

"Come on fella's, get a move on." Mac pushed the floating stretcher harder moving everyone along as fast as feasible. With a crunch, the stretcher slid up onto the sandy shore.

Mac turned back again to check on Dave and the bowman. They were now following fast. The shark was drifting in ever tightening circles. It edged closer to the men with each arc.

"Hurry up, will you?" Mac yelled.

Everyone jumped as a gun roared. Mac spun around to where the shot had come from the shore. Tanner stood with the smoking gun from the longboat in his hands. Mac looked back to sea. Blood coloured the water around the shark's head as it retreated. He turned his attention back to the wounded man on the stretcher.

The younger of the two women ran from the bedraggled group to crouch in the sand by the wounded man's head.

"Dad, Dad, you'll be fine now. We'll get you medical help."

Mac examined the slack face of the captain lying on the stretcher. He knew that not a word had been heard. While rolling up a cable, the bowman from the wreck walked over to Mac and introduced himself.

"I'm Donald Farley. This is my father-in-law, Captain Bruce."

Mac explained that the leg wound needed to have the bones pulled together. It must be cleaned and the skin sewn up if they were to have any chance of saving the man's life. "We'll take him aboard the *Northern Orchid* immediately. Our captain has considerable experience treating wounds. He'll need to examine the situation. We are a good distance from any doctor in this region."

As the men in the two boats hauled on the oars, the bow of the *Fleur* disappeared out of sight with the remnants heard crashing on to the rocks.

In the light cast from the hurricane lamp, Captain Sloan and Mac stood examining Captain Bruce's wound which was now clear of its coverings. In the first-class passenger cabin, the man's daughter sat stoically by her father's head speaking softly. A six-inch-long ragged laceration from which the blood trickled split his right lower leg. The upper part of the lower-leg-bone could be seen overriding the lower section of the lower-leg-bone.

"Put traction on the leg to pull the bone ends together and then sew me up." The voice was faint but clear. "Give me a few swigs of rum first. Then, just do it, lads."

The young woman's face pleaded with them to do as the man asked.

"His father, my grandfather, is a doctor. Dad has a fair knowledge of what must be done."

Mac and his captain shrugged. Captain Sloan nodded his head at Mrs. Farley before digging into the medical box on the table. He lifted his head to speak to the ship's mate.

"You'd best get Stretch and maybe the Dougall boys to help. Tell Josh to bring the bottle of rum in the right-hand drawer of the desk in my cabin."

Stretch stood near Captain Bruce's head, his hands rested lightly on the man's shoulders. Mac and Gus stood on either side of the wounded man's hips ready to reach forward and hold the leg steady at the knee area. Captain Sloan and Josh planned to exert pulling weight above the foot. If this was to work, they had to slide the bone ends apart then align them up together. The half empty rum bottle sat on the table next to the medical box.

"Do it." Came the whispered instructions from the patient.

Mac placed the roll of leather wadding between the man's teeth. Stretch leant heavily on the patient's shoulders, doing his best not to impede the man's shallow breathing while holding the two arms. Mac and Gus took a firm hold on the knee and lower thigh. Captain Sloan and Josh took hold of the lower leg and ankle. On the captain's word, they pulled slow and hard.

A scream slid around the edges of the leather wadding. Sweat beads stood out on the ashen face before the man passed out. Gus cringed as the bones scraped alongside each other. Sweat stood out on the brows of all those present. A fresh spurt of blood poured from the wound.

"Don't let go, Josh. Keep a tight hold. Pull a little more. Can you see anything there, Mac?"

Mac instructed Gus to hold hard as he released his right hand and felt inside the wound. "The bone alignment feels pretty good."

"Ease the pressure off slowly, everyone." Captain Sloan felt inside the wound. He grunted, then poured the remaining rum between the lips of the lacerated flesh. He grinned. "Not bad, not bad at all. Even the smaller bone is lying neatly in place. Now I'll see if I remember how to sew."

As he inserted large mattress stitches to the skin, he looked up to where Gus stood wide-eyed.

"Gus, I want you to go to my cabin. You'll find a small box on my desk. It has a bottle of fluid inside. A sheet of instructions is included. I want you to bring the box and its contents back here as quick as you can."

Mac lifted his head from where he assisted by cutting the thread using a cut-throat razor from the medical kit.

"What have you got in the mystery box, Cap'n?"

"It's a bottle of carbolic acid." Captain Sloan explained how he had acquired the item from Doctor Goldfinch, at Brisbane, via his friend Millie Carson. He reported on what he understood of its use as an antiseptic, while he finished bringing the wound together.

Mrs. Farley moved forward from where she had silently watched the complete process. She questioned the captain closely on what he knew of the antiseptic and its use.

"I understand that suppuration and gangrene are the two most dangerous complications following fractures like this one. Do you think it's possible to prevent this from happening using this fluid?" she asked.

The captain looked with sympathy at the daughter of his patient. Having seen many men die following compound bone breaks like this, he held out little hope for Captain Bruce.

"Mrs. Farley, I cannot promise anything but I do believe the doctor, who sent this to me, is well qualified in London and has experience using this solution."

Her head sunk to her chest for a moment. She then looked up and stuck out her chin. She thanked everyone present. As the carbolic acid was applied on linen bandages she watched intently. After all, was completed, she informed the captain that she and her husband could dress the wound and care for her father now.

"Before we finish here, I want to secure this lower leg with parallel pieces of timber. They will prevent this part of the leg moving and the broken bone being disturbed. When your father recovers somewhat, I will discuss with him where he wishes me to take him. We can return to Rockhampton; there is a small hospital there. Maryborough has a small hospital also. I can make a trip directly to Brisbane if he chooses, as my holds are full."

The moon shone out of a clear sky as they stepped out into the welcome light breeze. A bucket of sea water had been left at the door of the cabin. After the men had washed up, the contents were red with blood. Captain Sloan swiped the moisture from his face and wiped his hands down his trousers.

"Let's see if China has a feed ready for us. I'm starving. Josh and Gus, you can give a hand in the galley. Send meals, on a tray, into Mister and Mrs. Farley and see the others from the *Fleur* get a feed also. We'll weigh anchor first thing tomorrow. Hopefully, I will have spoken with Captain Bruce by then."

Josh and Gus headed to the companion-way leading to the lower deck and the galley. Gus turned back to ask Captain Sloan the question that filled his head.

"After all that, will he be alright; Captain Bruce, I mean, Sir?"

"That's all in the hands of the gods, lad. A doctor I once worked with in the navy firmly believed that he had a better success rate when he realigned the broken bones and sewed up the wounds." William Sloan rubbed his eyes. "Occasionally it is successful which is better than hardly ever successful, if not done."

Gus turned to move off but the captain's voice called him back.

"You and your brother did well in there, Gus. Tell Josh for me, will you?"

"Aye, Cap'n" Gus held his shoulders square and his head high.

When Josh and Gus entered the galley, they found Stretch with his knees on either side of a tub. Feathers floated around his legs. On the wall, two chooks hung from a hook. Blood dripped from the stumps of their necks into a dish. The third chook, in Stretch's hands, was almost denuded of its feathers.

"These three hens were drowned in the storm," Stretch explained.

"I make chicken soup for everyone; especially the sick man," China spoke from behind the cloud of flour where he was pounding a large damper into submission.

Captain Sloan threw himself onto his bunk with a sigh. The temptation to drift into a deep slumber tormented him. The loud knocking on the door gave him no choice.

"Enter!"

The door opened slowly. Evans' head peered into the cabin.

"Cap'n, sorry to disturb you but you may want to know that I put Mrs. Cousins and her son, Peter, into the third cabin on the top deck."

Captain Sloan's face stared vacantly at his bosun.

"Who is Mrs. Cousins?" His face cleared. "Oh, the other woman from the *Fleur*. I'd forgotten about her."

"Yes, Cap'n, her husband was drowned at the shipwreck. His is not one of the bodies recovered."

Sloan rubbed his eyes. He would have sworn they were full of sand if he did not know better.

"Whew, what sort of state is the poor woman in, Evans? I guess I'd better go and see her."

"You mayn't have to do that, Sir. China and I made her take some food and hot tea for herself and the child. After that, she said she'd like to be alone with her son. There's no lantern light in her cabin now so I assume they've retired."

The captain smiled and nodded his gratitude before Evans went on to report further.

“Sir, while you were busy with Captain Bruce, I took the opportunity to lay out the three recovered bodies awaiting burial. I thought you’d want to bury them first chance.”

“Yes, Evans, of course. Organize a sea burial first light tomorrow before we weigh anchor.”

THE MARINER'S REST

A cool breeze from the river blew in through the front doorway chasing the warmth of the evening. The dishes rattled in the sink as Sarah rinsed out the cocoa cups and left them draining on the bench. Miss Millie stretched and yawned. She pushed her chair back and stood up.

"Well, I'm off to bed. I'll see you both tomorrow morning. Don't forget, we have four of our guests requiring their breakfast early. They have to catch the coach to Toowoomba."

"I won't forget. Goodnight, Miss Millie." Sarah turned and smiled.

"Night, Miss Millie." Jacko stood and replaced his chair under the table before reaching for the lantern hanging on the post near the doorway. He lit a taper from the stove fire and set the wick alight before turning down the lamp on the table. "I'll just lock up before I walk you over to the shack, Sarah."

"Really, Jacko? All of a sudden I'm unable to find my way to the shack on a moonlight night?" Sarah's grin flashed for a brief moment and then her face became serious. "It feels nice to have someone care." She reached out and took his hand that was not carrying the lantern.

Jacko's hand slipped about her waist by the time they had stepped down from the verandah into the back yard.

"Do we really need that lantern, Jacko? The moon is extra lovely tonight."

Before Jacko made a move to turn down the wick of the lantern, they both heard the scream of a horse, a loud crash and the stamping of hooves. A dark shadow tore out of the stables on thundering feet. In the moonlight, the terrified eyes in Prince's tossing head reflected white. Both Jacko and Sarah ran together.

As they entered the opened doors of the stable it was the pacing of Emperor and Samson in the stalls that caught their attention. Their heads tossed their manes left and right. Snot flew from their noses as they snorted. Near the door, a lit lantern lay on the dirt floor. Some of the oil had leaked out and set alight scattered bits of stubbled hay. Jacko began stomping and kicking on the burning hay in an endeavour to forge a break between the small fire and the unburnt grass. He looked up at the urgent call from Sarah.

"Jacko! It's Ned, he's hurt."

With the threat of fire removed, Jacko ran to where Ned lay, unmoving, on his back in the dirt. Ned's eyes were shut. Blood ran from a large wound on the right-hand side of his head. Bloody hair matted the wound.

"I'll get a cloth." Sarah took the lantern that Jacko had rescued from the floor and disappeared into Ned's little room at the back of the stable. At the doorway, she paused holding up the light to see. A narrow cot covered with a grey blanket took up one side wall. A small cupboard and an old arm-chair on the other. The remaining space of the second wall contained a line of large nails on which various articles hung; including a bath towel. Sarah snatched it down. Her hands folded the cloth which she placed on the unconscious man's wound as a compress.

Jacko spoke quietly to Emperor and Samson while offering them a handful of oats. Gradually their pacing ceased. Every now and then one or the other tossed its head and snorted. Jacko held the light up to examine the rafters but there did not appear to be anything there that might have frightened the animals. He'd known the horses to be upset when an occasional python snake, stalking a meal, made its way up into the beams. Sometimes an owl roosted up there but the birds seldom worried the animals. Possums were always a pest. The horses hated their smell and were often restless if one of them prowled the area. Tonight, he could not see one at all.

Miss Millie burst through the stable doors. "What's going on? I heard all the ruckus."

"It's Ned, Millie. Something has frightened Prince. He's bolted right through the rails of his stall." Jacko pointed to where the broken timbers lay scattered about.

Millie knelt beside Sarah and looked at the man's wound. She tapped the side of Ned's cheeks.

"Ned! Ned!" But Ned was unresponsive.

"Jacko, you'll need to go for Doctor George. It might be quicker to run than try to quieten these two to the bridle. Duck out the short cut behind the wash house. Where is Prince, by the way?"

But Jacko was gone. Sarah answered.

"We saw him dashing out of here just as we arrived. I'm not too sure where he is now. It looked like he might be heading for Sydney the way he was going."

Miss Millie did not look too concerned. "Prince will not be too far. He'll be home for his next feed; you can depend on it."

Sarah pressed her palm against Ned's cold cheek. "His face looks grey, Miss Millie; don't you think?"

A neigh from the door caused the heads of both women to look up. Millie smiled and stood. She went to Ned's room and reached around the door. When she returned, she waved a carrot in her hand.

"Ned always has a bag of carrots hanging on the door there. He spoils the horses rotten but they will come when called."

Millie walked up to Prince and held out the carrot. Nervousness still showed as he reached forward then turned away. He threw his head and sniffed the air. He pawed at the ground with his front feet. Miss Millie spoke softly to the large animal that towered over her head. Eventually, Prince bit into the carrot. Holding it firmly in his mouth he then jumped backward.

"Something has certainly frightened Prince tonight. I think I might lead him into the outside enclosure."

Sarah watched Miss Millie disappear around the large double doors of the stable on her way to the horse pen at the back of the shed. Suddenly, she felt alone. Her hands ached with the effort of holding the towelling pad tightly to Ned's forehead. There was not a flicker of life in his face. How long would it be before Jacko returned with the doctor?

Miss Millie's reappearance coincided with the sound of a horse and buggy making its way into the hotel gardens. Thomas, Jacko and Doctor George alighted and moved to where Ned lay. Sarah stepped back and let the doctor examine the wounded man. Her heart wobbled when Jacko reached over and took her hand pulling her towards him. He put an arm about her shivering shoulders. Miss Millie did not miss the movement. Contentment filled her smile as she spoke to the doctor.

"I'm sure Ned was not kicked by the horse. It looks to me like he was caught on the side of the head by the top rail when Prince bolted. If you look closely you can see blood on the wood. It must be Ned's blood because there's no wound on Prince."

Doctor George looked up and smiled.

"Good evening, Miss Millie. You could be right. If a horse as large as Prince kicked Ned in the head, he'd have a broken skull at least. I cannot feel any grating bones under the wound. I'll sew this up now. We'll just have to wait and see when he wakes up if there's been any damage to his brain. No doubt he'll have widespread bruises."

The lantern wick was turned down low. Ned's unmoving body lay on his bed where Thomas and Jacko had placed him several hours before. Jacko lay across a bag of hay that he'd carried into the room. His head rested on the arm of the large chair where Sarah dozed with her hand across his chest.

"You awake, Sarah?" Jacko mumbled and turned his head to look into Sarah's face. His hand moved up to his chest to enfold her soft hand.

Sarah's eyes opened and her blue eyes looked deep into his dark orbs. She reached over to stroke his dark curly hair.

"Yes, Jacko. Are you comfortable there? Would you like me to go to the shack and bring you a hot drink?"

"Don't bother yourself, lass. Just lying here near you, feeling your hand in my hand, fills me with warmth enough." Their smiles merged.

Jacko pushed his body up higher until his shoulders were over the armrest. He twisted until he was facing her again. Calloused fingers lightly traced the outline of her face. Sarah took his fingers. She began kissing them slowly; one by one.

"Lass, I don't know if you should be doing that. You may start something that I cannot control."

Sarah's eyes dropped demurely but her lips smiled. She leant further forward and kissed his willing lips with the light touch of a moonbeam. She pulled back and peered again into the depths of Jacko's eyes.

It was Jacko's turn to bring his upper body closer and bend into his kiss; a deep and lingering kiss. Her lips parted under his touch. He felt the tip of her small tongue. He snapped back.

"Sarah, I'm sorry. I did say that I would not rush you."

"Yes, Jacko, you did. You said to tell you when I was ready to take you for my husband. I think that time is right now. I feel all a tremble. There is someone inside me whisking eggs to a froth. My body feels strange; like I've never felt before. I have a desperate yearning to lay with you right here and now and hold you so tightly until we are one. I don't know what to do."

Both Jacko and Sarah sprung apart at the sound of a cracked voice beside them.

"Lass, I'm sure Jacko will show you what to do but do you mind finding somewhere else to do it. A man's trying to sleep here."

"Ned, you're awake." Jacko and Sarah spoke in unison as they jumped up.

"Mate, I thought you'd carked it when I come into the stables and found you out to it on the floor with blood pouring from your head."

Sarah moved closer and checked the dressing. No wound ooze was visible on the cotton bandages.

"Ned, what happened to you? We found Prince bolting out of his stall and Emperor and Samson going crazy"

Silence was Sarah's only answer. Both she and Jacko stood staring down at Ned who lay again with his eyes closed. It was several minutes before he spoke again.

"Those blasted possums. They was fighting in the rafters. One flew down off the beams and onto Prince's back. The horse went mad and took off. That's the last I remember."

While Sarah poured a pannikin of water and supported Ned's head as he sipped, Jacko filled him in on what had happened during his unconscious spell.

As Sarah and Jacko prepared the early morning breakfasts, Jacko found his eyes drifting towards Sarah while she worked. Dark rings circled her eyes but a constant small smile touched her mouth. It was lucky for them Ned had woken up when he did because he may not have contained his passion in the face of her naïve revelations. By the time his friend had returned to sleep, both their passions had cooled enough that they were happy to make their way to their separate rooms. He grinned at the thought of the promise of what was to come.

TWENTY-FOUR

Captain Sloan sighed as he approached the cabins near the stern. He pondered on whether it had been worth recovering the bodies from the sea yesterday only to then return them to its depths earlier this morning? It was the vision of Mrs. Cousins, as she had stood with her son beside the remnant crew of the *Fleur,* that filled his head. Her face had been unreadable, yet she must be wondering what had happened to her husband's body.

Mrs. Farley's raised voice brought him back to the here and now. He heard a fear that was almost tangible.

"Donald, please talk to him. Make him see reason."

Her husband's voice was more restrained.

"Dear, he is your father. Anyway, he is a grown man. He knows the consequences following a broken leg. Surely it's his decision."

"He's still in shock. He must be, to be talking this way. Why would anyone in their right mind want to go directly to Brisbane? It will take at least a week. I cannot see any reason in that. Surely it makes more sense to stop in at one of the towns along the coast where there is a hospital and a doctor?" The woman's control was deserting her.

Captain Sloan stood for several moments looking out to the early sunrise in the east. The south-east wind rattled the rigging and the shrouds. It was going to be a good day for sailing. He drew in a deep breath before knocking on the door of Captain Bruce's cabin.

Weariness lay upon the face of Donald Farley.

“Ah, Captain Sloan, good morning.” He pulled the door back allowing the captain to enter the cramped cabin. A feeble light struggled through the open window. The dark circles under Mrs. Farley’s eyes stood out in her pale face. She sat erect on the chair in the corner. Captain Bruce lay quietly on the untidy cot. Pain was written in the lines of his grey face. Grey eyelashes lay on his cheeks.

Captain Sloan stepped over to the side of the bunk and touched the man’s wrist. He spoke quietly.

“You’ve made it through the first night, Captain Bruce. That has to be a good sign. You had a trying day yesterday.”

The eyelashes fluttered revealing grey eyes. A strained smile touched his lips.

“Ah, yes. At our age, it’s always a good sign when you wake up in the morning, Captain Sloan.” He paused to take several shallow breaths. “Call me Douglas, please.”

“I will if you call me, William, Sir. Now, it’s time for you to tell me what you wish to do.” Once again, the captain listed the three options he’d mentioned the evening before.

The man’s eyes closed again and he remained silent for several minutes. Captain Sloan thought he had drifted off to sleep and was in a quandary whether to wake him again or should he let the poor man rest. Captain Bruce gave a sharp cough. The eyes opened once more.

“William, you know what the risks are following such a fracture as this; not much chance of survival. Multiply those risks by a dozen, given the circumstance of how the fracture was acquired. Now I ask you, has medical science got an answer to reduce these risks?” Douglas Bruce answered his own question. “Not in my life, anyway. In a week, I will either be dead or alive depending on fate; definitely not on the care of any medics I have known. So, stopping off at a coastal-town hospital does not give me any more chance of surviving than staying on board this ship and making my way to Brisbane. If I'm still alive at that time, I can meet this man who is peddling the new wound solution you used. You recommend him, do you?"

"Douglas, I have to admit that I do not know him personally. He's a friend of a friend. He is young and not long out from London. He has had success using this new treatment. It is the first time I've heard of it being used."

"It seems to me that some chance is better than no chance. If it suits your schedule then sail directly to Brisbane. Maybe I'll live to meet this man and place myself under his care. If I don't, I will call it an honour to have you bury me at sea. What better place can an old salt end up, I ask you, William?"

Mrs. Farley's soft weeping was heard in the corner as Captain Sloan shook his patient's hand.

"Douglas, according to the instructions, we leave these dressings on for a couple of days and then replace them with a fresh dressing." William Sloan turned to Mister and Mrs. Farley. "If there's anything you want, please let Josh or Gus Dougall know. I'll have them take care of you all." He turned smartly and made his way out of the cabin and back to his wheel-house calling for the bosun as he did so. Having spoken to Mrs. Cousins earlier this morning, he knew she would receive their travel plans with gratitude.

"Let's capture some wind, Evans. We don't want to hang about here all day, do we?

Late on the sixth day, the *Northern Orchid* dropped anchor in Moreton Bay. The rhythmic swell of the seas rocked the ship as a mother might lull her child to sleep at the end of a long day. Ewan MacGregor stood at the cupboard of the wheel-house examining the manifest forms in preparation for the customs inspector on their arrival at the Brisbane River port. Captain Sloan stood tapping with his right hand on the lintel of the door. How long was he to wait until the sea pilot was available to take his ship into the river? Idly he watched the Dougall boys as they scampered across the yardarms securing the furled sails.

"Mac, can you remember when Jimmy Dougall's boys joined us at the beginning of this trip? Look at them now. They've grown so fast."

"How can I forget? Josh had only just begun chasing his voice from one octave to another. And do you remember how he was forever patting the chicken fluff on his top lip?"

William Sloan grinned. "Now, if given the chance, he fusses for hours in front of a broken mirror with his father's razor. What's Gus; nearly two years younger than Josh? He now has the occasional voice squeak and have you noticed he's started playing with his top lip. He'll be at the razor soon."

"Were we ever like that? I guess so." The ship's mate answered his own question before going on. "Those two have seen and experienced quite a lot in these past months." Mac looked up from his paperwork to glance out at the boys swinging like monkeys in the rigging. "Not as much as we went through in the navy, I suppose, but enough. They handled themselves well when we saved Captain Bruce and his crew from the *Fleur*. They didn't flinch when you re-aligned their captain's broken leg."

Captain Sloan lifted his cap and ran his hand over his hair and down the scar on the side of his face.

"Both boys had much to come to terms with when Bony nearly killed Gus. Josh had no option but to strike the fellow with that beam. Bony deserved to be killed but Josh was a bit of a mess for a while."

"Well Cap'n, it was lucky you were able to square it with the judge in Bowen."

"Remember, Mac, it was our crew's evidence that cleared the deal for the boys. It put Bony's partner in crime, Sykes, away also. Something like that has got to make you grow up quick."

"You know, I'm sure if there's a sailor's Heaven and Jimmy is looking down on his boys, he'd be mighty pleased."

"You and I would not be standing here if it wasn't for Jimmy Dougall, Mac. I often think of that, don't you?"

China arrived just at that moment with two steaming pannikins in his hands. He stepped into the wheel-house and sat the hot drinks on the bench. Both the captain and the ship's mate thanked him.

"Dinner tonight be poor fare, Cap'n. The cupboard is bare. I kill another chook this morning. Give Captain Bruce sustenance. Gus told me the man's leg healing good and clean."

"China, that stuff my friend sent is almost as good as your magic potions. There was no pus along the length of the wound at all when we took the dressing down yesterday; only a bit of clear fluid. In fact, the swelling in the whole leg seems to be reduced. By the way, the captain asked me to thank you for those small feathered cushions you made. He says those pads between his skin and the wooden splint have made him much more comfortable."

China's smile was wide as he stood tall.

After he had eaten his salted beef, potatoes and dry biscuits, William Sloan stood on the deck with his back resting against the main mast. The intermittent beam of the lighthouse on Cape Moreton stole the stars from the sky, but he hardly noticed. His view was inside his head. The russet-red curls surrounded the sparkling eyes. The heat of her smile warmed his body in the cool night air. A shiver raised the goose bumps along his skin as again he felt those fingers that spoke to his flesh.

"I'll go, Gus. You look beat." Josh's frown told of his worry. Gus's face was pale and dark circles rimmed his tired eyes.

Gus looked up from the stack of tin plates he had just dried. He nodded his thanks as Josh turned on heavy feet to make his way up the companion-way. On the top deck, he turned to the stern. Mister Farley stood near the door of Captain Bruce's cabin smoking a pipe.

"Excuse me, Sir. How is Captain Bruce?"

"Hello, Josh. The captain and my wife are asleep. I'll not be far behind them."

"Can I get you anything more tonight?"

"No thanks, Josh. Good night."

"Good night, Sir."

Josh held the opposing rails and slid down the companion-way back to the lower deck and the crew's quarters. Gus's hammock still rocked a little but the sound of soft snoring lifted on the air. He threw himself onto his own hammock.

The *Queensland* was the first ship to make its way out of Moreton Bay the next morning with the sea pilot guiding its course. The ship contracted to handle the mail, was on its way to deliver and collect from the coastal towns north.

On board the *Northern Orchid,* preparation was made to receive the sea pilot. The Jacob's-ladder hung over her side. Smoke billowed out of her funnel as the boiler built up its pressure. The engine was ready for use when the man climbed on board ship having seen the *Queensland* on her way. The crew was lined up at the capstan ready to weigh, first the stern anchor, then the bow anchor.

As they moved slowly in through the river-mouth, the dredge, widening and deepening the channel, was visible on their starboard side. Water and silt spewed into the tug boat, *Rainbow*. The river was thick with mud. When the *Northern Orchid* reached the mouth of Doboy Creek, six miles in from the river-mouth, she again had to wait. Echoes of the rattling anchor chains drifted across the water as the bow anchor dropped to the river bed. Once more the sea pilot returned to his territorial duties. Captain Sloan paced the deck as he waited for the river pilot to grace them with his presence.

It was the river pilot who delivered the news to Captain Sloan and Mac in the wheel-house as they chugged up the river to the harbour.

"The town is nearly deserted. It seems everyone has run off to try their hand in these new goldfields at Nashville. I believe they have since named the town, Gympie. All reports are saying it's the greatest discovery yet. We have four ships in harbour unable to move. Their crew abandoned them for the land of gold. Poor fools." The pilot almost spat out his disgust. "I once had a go at gold fossicking for a while; in Victoria. What a fool's chase that was. If I was you, I'd chain up your crew before you go any further."

William Sloan looked over at Mac. He could see his thoughts reflected in his mate's eyes. This fellow might be a garrulous old sod but what he said sounded all too familiar. They'd seen it happen in other places within this country and in other countries when ships were halted for want of a crew who had left to chase the golden dream.

Once they were anchored in the river just out from the Victoria Wharf, Captain Sloan called all the crew, including those who were from the *Fleur*, out on the deck below the wheel-house.

"No doubt, if you have not already heard, you will do so when on shore leave. There is a gold rush at a place called Gympie, just south-west of Maryborough. If any of you are wanting to chase gold, I suggest you let Mister MacGregor know as soon as possible. For those who will be signing on as crew, please let him know of that too. I'm sure you have all experienced short crews due to men rushing off to the different gold fields. Most return empty-handed and worse for wear. I want to know as early as possible if I have a crew for the next trip north."

When he stopped speaking the voices of the men erupted. Excitement spread like a bush fire through their numbers. William and Mac stood quietly watching the different reactions. The captain gave the men five minutes to settle before calling Josh, Gus and Evans up to the wheel-house.

"Which of you Dougall boys can run the faster?"

"Josh can fly like a racehorse, Cap'n" Gus did not hesitate.

The captain gave his instructions. "Well then, Gus, you are to row Josh to the south bank in the small tender boat. Once you have delivered him there, you can return here and help with launching the jolly-boat." The captain turned his attention to the older brother. "As soon as you reach land, Josh, I want you to run up the hill to Doctor Goldfinch's surgery. Ask the doctor to come and see Captain Bruce." His gaze turned again to Gus. "While Josh is away fetching the doctor, you and Tanner will use the jolly-boat to row China and Adams to shore to restore our food supplies; hopefully before night falls. Mister MacGregor will go with you to organize a water hoy to deliver as soon as possible. While there he will arrange for a cab to collect Mrs. Cousins in the morning. By that time, Josh and the doctor may be waiting at the river bank for a lift back to the ship." The captain turned to the bosun. "Can you keep an eye on them while you're sorting out the rest of the ship, Evans?"

"Aye, aye, Cap'n"

"Right, be off with you all." He tapped Josh on the shoulder and pulled him aside and spoke a few words into his ear. "On your way past the Mariner's Rest duck in and tell your sister you're home safe. Don't waste time."

"Aye, Cap'n."

Evans' voice seemed to come from all quarters of the compass as he sent the crew on the many tasks of preparing the ship for the end of a trip and unloading of cargo. The concentration of the crew was anywhere but on the job at hand. Gold, lots of gold and almost next door, filled the heads of many.

Mac called down the companion-way to China who was in the galley on the lower deck.

"You ready to go ashore, China?" He heard the thin reedy reply.

Mac went to see how the unloading of the jolly-boat was progressing. On his way, he dropped into where Captain Bruce sat up in bed writing a letter. The wounded leg in its splint rested on a pillow.

"Josh has just been sent with a message for Doctor Goldfinch. If the doctor is not busy on another call, he shouldn't be too long coming."

"Thanks, Mac." Captain Bruce smiled. He had much to smile about. He had given himself about a one percent chance of survival, yet here he was and feeling not too bad, all things considered.

THE MARINER'S REST

During the journey into town, Sarah had tried to reason with Miss Millie. They travelled via the ferry with the sign "Time Killer" written on a plank some joker had wired to the rails of the vessel. As the nickname suggested the ferry took its time to cross to the north bank. From there, they made their way to the main street. Sarah struggled to make her friend understand that she did not need lots of new things to start her married life. She could not afford them and she did not want Miss Millie buying these things for her. Her hands twisted in her lap.

Beside her, Miss Millie sat with a straight back and her competent hands on the reins. Prince looked smart as he lifted his feet and pranced along. His chestnut coat gleamed like bronze in the sun and the pale mane flew out behind his head. Millie swung the buggy around the corner of Queen Street and into George Street where she found ample room to park in the shade of a tree on a vacant allotment. Sarah sighed. It was no good ruining the day with an argument. Things may not be as bad as she thought.

As they climbed to the ground, Millie grimaced. Her vanity in wearing the fashionable flared-look with multiple petticoats did not make it any easier climbing in and out of carriages. She glanced with envy at Sarah who moved about unimpeded by such fripperies. The two women laughed as they walked along peering into windows of the shops on the street front. They welcomed the shade at those shops where awnings covered the footpath. When they reached the Emporium, Millie took Sarah's hand and led her inside.

Sarah stood agape. It was so big. Three long serving-counters ran the length of the building. Larger items were stacked against the slab-timber walls.

"Come, my dear. You don't have to buy anything but we can look and see what new things they have. Who knows, I may like something to titivate the hotel up a bit."

Sarah smiled and shook her head in resignation.

Millie spent a long time examining the many materials that had arrived on the latest shipment several weeks previously.

"Sarah, look at this." Millie fondled a pastel green linen. "This would make up into a lovely gown. You'd look so nice in this colour. You'll want something for your betrothal party."

Sarah managed to frown and smile at the same time. She shook her head slowly.

"Now, Miss Millie, what do I need a new gown for? I have a perfectly good gown that we made for the church fete. I plan on wearing that to the party."

Miss Millie reluctantly dropped that fabric but her fingers ran across the pile of other materials. They stopped at a white satin. Millie held a corner of the fabric to her face.

"Sarah, do feel that, please. Can you imagine that as a wedding dress?"

Sarah took Miss Millie's hand and led her away from the dress materials. She bent her head past the brim of Millie's bonnet and whispered in her ear.

"Miss Millie, it may be ages before Jacko and I set a day to be married. Jacko agrees with me it will only be a small party." She laughed and dragged Millie on to where the household items were stored. "You were saying that you wanted a new lamp for your room, didn't you, Miss Millie?"

Outmanoeuvred, Millie shrugged. There was still the drapery store in the block between Albert and Edward Streets.

"Yes, Sarah, I do." Millie held up a glass lamp which was one of a pair. "Sarah, if I bought the pair of these you could have one for the shack."

Sarah laughed and shook her head.

"Miss Millie you're at it again. A lamp like that just means extra work for me. It would need to be washed and polished every week to keep it clean. I'm quite satisfied with the old lantern in the shack. I can see enough to read in the evenings. I need no more."

By the time they had walked right up to the Skyring banana plantation and back, they were relieved to enter the coolness of the tea house. As they sat sipping their tea and nibbling scones, Sarah once again attempted to explain to Miss Millie that both she and Jacko needed to be responsible for their own debts.

"I know, Sarah, and that is commendable. I realize I can never be your mother but I love you like I would a daughter of my own. I want you to have all the things that I never had until I met my Christopher."

Tears stood out in Sarah's eyes as she reached over and took Millie's hand.

"Oh, Miss Millie, what a beautiful thing to say. I love you too. You have been a wonderful mother to the boys and me since our Ma died."

Samson, ridden bareback by Jacko, plodded along. Jacko held a lead rein attached to Emperor's bridle, which gave the animal just enough freedom to nibble at any long grass he could grasp. With Ned under doctor's orders, taking it easy for a week, it had been left to

Jacko to exercise the horses each day. As they entered through the back gate of the hotel, Jacko saw a man running full pelt through the front gate.

"You right there, fella?" he called.

The man bent double, his hands on his knees. He gasped, dragging air into his starved lungs.

"Hi, Jacko, it's me," Josh answered, some breath now restored.

Jacko slid from Samson's back and walked over to Josh. He stood wide-eyed.

"Look at you, you've grown a foot, at least. And Sarah is going to have the scissors to that hair before you know what happens." The two men laughed and shook hands.

"Is Sarah about? I just wanted to let her know we're back safe."

"Sarah and Millie have gone to town. Where's Gus?"

"Gus's on the *Northern Orchid.* I'm on my way to fetch the doctor."

"Is something wrong with Gus?"

"No, no; Gus's fine. It's the captain of the *Fleur.* We rescued him and his crew from a shipwreck up near Rockhampton. He has a broken leg and Captain Sloan fixed it." Josh noticed Ned standing at the stable door. They waved to each other.

"Hi, Ned. What happened to your face? It looks like one of your horses gave you a boot."

"Hello, Josh. Yeah, I had a bit of an accident. It's all fine now."

"Look, fellas, I'd like to stop and yap but I must get up to the doctor's place."

Jacko handed the lead rein to Ned.

"Here Ned, can you put Emperor into the enclosure out the back? I'll give Josh a lift up the hill on Samson." Jacko sprung up on to the back of the huge animal. He reached down inviting Josh to give him his hand.

"Without a saddle?" Josh was dubious.

"She'll be fine, Josh. He's only tossed about a dozen people and then stomped on them." Jacko and Ned both burst out laughing.

"He's only having you on, Josh," Ned called from the gate of the enclosure. "Samson's a sleepy old giant. He wouldn't hurt a fly."

When the two were seated, Jacko instructed his double-back rider to hold onto his waist. He warned Josh to keep his feet tucked in tight around the animal's belly.

"If you feel yourself slipping, don't go dragging us both off into a heap on the ground." He finished off with a laugh as he kicked the horse up and they trotted out the back gate.

When they rode into the yard of the doctor's surgery, Josh slid down off the horse and ran to the front door. Jacko tied Samson to a tree and went to talk with Thomas who was painting the new room they had built at the end of the house.

Josh moved his weight from foot to foot as he waited for his knock to be answered. At last, the door swung open and it was Doctor George who greeted him.

"Goodness me, it's Josh. I hardly recognized you. Is something wrong at the hotel?"

"No, Doctor George. Captain Sloan sent me; from the *Northern Orchid*." Josh went on to explain why the doctor's services had been requested.

"Josh, I want to see this man very much. It must have taken days to sail so far and yet you say the wound is looking good." He did not wait for an answer. "My sister and Jane have taken our buggy to the Telegraph Office. It may be a while before I can come and see your Captain Bruce."

Jacko and Thomas had joined the two at the front door. Jacko stepped forward.

"Doctor George, Josh and I can go back to the hotel and harness Samson to the dray. If he has a broken leg, this man will need something like a dray to carry him back here or to the hospital. I'll collect you and Thomas as soon as I've done that."

"That sounds excellent Jacko."

Mrs. Farley and her husband stood watching as Captain Bruce was lowered on the door- stretcher on which he'd arrived on board the ship a week before. Thomas, Jacko, Josh and Tanner were on the jolly-boat ready to receive the patient and secure him as comfortable as possible. Mrs. Farley turned to Captain Sloan.

"He will be alright, won't he, Captain?"

"Your father has done so well in this past week but as you are aware full recovery will take a long time. As far as I can see that is one fine doctor who is caring for him."

"The doctor recommended my husband and I stay at a place called The Mariner's Rest Hotel. Have you heard of it, Captain, and would you recommend it?"

"It is where I always stay. It is clean, the food is excellent and the prices reasonable. I will personally arrange to have a room reserved for you tomorrow if you wish."

"Thank you, Captain Sloan, you are most kind."

TWENTY-FIVE

THE *NORTHERN ORCHID*

The penny clunked onto the deck adding to the pile of pennies already there. Gathered around were several of the crew with well-worn cards in their hands. Other than their betting-calls, the discussion was almost exclusively about the current Gympie gold rush.

Reg's calloused hand rubbed his bald scalp as he explained that he'd be leaving as soon as the cargo was unloaded. While he spoke his blue eyes never left the cards.

"I ain't missing out on this find. The word is that it's a sure thing. There's more than enough for everyone who wants to work for it."

On the other hand, Dave was not convinced. Life on the sea suited him fine.

"Maybe when working the bilge pump, I may wonder why I didn't choose to go back scratching in the ground for a fortune. Most of the time, I know I'd rather be here on the sea with the wind at my back and the sails billowing overhead than picking at the dirt with a gun by my side. One does not easily forget the itch between the shoulder blades waiting for a bullet from some claim-jumping jail-bait wanting to make a sieve of my body. Worse still, I could be lying dying of cholera or typhoid in the dust and flies; or even worse than that, starving, thirsty and hungry."

Stretch who remained indifferent, grinned.

Reg's mind was made up. "Well, I'll be saying goodbye then, I guess. Two of the lads off the *Fleur* have asked me to join them in setting up a claim."

Dave shrugged.

In the chartroom, Mac, Guthrie Winston and Evans finished off their meal with a small drink of port.

"I wonder how Captain Bruce settled in at Doctor Goldfinch's surgery?" Mac asked no one in particular.

"He is one lucky man to be alive." Evans poured another drink.

"Where did Captain Sloan have to go this evening?" Guthrie asked as he swirled his drink around in the pannikin. "I thought he'd be wanting to join the end-of-trip celebration. Did he say when he'd be back?"

Mac stood and peered out across the river to the town, considering his answer. He smiled appreciatively as he noticed how the new gas lamps on the main street lit up like Christmas decorations. He turned again and reached for the jug of wine before he replied.

"The captain has gone to arrange accommodation for the Farleys; as a favour to Captain Bruce, I believe. You can guarantee he'll be back early, digging us all out of our bunks in plenty of time to shift to the jetty for unloading."

Evans, who knew exactly why their captain had rushed off to do the Farleys a favour, looked deeply into his glass and never commented. It was Mac who changed the subject.

"Guthrie, will you be looking to chase the gold when you get paid off or will you be staying with the ship?"

Guthrie smiled.

"Once upon a time, when I was younger, such a mad-cap scheme might have been my dream but these days, at my age, I think the quiet life on the ocean will suit me very well. What about you, Evans? You're the youngest one amongst us here. Will you run off to the goldfields?"

"Mister Winston, I've been shuffling my way around ships, in particular, this ship for over twenty years. I was apprentice to Jimmy Dougall, the father of the Dougall boys we have on board now, when he was alive. I guess I'll still be on the *Northern Orchid* for some years yet; unless we do some fool thing like sink to the bottom of the sea." Evans stood and moved towards the doorway. "Mister MacGregor, I'd best go and check the first watch is alert."

Indeed, Captain Sloan was on board the ship as the two bells into the morning watch sounded. The watch had not heard the tender boat move across the water from the river bank on silent oars. The watch had not heard the faint scrape of the captain's body as he slithered up the rope hanging over the side. It was not until he almost walked into the captain who dropped silently onto the deck, that Andrews gasped.

"Who goes there? Identify yourself."

"Geez, Andrews, you'll get yourself killed one day if you don't wake up. Who's in the crow's-nest this morning?"

"Gus Dougall, Sir."

The quiet words the captain spoke as he walked away to the wheel-house were not heard by Andrews.

"At least someone'll be awake on this blasted ship, then."

"You're not complaining, are you captain?" Mac's voice came from the dark. "I thought you'd be all smiles this morning. Don't tell me you weren't given the welcome you expected at The Rest."

The captain laughed aloud.

"Nosey, aren't you, Mac? That's my business anyway. I'll duck down to the galley and bring us back some hot tea."

When he returned, the captain asked the mate the most pressing question of the moment.

"Any idea yet of what our crew situation is going to be?"

Mac blew on the hot drink before taking a sip.

"Some are still undecided but I do know Reg will be leaving. The bosun from the *Fleur* is taking three of that crew with him to the gold and Andrews is in a quandary as to what he wants to do. The other two from the *Fleur* are hoping you'll take them on as crew on the *Northern Orchid.* Stretch and Dave are staying. As far as I'm aware the remainder of our stalwart crew will remain, including the Dougall boys." Mac sipped again at his pannikin as he watched the captain nod his head and a smile of satisfaction lift his lips. He went on. "While I was at the agent's office yesterday afternoon, he told me that he can fill our holds every day of the week with hopeful men heading, via Maryborough, to the goldfields."

Captain Sloan stood leaning against the mainmast in deep thought for some time.

"Well, as it seems that we are going to have a full complement of crew, it may pay us to do a quick run up to Maryborough. What do you think, Mac?"

"Should be an easy cargo with little time wasted in loading and unloading, William. You'd have to give China extra help in the galley, I suppose. A load of eating-cargo will really set him off. At least it's only a short run."

"That's what we'll do then. Whatever, we cannot leave here before Sunday. Josh and Gus's sister has become engaged to Millie's foster son. I'm obliged to attend the betrothal party on Saturday; it has been made quite clear my life depends on it."

Both men chuckled at the thought.

THE MARINER'S REST

The garden looked a picture. Ned and Jacko had been trimming and raking the area all week. Spring flowers brightened up many of the trees and shrubs. Gus and Josh had been busy during the morning hanging streamers crafted from coloured paper which added to the splendour. Millie had also charged them with the responsibility to ensure that the tables and chairs from the dining room were placed in the shade of the largest tree.

The dresses worn by the ladies added to the cheerful atmosphere. Doctor Goldfinch, along with his sister, Abigail Baldwin and her baby son, Henry, arrived with their loyal staff Thomas, Jane and Eve. All the guests from the A-Wing had been invited. These included Mrs. Keppel and Mister Boris, the permanent guests. Mister and Mrs. Farley, who had arrived on the *Northern Orchid* recently, gracefully accepted their invitation also. Mister and Mrs. Carrington, who had arrived the previous day from Toowoomba and were soon to sail to Sydney had joined the group. Millie was happy to welcome and introduce everyone including Captain William Sloan dressed in his best naval whites. Her eyes sparkled. Her face flushed bright pink.

On the central table, under a muslin cloth rested the betrothal cake. Millie had sat up well into Friday night in order to finish its decorations. Jugs of fruit juice were placed on the tables and Spud and Ned ensured that all those who wished to partake of ale were provided with the same.

A pathway had been worn in the grass from the kitchen to the front garden by the feet of Mrs. Hamilton and her daughter, Meg. Lizzie Randal, the daily cleaner, had taken on the task of assistant caterer. Her flamboyant skirts swirled about her legs as she bustled back and forth under Mrs. Hamilton's strict supervision. An explosion of brown curls was partially confined within a scarlet bonnet.

Gasps of admiration caused heads to turn when Sarah and Jacko rounded the corner of the building. Sarah's pale blue dress draped over several petticoats and set off by her matching bolero enhanced the blue of her eyes. Her skin was clear and several locks of her dark hair refused to be confined. They curled about her face. Jacko standing tall beside her was almost unrecognizable in his dark morning suit. His complaints of discomfort were little heeded by either Miss Millie or his future bride-to-be. Pride shone out like a lighthouse beacon as he presented his betrothed.

The rattle of cups, the rustle of clothing and the chatter paused during the interlude when Jane sang several modern pieces including the very popular Take Me Home Again Kathleen. An enthusiastic acclamation brought a bright flush to her cheeks when she finished. Spud Murphy surprised Sarah when he proved proficient with a fiddle and bow in his hands. Many of those present tapped their feet or clapped their hands.

With Sarah nudging him in the side, Jacko stood to make his speech. All week, he had protested at the need for him to say a word. How could he speak to all these people? What would he say? Millie and Sarah were adamant. He made a stumbling start. He stuttered. He coughed. Sarah stood up beside him and looked him in the eye. She took his hand. A gentle smile curved her lips. Jacko took a deep breath. His gaze held her eyes for some time before he turned to address his audience. He felt strong with Sarah at his elbow.

"Firstly, we wish to thank Miss Millie from the depths of our hearts for the wonderful party and for all her support. We welcome everyone here this afternoon. How lovely that the sun is shining upon us although, I'm sure, there are many farmers who would appreciate a few inches of rain. I'm here, to confirm before you all, that I have asked this beautiful woman to be my wife. I am proud to say that she has accepted. I fear one day she will wake up and ask herself what's she doing with an old bloke like me." At this point, Sarah grinned and kissed his cheek to everyone's delight. Jacko coughed. He took several deep breaths. He struggled to swallow the tears in his throat. "I have gained two brothers who have not yet taken me aside and delivered heavy warnings; maybe that will come later. Seriously though, they are stalwart friends and I can assure them both that I will care for their sister with every ounce of strength in my body." He turned towards where Josh and Gus stood under the Jacaranda tree, both with wide grins stretching their faces. Jacko went on. "Particularly now they have returned from their seafaring adventures twice the size they were when they left. Okay, that's enough from me." A cheeky voice from the back of the gathering, which sounded very much like Ned, warned in a loud whisper that once you get Jacko started talking, you'll never stop him. "I'll see you later, Ned, lad," Jacko called. "Anyway, everyone, Sarah and I wish to announce our betrothal. On behalf of Miss Millie, I invite you to please relax and enjoy yourselves."

His speech was an outstanding success. The guests cheered and laughed and clapped.

Dusk was falling when Jacko, Sarah and Millie saw the Goldfinch group into the buggy. Sarah ran up and took Abigail's hand.

"Thank you so much for the lovely tea-cloth. The fancywork and crochet are exquisite."

Abigail turned towards Jane and smiled.

"You have Jane to thank for the crochet work. My effort is in the needlepoint. The gift is from all of us at the surgery."

"Thank you all very much. Jane, enjoy the holiday at your Aunt's. Sydney should be so exciting. It is a much bigger town than Brisbane, I believe."

They waved as the horse led off into the evening.

Having everything cleared away, washed and dried, Mrs. Hamilton, Meg, Mrs. Randal, and Spud Murphy had long left for their homes. Ned disappeared an hour earlier mumbling that he was too old for this hullabaloo and he was so full he could not eat another thing.

Miss Millie, Captain Sloan, Jacko, Sarah, Josh and Gus sat around the kitchen table enjoying a nightcap. The sailors were to return to the *Northern Orchid* this evening.

"Ooh," said Miss Millie. "I nearly forgot." She rushed out of the room. Her footsteps clattered through the dining room on the way to her office. It was a few moments before she returned waving an envelope back and forth in her hands. "This came with the letter carrier yesterday. I had nearly forgotten all about it with everything going on. It's from Arthur."

"Arthur who? Oh, you mean Arthur Rankine?" Sarah asked.

"Yes, he wrote it from Maryborough. He tells how, after only two days, business took him and his partner to Gympie. Whilst there he witnessed a man murdered in the main street of the village. Someone stuck a knife into his gullet. You'd never guess who the dead man was." The faces around the table looked blankly at Millie. She sighed with frustration at their lack of guessing powers. "Edward Carson or whatever his real name is … or was, I guess now."

William Sloan reached over and gave her hand a squeeze.

"I know we should not speak ill of the dead but the world's a better place with him gone." Jacko did not apologize for his hardness.

When the group stood at the front of the hotel saying goodbye to the sailors, Millie held William's hand tightly. In the light of the lantern hanging at the front of the building, her eyes glistened with tears. Sarah hugged her two brothers, one on each arm. She kissed their cheeks.

"Oooh, Sis," the boys said in unison. "Do you have to?"

Everyone laughed. Sarah turned her attention to the captain.

"When will you be sailing, Captain Sloan?"

"The holds are full of supplies for the new village of Gympie. The final passengers will embark at first light tomorrow, Sarah. We leave on the mid-morning tide."

"God speed. Once again, Captain Sloan, I thank you for the magnificent bedspread that you gave to Jacko and me for our betrothal." Sarah dropped into a small curtsy.

The captain smiled. "It was nothing, lass. It's from both Millie and myself. It's an oriental cloth that a friend of a friend found for me in China."

Sarah stepped forward and reached on tippy toes to kiss the captain's cheek. She jumped back as if surprised at her own temerity. She grasped Jacko's elbow. The captain grinned and bowed slightly.

"I'll get another cloth for you if that is how one gets thanked."

The night shadows hid the flame of Sarah's face. Millie laughed and slapped the captain's arm.

The sailors turned and began the walk down the slope to the riverbank where the *Northern Orchid's* small boat awaited.

THE *NORTHERN ORCHID*

Gus could not believe what he was seeing. People, mostly men, lined the gangplank and reached out across the jetty. They waited for Mister MacGregor to check them off against the agent's list of passengers who had paid for a one-way ticket to Maryborough.

Late in the day, as the *Northern Orchid* made its way out of the river, the wind caught the reefed sails. It set them flapping and rattled the rigging. Captain Sloan and the ship's mate stood in the wheel-house with the sea pilot.

Up in the crow's nest, Josh threw out his arms and laughed out loud. Deep breaths of salt-laden air filled his lungs. He waved down to his brother who stood at the bow of the ship. Even from this height, he could see the white teeth and a wide grin on Gus's face.

He knew the rush of excitement, like exploding Chinese crackers, that filled his brother's chest. His own chest threatened to burst with the same thrill. He had been feeling that way since the captain had taken them aside this morning.

"You Dougall boys have done your father proud over these past months. If you are willing, I'll continue to support you in your studies and practical skills. When the time is right, I'll ensure you are enrolled to take the Master's Competency Test and the Engineer's Certificate examinations in a few years. All I need from you is your commitment and enthusiasm for hard work. Can I rely on that?"

Neither boy could speak but vigorous nodding of their heads relayed the message from both their wildly beating hearts.

As Josh hung over the crow's nest, he knew that if he lived to be one hundred years of age, he'd never forget how he'd felt at that moment. He'd forever feel the satisfied hand of his unseen father on his shoulder. Maybe the crew is right; Jimmy Dougall's ghost does walk these decks.

SHADOWS ON THE GOLDFIELD TRACK

To be released soon

Sequel to Shadow of the *Northern Orchid*

Part One

What compelling circumstances prompted the pregnant Abigail Baldwin to emigrate to Australia in the company of her brother, Doctor George Goldfinch?

In the antipodes, circumstances were a far cry from what they left behind in London. How did the Goldfinch entourage adapt in this new world as they built a medical practice?

Part Two

After six years, the Goldfinch entourage journey to Cook's Town seeking adventure as they provide assistance to a desperate new settlement.

Cook's Town in 1873, the gateway to the newly discovered goldfield at the Palmer River, two hundred miles inland, supports little infrastructure required to cope with the thousands of prospectors seeking their fortunes. No harbour was available on the Endeavour River. The town was no more than a tent city. Food and clean drinking water were in short supply. Access to a trained medical professional was rare. The monsoons threatened. Hundreds of miners died in their attempt to reach the goldfields or on their return to Cook's Town, starving and penniless.

After the death of her mother and the placement of her siblings in the Brisbane orphanage, sixteen-year-old Maureen Ryan must find her father. She arrives in Cook's Town on board the *Northern Orchid* in the company of the doctor's group. Foolishly, Maureen believes a ne'er-do-well packhorse handler, Silas, who promises he can take her to her father, Bert Ryan, at the Palmer River goldfields.

It is Josh and Gus Dougall along with China from the *Northern Orchid* and Bert Ryan himself, who begin the race to rescue the girl.

ABOUT THE AUTHOR

Elizabeth Rimmington

Elizabeth is an Australian author living in a rural area of South-East Queensland. During a career in nursing followed by several years driving a taxi cab, Elizabeth has met many and varied characters. Some good, some bad, some saints and some sinners, some cheery and some a misery, BUT all very interesting. If each individual was to be measured as a bucket of sea water, the *Northern Orchid* might have another ocean on which to bend her sails.

A new novelist whose story characters infiltrate the reader's heart by osmosis. Their laughter, their heartbreak and their pain will fill the booklover's soul with happiness, tears, fear and empathy.

Visit the author on her website. www.elizabethrimmington.com.au

Join the mailing list. lizrim007@gmail.com

Lightning Source UK Ltd.
Milton Keynes UK
UKHW020724310822
408116UK00005B/555